SLOW TANGO WITH A PRINCE

NICOLE BURNHAM

Slow Tango With a Prince

by Nicole Burnham

Cover design by Patricia Schmitt

Edition: May 2022

ISBN: 978-1-941828-01-4 (paperback)

ISBN: 978-1-941828-00-7 (ebook)

For more information or to subscribe to Nicole's newsletter, visit nicoleburnham.com.

For my aunt, Jan Burnham, who appreciated a rich cup of coffee, the experience of foreign travel, and all the good life has to offer.

PROLOGUE

TODAY'S ROYALS: THE LATEST
By V. Dempsey, December 1

SARCACCIA'S ROYALS COME CLEAN
Barrali Family Hosts Press, Addresses Recent Scandals

CATERI, SARCACCIA - In a first-of-its-kind event for the Barrali royal family, *Today's Royals* and other select media representatives were invited to what was termed an "informal press reception" in the palace's famed green parlor. While being served traditional Sarcaccian appetizers and wine from the Famiglia Barrali vineyards, the reporters were told they'd be given a half hour to ask questions about both matters of state and the rampant rumors that have plagued the monarch and his family over the past few months. As expected, when the family entered the parlor, media attention zeroed in on the flurry of reports regarding the family's romantic relationships and the apparent disappearance of Prince Alessandro, who is second in line to the throne after his twin brother, Prince Vittorio.

To the surprise of those gathered, it was Prince Stefano rather than King Carlo who raised his hand to quiet the room, declaring that he had an announcement to make before the family answered any questions.

He asked his rumored fiancée, Megan Hallberg, to join him in the center of the parlor before stating that the two are indeed planning to marry. Amid congratulations from those assembled, the prince explained that he proposed on a beach near Cateri in late July, but that the couple wished to have time for Ms. Hallberg to begin her new position managing Sarcaccia's conference center and to become better acquainted with the royal family before making a formal engagement announcement. Though the news was not a surprise, given that Ms. Hallberg has been attending family functions and appeared with the Barrali family at Independence Day festivities in September, the prince then stunned the crowd to silence by further announcing that Ms. Hallberg's ten-year-old daughter, Anna, is his biological child.

"Megan and I met in our early twenties, during my time working in Venezuela," the prince explained. "While I'm sure you have a number of questions about our relationship and what I knew of Anna's existence, what Megan and I believe is most important is that we found each other after many years of separation. We are very much in love and excited to be a family. On that note, our daughter is a wonderful girl, very bright and well-adjusted. She has lived out of the spotlight for her entire life. As her parents, we wish for it to remain that way. Therefore, we kindly ask all of you to give her space to enjoy her childhood." The prince went on to explain that he'd purchased his waterfront apartment and moved out of the royal palace in July in order to provide Anna as normal an upbringing as possible, not due to a rift with his parents as has been rumored.

Ms. Hallberg then showed off her diamond and sapphire engagement ring at a reporter's request. While the sapphire has been in Queen Fabrizia's family for over a hundred years, Prince Stefano designed its diamond setting with the assistance of longtime royal jewelers Conti & Fancetti.

A wedding date has not yet been set, but the couple say they will wed in Cateri's cathedral and are considering dates during which Anna will be out of school.

Following Prince Stefano's announcement, King Carlo reminded those present of Sarcaccia's strict laws concerning paparazzi coverage of minors, then took a question about the recent five-day trip he and Prince Vittorio took to the Middle East, where the king was involved in peace negotiations and the crown prince visited several schools funded by the Barrali Trust. However, the line of questioning quickly turned to Prince Vittorio's twin, Alessandro, who hasn't been seen in public since the early October funeral of Prince Vittorio's former girlfriend, Spanish actress Carmella Rivas, and was rarely seen during the two-week period preceding it.

Prince Vittorio told the media that there is nothing suspicious about his twin's absence. However, he admitted, "At the moment we're unaware of his location, though this isn't unusual. As you've reported on many occasions, Alessandro is an adventurer at heart and often travels to areas where communication is limited." When pressed, Vittorio did acknowledge that Alessandro has never been away for such an extended period. Asked point-blank if Alessandro was missing, the crown prince laughed and responded, "No. As I said, we are simply unaware of his exact location. If there is any cause for concern, we will of course discuss that with the Royal Police. However, I must reiterate that this is simply not the case."

A follow-up question noted unsubstantiated reports that Prince Alessandro was photographed in Croatia, but Vittorio stated that the family had no such information.

The crown prince then accepted a question about his former girlfriend and took the opportunity to once again extend his sympathies to the Rivas family on Carmella Rivas's tragic suicide. "It came as a horrible shock to us all and I hurt for her family. Unfortunately, there is no explaining it. We may never know what drove her to that place," he said. "However, it is my hope that the Carmella Rivas Memorial

Fund will help others who are contemplating suicide by offering them free professional counseling. No family should be torn apart by the loss of a loved one this way."

The event ended on an upbeat note when Prince Massimo was asked about his relationship with Kelly Chase, the American he employed as a closet designer in September, but who has not yet left the country...and whether Sarcaccia should prepare for a second royal wedding.

The question drew a burst of laughter from the entire Barrali family and a comment from Queen Fabrizia that, "One royal wedding is plenty to plan. Imagine the hours all of you in the media would have to work if there were a second. Impossible!"

QUEEN FABRIZIA SLID the emeralds from her ears and deposited them on a glass end table in the private palace apartment she and King Carlo shared. She hadn't wanted to wear them to the press event, as heavy earrings tended to exacerbate her headaches, but they photographed well and brought out the green in her eyes.

All the better to counteract the red.

Fabrizia prided herself on her steel spine and her ability to keep her large, powerful family together, but recent events tested her resiliency. Learning over the summer that she had a ten-year-old granddaughter—one who was her spitting image—and hearing Stefano declare he intended to break tradition and live outside the royal palace broke her heart.

Worse, though, was having to endure these weeks following Carmella Rivas's funeral. Carmella's deception and her subsequent suicide wreaked havoc within the family. It had taken every bit of Fabrizia's resourcefulness to keep the Barralis on an even keel, at least to the public eye. But if she continued to let it keep her awake at night, a sharp photographer would soon notice the evidence and the tabloids would pounce like buzzards on carrion.

"I certainly hope we never have to do that again. I abhor discussing personal affairs in a public forum," King Carlo said as he sank onto the sofa beside Fabrizia and put a comforting hand on her knee. Across from them, Megan and Stefano occupied a matching sofa while Massimo and his still-secret fiancée, Kelly, adjourned to the kitchen so Massimo could update Kelly on the afternoon's events.

Sprawled in a chair to the side, Alessandro held up his left hand, as if weighing an invisible object. "Hmmm…Mideast peace, or" —he raised his other hand, palm up— "rumors about the love lives of the royal family. Which did you think they'd want to address? I thought that was the point, anyway."

"Sit up," the queen hissed. "What if someone were to walk in?"

Physically, the twins were indistinguishable aside from the tiny white scar beneath Alessandro's left eye—now carefully concealed with makeup—and the location of their ears, with Vittorio's slightly higher and further back than his twin's. Even family members confused them from time to time. But once they opened their mouths, the differences were clear. Though the timbre of their voices was remarkably similar, Alessandro's relaxed, devil-may-care attitude and Vittorio's perpetually formal one gave away their identities as surely as if they'd been born with different hair or eye colors. While all the world thought it was Alessandro, rather than Vittorio, who'd disappeared, Alessandro needed to keep that fact in mind.

"No one will come in, Mother," Alessandro replied, though he straightened in his chair to mimic the carriage of his absent twin. "Umberto knows to keep the staff away for the rest of the evening. Besides, the press conference went exactly as planned. No one thought for a moment that I was anyone other than who I claimed. They were far more interested in Stefano's big news than in yet another Alessandro-has-taken-off story."

"I certainly hope so." Fabrizia sent an apologetic look across the coffee table to Stefano and Megan. "Thank you for being the sacrificial lambs. I know you were planning to make an announcement soon, but not in that manner."

"If it takes their attention off my delinquent brother" —Stefano flashed a look at Alessandro— "then it's worthwhile. Megan and I couldn't keep quiet much longer, anyway. The staff have been suspicious about an engagement for months. Besides—" an embarrassed smile lit his face— "Anna's started calling me Dad when we're at home. It'd only take one person to overhear her for that particular cat to be out of the bag."

"Oh, Stefano, I'm so glad." Tears pricked Fabrizia's eyes, though she blinked them back. How long had she wanted to be a grandmother? To see the joy Stefano took in Megan and Anna now that they were becoming a real family, one built on love and trust...it was everything she desired for her children. Yet, due to the public nature of their lives, such happiness was often as elusive as a butterfly in winter.

Megan shifted closer to Stefano at the same time he reached for her hand. "It's been a long haul, but Anna's transitioning well. She adores Stefano. You'd never know he hasn't been with her from birth."

Stefano and Megan made a handsome pair, Fabrizia decided. If only she could convince them to move back to the palace, the situation would be perfect. At the moment, however, pressuring the couple held a low spot on her priority list, given what was happening with Vittorio. And perhaps Stefano was right: the paparazzi were less likely to sneak photographs of Anna if she lived in a private home than if she stayed at the palace, which served as both a residence and government office.

"Let me know if the media becomes a problem now that they know Anna is your daughter," King Carlo told the couple, his thoughts apparently mirroring Fabrizia's. "I'll personally ensure that anyone who breaks the law is prosecuted."

After Megan thanked the king, Alessandro asked, "So what's next? Has anyone heard from Vittorio?"

"Not since he arrived in Argentina two weeks ago and called you," the queen said. Why Vittorio picked Buenos Aires as his escape, she couldn't fathom, but at least he was safe there for the time being. He could battle his demons far from the spotlight of Sarcaccia.

Sophia, the king and queen's only daughter, emerged from the kitchen in time to overhear Alessandro's question. "So what were the reporters saying about Croatia? I looked online and saw a photo of a man boarding a luxury yacht near Dubrovnik. It was taken from a distance, but it looked a lot like Vittorio to me."

"He's in Argentina," Alessandro assured her. "He gave me the name he's using at his current hotel in case of an emergency."

"Did you check to see if he was telling you the truth?" Sophia's forehead creased into a frown. "The way the man in the photo tilted his head to the side was just like—"

"Vittorio is not in Croatia." King Carlo's tone was meant to close discussion.

At the same time, Alessandro replied, "Of course I checked."

"Let's forget Croatia," Fabrizia said, rising from the sofa and smoothing the front of her dress. "The press is focused on Stefano and Megan for now. And Alessandro, you did a wonderful job both at the press conference and in the Middle East. I have every confidence Vittorio will return shortly, then we can all get back to business as usual with no one the wiser."

Then *she* could forget Croatia.

CHAPTER 1

Three Months Later

Nearly fifty people depended on Emily Sinclair for their livelihood. Given that pressure, she needed to focus on the shooting schedule and pages of red-inked notes spread across the breakfast table in front of her rather than allow her mind to wander. But the contrast between the serene scene surrounding her and the intense pressure of her job made concentration difficult.

Across the narrow street, in the outdoor seating area of a restaurant similar to the one in which she worked, a dark-haired man in crisp jeans and a white Oxford-cloth shirt sat alone, his face hidden behind the pages of the *Buenos Aires Herald*, a steaming espresso on the table in front of him. The smell of freshly ground coffee beans and warm pastry drifted through the air, mixing with the exhaust fumes of an early-morning city bus as it made its way up Avenue Quintana, which bordered the other side of the restaurant. A mother knelt to zip her son's backpack, then wave him off from his corner bus stop before picking up her own briefcase and heading in the opposite direction. Kiosk owners set out stacks of magazines, shop owners unlocked doors, and a lone black and yellow taxi idled at the corner, the yawning driver awaiting his next fare.

The residents of Buenos Aires' trendy Recoleta neighborhood were ready to start another workweek while Emily feared it could be her last. However, if there was any hope of *At Home Abroad* being renewed for a fourth season, it rested with her as the television show's host and executive producer. Because the program melded house-hunting with travel information and it focused on a different country each season, a bevy of local researchers, travel specialists, and real estate consultants drew a portion of their income from *At Home Abroad*. That was in addition to the usual salaried camera crew, film editors, and sound and lighting experts. She couldn't bear to let them down. The season finale had to be extraordinary and she had only a week left before the wrap deadline.

She stifled a sigh, forcing her attention back to the proposed shooting schedule. Somehow, some way, she had to make this work.

"You don't want to stop staring at him, either?" the show's director and co-executive producer, Rita Bragna, asked while she haphazardly spread fresh marmalade on her morning croissant, her eyes locked on the table across the street. She waved her knife in the man's direction. "I've seen plenty of hot guys since we arrived in Buenos Aires, but he wins the prize. Too bad we picked this place for breakfast instead of Café Luchana."

"Huh? Him?" Emily flicked her gaze toward the man, whose face remained hidden behind his newspaper, then turned back to Rita. Rita had been happily married for nearly twenty-five years, but she liked to look. Even more, she liked to point out good-looking men to Emily in the hope Emily would find the same happiness. But as Emily told Rita time and again, the lifestyle of a television host made it impossible, and she'd fought too long and too hard for her job to quit. She'd learned the hard way that it wasn't worth it to risk her career in order to pursue a relationship. Especially when her health history made a solid relationship a long shot at best.

"Yes, *him*. Didn't you notice when he lowered the paper to turn the page? I'd swear you were staring. The man is gorgeous."

Emily shook her head. "I wasn't staring at him so much as staring into space. I've been wracking my brain, trying to come up with a better hook for our final episode. What we have planned isn't going to generate the buzz we need to guarantee our renewal."

"Hate to say it, but I agree." Rita shrugged, giving up her match-making scheme for the moment. "The Winstons are a nice couple, but boring. We should've arranged for someone with his looks and an outrageous bank account as our finale's house-hunting ex-pat. Problem is, anyone who looks that good can't possibly have a budget to match. It'd go against the laws of nature."

"I'd settle for the budget alone." Unfortunately, every lead their network of real estate agents offered was for buyers seeking midrange properties. Leave it to Emily to select Argentina for season three just as the housing market took off and most foreigners moving to Buenos Aires were unable to afford anything luxe. Featuring midrange properties yet again in the finale would be a Yawn, with a capital Y.

Rita indicated the calendar on their breakfast table. "Whatever we decide, this schedule has to be finalized by tonight. We have the camera crew at six a.m. Unless your real estate contacts come through with a spectacular apartment that's going cheap, we should try to make the most of our other material."

In other words, cut the finale's real estate footage to its bare minimum and pad the show with the most interesting travel information they could muster. She bit back a sigh. "Are any of the places on the current schedule near tango? Perhaps we can work that angle. Show how deeply ingrained dance is in the local culture?"

"No way the Winstons are up to a tango, but maybe we can send them to a show." Rita tapped a few keys on her phone to pull up a map of the area. "Two of the three apartments on the current schedule are within a mile of tango bars. I'll make a few calls, see if we can get tickets for the Winstons, then get inside to film."

Emily scratched a few notes on paper, then said, "I was also hoping we could get some nighttime outdoor shots. Show the architecture of the buildings when they're lit, capture the music echoing up and down the streets in the evening outside the bars in San Telmo. Maybe show the way residents hold hands and smile while they watch the street buskers. If we can't show sexy real estate—or clients—we can certainly show some sexy street scenes."

"Street scenes. Atmosphere. Sexy. I'm on it." Rita waggled her eyebrows. "But it'd be so much better if I could get you to tango on camera with someone like him."

"You're hopeless," Emily said on a laugh as she reached for her coffee. She glanced across the street, then did a double take. The *Herald* now rested on the man's table, neatly folded beside a plate filled to toppling with French bread and an assortment of jam, leaving his face and upper body fully visible as he wrote on the page.

What a face and body they were. The man looked as if he should be gazing out from a billboard, wearing a custom-tailored suit in an advertisement for a sumptuous cologne or extravagant brand of Scotch, rather than sitting in an Argentine coffee shop in a white shirt and jeans. She was surprised to see he had a beard, but it did little to hide his sculpted cheekbones or the olive skin that set off his light-colored eyes to perfection. From this distance, she wasn't sure of their exact color, but the contrast with his jet-black hair and eyebrows was unexpected and sexy. Yet there was something oddly flawed about his face that made Emily want to study him from a closer vantage point, to determine just what it was that seemed out of place.

Perhaps it was the pen he held in his hand. A man who did the crossword over breakfast inevitably had brains, a trait Emily found even more appealing than his looks. Hell, a man who read an actual newspaper rather than spend his morning meal tethered to his electronic devices did it for her. Not that any man should be doing it for her when she had a season finale to produce.

"See what I mean?" Rita sighed. "Tell me you wouldn't want a guy who fills out a shirt the way he does to sweep you into his arms for a slow tango."

The mental image warmed Emily's cheeks. He was the embodiment of the word sultry. No doubt when he danced with a woman, he made her feel as if she were the only female in the world he'd ever held so close or gazed at with such intensity. And what woman wouldn't want to feel that way?

His hand moved across the newspaper page, making quick circles with his pen. As Emily watched the smooth movement, she drew in a quick breath.

"What?" Rita asked, instantly on alert.

"He's *exactly* the man I want. I'm going over there."

Emily set down her coffee, pushed back from the table, and strode across the street, leaving Rita in stunned silence.

VITTORIO BARRALI KNEW without raising his eyes from the newspaper that a woman approached. He'd always had a sixth sense for the presence of a beautiful female, but months of moving from hotel to hotel, constantly at risk of being recognized—or, more accurately, recognized as his "missing" identical twin, Alessandro—gave him defensive instincts he hadn't possessed in his life as Sarcaccia's crown prince, when most of those he saw on a daily basis were carefully vetted by security staff. The quick click of this woman's heels against the cobblestones meant she approached with a purpose.

Pretending not to notice, he kept his pen steady and his gaze directed at his newspaper. While he'd let his hair grow from its former close-cropped style, left a scruff of beard on his face, and changed his manner of dress, he knew it was only a matter of time before someone—a royal watcher, a reporter, a Sarcaccian national—recognized him and alerted the authorities, or worse, tipped off a media outlet like *Hello!* or *People*. He hoped the woman picked up on his Do Not Disturb vibe and opted to do exactly that.

"Excuse me? Do you speak English?"

So much for Do Not Disturb.

He raised his head slightly, intending to utter a curt no, but the woman's wide, hazel eyes and hopeful smile stopped him. She was a rare beauty, the type who took men's breath away simply by being in their presence.

Better yet, her earnest expression gave no indication she'd interrupted his breakfast because she recognized him.

Against his will, he smiled in return. Though she'd asked her question in flawless Spanish, she struck him as a well-dressed business traveler in need of directions. A rather beguiling traveler, at that. He'd spent time with some of the world's most attractive women—models, socialites, and one actress in particular—who poured immense amounts of time and money into improving their already-striking looks. Yet even without precise makeup, obvious designer clothing, or an artfully arranged hairstyle, this woman exuded a natural charm most of those women lacked and carried herself with a healthy self-confidence that didn't stray into arrogance.

Cautiously, he responded, "A bit. May I help you?"

She extended her hand. "I'm Emily Sinclair. I host an American television show called *At Home Abroad*. Perhaps you've heard of it?"

Television? Not the type of person he wanted to meet, in spite of her genuine manner and the fact she had a fantastic pair of legs. Tempting legs. He allowed himself a brief perusal before meeting her bright-eyed gaze and giving her a brief, dispassionate handshake. "I'm sorry, no."

Undeterred, her smile broadened. "You're not from Argentina, are you?"

"No. If you're looking for directions, I'm afraid I can't be of help." He needed to get rid of Emily Sinclair, American television host, and quickly, or risk exposure. Though next time he traveled to the United States, he might try to find her show. He could think of far worse ways to pass the time than admiring a beautiful woman from the solitude of his own sofa.

He reached for his newspaper, hoping she'd take the hint.

She pulled out the chair opposite his. "May I?"

He paused, his urge to learn more about the long-legged beauty warring with his sense of self-preservation. In that moment of hesitation, he caught a hint of vulnerability in her gaze, sensed that she was taking a risk, and was lost.

"I'm afraid I don't have much time, but go ahead." Emily Sinclair was a touchable woman. Honey-colored hair fell in gentle waves to her shoulders, her skin was porcelain smooth, and her full lips cried out for a man to run his finger over them. Though touching was out of the question, he decided to allow himself to indulge in the next best thing. What would a moment's conversation hurt?

As she slid into the seat, he caught the faintest whiff of her perfume. No, not perfume. She wasn't wearing a scent, at least not one from an ornate glass bottle, the way women did when they dressed up for the charity galas or state dinners he'd hosted alongside his father before leaving Sarcaccia. Her scent was soft, natural, like a ray of morning sunshine cutting through an ancient forest.

"I'm sorry, I didn't get your name," she said.

"Victor." It rolled off his tongue as easily as Vittorio once did. "You didn't get it because I didn't give it."

"I promise to be quick, Victor." She drew in a deep breath, confirming his guess that she'd been as wary of approaching him as he was of having her stay. "The reason I wanted to talk to you is that I noticed you were circling ads in the paper. Are you looking for an apartment to rent? Or to buy?"

Clever woman. Observant. "I'm looking at Buenos Aires real estate, yes." It was one of the few countries where property deals were handled on a cash basis, which would help keep the transaction below the media's radar…though apparently not this woman's radar.

"We're filming our show here in Buenos Aires this week. Our format for each episode is simple. We give our viewers a taste of Argentinean culture—say, the tango shows, the art museums, or the national obsession with *fútbol*—and show the exterior architecture of a local neighborhood. Then our camera crew follows a foreign house hunter, someone who's getting to know the country right along with our viewers, as he looks at a few properties in that neighborhood."

He knew where she must be heading, but kept his expression neutral. "I'm sure many people enjoy the show."

"Not as many people as I'd like." Her smile slipped a fraction and, despite himself, he wanted to bring it back to its full glory. "This episode is our season finale and I want it to be fantastic. Our network is about to make its decision on whether or not to renew the show and featuring just the right house hunter can make all the difference."

He said nothing, hoping his silence would forewarn her of his answer.

"If you're actively looking at properties, would you be interested in appearing on our show? We can make arrangements directly with your realtor, and—"

"What makes you believe I'd be the right person for your finale? You know nothing about me." Thankfully.

"First, you're a foreigner looking here in the city, so you fit our profile."

"As do dozens of others. You need only visit a real estate office."

"I realize that, but" —her cheeks flushed pink as she gestured from his feet to his face— "have you checked a mirror lately? You're extremely fit and you have a great face for television. Striking enough that I noticed you from across the street. When women peruse what's on, they tend to pause a few seconds on each channel. Someone with your looks captures their attention, just as you captured mine, and they watch long enough to realize they enjoy the show's content. They tune in again for the next episode and voilà, ratings go up."

He contained the grin that pulled at the edges of his mouth. In all his years, he'd never had a woman describe him to himself in such blunt fashion. "What about your male viewers?"

"Our audience is primarily women. However, male viewers tend to identify themselves with attractive men. Athletic men who look like they could tackle major home projects. You look like you've swung a hammer or two in your time." She shifted in the chair. "I realize this sounds like I'm flirting shamelessly, but—"

"You don't intend to flirt?" It was a dangerous question, but it'd been too long since he'd engaged in banter with an intelligent woman. Even then, those women knew they were with a crown prince, which changed the dynamic.

Her eyes lit with optimism. "Would flirting be effective?"

Oh, it'd be effective, but not in the way she envisioned. This woman's ignorance of his identity made her the perfect verbal sparring partner, which made her all the more tempting physically. He took a slow sip of his double espresso, making her wait for his response. When she didn't squirm, he realized that this could become something more, somewhere far more private, if he wanted a challenge. Despite the fact he'd hidden his royal identity for several months, he had yet to encounter the woman who didn't respond to easy flirtation or a quick smile, though he'd doled out fewer smiles than he could count on one hand in the time he'd been away. Even those were by rote, rather than drawn out by the recipient.

No, as enticing as it might be to see this particular woman's hair spread across a silk-encased pillow and her amazing legs tangled in his sheets, to savor the back-and-forth along the way to such intimacy —hell, to get back to actually *having* sex—he had to put a stop to it. The risks were too great.

"Enjoyable, yes. But effective? No, I'm afraid not for your purposes." He set down his cup. "While I like watching television, I have an aversion to being on it."

Unfortunate, because spending the remainder of his time in Buenos Aires with this woman would be far more interesting than what he needed to accomplish, finalizing his return to Sarcaccia and resuming his rightful place as crown prince without anyone the wiser.

Vittorio hadn't believed that Alessandro could pull off the duties of a crown prince, despite the fact that the switch was Alessandro's idea. Yet thanks to Alessandro, Vittorio had the opportunity to escape the palace and get his head on straight while Sarcaccia remained stable.

Alessandro vowed to continue standing in for Vittorio as long as was necessary, but the twins knew that eventually their deception would be discovered. Other than members of their immediate family, only Maria Cappalli, the Royal Police Chief Investigator, was told of their switch. While she'd promised to do what she could to protect their secret, she'd warned them that she couldn't keep inquisitive members of the media or her own police force at bay forever. When she'd called Alessandro last week to notify him that a group of police detectives were speculating about the length of the prince's disappearance and that it was high time they discuss the possibility of foul play with the king, Vittorio knew the clock on his return was ticking.

It wouldn't be to anyone's benefit for their actions to be discovered, which is why, as Vittorio told Alessandro just last night during a hushed phone call, in a few short weeks, he'd make his way home. He'd also hold the deed to a flat far from Sarcaccia to serve as a private escape should he ever want one. The very knowledge he owned such a place would make his return bearable, he'd explained to Alessandro. No longer would he feel confined to the fishbowl of the royal palace or be tempted by a false idea of home. With this retreat, he could be both the prince he was born to be and, on occasion, the private person his heart occasionally ached to be.

Alessandro claimed that what Vittorio needed was to get out and experience life, not hide away in a sterile flat, but Alessandro hadn't been able to argue the point before being called away to attend a reception for the King of Jordan. The way Alessandro mentioned the reception made Vittorio wonder—just for a moment—how his twin had managed to switch from club-hopping partier to the role of crown prince with such ease.

Perhaps because, in the end, the fate of Sarcaccia rested with Vittorio and his heirs, not with Alessandro. Vittorio's public behavior was subject to closer scrutiny than Alessandro's would ever be, his relationship missteps magnified. Acting as crown prince was just that for Alessandro. Acting. A temporary diversion rather than serious business.

Vittorio smiled at Emily, hoping to soften the blow of his refusal. It was too bad, really. In another lifetime, he might've enjoyed playing Alessandro's role, one in which pursuing women like Emily Sinclair was possible.

Emily leaned forward, unaware that in doing so she gave him a brief glimpse of cleavage. "You're certain I can't persuade you? The exact location of the properties you visit wouldn't be disclosed—we don't give out addresses—and your full name isn't used. We understand there's a certain need for privacy." Her head tilted as she grinned and said, "Believe it or not, most people we feature find the experience fun. It offers a unique opportunity to see behind the scenes of a television show. And I promise, my crew doesn't bite."

Bite? How could any man hear that word from her lush mouth and not be tempted?

On instinct, Vittorio reached across the table and took her hand, then raised it to his lips. His quick assessment of her had been accurate. She was very, very touchable. The places he could imagine directing that hand...if only he'd met her two years ago, before he'd made a life-altering mistake with another woman.

The memory left him cold.

But this woman...cold wasn't a word he could imagine being used to describe her. He felt, rather than heard, her intake of breath as his lips caressed her hand.

"Thank you again," he murmured against her skin before gently releasing her fingertips. "I'm quite flattered by the offer. It's...enticing. But I must decline."

"Oh." She was quiet for a moment, but the rise and fall of her breasts as her breathing sharpened betrayed an inner desire. When she spoke, her voice was thready. "Well, I promised I'd be quick. I'll leave you to your breakfast."

He stood as she did, giving her a polite nod. She covered her responding blush by tucking a loose strand of hair behind her ear. Reaching into a tiny pocket inside her suit jacket and withdrawing a business card, she said, "If you change your mind, Victor, I'd love to hear from you."

For a moment, he thought she'd hand it to him. Instead, she leaned forward and placed it on the tabletop beside his newspaper.

So she didn't trust herself with physical contact. Perhaps it was for the best.

She pushed in her chair and turned toward the street, then paused and looked back over her shoulder at him, a question in her hazel eyes. "By the way, it's Victor, you said? It's not Vittorio?"

CHAPTER 2

VVITTORIO FORCED himself not to react, despite the fact his chest closed in tight, just as it did when he'd taken a hard kick from Alessandro during martial arts training a few years ago.

Was Emily's entire approach a pretense leading to this singular moment? How, after all he'd experienced, could he still misread a woman's intent so completely? Certainly he'd fallen for a skilled actress before, and this woman flat-out told him she was on TV and had the business card to prove it. He internally cursed himself for making the same mistake he'd made in Sarcaccia and opened his mouth to utter what he hoped would come out as a casual denial, but Emily waved off her own question before he could answer.

"I'm sorry. That was unacceptably nosy of me. It's simply that we shot our first season in the Alps." Her lips pinched in a sign of discomfort that didn't look like acting. "We featured mountain villages in Italy, Switzerland, and Austria and…well, your accent sounds similar to our Italian real estate agent's, so I thought perhaps you were Anglicizing your name for my benefit. I shouldn't have—"

"I speak the language, but no, I'm not Italian."

He'd let his paranoia get to him. Emily had done nothing wrong, merely asked a question anyone in Buenos Aires might ask if they heard him speak more than a few words.

"I see. Well, thank you, Victor. Even if you aren't interested in doing the show and claim you only speak 'a bit' of English" —a teasing smile flickered across her lips— "I appreciate that you were willing to hear me out. It was a pleasure to meet you."

She turned, then crossed the street to a restaurant much like the one he occupied to join a woman who was seated at a table covered with pastry and what appeared to be business reports.

Pleasure. Yes, that was a good word for it. In another place, in another time, it might have been more.

Vittorio withdrew a few bills from his wallet and dropped them on the table, then folded the newspaper under his arm. Intentionally leaving Emily Sinclair's business card behind, he left without looking back.

SHE'D SAID SOMETHING WRONG. Emily sensed it the moment she'd asked whether Victor was Italian, though whether it was that he'd found her behavior rude or because he'd been caught off guard by the invasive nature of the question itself, she couldn't be certain.

"Wish I could read lips," Rita said as they walked toward the Recoleta office they'd rented for the season. "When he kissed your hand and looked at you like that, I was positive you'd finally gotten yourself a date."

"I told you, I only asked him if he'd be interested in appearing on the show. Nothing more. I haven't a clue why he kissed my hand."

"Bet it felt amazing, though."

"You're incorrigible." Though Rita was also right.

The moment Victor looked up from his newspaper and his eyes met hers, Emily's knees had threatened to give way. Right there, with Rita as a witness, she'd nearly swooned over a man. He was the kind of man who turned heads, even from a distance, but up close...a red-hot jolt of desire burned through her at the very thought of his intelligent brown eyes, so impossibly light in contrast to his jet-black hair she'd thought they might be green when she'd noticed him from across the street. He'd boldly studied her from head to toe, taking extra time to survey her legs before speaking to her. She'd forced herself to keep a calm, confident smile on her face, all the while feeling as if he could see right through her suit to assess every inch of her body.

His initial handshake was crisp, impersonal. But when he'd kissed her hand, allowing his warm lips to linger, she'd half expected him to turn her palm up and start working his way along her wrist. She wasn't sure she possessed the self-discipline to have stopped him.

She swallowed hard in an attempt to push the image from her mind. She'd approached a total stranger, an action that wasn't in her nature, in a desperate effort to save her show, and she'd come away from the attempt with nothing more than a case of mad lust. To top it off, she'd likely offended him with her question about his accent. She had to forget about her encounter with Victor and find a way to beef up the content they planned with the Winstons.

As the women rounded the final corner before arriving at the office, Rita's cell phone rang. A half beat later, Emily's phone rang as well. Emily reached into her handbag just as Rita said into her phone, "We're almost there. Yes, she's with me." She paused, listening, then said, "All right, tell us when we get there. Bye."

Emily glanced at her phone's caller ID and, seeing that her call also came from the office, she let it go to voice mail and frowned at Rita as the older woman rolled her eyes skyward.

"I'm not sure what's going on, but they need both of us right away." Rita let out an exaggerated sigh. "Welcome to another Monday morning."

Emily forced a smile. "Well, they say bad things come in threes. First, we strike out in our attempt to get an attractive house hunter. Second, we have an apparent meltdown in the office. One more bad thing and we're home free, right?"

"We don't know how bad the office is yet," Rita warned as she pulled open the glass door, then held it for Emily.

As Emily stepped inside the sunny space, a dozen somber faces greeted her. She strode to the center of the room, where a map of Buenos Aires was spread over a glass-topped conference table. After depositing her handbag in one of the chairs, she said, "All right. What happened?"

Maryam Tabrizi, one of the show's associate producers, grimaced. "It's not good. The Winstons' real estate agent just called us."

Emily put a palm to her forehead. "Don't tell me—"

"Their son had a bicycle accident while riding to one of his classes at Stanford. Thankfully he'll be fine, but he has to have surgery tomorrow morning for a badly broken thumb." Maryam shook her head. "Mrs. Winston asked if it's possible to delay filming for a week or two so they can fly back to California."

"What did you say?" Rita asked. "We've already pushed the schedule back as far as we can."

"There's no way we can do it, but I didn't want to tell her that, not until I'd spoken with you two." Maryam looked from Rita to Emily. "I simply told the agent that I'd have either you or Rita call as soon as possible. She gave me the number for the Winstons' hotel here in Recoleta, but said they were hoping to check out before noon so they could get on a flight this evening."

"Whew." This morning, Emily thought things couldn't get worse. Without the Winstons in town, there'd be no finale at all. The network wouldn't give her the budget needed for an extension, not when the show's fate was already up in the air. Network executives would likely greet any request for an extension with a cancellation of the final episode. On the other hand, never in a million years would Emily keep parents from an ailing son.

"Rita, call the Winstons. Assure them that they've made the right decision. Tell them we hope their son has a quick recovery and not to worry about the show, that we have contingency plans for just this type of situation. Then call their real estate agent and tell her the same."

"Got it."

To Maryam, she said, "Have one of the assistants find out which hospital is doing the surgery and arrange to have flowers delivered. In the meantime, I'd like you and Rita to get together to talk tango."

"Tango?" One of the cameramen, a lanky Australian named Mike, whistled from the back of the room. "Rita and Maryam? Now that'd make great television."

Laughter echoed through the office, prompting Emily to shoot a grin in Mike's direction. It raised her spirits to know the staff had a sense of humor about their situation. It was part of what she loved about working with them. Even when everyone was frustrated, they kept a positive attitude.

"Sorry, Mike. They're discussing a possible tango segment."

A chorus of "awwww" echoed through the office.

Emily made a show of plugging her ears against the sound. Once the room quieted, she turned back to Maryam. "Rita knows what we need. While you two get started on that, have the rest of the staff get on the phone and canvass our real estate contacts one more time. Maybe we'll get lucky and find a client who's willing to shoot this week. High-end properties are preferable, of course, but we'll take anything at this point. Expand the search area outside Recoleta and Palermo to include Barrio Norte and San Telmo.

"And Mike?" She turned toward the cameraman. "If you have time, maybe head to those neighborhoods and get some beauty shots while the weather's clear. That way we have the footage ready to go if we need it. But keep your phone close in case we need to go elsewhere."

As the staff scattered, Emily caught sight of the *Buenos Aires Herald* on Maryam's desk. The page was folded to the real estate listings.

"Mind if I borrow this?" she asked Maryam, who was already waving for Emily to take it.

Rita looked at her askance. "What are you thinking?"

"I have an idea. Give me a sec."

It probably wasn't the best idea, but how could she let her coworkers down? They'd spent almost ten months of the past two years away from home, giving up precious time with their families in order to film the show on location. They worked as hard as she did, yet received far less glory for their efforts.

"Anything Rita or I can do?" Maryam asked.

Emily shook her head. She scanned the page until she found the ad she sought, the one under the photo of a sparkling high rise, and then read the description. The figure listed at the end shocked her. Few people spent that amount of money on a one-bedroom apartment, even in pricier cities like Paris or London.

"I'm going out," she announced. "Call me if you come up with any leads."

She stuffed the real estate listing into her handbag and headed out the door before Rita, Maryam, or anyone else could protest. And before her own nerves got the better of her.

EMILY TRIED to appear relaxed and friendly as she discreetly scanned the well-heeled buyers strolling through the luxury apartment overlooking the Plaza Sicilia in Buenos Aires' park-filled Palermo neighborhood. Though she was unfamiliar with the real estate agent who hovered near the front door, Emily had managed to talk her way into the exclusive showing. She hoped that with the soft gray suit and ivory blouse she'd selected for work this morning she blended in with the other buyers, even if she didn't have their financial resources.

She'd been thrilled when she'd stepped inside. Not only was the apartment private, occupying the top floor of one of the area's tallest buildings, its gleaming hardwood floors, expansive views, and airy modern decor were certain to appeal to viewers of *At Home Abroad*. An attached rooftop terrace complete with a small swimming pool, teak chaises, and a living wall of potted bamboo would take the episode over the top visually. Who wouldn't want to imagine themselves sunning in such a divine spot?

However, much as she'd wanted to interact with the potential buyers and gauge their interest in appearing on her show, it was out of the question. No one entered an open house expecting to be approached by a television host, and she was certain the real estate agent wouldn't approve. *At Home Abroad* maintained its network of real estate contacts by allowing agents the ability to broach the subject with their clients privately, and only if they felt it appropriate.

On the other hand, there was nothing to stop an individual at the open house from approaching her, which was why Emily had spent the last twenty minutes circling the space.

It wasn't much of a plan, but it was all she had. Unfortunately, with only a half hour left until the real estate agent closed the doors, the specific individual Emily had in mind hadn't appeared. The only buyers remaining were a well-dressed older couple, and Emily suspected from the whispered conversation she'd overheard while they toured the master suite that they lived elsewhere in the building and had only come to see the penthouse out of curiosity.

Emily gave the couple a polite nod as they entered the spacious living room. Wanting to give them solitude to continue their conversation, she moved away from the floor-to-ceiling windows and into the apartment's sleek, European-style kitchen. An audible sigh escaped her as she allowed her hand to trail across the sparkling white quartz topping the ebony island. She'd give herself five more minutes, then she needed to head back to the office and check on progress. If she didn't have a shooting schedule finalized by tonight, she'd be forced to call her network's headquarters in New York to explain the situation.

It would be an out-and-out declaration of failure.

She closed her eyes, forcing down the bubble of despondency rising in her chest. She still had a few hours. If she couldn't make something happen, perhaps the staff could. They'd certainly worked miracles in the past. Or, if worse came to worst, perhaps she could tap into her savings and float the cost of the extension herself. Waiting for the Winstons to return from California would wipe out her account, but if it gave the show a fighting chance, she'd do it.

A shift in the air made her open her eyes. She stifled a gasp as she found herself eye-to-upper body with the very man she'd been hoping to see. How had she not heard his approach?

Victor stood less than three feet in front of her, his marked-up newspaper rolled in his hand. Despite the fact he wore the same loafers, dark jeans and white Oxford-cloth shirt as this morning, no one could doubt he belonged in an apartment as luxe as this one. He carried himself as if he already owned the place.

Taller, broader in the shoulder and narrower in the hip than she'd realized during their brief encounter, when a table had served as a buffer between them, he dominated the space between the island and the kitchen's rear wall of cabinets. He'd sent her heart into a slow flip this morning, but being this close to him fired every nerve in her body. If he spun her around and lifted her onto the counter behind him right then and there, she'd—

"Now you're stalking me?"

She met his gaze, but the chill in his eyes only served to emphasize the iciness of his tone.

Her fantasy died, the connection they'd shared this morning completely severed by his quiet, accusing words.

"No, it's not—"

"That's why you put your business card beside my newspaper instead of handing it to me." He stepped even closer, leaving her trapped between his body and the kitchen's massive island. "You wanted to see which ads I'd circled so you could follow me."

She shook her head, hoping he couldn't see how disconcerted he made her. She'd put the business card on the table rather than handing it to him because she'd been afraid he'd pull her fingers to his lips once more and he'd know how utterly desirable she found him. She hadn't thought twice about the ads she'd seen marked, not until she'd arrived in the office and heard about the Winstons. But how could she explain her action without admitting her intense attraction and looking like a fool?

"Then explain your presence."

"I will, if you give me some space." Why was he so angry?

He tossed the newspaper onto the island countertop and then surprised her by leaning forward, bracing a palm on either side of her. Her heart leapt into her throat as he spoke. "I'm not giving you anything. I want you to explain yourself. Who's employing you? How did you get in here? This showing required preregistration."

She blinked. Employing her? Who was this man, to have such a strong reaction to seeing her here? She ignored his second question and said, "I told you this morning. I'm the host of *At Home Abroad.*"

"And that's why you're following me?" His steady gaze bore into her as he spoke, as if he could draw out what was in her mind through sheer intimidation. "Or are you here for some other reason?"

It took every ounce of her fortitude to maintain eye contact. He'd imprisoned her in the space between his arms to compel her to respond, certainly, but there was something besides anger in his cold, assessing gaze, an emotion she hadn't expected.

Astonished, she said, "I make you uneasy."

His eyes narrowed a fraction. "I'm not afraid of anyone, let alone an oh-so-innocent-looking American in skinny high heels."

"I didn't say afraid. I said uneasy." Which was exactly the way he made her feel. Panicky, yet attracted and fascinated at the same time. But what could possibly make him uneasy around her? It wasn't sexual interest, though this morning she'd seen that, too. This was another emotion entirely.

His upper lip twitched as he stared at her, the same involuntary movement she'd noticed this morning when she'd asked if his name was Vittorio. What was it he thought she wanted? This wasn't about appearing on her show.

"You're trying to distract me." His strong, handsome face was only inches from hers now, so close she could kiss him with the barest of movement, if he didn't strangle her first for her perceived infraction. "Explain yourself or I'll have the real estate agent throw you out. I doubt she wants to risk a sale because of you, not on a property with a commission as high as this one."

"All right." Emily resisted the temptation to push him away. Putting a hand on his chest to give herself room to think would only worsen her predicament. "I admit that I saw which ads you circled."

"So you did follow me."

"No, not at first." At his look of consternation, she explained, "When I said goodbye to you this morning, I had no intention of coming here. I'd taken a chance approaching you at the restaurant. When it didn't work out, that was that."

"Then why did you inspect my newspaper?"

She couldn't help but show her exasperation. "It wasn't on purpose. I put it out of my head as soon as I left my card on the table."

"Yet here you are, which leaves my mind to all sorts of imaginings."

Was he flirting with her or threatening her?

Both options were decidedly hazardous.

"You're making it rather hard for me to concentrate, let alone explain." He had to realize it. Men with looks like Victor's knew the effect they had on women. She eased to the side in an attempt to escape the prison in which he'd trapped her.

He moved his right hand a few inches, but only so he could gesture for her to continue speaking.

What did Victor do for a living? she wondered as his hand came back down on the heavy quartz countertop. Not only did he apparently have the budget for this apartment, he acted as a man used to getting his way.

On an exhale, she said, "I went back to the office, fully intending to shoot the episode as planned. But when Rita and I walked in from breakfast—Rita's the show's other executive producer—we learned that the couple we originally scheduled asked to delay filming. Their son was in a bicycle accident and they wanted to fly home to the United States to be with him. Of course I thought they should go." Seeing the doubt in his expression, she added, "I'm not heartless."

"I didn't accuse you of being heartless. Only deceptive."

He pushed away from her and leaned his hips against the top edge of the opposite counter. At the same time, Emily heard the distinct sound of high heels striking hardwood in the adjacent living room. Before Emily could respond to Victor's accusation, the real estate agent rounded the corner, carrying a thick information packet emblazoned with the building's name. She greeted them both with a polite, professional smile. "I hope you're finding everything in the apartment to your liking. Do either of you have questions so far?"

Emily shook her head. "I'm sorry to be taking so long. Were you trying to wrap up?"

"You're the last, but please, take all the time you need. It's a stunning property." She turned her full attention to Victor. Handing him the information packet, she said, "This outlines the building's amenities. If you haven't had a chance to see this unit's private rooftop terrace, I'd be happy to show you its features."

"I'm still analyzing the features here in the kitchen," Victor replied, his gaze drifting back to Emily, leaving no doubt as to his meaning. He set the packet on the counter and told the agent, "I'll be sure to find you if I have any questions about the terrace. Thank you."

The dark-haired woman glanced from Victor to Emily, then back again. "Of course. I'll be in the den whenever you're ready. It's located just inside the front door." Though the woman's demeanor remained professional, Emily suspected the agent thought she'd interrupted a romantic encounter.

"I believe you'll have time to finish your explanation now," Victor said once the sound of the agent's footsteps faded. He didn't move to trap her again, yet the way he crossed his arms over his formidable chest left Emily no doubt about his determination.

Choosing her words with care, she said, "As soon as I realized our season finale was in jeopardy, I had the staff start calling around, trying to come up with other possibilities. That's when I remembered the ad I'd seen circled in your newspaper. It stood out because it was beneath a huge picture of this building. I decided to come here on the off chance you registered for the showing."

"I said no." The firm set of his jaw left no doubt he was a man who meant the word when he said it.

"I realize that, but I had to try. And I thought that, even if you weren't here, perhaps I could talk to the real estate agent afterward and get a lead. It's a gorgeous building, exactly what we'd like for the finale. And if we don't start shooting by tomorrow morning, everything we've worked to accomplish is lost."

"Lost?" A dark eyebrow arched. "Isn't that a bit dramatic?"

She shook her head. "We supposed to wrap by the end of next

week. The expense of keeping the staff in Buenos Aires until the Winstons return from the United States will blow the season's budget. If I ask the network for an extension and a budget increase, they'd likely say no and cancel the episode. Without a great finale to cap off the season, they're almost certain to cancel our series." There. She'd said the words aloud and managed not to choke on them.

"I'm sorry to hear that." His expression softened for a moment. Turning to look out the window at the end of the kitchen, he said, "There are views from every room in this flat. I can even stand at the cooktop and see parks. The botanical garden. The city skyline. And because it's higher than the surrounding buildings, with glass that has been specially treated, no one can see inside. It's completely private. And it's a one-bedroom unit. No guest room, no guest bath."

He turned back to face her. "It didn't occur to you after I explained that I had no desire to appear on television, and after you read the description of this flat, that what I'm seeking is privacy?"

"Of course, but" —how could she phrase this?— "when we met...well, I can't put a finger on it, but you struck me as someone with a lot of warmth." No man who kissed her hand the way he had, with such fire in his gaze, could be as coldhearted as he wanted her to believe. "When our plan for the finale fell apart, I thought I might be able to talk you into helping me out of a jam. That's all."

"In my experience, women who use deceptive means to get help—out of a jam, as you put it—never, ever have a man's best interest at heart. Especially mine."

CHAPTER 3

W_{ELL}. A woman had obviously done a number on Victor to make him distrust all other women. She took a step toward him. "Victor, I—"

"You are an enticing woman." His forehead creased as he waved off her words. "The answer is still no."

He turned on his heel and strode out of the kitchen, leaving his newspaper and the information packet behind.

Emily let the breath whoosh from her lungs. As much as she'd felt drawn to Victor, as much as she was certain he'd felt the same, she'd obviously wasted her time in coming here. She hadn't thought she could feel worse than when she'd arrived at the apartment, but his distrust—and curt dismissal—accomplished it.

Tears pricked at her eyes for the first time since she'd landed the hosting gig. Whether it was frustration over the episode or disappointment in the way things had gone with Victor, she didn't know. Maybe it was both.

Or maybe it was the fear of seeing so many people—good, talented, hardworking people—lose their jobs after they'd poured their hearts and souls into making the Argentina season spectacular.

At that moment, she felt a vibration from her handbag. Digging inside, she withdrew her phone and read the new text message from Rita.

No luck yet. You?

Grateful for the momentary distraction from thoughts of Victor, she typed back *Working on a Plan B, will call shortly.*

Once she got downstairs, she'd make two calls. First to her bank, and then to Rita.

VITTORIO UNCURLED his fists as he crossed the apartment's threshold to stand in the penthouse's circular elevator lobby. So much for the pleasant memory he'd hoped to retain from this morning's breakfast. Emily Sinclair—assuming that was really her name—had gall.

In front of him, a sleek electronic panel marked the floors as the elevator made its ascent. Behind him, he could hear Emily saying all the right things to the real estate agent, thanking the woman for allowing her extra time to walk through the flat.

He wondered what lies Emily had told to gain access.

He wondered whether to believe anything Emily said.

Now that he considered the idea, it seemed farfetched that of all the people to notice him sitting in a near-empty Buenos Aires café scanning property listings, it'd be the host of a real estate show. Despite what his gut said about Emily, with her honest face and beguiling smile, logic told him it was far more likely she was one of the long line of private investigators and paparazzi who'd tried to locate Alessandro, hoping to get the first confirmed photo of the missing prince, and that she'd managed to track him to Argentina and come up with an original approach in hopes of doing just that.

All Emily had to do was ascertain his identity by whatever means necessary—a carefully dropped question, a glimpse at his identification—whip out a camera, and she'd be an instant millionaire. When she'd asked if his name was Vittorio, he should've known she was fishing for information, hoping that "Alessandro" might react to the use of his twin brother's name.

He might be sporting an uncharacteristic beard, a deeper tan, and longer hair than when he'd last been photographed, but anyone looking for Alessandro's features when studying his face would believe they had their man. Worse, what if after sitting across the table from him she realized that it was he, rather than Alessandro, who'd disappeared? Surely a stranger wouldn't have the ability to tell them apart, let alone after such a brief meeting. His own mother occasionally had to look twice to be certain which son had entered the room. Then again, he'd been foolish enough to identify himself as Victor. He shouldn't have been so trusting, no matter how harmless she appeared.

His gut had been dead wrong about a woman before and it had almost cost him everything. No reason to think his gut would be right now.

The light on the electronic panel froze on the third floor. Vittorio ran a hand through his hair in frustration and willed the elevator to move so Emily wouldn't have the opportunity to study him again. He'd have been better off if he'd turned and walked out of the apartment the moment he'd seen her in the kitchen. But when he'd rounded the corner from the living room and noticed her standing alone with her eyes closed, a heady mixture of beauty and vulnerability, he couldn't resist approaching her. It wasn't until he'd taken those few steps forward that he'd realized her presence couldn't be coincidence.

He could kick himself for failing to call Maria Cappalli as soon as he'd left the restaurant this morning. The Royal Police Chief Investigator would have run a quick background check on Emily, and he'd have known in minutes whether his breakfast companion was who and what she claimed.

He punched the button again a split second before he heard the click of the apartment door. He didn't need to turn around to know that Emily now stood behind him. A few painful seconds ticked off before she spoke, a slight tremor edging her words. "I wanted to let you go ahead, but I couldn't stall any longer without looking suspicious. The agent needed to do her final walk-through before locking up."

He said nothing, despite the temptation to mock her use of the word "suspicious," keeping his attention focused on the elevator panel. When the doors finally swished to admit them, he propped open one side with his arm and gestured for Emily to enter.

"No, I can wait."

"Get in," he ground out, allowing himself a quick look at her. Though she stood tall, shoulders back and proud, pinkish streaks tinged her cheeks and her eyes were bright with restrained tears. She paused, considering, then strode past him into the mirrored, walnut-inlaid carriage.

He shouldn't have looked. Her defiant, I-can-handle-anything demeanor reminded him of his sister, Sophia.

Once inside the elevator, he turned away from her and hit the button for the ground floor. They were nearly to street level when she spoke again, her voice steadier this time. "If it makes any difference, I'm sorry. I thought I was doing what was best for the show and for my employees. I didn't mean to intrude. The rest of my team doesn't know I'm here. Other than Rita, who was eating breakfast with me this morning, they don't even know you exist. So I promise, you won't have to worry about seeing me—or anyone from my show—again."

Good to know—assuming she told the truth—but he only tipped his head in response.

The elevator reached the ground floor with a light bounce, then the doors opened. Once again, Vittorio moved to the side so Emily could exit before him. Much as this woman drove him to distraction, certain acts were ingrained from birth.

"Thank you," she said as he moved ahead of her to hold open the glass door leading out to the street. "You're very polite."

"And apparently a rotten judge of character," he muttered as he blinked against the bright sunshine. The walkways of the popular neighborhood had thickened with the noontime crowd while he'd been indoors. Many moved purposefully in the direction of the neighborhood's shops and restaurants, while others carried bagged sandwiches and drinks in search of an open bench in one of the area's many parks.

He was about to turn to walk down the sidewalk, heading whichever way Emily Sinclair was not, when she surprised him with a quick, "You're right. You are."

At what must have been a look of astonishment on his face, she planted a fist against her hip. There was no sign of the threatening tears he'd noticed a few minutes earlier. Much like Sophia, Emily seemed to rally in the face of a challenge. "Look, I was wrong to invade your privacy and I've admitted that. But I'm not a bad person. I don't know who made you think that every female in the world is out to get you, but they're not. At least *I'm* not." She checked her watch before pulling a phone from the side pocket of her handbag. "I have to get going. I have a show to put on and a limited amount of time in which to handle everything. Goodbye, Victor. I do hope you find your dream apartment…and whatever else it is you're trying to find."

She spun away from him and threaded her way down the crowded sidewalk, raising her phone to her ear as she went.

His stomach clenched. She'd said it to bait him. Still, there was truth to her words, and that truth made him feel like an ass.

Let her go.

He slipped on his sunglasses and turned in the opposite direction, trying to remember the address for the next flat he'd planned to view. He'd been so distracted by his encounter with Emily that he'd left the newspaper behind. Had it been two blocks away? Or three? He groaned inwardly. Even if he knew where to go, he'd lost the desire.

After nearly five months of globetrotting, he'd finally prepared himself to make his return to Sarcaccia and be the heir to the throne his country deserved, the type of heir he'd been until Carmella's death —focused, determined, and hard-working. It'd taken that long to convince himself that Carmella's actions were a reflection on her, not on him or his ability to lead. But in a matter of hours, a woman with innocent eyes and sinful legs made him question everything.

Turning back, he was able to pick out Emily amongst the crowd waiting for the walk signal at the next intersection. She stood a few steps apart from the rest of the pedestrians, listening to a call on her cell phone.

Was she calling someone about filming her television show, as she claimed? Or was she reporting her actions to a superior at a tabloid? He had to know.

Taking quick strides, he covered the half block between them, coming up a few steps behind her just as the light changed and she crossed the street. She shook her head as she listened to someone on the other end of the call.

"No, Rita." Stress and fatigue filled her voice. "Don't tell anyone the funds are coming from my account." A pause, and then, "Don't worry, I'll be fine, I have enough to cover it. I appreciate the offer, though."

He lost track of the conversation while he skirted around a woman whose dog stopped to sniff a signpost, but caught up again as Emily approached another intersection.

"Look, this buys us another ten to fourteen days," he heard as Emily stepped to the curb, then waved for an approaching taxi. "I'm confident we can pull off a great show in that time. When we're renewed, I can talk to the network about a reimbursement. It'll be worth the gamble...okay, okay...I'm catching a cab now. I'll be back in fifteen minutes."

He ground his teeth. Emily was one hundred percent right. He was a rotten judge of character. If he hadn't been born a Barrali, he never would've thought the worst of her. That she was, in her words, out to get him.

Then again, if he hadn't been born a Barrali, he wouldn't have had a reason.

The taxi slowed before rolling to a stop alongside the curb. Emily smiled her thanks to the driver before opening the door to the back seat.

Swearing aloud, Vittorio jogged to the other side of the taxi before it could pull out into traffic, yanked open the door, and slid inside.

Emily flinched as the door on the opposite side of the taxi flew open and a large, well-muscled body slid into the empty space where she'd been about to set her handbag. "What the—"

"Tell me why you need money."

Emily stared at Victor, dumbfounded.

"Tell me." His tone was lower this time, commanding. She wondered if he kept the beard because it made his face as intimidating as his voice.

"You not only followed me, you listened in on my phone conversation?" she managed, hoping she didn't appear as shocked and disoriented as she felt. "Now who's invading whose privacy?"

The taxi driver shot Emily a questioning glance in the rearview mirror before shifting in his seat to turn and frown at Victor in warning. She assured the driver she was all right, then asked him to hold on for a moment.

"I didn't mean to startle you, but I didn't want you to get away, either," Victor said, his demanding tone softening a few notches. "Tell me why you need money. Please."

Get away? The man was positively infuriating. Despite his effort to ask more gently, he continued to stare at her as a parent might at a teen caught sneaking out of the house.

She set her handbag between them as a buffer. "I told you, the network is not going to give me an extension. I'm creating one. Not that it's any of your concern."

"With your own money?"

"Yes, with my own money."

"You have enough to do that?"

"I can get it." Why she told him that, she didn't know. She rarely discussed finances with anyone, let alone with a total stranger. Maybe it was out of a sense of pride. Or to prove to him that she wasn't desperate, that she was resourceful and strong.

Victor ran a hand through his dark hair as he glanced at the driver, who was still watching from the front seat, wary of the man who'd barged into his cab. "Tell the driver where you're headed. I'll come with you."

When Emily hesitated, Victor shot a pointed look in the direction of her cab window. "There are two people on the curb who want the taxi. If we don't get moving, we're costing him a fare."

Fine. What'd she care if he rode along? She gave the driver the address of the show's office in Recoleta. The burly man shrugged, then eased out into traffic.

Victor slid the glass panel between the front and back seat closed, cutting off the driver from their conversation. He gestured toward the phone she still clutched. "Have Internet access?"

"Of course."

He held out his hand, palm up. "May I use it for a moment? I'd like to check some information while we're en route."

"You don't have your own phone?"

An odd look crossed his face, but was gone in a flash. "Left it at my hotel this morning."

She wasn't sure she trusted him, but since there was a pass code that would bar him from accessing any of her personal information, she tapped the screen to open her browser and handed over the phone.

"Production costs on a show like yours must be considerable," Victor commented as his fingers moved across the screen with quick, light movements.

"I don't have to fund the production itself. That's already covered. Just the expense of keeping the staff here an extra week or so while we wait for the Winstons to return. They're the couple we'd originally planned to use in our finale."

"Still a lot of money."

She turned to face him. "First, I'm not sure why you're so concerned with my budget. And second, if you were responsible for the livelihoods of so many people, I suspect you'd do whatever you could to help them, wouldn't you?"

His lean fingers stilled over the screen, but he didn't meet her gaze. "I ask because I've wrestled with a budget or two in my time. I've also been responsible for the livelihoods of others, and yes, I do what I can to ensure their well-being. In fact, I'm quite good at it."

"Well, so am I. And that's all I'm doing." She knew it would sound defensive, but she explained her reasoning to him anyway. "It's not as if I'm throwing the money away. When the finale goes well and we're renewed for another season, I can recoup the investment."

His brow puckered as he studied her phone, then tapped the screen a few more times. "From my understanding of television production—and I admit, it's limited—it's rare for one person to be responsible for everything. I doubt your staff would blame you if the show is cancelled."

"I'm not worried about blame. I'm *responsible*. There's a big difference." She snagged the phone from Victor's grasp, holding it away from him so she had his undivided attention. Irritation flashed in his gaze, but he made no move to reclaim the phone.

"Rita and I are the show's executive producers," she explained. "The network might dictate the show's budget and have final approval on what actually airs, but we're the ones who came up with the concept and pitched the show to the network. We hired the staff. We make the decisions about where to film, what aspects of the local culture we want to include, and who we'll feature. Since I'm the host, I'm also the public face of the show. That's what I mean when I say I'm responsible. The people Rita and I hired trust us to make good decisions, decisions that will keep them employed so they can pay their mortgages and feed their families. Now do you get it? It's a bit like running a small country."

One side of his mouth hitched up in a blend of curiosity and doubt. "Your concern is entirely for the staff? You're not worried about your own career?"

"I probably should be, but at the moment it's not my priority."

It was far easier to focus on everyone else. She'd already faced one big failure in her career, thanks to her stupid decision to quit her last job as a concession to her ex, Paul. She'd been forced to rebuild her career from scratch and she'd done well—at least until this season—but she knew the chances of starting over a third time and being successful were slim. Yet to dwell on the worst possible outcome would cripple her ability to focus.

"You think that when these people—the Winstons?—come back, you'll have a good show with them?"

"I'll find a way. Nothing leaves my hands for the network unless it's of the highest quality." What did he expect? "Quality keeps good people employed, myself included. I won't settle for less."

The taxi slowed to round a corner. Victor leaned away from her, craning his neck to see past the driver and down the street in front of them. "We're going back to Recoleta?"

"The office space we rented for the season isn't far from Café Luchana, where you were having breakfast."

She followed his gaze and realized they only had a few more blocks to go. As she moved to open her handbag and retrieve her wallet, she noticed the screen on her phone. There, right in the center of the display, was her picture. Below it were her name and title, followed by similar information for both Rita and Maryam.

Victor had pulled up the credits page of the *At Home Abroad* website.

Emily drew in a sharp breath. "You said you needed to check some information. You didn't say you were checking on *me*."

"I needed to be absolutely sure you were who you claimed to be—"

"And on my own phone, no less!"

"—and that your motives for approaching me were what you claimed—"

"After jumping in *my* cab! Why? You planning to turn me in to the cops for following you to the apartment or something?"

"—before I agree to appear on your show."

The taxi pulled into an open spot across the street from the *At Home Abroad* office. Emily stared at Victor, stunned into silence.

"If you're still interested in me, that is."

Before Emily could recover, Victor slid open the glass panel in front of them and paid the cabbie, including a generous tip. She started to protest, since the ride was her business expense, but he enveloped both her hands in his stronger ones and moved closer to her on the narrow seat.

"Are you?" he asked, his gaze intense as he waited for her answer. "Interested?"

CHAPTER 4

"You...you're saying you want to be on the show?"

His brows rose fractionally. Sitting this close, she noticed golden striations radiated from his pupils, adding depth to irises the color of sweet honey. Fascinating eyes for an utterly confusing man.

And his hands were still wrapped around hers, though she fought to ignore the warmth that flowed through her as his thumb grazed her knuckles.

"'Want' is a strong word. But yes, I'll visit your fancy properties and rave about the fixtures and floor tiles. And I can film right away, so you won't need to tap your own financial resources. However, there will need to be a few conditions." He regarded her for a moment, then released her hands and leaned back, reaching for the door handle. "Shall we adjourn to a café or to your office to discuss?"

"Café." Until she knew exactly what his conditions were, she wouldn't walk him into the office and give the staff false hope. "And I have a few conditions of my own."

A wry smile curved his lips. "You believe you're in a position to negotiate?"

"It's not a matter of negotiation. The network has a standard contract for anyone who appears on the show."

"Then let's find a café. My treat."

She allowed Victor to lead the way back to Café Luchana, where a hostess guided them to the same table where she'd spied him having breakfast. Once they were seated with menus in hand, Emily waved to encompass the outdoor space. "Twice in one day?"

"I wasn't expecting this particular table, but" —he shrugged— "when I find things I like, I tend to stick with them. My siblings tease me about being a creature of habit, but I prefer to think of it as being consistent and reliable."

"Siblings, plural?" It was her first glimpse into the man's life, and she was intrigued. "Do you come from a large family?"

"Very." He shut his menu as if closing the door on further personal discussion. "Now, my conditions. You said this morning that I could use a different name for privacy's sake?"

"I believe I said that we don't use last names, but I'm sure using a different first name on air won't be a problem as long as the network has your legal name for the release and to pay your stipend."

"I don't require a stipend."

"It's not much, but we're happy to do it. And as I said over breakfast, it can be a lot of fun to be in front of the camera. An adventure you talk about with friends and family when it's all over."

A laugh escaped him, but before she could comment, the waitress approached to offer a large bottle of sparkling water and to take their sandwich orders.

"No stipend," he said once the waitress left. "And no release."

"It's mandatory for the show's insurance carrier. No release, no show." And back she went to the Winstons.

He took a slow sip of his water, his eyes narrowing as he studied her over the rim of the glass. In those seconds, she felt each beat of her heart.

"All right," he said at last. "I'll sign a release, assuming it doesn't contain any terms that are out of the ordinary. But I must insist upon remaining anonymous. And that includes to your crew. Can you do that?"

Relief coursed through her. "Done."

A group of college-aged women with shopping bags walked by arm in arm, laughing as they made their way toward Avenue Quintana, one of Recoleta's main thoroughfares. A brunette with her hair in a casual twist glanced back over her shoulder at Victor at the same moment he slipped on a pair of sunglasses and turned away as if he hadn't noticed. But Emily knew he had.

The man grew more interesting by the moment. She leaned forward and asked, "So what changed your mind, oh creature of habit?"

"You told me I was a poor judge of character, that's what." Though she couldn't see his eyes, his tone and the self-deprecating lift at the edges of his mouth made her realize he was serious. "No one's ever told me that before. I appreciated the honesty when you had nothing to gain and everything to lose. That's uncommon."

"Thank you, I think." When he'd walked away, she'd have sworn she'd seen anger in his expression. In her experience, men with stunning looks like Victor's didn't often hear anything from women but compliments. Apparently, her words had penetrated, though now she could feel him studying her from behind his dark lenses as if attempting to discern what else she thought of him.

He merely angled his head, as if waiting to hear what she'd say next. While she wasn't one to back down from a challenge, she desperately needed to find a restroom. After locating a copy of the release in her handbag so he could take a moment to peruse it, she excused herself, promising to return before the waitress appeared with their lunch.

Vittorio watched her go, then gave the release a quick read. Seeing nothing alarming on the single sheet of legalese, he dug in his pocket for his cell phone...the throwaway he hadn't wanted Emily to know he had.

A moment later, a groggy voice nearly identical to his own answered in Sarcaccian-accented Italian. "What's wrong? It's the middle of the night."

"What's on your schedule this week?"

A muttered epithet, then the rustle of bedsheets came over the line.

His sheets, given that Alessandro had moved into Vittorio's palace apartment. "Does this mean you're on your way home?"

"Not quite yet.'"

A pause. More shuffling, then feet hitting the floor. The flick of a light switch followed by more footsteps, as if Alessandro had walked from the bedroom to the living room for privacy.

Vittorio closed his eyes against his brother's idiocy. "Are you *with* someone?" And if so, who was he claiming to be?

"No. God, no, or I'd be in a better mood. I'm trying to find my calendar." After heaving out an exasperated breath, Alessandro said, "Nothing but social events. I'm visiting a hospital tomorrow, then a halfway house on Wednesday. Otherwise, there's a movie premiere, a few dinners, and yet another art exhibition. You can imagine my delight. Oh, and Megan and Stefano want the family to get together to discuss wedding logistics. You do remember that they're getting married this summer? Of course, since you missed Christmas, you might not—"

"No political engagements? Nothing where you'll be acting on behalf of the government?"

"Not for almost two weeks. The Indian Prime Minister is stopping here on his way to speak at the United Nations. Why?"

Vittorio kept his gaze moving, ensuring no one was within earshot as he spoke. "When I left, you encouraged me to live like you do. I told you that wasn't possible, that I needed solitude. Hell, even *you* shouldn't live like you do. It's a wonder you've survived." Nightclubs. Parties. Adventure travel. All the wealth and access a man could desire, yet with none of the responsibilities of the heir.

"I didn't think it was possible I could survive an art exhibition, yet here I am," came the droll response. "You'd be surprised what humans are capable of enduring."

"I also told you that if I lived the way you do, we'd be caught." Vittorio ran a hand over the thick growth covering his jaw. "Let's just say that if we're ever discovered, it'll be due to my activities this week. Given that risk, I'd prefer it if you have Father handle any political events. Then, at least, the scandal will be minimal. No harm done.

We'll look like brothers who decided to pull a prank by having you attend a dinner or two in my place." He'd switch his accommodations again tonight, just to be safe. If anyone traced him to the date he agreed to appear on the show, it'd look like he'd just arrived in the country.

Silence reigned on the other end of the line.

"Alessandro? Did you hear me?"

"What. Have. You. Done?"

"Nothing salacious. I'm simply helping out someone who's in a tough spot. However, it will put me at risk of being recognized."

"Is this someone a woman?"

"It's not what you're thinking." His denial came out more forcefully than he intended. Across the café, he noticed Emily speaking to the waitress just inside the door. "I have to go. I'll update you when I can."

"Understood. But Vittorio? I'm glad you're interacting with someone. Anyone."

"You may change your mind."

"Come home soon. I prefer my own bed."

He pocketed the phone before Emily noticed it. While his sense of self-preservation warned that it was ridiculous to have agreed to appear on television, simply watching Emily Sinclair as she resumed her seat made him believe he'd done the right thing. It wasn't the hopefulness in her expression this morning or that she'd noted he was a bad judge of character, which no one had the guts to say to his face after his Carmella fiasco, though it'd put the entire family at risk. Rather, it was that Emily had stood up for herself. Risked his ire to make her point that she wasn't a bad person and that the world wasn't out to get him. That steel spine, more than her plea for help, convinced him she was worth helping.

He picked up the bottle of water and topped off both of their glasses. All his life, people had deferred to him, even when he knew he was in the wrong. He'd left Sarcaccia for much-needed clarity, and it didn't come in any more pure form than a woman with the determination to protect those around her and the backbone to speak freely when it was important to do so. Spending a week outside his comfort zone with Emily might give him the sober perspective he craved.

Once she'd draped her suit jacket over the back of the chair and turned to face him, he pushed the signed release across the table. "There. We're official."

She glanced at it, then frowned.

"It's Barr," he said before she could ask him to decipher the scribble he'd used for his signature.

"It looks longer."

"Let's just say it's Barr, all right?" Close enough to Barrali, but more common. And safer. "I imagine you won't be the only one to see this paper, and as I said, I wish to remain anonymous. If there's ever a legal issue, you'll be covered by that. So tell me what this filming entails. And remember, I appreciate honesty."

The comment drew a smile from her, despite the fact she couldn't know the full extent of its irony. He sat back and allowed himself to study her from behind his sunglasses as she spoke. Though her doubts about the release were apparent, she went on to describe the schedule for a typical week of filming, assuring him that he wouldn't be needed all day, every day, and that she'd try to keep everything as streamlined as possible. "We call ahead to the locations to ensure we can film and we keep to set times. It's easier for the cameramen if we can shoot during the hours with the best lighting. Since we're supposed to have good weather all week, that makes it easier."

She then explained the tourism angle of the show, which would encourage viewers to visit the country being filmed even if they weren't interested in moving there. "It's a great dream, to live abroad. We want our viewers to experience the richness of the culture, explore the nooks and crannies of a new place, and come to appreciate what it would be like to live in a particular country, even if they're only planning a quick trip. This whole season has been about Argentina. So when we filmed in Patagonia, we talked about the climate, the wildlife, and the locals' favorite water sports and hiking trails. In Córdoba, it was all about the rise of a modern city that acknowledges its colonial history and Jesuit traditions. For Buenos

Aires, our last episode gave an overview of the museums and cathedrals—the touristy spots—but in the season finale, we'd like to dive into one or two places tourists might not see, but that have deep meaning for those who live here."

He couldn't help but absorb the excitement she radiated. Much as he enjoyed the work he did for his country, it'd been ages since he'd felt the kind of enthusiasm Emily showed when describing her job.

"What are you planning?"

"Our camera crew is tentatively scheduled to shoot at a major *fútbol* game tomorrow. I want to capture the vibrant atmosphere of a stadium crowd, the way fans sing at the matches and consider their team's performance a point of national pride. And" —she accepted her sandwich from the waitress, offering the woman a smile in thanks— "if you're up for it, later this week we're considering filming inside one of the city's tango bars at night. Give our viewers a sense of the passion the dance entails and show how much Argentinians value it as part of their heritage."

"You expect me to...to tango?" he asked once the waitress departed. He'd figured all he'd have to do was walk around a few properties, ooh and aah over the crown moldings or kitchen appliances, and he'd be done. Not participate in what was arguably the most sexually suggestive dance performed outside a strip club.

"No, not unless you want to," she assured him. "But if you'd be willing to go to a tango show, we could air portions of the professionals' performance and mention how much you enjoyed learning about the culture. The same goes for the *fútbol* game. Part of what gets our viewers invested in the show is seeing *your* interest."

"I see." He lifted his sandwich to take a bite, but a whiff of onion led him to set it down and pick out the offending vegetable. "I suppose I could do that."

"Great. So how about we discuss what you're looking for in an apartment? That way we make sure to see properties you'd seriously consider." She paused as she noticed the growing pile on the edge of his plate. "Not an onion fan?"

"Smell bad, taste worse. I should've read the menu more carefully."

"I'll warn you if our food delivery service brings any." She grinned as she lifted her own sandwich for a bite.

"Add that to my conditions." Given what happened the last time he'd consumed onion, they'd both be safer. It had been the worst night of his life.

IT WAS his mother who'd broken the news of Carmella's suicide.

Vittorio had missed dinner, having just returned to his palace apartment from a meeting with the chancellor of the University of Cateri. Needing to stay awake another hour or two in order to review the proposed expansion project for the campus, he phoned the palace kitchen and asked to have a light dinner delivered. He'd loosened his tie, settled into the sofa, and read the first few paragraphs of the report when his mother knocked, then slipped into his apartment without waiting for his response.

"I know it's very late," she'd said, then hesitated. It was the hesitation that unnerved him. And he knew.

"What has Carmella done now?" More than another painting or bauble showing up in the market.

"She's passed away. Her body was discovered about an hour ago."

Even now, he remembered the horrifying sensation as his stomach dropped and his mouth went bone-dry. He remained immobile while his mother gave him what few details she had: Carmella had hung herself. A neighbor heard a crash from the actress's Madrid apartment, followed by silence, and had knocked to no avail. Firefighters eventually broke down the door. No note had been discovered. The crash had apparently come when Carmella kicked over a large ornamental vase.

"I'm sorry, Vittorio." He'd blinked, realizing Queen Fabrizia had come to kneel before him. "Despite everything, I know you cared deeply for her."

"Thank you."

She'd squeezed his knee and left him alone. A few minutes later, his dinner arrived, followed by Alessandro. Unlike their mother, Alessandro didn't bother to knock. Nor did he speak for several long minutes.

"Mother told me the news."

"I assumed as much."

"She also told me to leave you alone." He hesitated a moment before adding, "I waited until she was around the corner. I decided that was long enough."

"I'm surprised you waited that long."

Alessandro had bucked authority since they were toddlers in the nursery. If the children were told not to touch the fireplace tools, Alessandro would stick out a finger the instant the nanny's back was turned.

"I was attempting to be respectful," he deadpanned.

Vittorio stood and crossed the room to the table where his soup and salad had been placed. With deliberate motions, he unfolded his napkin and placed it in his lap. Without meeting his brother's eyes, he said, "This will be difficult."

"I know she meant a great deal to you."

"It will be difficult for more reasons than that." A tough admission, but true.

"Yes." Alessandro cleared his throat. "She is—was—well-loved in Spain. Beautiful beyond words with a career on the upswing. The gossip rags will want a story to explain her death."

"I know." On autopilot, he lifted his fork and took a bite of salad. "I'll go to the funeral. If her family wishes for me to speak, I'll do so in glowing terms."

"Can you do that?"

"Of course." He could speak to a crowd in his sleep. Say all the right words, smile at all the right people, console those who needed consoling. He'd been trained from birth for exactly such situations.

A knock at the door interrupted his dinner. Assuming it was another of his siblings, he waved for Alessandro to answer it, but was surprised to see one of the palace guards. "Your Highness," the man said, bowing deeply, "I was handed a letter about ten minutes ago at the front gate. Normally, I wouldn't accept such a thing, but it came from Ms. Rivas's personal assistant. She said that Ms. Rivas gave it to her yesterday and asked that it be delivered to you personally this evening."

"Is she still here?"

"No, sir, she left as soon as I accepted the letter. Should I take it to security to have it scanned?"

"No, I'll take it." He thanked the guard for his discretion, then had another a forkful of salad before opening the envelope. Immediately, he recognized Carmella's handwriting.

The words inside left him sickened. He read it again, slowly, trying to absorb the double blow of both Carmella's death and her final missive.

"Dear God, Vittorio. What is it?"

"Nothing." Hoping he appeared calm, he folded the letter in thirds and slid it back into the envelope. Setting it to the side, he took another bite of salad, then realized what was in his mouth a split second before he swallowed. Onion. Nasty, odiferous, crunchy onion. Bile rose in his throat. Who the hell put onion in his salad?

Rage, hot and potent, wound its way through him, tensing his muscles. He gripped the fork tighter and began flipping through the greens in search of the offending vegetable.

"Put down the damned fork and look at me." Alessandro's voice was low and dangerously accusatory. "We both know it's not nothing."

CHAPTER 5

IT WAS the wrong thing to say. *Anything* was the wrong thing to say.

Without thinking, Vittorio sprang from his chair and hurled the fork against the wall behind Alessandro's head, then grabbed the bowl and launched it in the same direction, unleashing his fury with every ounce of force his shoulder and arm possessed. Shards of china sprayed outward, leaving a bomb blast of arugula, tomato, almonds, dressing, and the infernal diced onion clinging to the brocade wallpaper and splattered across the hardwood floor below. The base of the bowl somehow remained intact, swiveling on the floor in lopsided circles until it hit the leg of a chair. Still, it wasn't enough. He kicked the back of his chair hard enough to send it sailing across the room, then slammed a fist into the heavy dining table, causing the thick, centuries-old top to shudder as if rocked by an earthquake.

Alessandro turned toward the carnage, ignoring his brother as he ran a finger down the wall, then inspected the battered vegetables on the floor at his feet. "Shall I order another? Perhaps one without onion?"

Vittorio quaked with a mix of anger and bone-deep grief, but the urge to smash the rest of the apartment's contents was diffused by Alessandro's attitude.

"I believe I've had my fill."

"Just as well," Alessandro flicked a stubborn piece of arugula from the wall. "Most of the staff have left for the evening. You won't mind if I give this a quick wipe? Save having to call housekeeping?"

Vittorio balled his fists, took a deep breath, then strode to the sofa, settling into it with an uncharacteristic oomph. He stared at his brother and the stained wallpaper without seeing, lost in the haze of his wretched emotions.

"May I?" Alessandro asked some time later.

The quiet words snapped through Vittorio like an electric shock. He blinked, realizing that the wall was now clean—though damp— and that Alessandro held Carmella's letter aloft. Knowing the contents would go no further, he nodded.

A tremor went through Alessandro's jaw as he read, but he said nothing. When he finished, he set the letter on the coffee table and took the seat opposite Vittorio.

"What will you do?"

"Nothing." Vittorio answered. He rested his elbows on his knees and tented his fingers to his forehead. There was nothing to do. Carmella's decision rendered him powerless. "And yes, I truly mean *nothing*. Attend the funeral. Pay my respects. But I can't change what happened."

"I'll go with you."

"It will likely take place in Madrid. There will be cameras. And Carmella's family."

"I'll go with you."

He nodded, grateful for his brother's rare show of support. "I shouldn't have thrown the salad at you. I apologize."

"You threw it at the wall. If you'd have really wanted to hit me, you would've."

"Nevertheless, it was wrong of me."

"Always so formal. Fine. You're forgiven." He expected Alessandro to say more about the letter's contents, or to simply leave and give Vittorio time alone with his thoughts. Instead, the younger twin said, "When it's over, go away. Get out of here."

"Of course. That was my first thought."

"Vittorio." Alessandro leaned over the coffee table and grabbed Vittorio's forearm, forcing Vittorio to meet his gaze. "I mean it. Go laze on a beach or climb a mountain. Get out of your own head. Stop being so damned responsible."

The idea was ludicrous enough to bring a smile to Vittorio's face, despite the ache in his chest. "Easy for you to say. I'm responsible because it's my duty to be responsible, but everyone expects you to disappear for weeks at a time."

"Exactly. *I* can disappear. What good is it for you to have the perfect body double if you can't take advantage of it now and then? Go be me for awhile." He released his grip on Vittorio's arm and grinned. "I'll cover for you."

"Very funny."

"I'm serious." Alessandro stood, spreading his arms wide. "Let's do it. Hell, I can fool anyone into thinking I'm you."

"Not our parents. Or our siblings." He shook his head at the impossibility. "Not that I'd even consider—"

"From now until the funeral, I'll be you. You be me. See if anyone outside the family notices. If not, then take off. No one should have to endure what's happening to you, let alone endure it in the public eye." He shot a pointed glance at the wallpaper. "Even you, dear brother, are not perfect, and the coming days will be harder. The media will pick apart your every utterance and facial expression. They'll conjure up all kinds of interpretations in terms of your private life and your ability to govern."

"I've always acted professionally, and I'll do so now."

"Until life hands you a bowl of onions at the wrong time." Alessandro barreled on, despite the threatening glare Vittorio gave him. "I've never seen you lose your temper, even when we were little. Go. Live my life for a few weeks. Trust me, it'll help you refocus. It'll make you a better...well, *you*. And it'll be better for the country in the long run if you get all that angst out of your system."

"First, I don't have *angst*—"

"Or a complete set of china."

"—and second, it's impossible." He flattened his hands on the coffee table and took a deep breath. "Even if I wanted to do it, you couldn't be me for the funeral."

Alessandro's eyes glittered with the realization Vittorio was considering the possibility. Vittorio didn't deny it. Despite its ridiculousness, the idea held its allure. Vittorio wasn't one to lose his temper. His control was a point of pride, and the tidal wave of emotion that caused the breach in his control...he had to stem it. Somehow. Because Alessandro was right. If Vittorio stayed, he couldn't simply lie low, not without raising questions, which meant he'd be faced with Carmella's betrayal over and over again for the next few weeks. A betrayal so deep and personal only he and Alessandro—and God forbid, possibly a coroner in Madrid—knew of it.

How would he react when faced with endless inquiries from reporters, reporters who didn't—and couldn't—know the full extent of Vittorio's anguish?

For the next few hours, they talked about the logistics. About the insanity of it. About the strain on Vittorio and ramifications for the country if they didn't. How they'd convince their parents to go along with the plan. Then for two weeks before Carmella's funeral, during the investigation into her suicide and the resulting media attention, Vittorio stayed out of sight as Alessandro took his place, acting the role of the polished crown prince. A minor snag occurred when Alessandro stood a hair too close to a French pop singer and shot her a flirtatious smile during a palace garden party, but thankfully Sophia noticed and interrupted before Alessandro's slip was caught by a photographer.

Much as Vittorio loved women, he didn't flirt with the devilish flair of his brother. Vittorio considered his approach to be more straightforward and refined. Appreciative of a woman, her intelligence, and her unique personality traits...not merely her figure or the ease with which he might get her into bed, which seemed to be Alessandro's priorities.

But Alessandro handled the funeral itself with aplomb. No one knew that the brothers, sitting side by side in the rain, had switched places. That it was Alessandro, rather than Vittorio, who went to the podium and spoke the heartfelt words Vittorio had prepared for the emotional event.

Two days after the service, Vittorio left, a thick scarf over his face and wool cap covering his head as he took a late evening ferry to Italy, then an overnight train to Vienna where he boarded a flight to Montreal. No one was the wiser. After a few days in Montreal, he made his way to Buenos Aires, simply because it was the most interesting city he spotted on the airport's departure list and there were seats available.

All thanks to onions.

During the first two weeks he considered going home more than once, certain he and Alessandro would be found out. He changed his accommodations nightly, keeping to less popular hotels and apartment rentals so he wouldn't be noticed. Used different names, kept a disposable cell phone, and only answered calls from Alessandro. Grew out his facial hair and chose clothing that wouldn't give away his wealth or status, ensuring he could blend into any crowd. Avoided restaurants and museums frequented by the glitterati or recommended by Italian-language travel guides, given that tourists of Italian and Sarcaccian heritage would be more likely to recognize him than those from other countries.

As the days lengthened into weeks, he grew more comfortable, not simply with the fact his disappearance had gone unnoticed, but in his own skin. He'd explored Buenos Aires, discovering what it meant to be completely free for the first time in his life. Reveled in the ability to walk anywhere he pleased, visit the city's famous cemeteries, and eat ice cream from walk-up windows. He'd spent more than one afternoon on a rented bicycle, pedaling his way through parks and along trails. Taken public transportation for the sheer joy of it, looping through the city and observing people he'd never have interacted with in his day-to-day life as a wealthy crown prince. And not once had he needed to make a speech, present a head of state or local dignitary with a gift, or pose for a photograph. He had no schedule. No expectations. Not even an alarm clock.

And while he wasn't exactly excited about the prospect of returning to Sarcaccia and resuming his role as crown prince, at least he now knew he could handle a surprise onion.

Women, on the other hand, were another matter. Carmella's unexpected deception exorcised that part of him. He had no interest since the day he'd discovered her real reason for pursuing him and he'd ended the relationship.

At least not until he met Emily Sinclair.

AS VITTORIO LAY with his head on his pillow the night following his lunch with Emily, listening to the hum of street noise below his hotel window, he convinced himself his attraction to her was a freak occurrence, the result of months with only brief, necessary female contact.

Thinking of her as *touchable*. Flirting with her. Kissing her hand. It wasn't like him, especially not the person he'd become since opening Carmella's letter.

But as Vittorio walked into La Bombonera stadium behind Emily and her crew in the bright light of day, it took only a glimpse of the fall of golden hair against her tailored white blouse and watching the sway of her hips in a pair of curve-hugging slacks to discover his libido hadn't died with Carmella, it had only gone dormant. The radiance of Emily's smile as she turned to wave to the stadium's head of operations, who'd given them permission to film, sent a surge of heat through Vittorio he hadn't experienced in a long, long time, one that made him realize that his response to Emily yesterday wasn't a fluke.

He exhaled, resolving to enjoy the entire experience...the television cameras, the jubilant noise, the scent of freshly grilled meats that permeated the air, and even his reborn sense of desire. It might not be quite the way Alessandro would've embraced the day, but it was adventure enough for Vittorio.

They paused at the edge of the field, where a local makeup artist quickly touched up Emily's lips with a thin brush, then fluffed powder over her nose and forehead. He'd had his own face touched up for a camera more than once, particularly before hosting televised charity events. Necessary, he knew, but awkward. Yet there was an effortlessness to Emily's last-minute preparations—the makeup check, a review of her script with Rita, a discussion with her cameraman, Ignacio, about the angle of the sun—that put Vittorio at ease when the makeup artist approached him and asked to do a quick shine check before she left for her next job.

Vittorio's attraction to Emily was more than the physical, though. When she introduced him to Mike, the gregarious Australian cameraman who would capture Vittorio's experience at the game between the local Boca Juniors and their cross-town rival, River Plate, he found himself admiring the way Emily interacted with her coworkers. Her confident demeanor and the respect with which others spoke to her left no doubt she was the star of the show, yet her lack of hubris and the efficiency with which she'd scheduled the filming proved she was willing to do the hard work necessary to make the production a success.

She did everything so effortlessly, he almost didn't notice that she'd introduced him to everyone as Bob.

After ensuring everyone knew their duties for the day, she turned to him with a smile. "You ready to have a good time, Bob?"

His responding grin came naturally. "With a fired-up crowd like this? Don't think I have a choice." Then he added in a whisper from the side of his mouth, "Do I look like a Bob?"

"No, but it's what popped out of my mouth." Louder, she said, "Just beware of the troublemakers. I'm sure you've noticed that there's plenty of partying going on. I hate to think how much alcohol they'll consume by halftime."

"I've attended games in Europe. I think I can handle myself."

"I never doubted it." She gestured toward the side of the field. "I'll be over there with Rita and Ignacio to film a segment about fan traditions and the popularity of the sport. Mike will be with you, about ten rows above us. All you need to do is have a good time and be yourself.

Feel free to chat with the fans around you, have something to eat, or cheer along with the crowd. Whatever comes naturally. Mike will get what he needs."

"You won't be in the stands?"

"No, but I'll find you at the end. While we're filming, one of our associate producers, Maryam Tabrizi, plans to contact some tango clubs and restaurants. She's also talking to real estate agents about doing walk-throughs of a few apartments that meet the criteria we discussed at lunch yesterday. If we can hit one of the apartments later today, it'll give us more flexibility. Sound good?"

He nodded, surprised at his regret over witnessing the soccer match without Emily at his side. Her cameraman pointed out a spot near the corner of the field with good light where she'd be away from pregame foot traffic. Checking the time, she flashed her press pass to a security guard at the edge of the field, then moved to film the introduction to her segment. Vittorio watched in admiration as Rita stood behind Ignacio and signaled Emily to begin. Emily's face transformed, her stance took on an air of casual comfort, and she hardly looked at her cue card as she spoke, noting the history of Argentine *fútbol*—better known to Americans as soccer—the passion of the spectators, and the distinct characteristics of La Bombonera stadium. Finally, she said, "Expat Bob White took a break from his apartment hunt to soak in the experience today from a prime seat at midfield, where he was welcomed by stadium regulars as they cheered on the local Boca Juniors against their rivals from River Plate in a game known throughout Argentina as the *Superclásico*."

After the cameraman cut, she waved to Vittorio and Mike, then moved a few feet down the field, where she and Ignacio would capture scenes from the game itself. Mike handed Vittorio his ticket, and the two of them ascended to their seats. As with the games Vittorio attended in Europe, energy rippled through the crowd. A man in the row in front of Vittorio taught him the words to one of the team's cheers, and by midway through the first half, Vittorio was singing along with the crowd, lost in the spectacle. As he'd told Emily, he'd been to matches in Europe, having cheered on Sarcaccia against their rivals from Italy, Germany, and France, in particular. But he'd always been in the royal box at home games and in a secure, VIP guest area when at foreign locations. A certain level of decorum was expected in both his dress and his demeanor. But today, he wore light, casual pants and a white shirt, roared with the crowd, helped a fan sitting beside him hold a flag aloft, and happily downed a beer.

Then a second.

A lean man sporting blue and gold face paint to match his Boca Juniors team jersey clasped Vittorio's shoulder, urging him to sway back and forth with the rest of their section as a new cheer began. Though Vittorio didn't know the words, by the second time through, he picked up enough to sing along. Beside him, Mike paused in his filming to join in, his Australian accent booming through the row.

A sense of lightness filled Vittorio, and not as a result of the alcohol. He couldn't remember the last time he truly sang. At public events in Sarcaccia, he frequently joined in the singing of the national anthem, but he'd always been careful to keep his voice low so it couldn't be recorded. Here in La Bombonera, he was anonymous. No one cared whether their seatmates could carry a tune. It was all about the enthusiasm with which one let their voice be heard. There was a camaraderie rarely shared by strangers outside of sport, and he reveled in it.

When the refs made a series of controversial calls resulting in a penalty kick—and goal—against the home team less than a minute before halftime, he joined in the fans' rowdy jeers, careful to keep his comments family-friendly in case they were aired.

"I think we have plenty of good footage," Mike said at halftime after checking his cell phone. "Maryam locked down an apartment we can see tonight if you're up for it. Rita and I are going to head there now to get some daylight shots. Emily will finish up her on-field work with Ignacio during the second half and then meet you at the gate where we entered."

Vittorio thanked Mike, then followed him up the stairs to the refreshment and restroom area for a quick break before returning alone to his seat. He chatted with the men and women around him, but found himself scanning the field for Emily as the second half began. Almost immediately after kickoff, two players collided while jumping to head the ball, resulting in a brief shoving match. A few minutes later, a bad slide tackle resulted in a yellow card for a popular Boca Juniors midfielder. The crowd went crazy, with most fans yelling obscenities at the referees over the perceived bad call. On the sidelines, the players began gesturing that the midfielder's tackle was clean, which only served to further inflame the crowd.

Finally, Vittorio caught sight of Emily and Ignacio standing a few feet to the side of the visiting team's bench, which was directly in front of his section. She seemed safe enough, given the security detail standing behind the players, but a niggling feeling caused him to survey the stands behind her. A group of intoxicated men in their twenties waved their arms while shouting obscenities in the visiting team's direction. Two middle-aged men dressed in River Plate colors yelled back from across the aisle, using colorful Spanish to tell the group of drunkards to go home. One of the security officers eyed the fans and spoke into his radio at the same time Emily turned toward the group and frowned. Ignacio lowered his camera and said something to Emily, but she didn't appear to hear him.

Vittorio made distracted excuses to those around him as he cut out of his row and moved toward the field, dodging the cheering fans who filled the stairs as River Plate lost the ball on a bad throw-in and the Boca Juniors sent it flying to an open player down the field. The River Plate goalie leapt for the ball, snatching it from the air and knocking the Boca Junior striker flat on his back in the process.

At once, the crowd erupted, a wave of anger carrying their fists skyward as they called for the goalie to be ejected. The young men Vittorio had spotted before surged into the aisle, attempting to grab the duo who'd chastised them a moment before, even as a surrounding group of calmer fans struggled to hold them back. One of the security guards leapt the barrier separating the stands from the field at the same time Vittorio ducked past a burly River Plate fan to reach Emily.

From nowhere, a scrawny male with sharp elbows knocked into

Vittorio's back, then a woman attempting to move up the stairs smacked into Vittorio's knees. He braced himself against the railing so he wouldn't fall forward and crush her, but lost his footing and careened backward instead. Pain split his vision as the back of his head slammed into the concrete. He managed to get a hand up to stop the woman from falling on top of him and give her space to step to the stair above him, but in the next second, a large male body landed on top of him, knocking his head against the cold, hard edge of the stairs once more. His sight blurred, but his peripheral vision registered a moving fist. Vittorio jerked and it missed him, instead sinking into the soft side of the man struggling to get off of him.

Vittorio gave the man a mighty shove, but the effort was fruitless. Twisting his head to the side, Vittorio looked down to see at least a half-dozen security guards and police ascending the stairs. One grabbed a man by the back of his jersey, then pushed him face-first over the nearest seat and slapped a zip tie around the man's wrists to secure him.

The officer glanced up the stairs, locking eyes with Vittorio just as Vittorio gave the man on top of him another shove. In that instant, Vittorio realized that if he didn't move, and quickly, he'd end up leaving in the back of a squad car.

CHAPTER 6

EMILY WATCHED in fascination as River Plate's goalie drop-kicked the ball, sending it further than she thought possible to land at the feet of one of his team's strikers. While the members of River Plate's team cheered from the nearby bench, the odd rumble of voices throughout the stadium made her realize that few others were watching the game. Instead, fans craned their necks to see the section immediately behind Emily. She spun, amazed at the change in demeanor in the section behind her. Where fans had been singing moments before, security guards and several police officers now scampered over the wall to break up a fight that had erupted in the lower stands.

As if pulled by an invisible force, Emily's attention sliced from the commotion near the field to the seats a few rows back. Early in the game, she'd glanced up at Mike and Victor to ensure all was well and had been rewarded with the sight of both men's jubilant cheering. While she was used to Mike's perpetual good humor, the unabashed joy on Victor's face took her aback. She'd thought him good looking from the moment she'd caught sight of him in the café, but his dark, forbidding aura made it clear he preferred to keep others at arm's length. However, the genuine smile that lit his features as he drank in the sights and sounds of the game transformed him, making him seem both approachable and—if such a thing were possible—more deeply attractive than before. She found her gaze drawn to the tenth row whenever the fans reacted to a play on the field, craving the sight of Victor's reaction. Now, however, she saw no sign of Victor's dark head amongst the stunned fans, all of whom were fixated on the chaos unfolding before them.

She frowned, scanning the stairs extending above his seats toward the concession area, but there was no sign of him, only a security officer descending, urging fans to stay clear of the disturbance below.

Then she spied him in the midst of the scuffle. Her heart went to her throat as he wended his way against the tide of fans attempting to flee the lower seats, until two battling men flew out of their row and into his path. He slid sideways to help a woman out of harm's way, then disappeared beneath the men and a blur of fists and pulled clothing.

"Come on," Ignacio urged, wrapping a hand around her elbow and pulling her toward the gate. "I have enough footage. Let's get out of the way of security so they—"

"Wait!" She ripped free from Ignacio's grasp and headed for the stands. "Victor's down there! Under those men!"

"What?"

"Bob. I mean Bob. We need to get him."

Even as the words left her lips, the bigger of the two men slipped, dragging the other with him down the stairs at the same time Victor shoved them both in an attempt to extricate himself. While using the railing to stand, he offered a hand to the woman he'd protected a moment before, sending her up the stairs and away from danger before he descended toward the field.

"What's he thinking?" Ignacio muttered.

Emily couldn't answer. She took another few steps toward the wall separating the spectators from the field as the police set upon the two out-of-control men. At that moment, Victor's hand went to the back of his head.

Horror squeezed the air from Emily's lungs as his fingers came away covered in blood.

A low whump, then a torrent of apologies in Spanish came from behind her as an armed police officer with the build of a bull collided with Ignacio from behind, sending his expensive camera equipment to the ground. From the corner of her eye, she saw Victor leap the barricade and take three long strides in their direction. The officer's attention swiveled from the camera equipment to Victor. The heavy-set man reached for the weapon at his waist at the same time he commanded Victor to stop.

"He's with us. It's all right," Emily pleaded in Spanish, stepping between the gigantic officer and Victor. Her heart thumped audibly in her ears as the officer paused, eyeing the press credentials hanging from around her neck before scrutinizing Victor once more to assess the potential threat he posed.

The officer's hands dropped. He jerked his head in the direction of the gate and grunted for Emily to get Victor to the emergency aid station, then strode past them to take up a spot at the bottom of the section to stop others from climbing over the barricade and to ensure a clear pathway for the other officers, who now had several of the fans in handcuffs and were leading them out of the stands.

"What the hell was that, Emily?" Victor's eyes blazed as he spoke. "You should've stayed where you were. You could've been hurt!"

"I could say the same to you." She grabbed his hands, flipping his bloody palms upward. "And you *were* hurt. Come on, let's get you to a medic."

"I'm fine. Head wounds bleed a lot. You, on the other hand, could've been shot."

An odd note crept into his voice on the final word. She glanced up, meeting his eyes for a split second before Ignacio moved behind Victor and angled the taller man's head down to inspect the wound.

The mixture of concern and anger she saw in Victor's brief look was nothing like the anger he'd displayed when he'd cornered her in the Palermo apartment. This was protective. Caring. And not caring in the manner one might care for a child or a friend, but in the manner a man fought to protect a woman he treasured.

The shock of it clogged her throat and caused tears to well in her eyes. She blinked them back, embarrassed, before the men could see.

"It's not too bad, despite the blood," Ignacio said as he stretched for a better look. "Only a small cut."

"I wasn't about to be shot. He wouldn't have drawn the weapon," Emily argued, though it came out sounding weaker than she'd anticipated. "But you could have a concussion."

"I don't." Before she could say another word, he added, "I've had one before. This doesn't compare. However, a bandage might be in order if we want to go look at that flat later."

"More likely a stitch or two," Ignacio said. "Let me grab my equipment and we'll head to the medical area."

"Are you kidding? No apartment tonight."

Victor shrugged. "It's your decision, of course, but I'm up for it if you are. Until the last five minutes, I was having a fantastic time. It's been ages since I've had a day like this."

"You're crazy."

Whoops and applause rattled the stadium as the Boca Juniors put the ball in the net to tie the game. A slow, incredibly sexy smile spread across Victor's face as they walked off the field. "I could've suggested we stay to watch the rest of the match and get the bandage later. *That* would be crazy."

"Now I know you've hit your head."

Once they entered the first aid area under the stands, a young female medic quickly took stock of Victor's cut. As Ignacio had guessed, it needed a couple of stitches, but a thorough check by the supervising doctor convinced Emily that Victor wasn't suffering from a concussion. As the medic stood behind Victor and cleaned the area to be stitched, Emily offered him an apology. Never in all her years of work had anyone been injured filming one of her shows. No guest had dealt with so much as a splinter.

"Of course we'll replace your shirt," she said. "And if there's anything else we can do—"

"You're forgiven." He waved a freshly-washed hand in dismissal. "I was serious about this being fun. More than I expected. And don't worry about the shirt. Blood washes out."

Another roar came to them from above. The medic glanced at a television screen showing a feed from the stadium and informed them that the Boca Juniors had scored again. She finished her stitching and put a narrow protective covering over the wound, then handed Victor a set of instructions for keeping the area clean. Though it was written in Spanish, he assured her he could translate and slipped the paper in his back pocket.

"I think this is fine, but I'd like to take it back to the office to test it," Ignacio said to Emily, indicating his battered camera equipment. "Are you two going back to Recoleta or joining Mike at the apartment?"

"Recoleta."

"Apartment."

Emily eyed Victor. "We can do the apartment tomorrow, you know."

"I'm confident I can keep the back of my head out of the shots as easily tonight as I can tomorrow. Let's do it."

Humor glittered in his eyes. She wondered if he'd enjoyed attending soccer matches in Europe this much, and if not, what explained the difference.

"Fine," she acquiesced. "Apartment, then. But you'll need to change clothes. And if you feel the least bit headachy—"

"I'll inform you. Or you'll question me so much I may develop one." He put a hand on her shoulder and turned her toward the exit. "Come on. Time for you to dress me."

FOR THE FIRST time in months, Queen Fabrizia went through her bedtime routine without an upset stomach.

"I had a phone call," Alessandro had whispered at the dinner table a few hours ago. "He'll be home soon."

"When?"

"Didn't say, but I suspect any day." Alessandro changed the subject as a member of the kitchen staff entered the dining room to clear the table, but once the family was alone again, he added, "I believe him."

Optimism lit Sophia's eyes before a happy smile danced across her face. Massimo took a long sip of his wine, then glanced at his future wife, Kelly, who'd joined them for the meal, and exhaled in relief.

"Let us know if you hear anything further." King Carlo's voice held none of the emotion exhibited by his children. He forked a bite of tenderloin into his mouth, then asked Massimo about the tour he'd taken of a veterans' outpatient clinic that afternoon.

They all understood. Not only was the subject not to be discussed where they could be overheard by the staff, Carlo felt it wasn't worth discussing until they had hard evidence Vittorio's plane was wheels up, on the way back to Sarcaccia. The crown prince's absence had gone on too long and been too deeply felt for the king to assume it would end soon.

Still, as Fabrizia returned her toothbrush to its crystal case and reached for her favorite nighttime moisturizer, hope filled her. Vittorio wouldn't have told Alessandro of his intention unless he meant it. Nor would Alessandro have repeated it.

"I'm going to take a shower," Carlo announced as he entered the expansive marble-floored bathroom, then walked up behind Fabrizia to plant a kiss on her shoulder, just beside the thin strap of her peach nightgown. He stripped off his workout clothes, tossing them into a hamper hidden inside the room's built-in cabinetry. "By the way, we need the treadmill inspected. It squeaks when it gets over a five percent incline."

"I hadn't noticed. I'll let maintenance know." She turned to admire her husband as he removed his watch and placed it on the countertop. After all their years together, the sight of him naked sent a shiver through her. More so now than when they first married.

"Care to join me?" He took a step closer, then cupped her face in one large, strong hand. "I'm sensing something…dirty…that should be addressed."

"Give me a minute and I will." She dropped a quick kiss on the inside of his wrist, then watched in open admiration as he entered the glassed-in shower before she turned toward the bedroom. A smile lifted the edges of her mouth.

He might not be willing to admit it, but Carlo harbored hope, too.

She removed the diamond studs from her ears while she walked to her closet, then placed them in the velvet-lined box her husband had given her as a first anniversary gift. After selecting a dress for the next day and setting out matching shoes and accessories, she made her way back to the shower. Even from the bedroom, she could smell his masculine shampoo. He should be ready for her by now.

A low buzz made her pause. She glanced toward the nightstand to see the screen lit on Carlo's private cell phone. Only the family and a few important members of parliament had that number.

Please, God, let it be Vittorio. Let him come home. The blocked number displayed on the screen sent her pulse racing. Knowing Carlo would want her to answer, she clicked the appropriate button.

"Hello?"

For a few long seconds, no one spoke, though she could hear the wail of an ambulance or police siren in the distance.

"Fabrizia?"

She sank onto the bed. It had been years since she'd heard the throaty, feminine voice, but it was etched on her memory as if engraved with a knife. "Yes."

"You answer his phone?"

And you refuse to use my title? "He's in the shower. Is something wrong?"

"Of course something is wrong. What, you think I call him for fun? Those days are long past."

So this is how it's going to be. "What can I do to help, Teresa?"

"Get your son home."

Carlo's voice echoed against the bathroom tiles. He was singing. So happy.

"Do you see the news, Fabrizia? Ever go on the Internet? Or do you have an assistant who does that for you?"

"Of course I see the news." She sounded much calmer than she felt, thank goodness. It's what Carlo would want.

"Then you know my oldest son has been photographed."

"Yes. Carlo and I have discussed it." Though it was in December and no more photographs of Rocco Cornaro had appeared, at least to her knowledge. She'd been monitoring the situation carefully.

"Yesterday, Rocco was approached at the market. A man stood beside him, looking at the spinach. He asked my son if he had bought from that particular farmer before. When my son said yes, the man said, 'Interesting. How long have you been here, Alessandro?'"

"How did he respond?"

"He told the man that he must have him confused with someone else, as his name is not Alessandro. But the man said, 'Forgive me, my mistake. You look very much like a man from Sarcaccia named Alessandro. I saw you yesterday, as well, when you visited your lover, and I made the wrong assumption.' Then the man apologized again and left."

Fabrizia clenched her back teeth. She could feel Teresa's fear and understood it. But what could she do?

"Whoever that man is, Fabrizia, he thinks my son is yours. And he obviously followed my son to his wife's apartment the day before yesterday—"

"His wife's apartment?"

"They are separated. Not that this is your concern." Teresa's voice held a mixture of anger and fear. "Get Alessandro home. Otherwise, we're all in danger. This man could go to the press. He might *be* the press. And if he digs too far—"

"I understand. I'll handle it."

"—he will discover that Carlo has left his children all over the globe."

Fabrizia rose from the bed. In a deliberate, commanding tone, one she rarely wielded, she said, "Teresa, I said I would handle it."

A snicker came over the line. "You don't frighten me, Fabrizia. You have far more to lose than I do. And I'll do whatever it takes to protect my son."

"As will I, Teresa."

But Teresa never heard the words. She'd already disconnected the call. Fabrizia shook her head and returned the phone to the king's nightstand. To the air, she said, "And you lost Carlo long ago. I never will."

In fact, she intended to make love to him this very minute. When they finished in the shower, they'd make love again in the bedroom. Then, when they were fully sated, she'd tell her husband about the call. They would come to a decision together on what to do about their son.

And what to do about Teresa's.

CHAPTER 7

THE MAN WAS sexy as all get-out, shaved area and stitches in the back of his head or not.

Emily sat patiently, her hands in her lap as she perched on a leather settee and waited for Victor to come out of the dressing room. Rather than stop for a change of clothes at his hotel, which he claimed was well out of their way, he suggested they swing into a men's shop close to the apartment they intended to view, which was located in the fashionable Puerto Madero district.

While the idea made sense on the surface, it was another thing in practice. Shopping with a man turned out to be a rather intimate experience. It was all the male clothing. The smells of cologne from the nearby men's grooming counter. The photographs of male models on the walls...men who didn't compare to the dark, sexy Victor, let alone the smiling, affable Victor she'd glimpsed at the soccer match.

She wondered what he'd look like without the close-clipped whiskers covering the lower half of his face.

"Tell me about this apartment," Victor said over the faux walnut door of his dressing room stall.

She welcomed the question. Talking business helped keep her mind off the fact Victor was likely shirtless at the moment. "It's just off one of the main thoroughfares, not far from public transportation. Fiftieth floor in a fifty-two story building."

"Not the top?"

"It's the top as far as apartments go. There's a spa on the fifty-first floor and the fifty-second has a gym, swimming pool, and entertainment space." She wracked her brain, trying to remember what else Maryam had said when she'd called to describe the place. "It's modern inside, like the apartment building in Palermo. Security at the door. There are only three apartments on the entire floor, so you'd have a great deal of space and privacy. And it's under budget."

"That's a plus."

"Yes." She flexed her fingers, deciding it was easier to broach the subject now, when she didn't have to look Victor in the eye, than when he'd discussed his wish list with her over yesterday's lunch. "By the way, you know your budget is high, even for Buenos Aires. You have your pick of most anything in the city. Are you sure that's what you want to spend, especially given that all real estate purchases in Argentina are on a cash basis?"

The amount he'd given boggled her mind. While the Palermo apartment they'd visited yesterday morning was one of the priciest she'd visited for the show, his budget could stretch further. A lot further. What single man spent that kind of money on an apartment outside of a wealthy few in Manhattan or Tokyo? What did he do for a living? Most people in Buenos Aires with that kind of budget kept a modest city apartment, then used the money to purchase a more spacious house out in the country.

And they had the money to spend.

"I thought you said that's what you wanted for the finale."

"I did?"

"You did. When we were in the Palermo apartment, you remarked that it was a gorgeous building, exactly the type you wanted." He stepped out of the dressing room, then turned slowly in front of her, his arms spread, showing off a lightweight cotton shirt in a shade of olive that emphasized both his Mediterranean complexion and a well-muscled pair of shoulders. Wickedness tinged his smile. "Camera ready?"

She swallowed. He could grace a magazine cover. "That'll be fine."

"Fine?"

"Yes, you look nice. The green is a good color for you."

His brows rose. "*Nice?*"

How did he make her so uncomfortable with such a simple question? "Is nice bad?"

"Nice is boring. How about, 'you look extremely fit and have a great face for television.' Or perhaps something along the lines of, 'women will tune in to see you.'"

Warmth suffused her face as he delivered the very lines she'd used at the café while trying to convince him to do the show. "Now *you're* flirting with *me?*"

At his raised brow, she said, "All right. Yes, you look extremely fit and have a great face for television. Women will tune in to see you." She couldn't help but add, "And green is a good color for you."

"Then I'll get it."

He ducked back into the dressing room. Though she couldn't see him changing, the top of the door was low enough for her to catch the sight of his arms stretched overhead as he pulled off the shirt. She shifted on the settee, averting her eyes. Yesterday, after breakfast, she'd suspected he was attracted to her, even if he'd turned her down for the show. Seeing him at the apartment blew that thought out of the water. But in the cab and at lunch afterward, he'd been kind—if businesslike—so she'd eased her mental pendulum back to the center, deciding he liked her, but wasn't attracted to her. Now she didn't know what to think.

Maybe Mike had plied him with more than one beer during the game.

Victor's rich voice came to her over the door. "In answer to your budget question, yes, I'm well aware of what that amount buys in Buenos Aires right now. I have the cash available, if that's your concern, but I don't need to spend that much. A prestigious address isn't my priority.

Nor is owning an obscene amount of square footage or swanky kitchen appliances I'll never use. I don't want a showplace or an entertaining space." There was a shuffling of fabric, then the sound of hangers bumping against the door. "This is a vacation apartment for me. I want light, I want a view, and most of all, I want privacy. Problem is, privacy usually means spending more for a corner or penthouse unit. And buying furnished, so I don't have to deal with salespeople and delivery people."

He made it sound like he'd planned a hermit's life while in Argentina. "I'll keep that in mind."

He emerged with the shirt on its hanger and placed two others on a returns rack outside the stall. "I'll change back into this after I've paid for it, then we can head to the apartment."

Emily shook her head as she stood. "I told you, the show can buy—"

"I wouldn't hear of it." He wrapped his hand around the top of her arm, deepening the sexual awareness already thrumming within her. "This is mine."

Much as she wanted to argue, she didn't. Not only was she unsure of her voice, there was a confidence in his gaze, as if he knew that when he used that particular tone of voice no one would question him. She stood by as he handed the gray-haired gentleman at the register the required amount of cash, spoke a few polite words in Spanish, then headed back into the dressing room to remove the tags and change. He emerged a moment later with his bloodied shirt folded into the shopping bag, then gestured for Emily to lead the way back outside.

Despite the setting sun, the air remained warm and a light breeze carried the fresh green scents of nearby grassy parks and the Río de la Plata through the streets that connected the neighborhood's modern high rises and upscale restaurants. Emily took in a deep breath and sighed, grateful for the chance to walk the two blocks to the apartment rather than be confined in a stuffy cab.

"Something amiss?" Though she suspected he usually walked faster, given his long legs, he matched his pace to her leisurely one.

"No. The opposite, in fact. I'm enjoying the weather. It might be summer here, but it's still chilly at home."

His eyebrows angled in query. "It can't be that bad in southern California, even in early March."

"Probably not, but our show is based in New York."

"Ah." He tipped his head as he studied her. 'You don't sound like you're from New York, though. At least not from any of the boroughs."

"Born and raised in Oregon. The land of no accents." They rounded a corner and she dodged a man cupping his hands to light a cigarette before coming to stroll beside Victor again. "But I've been in New York since I graduated college and landed my first job with a magazine. Early March can be bitter. The spaces between buildings create wind tunnels. *Icy* wind tunnels." She took note of a young couple walking in the opposite direction, the woman in a short skirt. Once they went by, she added, "I certainly couldn't wear that this time of year."

"You're not wearing that now."

"True. Can't get away with it for work." She paused a moment before asking, "So what about you? Or is that too intrusive a question?"

"No miniskirts for me, any time of year." Emily couldn't help but shake her head before Victor explained in a more serious tone, "I've spent most of my life in southern Europe. Warm weather suits me."

"So if not Italy…Greece? Or southern France?"

The more time she spent with him, the more he piqued her curiosity. She ached to know where he was from and what he did. About his large family and whether they were the reason he craved solitude. Why his manner led her to believe he tended toward the traditional, yet he claimed he wanted a modern apartment.

Rather than answering her question, he simply nodded. "It's part of what drew me to Argentina. It's sunny here when it's cooler at home."

She suspected it was the most she'd get from him, so she didn't press. Above them, the streetlights that arced over the broad sidewalk flickered to life. A cyclist went by wearing a dark brown suit, his pants legs rolled up slightly and a messenger bag slung across his body.

"Looks like the end of the workday. People who didn't play hooky to watch the *Superclásico* are heading back to their apartments." Victor's gaze followed a woman in a suit as she dashed into the front entrance of the high rise across the street, a restaurant carry-out bag in one hand, a bright red leather satchel dangling from the other. "It's a very young section of town, isn't it?"

Emily nodded. "Puerto Madero was built on the former dock-yards. It was in rough shape for decades—abandoned brick ware-houses, empty lots full of weeds, bridges in disrepair—but the city hired a developer to oversee the revitalization of the whole area. Now it's all high rises and green space. And nightlife." She stopped walking as they approached a silvery, glass-fronted building with a revolving door. "Well, this is it. Your possible future home."

He glanced up and down the street, taking in the storefronts and restaurants, then looked skyward, assessing the contemporary archi-tecture of the building before he swooped a hand toward the entry and bowed, his Old World charm a stark contrast to the surroundings. "After you."

SHE WORRIED ABOUT HIM.

Vittorio waited on one of the chrome and leather barstools in the apartment's sleek kitchen while Emily strode through the apartment, discussing the shoot's logistics with Mike and Rita. She glanced his way when she thought he wasn't looking, her forehead creasing in concern when she caught him feeling the bump on the back of his head.

It wasn't bad. He'd suffered worse cuts from Alessandro and their younger brother, Stefano, when they were kids horsing around in the nursery or the palace gardens. Then there'd been the concussion he'd sustained during martial arts training with Alessandro, when their instructor had accidentally caught Vittorio off balance and sent him careening off the mat, where Vittorio had slammed his head against a wall. Vittorio only put his hand there now out of curiosity, making sure the wound wasn't too obvious. Still, Emily worried. And she continued to steal looks at him.

He was used to being watched, of course, and by millions. This was different, as if he were finally being seen rather than watched, and by a woman with the instinct to leap in front of an armed officer in an effort to protect him, even when he didn't need the protection. Even when she had no idea of his identity.

It unsettled him.

Rita approached with a smile. "I think we're ready. I'll hang back, out of the line of the camera. Emily will walk through the apartment with you. Say whatever comes naturally. If you like the shower, the tile, the views…anything, really. We can edit it as needed. Mike will follow behind for most of it. When it's time for the bedrooms and master bath, he'll go in first, then he'll film you opening the door and walking inside. Pretend he's not there."

"Sounds simple enough."

She reached behind him and picked up the water bottle he'd left on the counter. "Mind if I put this in the fridge? That way it's out of the shot."

"Not a problem." He frowned. "Wait…you sure you want me to comment on the view? I can still see well enough to determine what it'll look like during the day, but I can't imagine it'll translate on camera."

"Mike filmed the views when he arrived. We'll intersperse his earlier shots with what we get now. It's all about angles and editing." The dark-haired woman gave him a conspiratorial wink. "The magic of television."

"The same magic that makes all Hollywood leading men appear to be six-foot-two?"

"The very same. Though you don't seem to need that magic." She gave him an obvious perusal, tossing her dark hair over her shoulder as she did so. "You've got tall, dark, and handsome down pat."

"I forgot to warn you that Rita's a terrible flirt," Emily said as she approached. She gave Rita a light elbow to the ribs. "Now step aside so I can powder this tall, dark, and handsome man's nose."

A wide smile spread across Rita's face. "You go right ahead."

Emily moved to stand between his knees, wielding a large, fluffy black brush and a compact. He raised an eyebrow. "Twice in one day?"

"I might've gotten away with blotting if you hadn't sprinted down the stairs and jumped the barrier at the stadium." She shrugged. "But in this case, film twice, powder twice. Unfortunately, we only booked the makeup artist for this morning."

He held still while she swirled the brush against the compact, tapped it, then swept the soft bristles over his nose and forehead. In the quiet confines of the apartment, the action felt more intimate than when the makeup artist had dusted his face in the corridor leading to the soccer field.

"Close your eyes."

He did so. Her wrist moved close to his cheek. Warmth radiated from her and he caught a hint of her soft scent. The light, airy fragrance suited her perfectly. As she shifted to dust the other side of his face, he detected another, more natural layer, one that made him want to bury his face against her skin and inhale. The mental image that conjured stilled his breathing.

"Open."

He found her scrutinizing him, an odd expression on her face. She smoothed a stray lock away from his temple, then stepped back for a better look. "Huh."

"Huh?" he repeated. "That's your assessment? How did I go downhill from nice?"

"Never fear, you still look nice." Crinkles formed at the outer edges of her hazel eyes. "It's the strangest thing, but for a moment there, you looked familiar to me. Like I should recognize you from somewhere. But then I lost it."

Shock left his gut in a hard knot. It took every ounce of his training to keep his expression neutral and his tone easy. "All tall, dark, and handsome men look alike, don't they?"

"Very funny." She shook her head. "You've never lived in New York or Oregon, have you?"

"Never. I've only visited New York twice and have never set foot in Oregon."

She couldn't possibly recognize him. Most of the time when he entered a room, he was announced. It was the only way those outside southern Europe knew him. The only Americans who ever placed him otherwise were die-hard royal watchers or tourists who'd studied Sarcaccia's travel brochures just before visiting his country.

"Didn't think so." She signaled Mike that they were ready to begin, then walked Vittorio out the door to the apartment's vestibule so Mike could film their entrance. While they waited for the signal to enter, she shot him an easy grin, one meant to put him at ease. Nevertheless, throughout their tour of the apartment, he remained on edge. Emily had intentionally kept him in the kitchen prior to filming in order to capture his first reaction to each of the apartment's rooms, and it'd been a smart move. Despite his lifelong media training, he needed every aid possible in order to appear natural on camera. The idea Emily might identify him—or worse, say something in front of the others—distracted him from the apartment's numerous amenities. It wasn't until they were on the final rooms that he felt like himself again.

Once they'd walked through the entire apartment, Emily called for a break so Mike could use the restroom before their second take. Once again, she surprised Vittorio by brushing the same stubborn lock of hair back from his forehead.

"This always fall in your face?"

"It seems determined." He couldn't tell her that until a couple months ago, he'd never kept his hair this long.

The odd expression she'd worn before the walk-through reappeared as her hand fell back to her side. "You seem very relaxed in front of the camera. Done this before?"

"Nothing like this, no." Sharing his thoughts on camera about living arrangements didn't compare to discussing politics or the charities his family supported. Frankly, he found it more challenging.

More intimate. And if he wanted to avoid discovery and the scandal it would cause, intimate was not the way to go.

And that went for the intimacy of having her constantly touch his hair.

"It's good that you're mentioning the pros and the cons of the place, like the size of the bathroom in comparison to the bedroom. It prompts viewers to debate the same features, which keeps them engaged."

"You're very good at this, you know?"

"I do my best, but a lot depends on who we feature." Her lower lip twitched, then she tilted her head to indicate he should follow her from the living room toward the bedroom. In a voice low enough to keep Rita and Mike from overhearing them, she said, "I know you want your privacy, and I truly wish to respect that. But can you give me anything to work with editorially as we do our second walk-through?"

The words *your privacy* pinged his internal radar, putting him on alert. "Such as?"

"During the house-hunting segments, I like to give our viewers information about why we're visiting a particular home or apartment. For instance, I might say you're an architect who appreciates the building's free form shape and the apartment's open floor plan. Or that you're a painter who needs a living area with plenty of light. It doesn't need to be too personal." She gestured toward the windows. "You'd think anyone would want this, but last season, we had a woman who didn't like heights and decided against an apartment that hit everything on her wish list because it was on the tenth floor. In the end, she asked to be put on a waitlist for a unit on a lower level in the same building, even though that floor didn't offer very good views. Any tidbit like that would work."

"I see." He wasn't about to explain that he wanted the apartment so he'd have an escape from the watchful eye of paparazzi cameras or that he requested a modern space because it was the polar opposite of his centuries-old apartment in Sarcaccia's royal palace. But as Emily's expressive eyes searched his, Vittorio experienced an overwhelming urge to tell her exactly that. He wanted her to understand him just as he burned to understand her. To discover why she gave up the beautiful vistas of Oregon for the intensity of life in Manhattan. What drew her to work at a magazine, then sparked the idea for *At Home Abroad*. About the struggles she must have faced to convince a network to pick up the show. About the strain of being on the road for months at a time, with only her coworkers for company. People for whom she felt responsible.

Though it didn't seem so on the surface, in many ways their lives were similar.

She stepped closer and rested her hand on his forearm. "You mentioned that your siblings tease you about being a creature of habit. Does that figure into your apartment criteria at all? Are you happiest in modern surroundings? That's an easy thing to mention." One side of her mouth jerked up. "The modern surroundings part, not the teasing, that is."

"Anyone with siblings has endured their share of teasing."

"I imagine."

"You don't have any?"

Her fingers tightened fractionally before she released his arm. "My parents married in their forties. It was a second marriage for each of them after short first marriages. They had me a couple years later. Even if they could've had more children, I suspect I wore them out. I was a rambunctious toddler. Liked to push buttons, open cabinets, climb furniture, you name it."

Her answer conjured a mental image of a tiny Emily perched atop a dresser. "They still alive?"

"And kicking, no thanks to me. Yours?"

"Same. Though these days, they'd kick me if they could get away with it."

"I doubt that."

"I haven't visited recently," he explained, though it skimmed over the fact they lived under the same roof. "They're entitled."

"I suppose parents want to keep track of their kids, no matter their age."

Her voice held a hint of wistfulness, though she covered it with a broad smile. He wondered why she didn't have children, though it was obvious she'd be an attentive, loving mother. Was it the job? Or something else?

It made him wish he were anyone other than the crown prince he was, that he could speak to her as two normal people might while getting to know each other, without dancing around reality. But if he wasn't royal, he wouldn't have met Carmella, wouldn't have needed an escape far from Sarcaccia, and certainly wouldn't have met Emily. Wouldn't be standing here now, looking into her caring hazel eyes, envisioning her holding a bouncy, giggling infant. Or handing the baby off to him.

CHAPTER 8

Noises from the adjoining living room indicated that Rita and Mike were getting ready to do a second run-through on the apartment. He blinked. What was he just telling himself about intimacy?

And dear God, a *baby*? Much as it was his duty to beget heirs, he'd never visualized a woman as the mother of his children, even for a split second. Maybe he really had hit his head harder than he'd thought.

"So…any editorial ideas?" Emily asked, sensing the change in his mood and taking a step back. "If not, no worries. I can wing it."

He ran a hand over his beard, thinking. "How about this: I was raised in a home with antiquated floors and windows, heavy crown molding, and electrical and plumbing systems older than my grandparents. So while I'm nostalgic about traditional design and enjoy having access to Argentina's historic neighborhoods, which have a distinctly European feel, I want the experience of living in a contemporary residence, one with an abundance of light and clean-lined decor."

"Wow." She let out a low whistle of appreciation. "When I said I wanted editorial, I never expected you to deliver actual content. That's very good."

"Agreed," Rita said as she entered the bedroom. "At least the part I heard. So you ready to roll?"

The second take went quickly. When they finished, Rita called the building's security office to let them know they'd be leaving shortly and to thank the management for giving them such latitude for filming. As Mike packed his gear and Emily walked back through the bedrooms to ensure they'd left everything as they'd found it, Rita handed Vittorio a few sheets of paper.

"What's this?"

"Our schedule for day after tomorrow. We'll film that day and the next, then we'll be done."

He glanced at the papers, which also contained the descriptions of two more apartments. The first looked like nothing he'd described when he'd talked over his wish list with Emily.

"I know," she said, grimacing at the first one. "It's an old-fashioned colonial, rather than a modern building. It's in the neighborhood of San Telmo, not far from the soccer stadium where you went today. But it's in an amazing location, has a secure entrance for privacy, and is near a lot of tango. I can get us in there for a walk-through in the daylight, then we can either visit a tango instructor that afternoon or a tango bar that night."

She flipped the papers to show him the second apartment building. "This one is more your style. It's a recently renovated Belle Epoque building in Barrio Norte. The exterior was left intact, but the interior was completely modernized. There are a number of units available and they're all open, so we have a lot of options for filming. We'll do that on Friday, then we'll be finished. And you'll be free of us."

The San Telmo apartment didn't interest him, but the Barrio Norte units were similar to one he'd admired in that district the day before he met Emily. "What about tomorrow?"

"The sky is supposed to be clear, so Mike and Ignacio are going to film our outdoor scenes. Emily and I like to pick a theme for each episode. Sometimes it's stated outright, sometimes not. For this episode, we're going with passion."

"Passion?" And he was being featured?

Rita nodded. "When Emily does the voiceovers, she ties what's depicted on screen to our theme. It helps give each episode a cohesive feel and makes it more memorable. For instance, during your episode she'll talk about the passion of soccer fans, the passion of the tango, and the passion the government had for the reclamation project that brought Puerto Madero back to life. In keeping with that, tomorrow we plan to capture some shots of the tango parlors in San Telmo. Emily's also filming a short segment on drinking like a local."

"Now that sounds like a topic to get passionate about," he said with a grin.

Emily walked up behind him. "It's not what you think. I'm interviewing a café owner about the Argentine obsession with *mate* tea, then he's going to demonstrate how he makes his. I'll say that while I like *mate*, I'm far more passionate about the Argentine *submarino*."

"Isn't that…milk?"

"Oh, it's much more than milk." Her eyes lit with humor. "It's a submarine-shaped chunk of chocolate *dunked* in hot milk."

Rita's laugh resonated through the apartment. "Mention chocolate and every woman instantly ties it to passion."

"I'll have to remember that," Mike called from the front hall, where he was holding the door open for them to exit.

Emily rolled her eyes, then turned to Vittorio. "The bottom line is that we won't need you until Thursday. But Thursday will likely be a long day, since the tango parlors don't get into full swing until late at night, assuming we do that instead of an early show or a visit to a tango school."

"I can handle a late night," he assured them.

Rita swirled one hand in the air, then drew an imaginary rose through her teeth. "In that case, I expect you two to put on a fine performance. One with passion!"

"I should apologize for Rita, though if she ever discovers I did, she'd kill me."

Emily said the words through clenched teeth as she waved from the cab window, watching as Rita keyed into the front door of a small apartment not far from the *At Home Abroad* offices. Though the rest of the staff members were staying in one of two bed and breakfasts, Rita had opted to say with an aunt who lived in the city.

"You don't need to apologize," Victor replied. "She's a flirt, but she loves her husband dearly."

Emily gave the driver the address for the bed and breakfast where she was staying, then turned to Victor with interest as the driver pulled away from the curb. "How do you know that?"

"Because her exact words to me were, 'I love my husband dearly.'"

She wondered what compelled Rita to speak so bluntly. Had Victor flirted back while Emily was in a different room?

Victor leaned against the taxi's cracked leather seat, stretching one powerful arm along the edge of the window. "She also told me she wishes you'd flirt more, then maybe you'd be lucky enough to find a husband as adoring and perfect as hers. Of course, she was also trying to convince me I should give tango lessons a try, rather than watching from the sidelines on Thursday at a show."

Now it made sense. "Rita should've been a matchmaker instead of a television director and producer. Some days I think she gets a bigger kick out of trying to find partners for her friends than she does in her real job."

"Is she as successful at matchmaking?"

That drew a low laugh from her. "She's a great director, while Mike, Ignacio, Maryam, and I are all single, despite her best efforts. So I'd say no."

"Then perhaps it's best she sticks to her day job."

"Better for me, for sure." The last thing she needed was a boyfriend, one she'd eventually have to tell about her health history. When she was a few years older, perhaps it wouldn't be such a relationship killer. But for now, Emily had the show. That was enough to keep her challenged and fulfilled.

She leaned forward to ask the driver to pull over, then turned to Victor. "My bed and breakfast is in that narrow white building on the other side of the park, so I'll get out and walk from here. You know how to get to the apartment for filming on Thursday?"

"I do." The space between his brows wrinkled as he looked across the park. "You shouldn't walk alone at night. I'll go with you. My hotel is only a few blocks beyond your bed and breakfast."

"I appreciate the offer, but I've made the same walk every night I've been in Buenos Aires. It's perfectly safe. You go ahead and take the cab." She patted his arm in thanks, then handed a bill to the cab driver and told him to keep the change. When she stepped out, Victor did the same.

"You don't follow directions, do you?" she said over the top of the cab.

"Nope. I prefer to manage rather than be managed." The devilish grin lighting his face made her weak in the knees.

"You know that's how you ended up with that lump on your head, right? You don't stay put when you should."

"Ease your guilt by allowing me to walk you home." Without waiting for an answer, Victor tapped on the roof of the cab and sent the driver on his way. Once they'd crossed the boulevard and entered the park, a wave of calm washed through Emily. Though they'd filmed all over the country, Buenos Aires was the show's home base for the season and she'd come to relish breathing in the crisp, summery night air and the mossy scent of the park's old trees after a long day of work.

"Refreshing, isn't it?" he asked. Victor walked on her left side, less than an arm's length away. "When I arrived in town, I rented a bike and rode all over this neighborhood. I stopped at the lunch cart at the northern edge a few times. Great, quick food. I sat on a bench over there" —he pointed toward a fountain in the distance where a number of young couples sat eating late-night ice cream cones and chatting— "and people-watched while I ate."

She sliced a glance sideways. "Yellow cart run by a guy named Franco?"

"One and the same. Great sausage sandwiches. You like them, too?"

"*Choripán*? No." She shuddered. "Mike and Ignacio like to bring them to the office smothered in *chimichurri* sauce, then breathe their garlic and onion fire-breath on the rest of us."

"Doesn't surprise me. I suspect they eat them in the office rather than the park specifically for the entertainment value of torturing you."

"I suspect you're right." After a moment, she said, "I'm surprised you like *choripán*. I'd have guessed you'd choose something else from his cart."

"I get mine without onions or sauce. They're not nearly as tortuous as what Mike and Ignacio eat."

His lighthearted tone drew a smile from her as they strolled through the park center in silence. A stray dog lay sheltered in the raised, twisted roots of the massive ombu tree that dominated the square. The furry creature blinked at them as they passed, then turned its attention to a group of old men who sat on the low edge of a nearby brick wall, where they debated politics with an abundance of hand gestures.

"The park is completely different at night," Victor observed as he glanced up at the tree's sprawling, umbrella-like canopy. "Quieter, but still full of activity if you take the time to look."

"I've never been here in the middle of the day. Always early morning or late at night, when it's like this. It's why I'd rather walk than take a taxi the whole way. I can forget work worries for awhile and let my mind drift." She pointed out an elegant, amber-toned building on the far side of the park. "When I see the lights on in that window and the thick curtains to the side of that balcony, I can't help but sing 'Don't Cry For Me, Argentina.' In my head, of course."

Even in the semidarkness, she read the amusement in his expression. "That doesn't strike me as very relaxing. I always found that song depressing."

"Not me. I saw it on stage in New York and I was blown away by the power of the song and the image of a woman standing on a balcony, singing her thanks to people who care for her. There was no resentment of her cancer or the fact she wouldn't have a long life with her husband, let alone a family." Emily's gaze returned to the gracious old building. "When I see that building after a long day of work, it reminds me of the fact I've had the opportunity to travel the world, and it makes me grateful."

They were nearly across the park now. Both their steps slowed, as if neither of them wanted the conversation to end.

"I saw *Evita* in London," he said. "I'd spent the entire day at work functions and had little sleep the night before, so I was exhausted. It was all I could do to stay awake when I took my seat and the lights went down, even though I was surrounded by the...by colleagues... and I needed to stay sharp." His voice deepened, as if he were concentrating on the memory. "But when Eva first arrived from her rural village and began singing, 'Hello, Buenos Aires!' I got my second wind. I don't remember most of the lyrics, but there was a vibrancy and freedom to the music that appealed to me. A sense that everything could be new again. So it was that song I found most powerful. When I got back to my hotel it took me a long time to fall asleep."

The canopy of trees gave way to a wide sidewalk fronting one of Recoleta's main streets. The buildings on the opposite side housed hotels, bed and breakfasts, and private residences. Though the lights twinkling in the windows gave the entire street an elegant, romantic feel, it didn't exude the same magic as the park.

Victor's voice floated to Emily as he glanced over his shoulder, taking in the sight of the tree-covered path they'd just traversed. "When I arrived and took my first bike ride through this park, it was the chorus of 'Buenos Aires' that went through my head." He cocked his head and smiled at her. "Funny how the park and surrounding buildings make us both think of *Evita*, but the songs we hear are so different."

It was a surprising revelation from the man who, when she first approached him, unnerved her with his cool, distant demeanor. He'd done it again when he trapped her between his arms in the Palermo apartment, demanding to know who employed her and why she'd followed him, but then it was with the heat of his anger. Now he struck her as a man who'd come to Buenos Aires craving vibrancy and freedom, a man who needed his faith in the world renewed. The thought spoke to an inner anguish she'd never have predicted when they first met.

Keen to understand him, she stopped walking and faced him fully. "Victor, tell me something. How long have you been on your vacation?"

CHAPTER 9

SHE'D ASKED the question softly, but wariness leapt in his eyes before he covered it with a shrug. "A while."

She waited. A group of twenty-somethings cut through the park behind them, their voices giddy as they crossed the boulevard and made their way toward a nearby street known for its dance clubs.

"Mid-October," he finally admitted. "Almost five months."

"Five months is a long vacation." Sensing that she treaded on dangerous ground, she shifted to a gentler approach. "You likely know more about Buenos Aires than I do. The irony of *At Home Abroad* is that I'm never in one city long enough to actually be at home in it."

He remained still, but the air between them felt thicker, imbued with tension. She took a risk and asked, "Did you intend to stay so long?"

"Are you asking for the show?"

"I'm asking because I'm curious."

The edge of his mouth twitched, but he didn't look away from her. Rather, she felt he looked right through her, as if attempting to discern her motives and determine whether she could be trusted. "I've enjoyed my time here more than I expected I would. The cobblestone streets, the Italian eateries, the passion for *fútbol*…they all appeal to my European heritage. But it's far enough away from my real life that I can escape the pressures of work."

"Your job sounds stressful."

"You could say that."

"Have you considered changing?"

His mouth quirked as if her question were unintentionally funny. "Much as it can be exhausting, it's also very rewarding. Like you, I have a lot of people who count on me and it's gratifying to see their lives improve as a direct result of decisions I make." He shrugged. "This vacation is a first for me. I suppose that's why I've been away as long as I have, though I'm planning to return soon."

"You've never taken a vacation before?" Victor had to be in his mid-thirties. Who went that long without a break? No wonder he vividly remembered the night he'd spent at *Evita*. It was—literally—a wake-up call.

"I've vacationed, but never without family and at least some time devoted to work. And never for more than a few days."

She thought back to what he'd said about his family while he was touring the Puerto Madero apartment. "If you're that close to them, they're probably more worried that your job stress is getting to you than about how long it's been since you've visited."

His eyebrows rose slightly and she knew she'd hit the mark.

"Maybe you could give them a call tomorrow morning. It'll be afternoon in Europe then."

"I believe I will." He put his hand to her lower back and began walking again, encouraging her to fall into step beside him before letting his arm drop to his side. "I'll tell them I'm considering buying a vacation place here."

"Describe the apartment we visited today and they'll end up wanting to visit."

"I suspect they'd rather have me home, but it's a nice thought."

They crossed the street and approached the narrow buildings that housed the *At Home Abroad* staff. The light in Maryam's third floor room burned bright, but Emily could see from the darkened windows a few doors down the street that Ignacio and Mike weren't back to their bed and breakfast yet. They'd likely gone out to have a beer and swap stories about what happened at the soccer match.

"You're under a good deal of pressure yourself," Victor observed. "Enough to tap your own financial resources to save everyone's jobs if necessary."

"Since my job is one of those in need of saving, there's a certain amount of self-interest involved. It's what anyone would do."

"That doesn't make it any less stressful. Yet here you are taking the time to ask about my family and you hardly know me." He stopped and turned so abruptly she nearly crashed into his chest. He took her elbow and leaned against the wrought iron railing of her entry stairs. The warmth of his fingers radiated through the thin fabric of her blouse, sending heat to pool in regions where she had no right to feel it. Not for this man, a guest on her show. A man who, as he pointed out, she hardly knew.

His light brown eyes searched her face, and she again experienced a feeling of déjà vu, as if she *had* met Victor before. As if she should not only know him, but should trust him.

Before she could process the thought, his quiet voice pulled her back to reality. "You always take care of those around you, don't you?"

"Some care," she scoffed as she reached to the side of his head and angled her gaze, trying to get a glimpse of what must now be a sizable lump on the back of his head. "You ended up with stitches in your head. Or did you hit it so hard you forgot?"

His thick, dark hair felt soft as down beneath her fingertips. Suddenly conscious of touching him, she withdrew her hand, though he didn't shift his gaze or let go of her other elbow. If anything, his scrutiny of her intensified.

"That was my own fault. I chose to go down the stairs. And I'm fine."

"Still, it shouldn't have happened—"

"You're the one who shouldn't have stepped in front of a police officer."

"It's not a big deal. Anyone would've spoken up. I was afraid he'd hurt you before he realized you weren't a threat."

They stood too close, more like lovers than acquaintances; she could see the variation of color in the dark hair that dusted his cheeks and chin and sense the rise and fall of his chest as he breathed. She could even smell his warm, masculine skin. Her throat tightened, but not with the same trepidation she'd experienced when he pinned her against the kitchen counter and she struggled to gain the space she needed to think. Now she wanted to bury her face against his strong shoulder, to inhale his blissful scent and feel his light beard against her cheek to see if its texture differed from the hair on his head.

"Liar," he whispered. "You didn't simply say something, you did something."

He didn't let go of her elbow as he eased off the railing. Instead, his hand moved higher to stroke the back of her arm. A split second before he leaned in, she knew he was going to kiss her. His unhurried approach afforded her the opportunity to pull away. She didn't. He hesitated again with his mouth a breath away, then shifted to delicately brush his lips across hers. The faint, controlled touch sent her senses into overdrive. Then his hand cupped the back of her head and his mouth covered hers completely. The rest of the world faded away —the streetlights, the distant noise of the nightclubs, the low conversation of a couple passing them on the sidewalk—and Emily's entire being succumbed to the sensation of his kiss.

Her hands went to the front of his shirt as if it were the most natural motion in the world. The broad expanse of muscle beneath her fingertips combined with the heady sensation of his warm, skilled lips moving against hers to elicit a sigh from deep within her.

He growled against her mouth at the sound. Then he really kissed her.

His other hand came up to frame her cheek, cradling her face as if she were a precious treasure even as he did wicked things with his mouth. Against her better sense she opened to him, kneaded her fingers against the fabric of the shirt they'd bought together only hours earlier, and allowed herself to savor the feel of his powerful thigh pressing against hers, locking her in place.

She had no right to kiss him. Rita might've encouraged a flirtation, but nothing like this. This made her want to pull at his clothing, to explore the hard planes of his chest and what was undoubtedly a spectacular set of abs, then…oh, and then…what she wanted was completely unprofessional, especially before the show wrapped.

And once the show wrapped, there'd be no point. She'd be back in New York and he'd be…wherever he came from.

His hands slid down her shoulders, then caressed the sides of her body to rest at her waist for a moment before he pulled her hard against him. Sensation drowned out sense as she kissed him back, her tongue discovering his, her fingertips drifting over the rounded, firm expanse of his shoulders before she wound her arms around his neck.

Then, as gently as he'd begun the kiss, he ended it, leaning back against the railing again even as he held her lower body flush to his. He blinked, as if shaking himself awake from a lust-filled dream. A chaos of emotions flickered across his face before his gaze shuttered.

"You haven't kissed anyone in a long time, have you, Emily?"

Shock left her agape.

"I suspect it's because you work too hard." His voice was low and knowing. "You've sacrificed your personal life to ensure everyone else is all right. It's not good for you or anyone else in the long run. I speak from experience."

"Experience?" she managed, her lips still singed from physical contact. "What kind of experience could you possibly have that would give you any insight into whether or not I've been kissed recently?"

He raised his fingertips to cradle her face. His golden gaze followed his thumb as he slid it from her temple to rest over the center of her lips. With a faint smile, he let it fall away. "Perhaps it was your…extraordinary passion. You should go around kissing men more often."

"I believe *you* kissed *me*." She shook her head and stepped back from his embrace before he could respond. "Look, Victor…I shouldn't —" It aggravated her that she couldn't think straight with him standing so close. "Regardless of who kissed whom, it's not appropriate given that you're appearing on the show, and that's aside from the fact that my coworkers could look out their windows or walk up behind us at any time."

"Are you saying it was a mistake?" His easy, teasing smile bloomed into a full-fledged grin.

"No, not a mistake." When Victor looked at her with such life in his expression, she couldn't have regrets. Nor could she fail to smile in return. "But it shouldn't happen again. It's not professional of me."

He regarded her for a moment before saying, "I'm learning that life isn't all about one's career or position, no matter how many people are watching you or expect you to act in a certain manner. It's not an easy lesson to learn. I've been at it for almost five months."

She forced a smile, though she knew it wasn't convincing. Victor's situation wasn't the same as hers. She'd given up her job once before to have a so-called life, and it hadn't worked. But even if the man existed who could accept her travel schedule, he'd also have to accept her other limitations, limitations that weren't her choice. Limitations her ex, Paul, hadn't been able to accept, no matter how much he'd loved her. There'd always been an, "I love you, but…." It was the "but" that drove her to build a life—a very happy life—around her career and the friends she'd made of her coworkers along the way. A life that made her damned proud.

"Victor—"

He held up a hand to forestall her argument as he pushed off the railing and moved past her, down the staircase. "I'll respect your wishes. I even understand them. Hope your filming goes well tomorrow. I'll see you Thursday in San Telmo."

"Thursday."

Her legs went to jelly as she climbed the stairs and punched the keypad code that would let her inside. He'd kissed her. And he was right…she hadn't experienced a kiss like that in a long, long time.

She hadn't experienced a kiss like that *ever*.

"Emily?"

Slowly, she turned. He was walking backward on the sidewalk, hands in his pockets. "I'll contact my family to let them know I'll see them soon. Thank you for the suggestion."

He spun on his heel and was gone into the night.

"Did you have a late night, my dear?"

Fabrizia felt her husband's presence before the playful question left his lips, despite the fact he moved soundlessly across their apartment's inlaid wood floors and dense Persian rugs. She also knew without looking behind her that he saw the image of Rocco Cornaro on her computer screen. His eldest son—Teresa's eldest son—photographed boarding a luxury yacht near Dubrovnik a few months ago.

"I would've assumed you'd prefer to read today's weather report over breakfast." He reached past her to pick up her teapot and top off her cup. "Better for the digestion than gossip. And old gossip, at that."

His playfulness made her smile, but only for a moment. The matter was too serious to take lightly. "Perhaps I should send one of my private investigators to Croatia. We should find out who approached him in the market."

"No." The single word, spoken quietly, was intended to hide frustration and—only because she knew her husband so well—a dose of fear.

"We need to protect our family," she argued. "If Vittorio isn't coming home soon, if he's not in the frame of mind to carry out his duties—"

"Absolutely not."

Slowly, the queen turned in her chair. Even after more than forty years spent together, some happy, some not so happy, she couldn't look at Carlo in one of his bespoke suits without a pang of lust coursing through her. And last night, as they'd sprawled across the bed, her head nestled against his chest while they discussed the situation, she'd felt an immense amount of love. He wanted what she wanted, even if they didn't see eye to eye on how to achieve it. "Are you saying this as my husband, or as my king?"

"Both. Whichever will get you to stop this nonsense. Sending your cadre of spies would draw more attention to him, even if they're discreet." He put his hands on her shoulders and ran the pads of his thumbs along her collarbone, warming her through the red silk of her favorite wrap dress. "Besides, that's our past."

"I know that. However, our present could fall apart if we don't—"

"Fabrizia, the man is a multimillionaire and a clever one, at that. He has the ability to take care of himself." The king's intelligent brown eyes flicked to the screen, then back to her. "But more important, I don't want to reopen that wound. It took us years to get beyond it. I can't risk losing you again."

She placed a calming hand on his lapel and smiled. Carlo rarely showed vulnerability. When he did, her heart ached for him. He wasn't the man he'd been all those years ago, but on occasion he still felt the sting of his youthful failures. "You won't."

"Then trust me to handle this?"

She bit back an argument and nodded. What choice did she have?

"We'll give Vittorio a few more days. Then he'll return to his duties, ready or not."

"If you try to force him, he'll resist."

Carlo placed his hand over his wife's, holding her palm against his heart. "I resisted, too, once. I was even younger and my mistakes more grave. In the end, I knew I was a Barrali first and obligated to my country. That duty—and the unconditional love I had from you—kept me from the harm that would've occurred had I stayed with Teresa. Vittorio will do what's right, just as I did, and without coercion. He has no choice. He knows this. We will give him the support he needs."

Behind her, the computer pinged. Carlo started to say something, then paused and turned his attention to the screen. His eyes brightened. "My dear wife, I told you to trust me. The timing is rather coincidental, but—"

She twisted in her seat to see the e-mail box she'd left open on one side of the screen. Foreboding crept through her as she clicked on the new message.

Late Monday night. Looking forward to it.

She sat back in her chair and put her hand to her stomach. The signature indicated it was sent from a temporary account created at an Internet café in Argentina.

"Oh, Carlo." Fabrizia reached up to stroke her husband's cheek and pull him to her for a kiss. She could only hope that when Vittorio returned, he would find the same strength Carlo had.

CHAPTER 10

VITTORIO DROPPED a tip into the open case of an accordion player not far from the address Rita had given him in San Telmo. Emily would be there already, along with Rita, Mike, Ignacio, and perhaps others. A makeup artist. Lighting specialists. The real estate agent. All people who'd notice if he acted like a man who wanted to have his way with the show's host.

He'd accused her of extraordinary passion. Of putting her job before her own desires.

But that wasn't the problem, was it? It was his own passion.

He'd intended the kiss on her doorstep to be quick and gentlemanly. An expression of gratitude for the risk she'd taken for him at the stadium and a recognition of her caring spirit. But when he'd experienced the heady sensation of her soft, yielding mouth beneath his own, then felt her palms against his chest, her fingertips bunching the fabric of his new shirt much as a cat's paws might bunch a rug in bliss following a long, sun-soaked nap...he'd burned for her. Wanted her beneath him, arching her back, clawing at him in the throes of ecstasy. The speed and intensity of that fire had shocked him.

Even now his jaw tightened at the memory.

The scent of freshly baked croissants and hot coffee filled the air as he passed a café. Across the cobblestone street, a man washed the windows of an antique shop while next door, a bookseller shook out a small rug before placing it at the entry to her store. It wasn't so different from a morning in the streets of Cateri's medieval center, though he couldn't walk the streets of Cateri as freely as he could here. He moved to the edge of the sidewalk, allowing a man pushing a pretzel cart to pass, then crossed to the narrow side street Rita had described when she'd given him directions.

In the light of day, he could understand why Emily had launched into her speech about appropriateness. Hell, he'd said virtually the same thing to Carmella once when they'd shared a brief kiss outside the palace ballroom last summer. It wasn't appropriate, not at that time or location.

But there was a difference. With Carmella, he'd been content to wait for a better time and place, as had she. With Emily…he suspected he'd never describe himself as content to end a kiss with her, at any time or any place, and every instinct he possessed told him she'd experienced the same conflagration of lust he had. It wasn't simply in her exquisite surrender, when she'd reached her arms around his neck and sighed against his mouth. He'd seen it in the flush that crept up her throat and reddened her cheeks. In her quick defensiveness when he observed that she hadn't been kissed in awhile, then in the bobble of her knees as she'd climbed the stairs afterward. It was that slight loss of balance that nearly did him in.

He'd known Carmella for years and never experienced the inner satisfaction he had in that moment, knowing he'd affected Emily as much as she'd affected him. And he'd been acquainted with Emily for what, forty-eight hours?

It wasn't like him at all. Then again, neither was a five-month disappearing act. Or lying about his identity before sharing a lust-filled kiss with a woman who could place him.

He skipped over a puddle created by a shopkeeper's hose before stepping onto the curb. When Emily scrutinized his face after dusting on that infernal powder at the apartment in Puerto Madero, he'd experienced a flash of regret about appearing on her show. But kissing Emily that night reinforced the appreciation of life he'd grasped during his months in Buenos Aires. It proved he still possessed a soul that could be moved. It also proved a woman could want him for more than his title or his wealth.

He'd walked back to his hotel feeling energized. And what was the harm in that, given that he'd left Sarcaccia specifically to reenergize? Besides, it was perfectly natural to kiss a woman who stepped in front of an armed cop for you.

The realization he was making excuses to himself made him grin as he approached the crumbling brick building bearing the address Rita provided and pushed the appropriate button on the panel outside the entry. He wouldn't have planted a kiss on a member of his security detail in Sarcaccia if they'd jumped to his defense.

Then again, they were paid to do it. They were protecting what he represented to his countrymen rather than him personally. Emily was…well, Emily was something else entirely. A great risk, but one that was only temporary, given his schedule. He'd occupied part of his time yesterday determining the best way to enter Sarcaccia without the press catching wind of it until he was inside the palace and could ensure a smooth switch with Alessandro. The plane reservations were made, he'd arranged low-key transportation from the airport to a discreet drop-off spot near the palace, and he'd even notified his mother.

He ran a hand over his beard. He'd need to get rid of it when he arrived home and hope he hadn't gotten so much sun in Argentina that shaving would leave a line of demarcation.

"It's me," he said into the ancient speaker when the intercom buzzed to life, unsure whether it would be Emily or one of her coworkers on the other end.

"Bob? Fantastic. Come on up to the top floor," Rita's familiar voice crackled through the speaker at the same time the door lock clicked open.

The narrow entry hall had apartment doors on either side and a windowless staircase in the center. Vittorio took the worn marble stairs at a jog, passing two more apartments on the next floor before arriving at the top of the staircase, which boasted a landing only large enough for two people and a sizable wooden door that looked more appropriate for a barn than an apartment.

Rita opened the door, coffee in hand, and waved him inside. "I know, I know. It's not much to look at on the outside, but you'll love it. Grab a cup of coffee in the kitchen. Ignacio is on his way back from filming one of the nearby churches. Once he's here, we'll get started."

She walked him to the kitchen where he was greeted by the makeup artist and introduced to the real estate agent, a balding, affable young man named Enrico who was busy wiping the counter to a high shine. Though Vittorio made small talk with the group while he located the coffee cups and gave himself a healthy pour, he couldn't help but listen for Emily. He'd fully expected her to greet him at the door.

Until she failed to appear, he hadn't realized how much he'd craved seeing her face this morning. It shouldn't have surprised him. Yesterday he'd been about to check out of the Internet café, having booked his travel and contacted his mother, when, on a whim, he'd looked up *At Home Abroad*. He'd skipped the staff biographies he'd seen on Emily's cell phone the morning they met and discovered a wealth of information. Fan sites, message boards, and even—to his surprise—a few men's magazines' lists of hottest women on television that included Emily. What kept him glued to the computer screen, however, was an interview published a year earlier by a popular home decorating website. The main photo showed Emily leaning against her kitchen counter with a mixing bowl nestled in the crook of her arm. Her hair was tucked behind her ears and worn shorter than she had it now. Her feet were bare. She wore weathered jeans and a gray T-shirt topped by a tacky white apron sporting a wedding photo of Prince Charles and the late Princess Diana. He'd laughed to himself at that, as his mother had a similar apron hanging in a discreet spot in the palace kitchen. His mother found the royal wedding souvenir so horribly tasteless she couldn't resist owning it, and she'd even worn it once while baking cookies with her granddaughter, Anna.

He'd read the article with interest. It claimed that Emily liked to bring something from each of the countries she visited back to her own home. However, rather than decorative vases or art pieces, she preferred items she could use every day. The countertop basket holding pears and apples came from Japan. The mixing bowl had been a find at a village market in Switzerland. A magazine assignment in Turkey led her to the artisan from whom she purchased her spice rack. The apron, however, was a parting gift from coworkers at her last job, not an item she'd picked up on a trip. She told the interviewer she loved the kitsch factor and wore it whenever she hosted summertime barbecues, despite the odd looks it garnered from her guests.

It was another insight into a complex woman.

He rested his hips against the kitchen counter and took a deep swig of his coffee. Shouldn't Emily know he was here by now?

"Emily's on the phone in the other room," Rita said, making him wonder if she read the direction of his thoughts. He kept his expression neutral as Rita explained that Emily had missed an early morning call from the network and decided to return it while they were waiting for Ignacio.

"No problems, I assume?"

"I doubt it. We're at the end of our production for the season, so the brass like to check in often."

Vittorio took another sip of his coffee as the real estate agent asked Rita a few questions about the show and how the apartment would be presented. Rita's attitude throughout the discussion was upbeat, but Vittorio wasn't fooled. Whatever the nature of Emily's call, it rattled Rita.

Less than five minutes passed before Ignacio returned. He shot a meaningful look at Rita, who angled her head in the direction where Emily had disappeared and shrugged.

"Everyone's back? Great...let's get rolling." Emily appeared her usual, cheerful self as she entered the kitchen a beat later. Her hair was worn up in a loose but elegant bun that highlighted her long neck and the smooth expanse of skin at the vee of her bright pink dress. Perfectly applied lipstick matched her outfit and made her face seem alight. Rita pushed a cup of coffee her way, but Emily waved it off.

She smiled as she turned his way, every bit the professional. "You haven't peeked outside the kitchen yet, have you, Bob?"

When he assured her he hadn't, she said, "Then you know the drill. We'll head out to the hall until we get the signal, then Ignacio will shoot us as we walk in. Give me your thoughts on the apartment, good and bad, and we'll go from there."

After he received a thumbs-up from the makeup artist, Vittorio followed her out, shutting the wooden door behind them so they were alone on the small landing. "Everything all right?" he whispered as they waited for Ignacio's signal to enter.

"Of course. Why?" An immediate blush rose in her cheeks. As if she realized he could be asking about their kiss, she diverted him by finishing, "Are you concerned about the apartment?"

He waved off the idea. "I meant the call. Rita seemed to think it was important."

"Oh. No, nothing to worry about." They heard Ignacio and she swept a hand toward the door. "After you."

He paused, frowning. Her tone sounded casual, but he noticed the tightening of her jaw before she answered. He didn't buy her all-is-well routine for a second. Hoping to put her at ease, he allowed the conversation to follow her earlier direction. "You don't think I'm going to like this place, do you?"

One of her shoulders hitched, then lowered. "Let's find out."

Now that he knew the routine, it wasn't difficult to determine where to stand for each shot, what observations to make, or the appropriate amount of banter to exchange with Emily and the real estate agent. They began in the kitchen, since it wasn't far from the entry. As Vittorio had observed when he'd come in for coffee, it boasted state-of-the-art appliances and an efficient layout, but the cabinetry choices and wall tiles harkened to the building's roots. He entered the main living space expecting more of the same and found that the modernity had been reserved for the kitchen.

"San Telmo is Buenos Aires' oldest neighborhood, and this partic-ular building dates back nearly a hundred and fifty years. Care was taken during the renovation to preserve as many of the original features as possible while adapting it for modern living." Emily addressed her comments both to Vittorio and the viewers. "The beams and the brickwork are original, while the chandelier was salvaged from a nearby colonial-era mansion after the structure fell into disrepair. It was crafted on the island of Sarcaccia and brought over on a cargo vessel by the mansion's Italian owner."

Vittorio tilted his head to take in the details of the antique piece. Not only was it massive and exquisitely designed, it reminded him of home. Having seen similar creations in several of Sarcaccia's historic buildings, he'd have known its provenance anywhere.

Emily gestured to the series of French doors at the far side of the room. "The wooden shutters are also original to the building and were refurbished by a local craftsman. When we return to this room, I'll let you take a peek outside."

Surprises waited around each corner. A table and chairs purchased from a neighborhood antique shop. Sumptuous Persian rugs that echoed the designs of those in Sarcaccia's royal palace, though on a smaller scale. A massive, hand-carved headboard recovered from the same mansion that once housed the living room chandelier. Yet for all the finery, the apartment had a comfortable, lived-in atmosphere. The rustic wood floors had aged naturally, the bathrooms were updated, yet with fixtures designed to mimic the originals. Enrico took pains to prove that the shower did work and the toilets flushed, and explained that all the plumbing and electrical systems were above code.

The greatest surprise of all, however, lay outside the living room's French doors. He suspected from Emily's look of anticipation that the view would impress. And as he approached the heavy, floor-to-ceiling glass, he was provided an intimate view of the cobblestoned neighborhood, complete with a glimpse of the cathedral between the two buildings on the opposite side of the street. However, it wasn't until Emily opened the doors inward that he saw the apartment's biggest selling point.

Three wide stairs led down to an ornate balcony crafted of iron. Wide enough for a small table and two chairs, it was surrounded with iron flower boxes spilling over with vibrant red blooms.

It wasn't anything like the sleek rooftop terrace he'd seen in Palermo, with its carefully arranged teak chaises and wall of bamboo, or the Puerto Madero apartment, with its expansive views of the river and adjacent high-rise buildings. This was lived in. A balcony designed for close conversation, romantic dinners, and people watching. He could imagine the original inhabitants, years ago, hanging their laundry here. Calling down to their children, waving to the local baker as he closed up shop for the day, and even watching the holiday processions at Christmastime.

"This balcony is also original to the building," Emily explained. "The neighborhood is known for its variety of balconies. If you look across the street, the building on the right has a balcony constructed of balustraded stone. On the left, there are a series of balconies made of wrought iron, decorated with a bird motif. Every building is slightly different. *Porteños*, which is what Buenos Aires locals call themselves, take great pride in the distinctiveness of this neighborhood."

"What do you think of the apartment?" Enrico asked.

"I've never seen anything quite like it," he said, truthfully. The place embodied all he'd loved in Sarcaccia, but it had a distinctly Argentinian flair. The neighborhood was beautiful and gritty and bursting with life all at once. This apartment put its owner in the center of it all.

"San Telmo is quite a melting pot." Emily led the way back inside the living room as Ignacio angled the camera to catch her movement. "Italians made up the bulk of the immigrants here in the 1800s, but many other nationalities have settled here in subsequent years. Now it's a thriving center for musicians, antique shops, and tango. We'll learn more about tango tonight. Until then, you have another wonderful apartment to add to your list of possibilities."

Rita, who stood behind Ignacio, signaled to wrap. "Ten minute break, then we'll do it again."

After a moment's small talk, the two women adjourned to the kitchen while Enrico left to take a phone call from his real estate office.

"How's the head?" Ignacio asked as he tinkered with his camera. "You spend yesterday recovering from the *Superclásico?*"

"I'm perfectly fine. Spent my time running errands." Which reminded Vittorio of a tidbit he'd overheard when he'd stopped for dinner at a local bar last night. "How did you guys manage tickets for the match? From what I gather, it's been sold out for months. Resale prices were through the roof, even for the nosebleed seats."

"We were lucky enough to be given tickets by the tourist board."

Given the extensive work Vittorio had done with Sarcaccia's tourist board over the years, the idea intrigued him. "How'd that come about?"

Satisfied with the state of his equipment, Ignacio set down his camera, then lounged on the sofa to wait for the next take. "Once Emily and Rita select a country to feature on the show, there's a lot of pre-production work, selecting sites to film. We make a point of contacting the national and local tourist boards to let them know we're coming and they fall over themselves for us. A television show like ours is the best kind of advertising they can get, so they clear the way for us to film in museums, parks, and other tourist attractions. When Emily put La Bombonera on the list of sites we might want to see, we were sent tickets and a press pass."

Vittorio settled into a carved chair near the windows and relaxed into its comfortable contours. "Does the tourist board offer suggestions of places to film?"

"Very good ones, at times. Sometimes we take them, sometimes we don't. Depends on our needs, the theme of the show, what we've covered in earlier episodes…you catch my drift." A wry smile slid across the cameraman's weathered face. "The Winstons—the couple we were originally going to film for the finale—wouldn't have done so well with the match. If we'd featured them instead of you, I'd only have filmed a couple minutes of the game from the press location at the side of the field and saved the tourist board the cost of the tickets. We'd have used a short clip in the episode and taken the Winstons to a modern art exhibit instead."

"And highlighted the Argentinian passion for art and architecture over *fútbol*?"

He placed a hand over his heart. "Exactly."

The information slipped into Vittorio's mental files as Emily and Rita emerged from the direction of the kitchen. Though Emily appeared her usual self, Rita seemed preoccupied. Ignacio picked up on it as well, sending Rita a discreet, meaningful frown. Rita gave a faint shake of her head just as the real estate agent returned from his call and asked if they were ready to do another walk-through.

The second pass went smoothly. Vittorio acted as if he were seeing the apartment for the first time. When they finished, Enrico handed him information on additional properties and thanked Vittorio for taking the time to tour the apartment.

Emily urged everyone outdoors to allow the real estate agent to close the apartment and the makeup artist to meet the car that would take her to an afternoon appointment. Once they exited to the street, she said, "We have a few options for filming tonight, Bob, but I want to get your take on what will make you the most comfortable."

Hearing himself referred to as Bob still struck him as ludicrous. *Roberto* he could understand, but *Bob* for a man with his apparent heritage and accent? Rita's forehead creased at Emily's use of his name, but since no one else seemed to find it odd, he played along. "Tango is on the schedule, right?"

"It is," Emily replied. "Our first option is to see a stage show. They're frequented by a lot of tourists and we have access to good tickets and permission to film. Our second is to watch tango at one of the *milongas*. They're social events where both locals and tango-focused tourists go to dance. There's a certain etiquette involved for the dancers, though different locations have different levels of formality."

"But don't worry," Rita interjected with her usual playfulness, "they're all incredibly sexy."

"True," Ignacio said on a grin. "Which is why you get Mike on the camera tonight instead of me."

"At least that's what we tell Mike. It's good for his ego."

Emily ignored Rita and Ignacio's banter, keeping her focus on Vittorio. "Our third option is to attend a seminar this afternoon where you learn the basics of tango from a local expert, then we'd combine that with some film of locals at a *milonga*."

Though the third option sounded like an adventure, he wasn't sure he wanted to be captured for all time looking like a fool at a dance lesson. He'd suffered through plenty of dance tutoring throughout his teen years and was relatively competent—his parents had insisted, given that he'd attend and host balls as the future monarch—but the tango was the rustiest part of his skill set.

And if he ever were found out, the press would run that footage over and over again.

"Then there's a final option." Emily glanced at Rita before she said, "We attend the seminar, get a crash course, then go to what's known as a *practica*—a public practice session—where you'd actually get out and dance. Since there are a lot of beginners, it's more forgiving than dancing at the *milongas*. Now, we can still observe at a *milonga* or attend a stage show afterward, but this would give us more flexibility in what we air."

"And our female viewers would love it, which would help the ratings." Rita actually wiggled her eyebrows, which earned her a look of faked exasperation from Ignacio and a flash of the real thing from Emily.

"It's entirely up to you and your comfort level," Emily told Vittorio. "We've made arrangements that allow us to work with whatever you're willing to give us. For our part, we're very appreciative of your willingness to appear on the show on such short notice and give us so much of your time."

A taxi stopped at the side of the street to pick up the makeup artist, who gave Rita a quick hug before she stepped into the vehicle. Vittorio used the momentary distraction to decipher what was happening between the staff members. He sensed that Emily's expression of gratitude was as much a message to Rita and Ignacio as it was a thank you to him. An uneasy feeling slithered along his spine.

Could it be possible they knew his identity? If so, they certainly would've checked in with the network about how to handle it. Emily's subtle *no* signals to Ignacio and Rita as they'd filmed in the apartment could mean she didn't want them to let on. And it would certainly explain their sudden deference to his wishes.

"Since I'm apparently in the driver's seat" —he looked to both Rita and Emily for confirmation— "I'd like a little more information before I decide."

"We'll answer whatever questions we can," Emily assured him.

"Tell me about the phone call."

CHAPTER 11

EMILY'S HEAD JERKED BACK. Though Victor's question was asked in a level tone, the hardness in his amber gaze suggested he believed she was hiding vital information. It left no doubt in her mind that he was used to commanding people and getting exactly what he wanted from them. But what could he possibly think she discussed that would involve him?

"I realize you three have only known me a few days," Victor continued, "but it's obvious that phone call threw all of you for a loop."

Emily knew it was too late to cover her surprise at his question, but she made the attempt anyway. "It was a simple call about programming. Completely expected."

"If it was so simple and expected, why all the odd looks between you? There's more to it than you want to say."

Rita let out an exasperated sound before turning to Victor. "The network released the list of shows it expects to renew for next season. We weren't on it. That's all."

A strange look flickered over his face, as if Rita's revelation was the furthest thing from his mind. He glanced from Rita to Emily. "Does that mean you're being cancelled?"

"No," Emily was quick to tell him. "Not at all. It's an early list. It would've been nice to be on it so we'd know where we stand, but we weren't expecting it."

Rita hmmed her agreement. "Not many shows make the early list. Thankfully, not many shows are outright cancelled this soon, either—"

"Including us," Emily finished. "Which means the network is waiting to see the numbers on our last few episodes to decide if we have the viewership to justify another season. I'm confident we will."

Victor looked at her askance. "That's a lot of pressure."

"It's the nature of the business. We're used to it." Thankfully her voice sounded cheerful. It wasn't his problem to tackle; it was hers and Rita's. "So what say you? Stage show, lessons, what's your pleasure?"

He shaded his eyes against a slant of late-morning sun. "A croissant. Would any or all of you care to join me? I spotted a promising café just around the corner."

"I need to head back to the office," Ignacio said. "Rita? Emily?"

Rita checked her watch. "Depends on what we're doing this afternoon. Maryam and I need to notify the venues of our plans and send Mike ahead to do his thing. And I'd like to get an afternoon nap if I can. If we do a *milonga* it can go until the early morning hours. And if not, I promised a cousin I'd call about catching a late dinner."

"All right. You two call a cab back to the office," she told them. "I'll take Bob for a late breakfast, discuss the options, then call you with a decision." Victor had a mission. What it was, Emily could only guess, but given what happened with the man on her doorstep last night she didn't want to risk any hints in front of Rita and Ignacio.

Agreed on the plan, Emily and Victor made their way to the café while Rita phoned for a taxi.

"You didn't eat breakfast," Victor said quietly as they approached the corner. He walked with his hands in the front pockets of his light, khaki-colored slacks, his face revealing nothing.

"What makes you think that?"

"Perfect lipstick."

"Having a professional makeup artist will do that."

"So will skipping breakfast." He paused at the café entrance to wait for the hostess. "Your lipstick was immaculate when you came back from that call, before the makeup artist checked you. And I noticed an untouched cup of fresh coffee on the counter. Rita pushed it in your direction, but you left it."

A bent, gray-haired hostess approached. They followed her through the narrow restaurant to a tiny wood table etched with scratches and cigarette marks that evidenced decades of use. Victor ordered croissants and two coffees before the hostess could shuffle away, then turned to Emily. "Now, tell me I'm wrong."

She wanted to protest, but he wasn't wrong. She'd been too anxious about the network call and nailing the apartment walk-through to eat. Instead, she asked, "Why are you so concerned?"

"Because I know what you're going through." His hands covered hers on the tabletop. Afraid of being seen, she turned to glance at the street, but he assured her Rita and Ignacio were long gone. "I told you earlier that I have a job where I manage a good number of people. I understand how hard it is to keep everyone around you feeling secure when you know the situation is anything but."

Against her will, a hard lump formed in her throat. She willed it back, but the effort only made her eyes burn. She was not a crier, damn it, and she would *not* cry in front of this man; not only because she'd spent nearly the whole night lying awake, reliving the blissful experience of being held in his strong embrace and wondering how it'd feel to have his arms around her all the time, but because travel show hosts didn't bawl in front of a guest. *Any* guest. Even one who'd kissed her senseless.

"Be honest with me. You were bothered not to be on that list, preliminary or not."

"Of course, but—"

"Were you on it last time around? Or did you have to wait?"

"We were on it our first season, but had to wait at the end of last season. And we ended up renewed."

Long, strong fingers flexed around hers before he released her. "I suspect you weren't compelled to take the risks you had to take this time. Approaching me blind, scrambling to finance an extension using your personal—"

"I told you, I believe in *At Home Abroad* and the quality of what we've produced. The finale will be fabulous."

His brow puckered. "Fabulous or not, it needs to draw viewers. And before you can increase your viewership, you have to impress the network executives with what you've created so they feel it's worthwhile to invest in advertising it."

He leaned back in his battered wooden chair as the hostess returned with two fluffy croissants on ceramic plates and richly scented cups of coffee. Once she'd departed, Victor asked, "Given that, which tango option would you choose?"

Emily picked off a corner of her croissant and popped it in her mouth. The impossibly light, buttery layers melted against her tongue. Until that moment, she hadn't realized how ravenous she'd become, how desperate for sustenance. She exhaled, then met Victor's penetrating gaze. "Why are you being so generous? And how do you know about network executives?"

"First, because you've been kind to me and I like you."

Given his self-contained demeanor, she doubted he said such a thing often. She rearranged her napkin in her lap, hoping he couldn't see the effect his straightforward statement had on her.

"Second, anyone who's ever had a favorite television show knows what it's like to have it cancelled. Usually fans complain that it wasn't promoted enough to find a following." He took a bite of his own croissant. Instantly, he made the satisfied sound of a man who'd found a new favorite.

"Phenomenal, aren't they?" She savored another piece of hers before turning back to the subject of tango. "The seminar followed by the *practica* would likely be the most interesting. As I said before, viewers want to put themselves in your shoes and see what it would be like if they were to take a class. Interspersing that with video taken at a tango show or a *milonga* would make for a colorful segment. But I also understand it's a lot to ask. Dancing tango can feel very personal. If you're not comfortable, it won't work on the screen."

He regarded her over the rim of his coffee cup. He had an interesting face, especially in the muted light filtering through the café's old, bubbled windows. Crinkles at the edges of his impossibly light brown eyes betrayed the weighing of pros and cons going on in his mind. The wavy, coal black hair, the full lips that hid straight, white teeth, so cheerful when he smiled. The model-perfect ridges of his cheekbones and the dark beard beneath them. The guarded manner in which he seemed to see everything in a room at once. All of it fascinated her.

She wondered if his siblings shared his traits. She wondered how many siblings there were. Male? Female? Older? Younger? Both? Which reminded her of his parting words last night.

"Before I forget to ask…did you call your family?"

"Well, there's a change of topic." He set down his cup. "I e-mailed my mother last night. I'll see her in a few days."

"A few days?" Emily couldn't keep the note of astonishment from her voice. "Is she coming to Buenos Aires?"

"No. I'm going home. Bought my plane ticket yesterday."

Disappointment rippled through her, followed by consternation that she'd experienced the emotion. After all, she was leaving soon, too. "I'm sure she was pleased to hear it."

"I'm sure she was." He finished his croissant in two bites, then said, "Call Rita. Tell her I'll attend the seminar and the *practica*. But on one condition."

"You're full of conditions, Bob."

"About that—"

"Terrible choice," she admitted. "Doesn't fit you at all. But it's what popped out of my mouth at La Bombonera."

"Even worse, when you filmed your segment on the field you called me Bob White. Isn't that an American bird?

Her face heated. "As I said, terrible choice."

It had taken a moment for Emily to realize what she'd said, but by then she wasn't sure how to correct it without raising questions amongst the crew. Today, though, she could swear Rita picked up on the fact it wasn't his real name. As soon as Emily found a moment, she'd explain Victor's request to remain anonymous from the crew as well as the audience. Rita would understand.

"The price of embarrassing me with that moniker is to suffer some embarrassment yourself. You're going to tango with me."

"Me?" She did *not* dance.

"I'm going to need a partner. Why not you?"

She held her hand palm out in the universal signal for *no way*. "The tango school has promised to take care of that. Then at the *practica* there will be dozens of beginners—"

"That's my condition. If I'm going to spend the afternoon dancing with a woman, I want to ensure it's not one who'll want to make small talk between sets and ask a dozen questions about my background, why I'm in Buenos Aires, or about my apartment hunt. Deal?"

The hostess seated a young couple at a table behind them, then ambled over to offer more coffee. Emily gratefully accepted a refill, but Victor declined, asking instead for the bill. Emily was about to protest, but his quick look made her realize it was fruitless to argue. She waited for the hostess to depart before asking, "Do you always get your way?"

"When I make a request, yes, people tend to do what I ask. But I wouldn't say that's the same as getting my way. I rarely get my way."

His cryptic statement made her wonder once more what he did for a living. Perhaps he ran a business where he was subject to circumstances of the market...but those who worked for him did what he asked.

"My way or not, you can't tell me that viewers won't tune in to see their beloved host tango," he continued, shifting in his seat. "In fact, I'd be surprised if Rita hasn't already suggested it to you."

"I see why you often get your way." The man had a knack for saying the right thing at the right time. He'd slipped in the word *beloved* on purpose. "But the answer is no. My job is to host. I can't intrude by becoming part of the story." She swept a hand toward the windows, encompassing the view of the cobblestoned streets. As if on cue, cathedral bells rang out through the narrow streets. "This is your adventure. Not mine."

He crossed his arms over his chest and leaned back as if to say, *we shall see.*

———

"COME ON, Emily. Where's your sense of adventure?"

Rita stood with her hands on her hips, angling her head to take in the full effect of Emily's outfit. Maryam had sent a clean-lined strapless top with black sequins along with a black skirt in a lightweight fabric to the tango studio. Emily was grateful not to be in overtly sexy fishnets and the shiny fabrics often worn in tourist-oriented tango shows, but felt naked with her shoulders bare.

"Adventure is one thing. Embarrassment is another." She ran her hands over her arms as she stepped the rest of the way out of the bathroom that served as the tango studio's dressing room. "Are you sure there wasn't a shawl in the bag?"

"Part of the allure of tango is the visibility of a woman's back. It also helps the instructor see the position of your shoulders." At Emily's glare, Rita added, "Or so Maryam says. She did the research and selected the wardrobe."

Emily bit back a retort and sat down on a nearby bench to slip into the tango shoes Maryam provided. The soft soles were impeccably crafted and the patent leather uppers molded to Emily's feet, making them more comfortable than she'd imagined when she'd been handed the strappy heels ubiquitous to the dance. She looked up at Rita, hoping for a last-minute reprieve. "I can't believe you think this is a good idea."

"The tango instructors thought so, too, when I talked to them. Besides, you know in your gut it'll get the attention of the network. That's what we need, more than anything. We have to throw them a curveball if we're to have any hope of renewal."

She cinched the buckle on her left shoe, ensuring the strap wouldn't come undone. "You could've danced yourself, you know."

"They don't want to see a stranger. I'm strictly behind the camera." Rita dropped her voice to a whisper. "Besides, Bob doesn't look like the type to trip over you. It could be a lot worse."

"How?"

"We could be watching the Winstons. Or Bob could be the type who'd take the opportunity to grope you." Rita's eyes twinkled in unconcealed mischief. "Though maybe it'd be better if he did. The man is stunning. I wouldn't object if he tried—"

"Rita Bragna! You most certainly would."

The women shared a smile, though Emily hoped Rita couldn't see through hers to the true thoughts percolating in her head. How could she dance in the traditional close tango embrace without betraying how attractive she found the man? It was the last thing she wanted her coworkers to see, let alone a nationwide viewing audience. Or—God forbid—James Owens, the network head who had the final say in whether or not *At Home Abroad* would be around next season.

Then there was Victor himself. Spending yesterday apart hadn't dimmed the pull she'd felt toward him. All morning she'd been aware of his presence, even when he'd been in the next room. Each step he took, each observation he made about the apartment, magnified itself in her mind. Between her hyperawareness and the we-can't-let-this-happen-again talk she'd given him following their kiss, the tension between them during a tight tango would be unbearable.

Emily ran her hands down her thighs, drying the sweat from her palms and willing her nerves to behave.

"Have fun with it." Rita leaned down to brush a stray thread from the side of Emily's skirt. "Imagine you're here as a tourist yourself. It's not as if you're not due for some vacation time."

"We'll all end up with more vacation time than we want if this doesn't work."

"Then make it work." Rita straightened as her eye caught movement in the mirror behind Emily. "Here come our instructors."

An elegant, fit-looking couple in their mid-fifties entered the room and introduced themselves as Hector and Eva, the owners of the studio. While Rita gave them the rundown on her goals for the segment, Victor slipped into the studio from the other bathroom. Though *slipped* wasn't the right word; the man might move silently, but he knew how to make an entrance. His black and white tango shoes, the fall of his dark pants, and the smooth fit of his cream-colored shirt made him look as if he were the teacher rather than the student. The slight angle of his brow in Emily's direction said, *I told you so.* She fought not to roll her eyes as he scanned her from head to toe, taking in the white flower Rita had pinned into her hair—for the camera, she'd claimed—the sensual lines of her clothing, and the classic design of her own tango shoes.

Hector greeted Victor, then declared it time to start. "First to learn in tango," he explained in a rich voice, "is that you must walk before you run. The walk is your foundation."

Eva demonstrated the slight bend of the knees that prefaced each step a dancer took forward, then to the side, before asking Emily and Victor to stand beside each other and do the same. "Not too much bend in your knees," she corrected Emily. "Light. Sensual. With your head high and no rebound in your step. Yes!"

Classical tango music filled the airy studio as Hector fiddled with buttons on a small player mounted to the wall near the door. Eva watched as Emily and Victor moved back and forth, mimicking the walk Eva had demonstrated, while Mike crouched in one corner to get the best angle. Much as Emily felt spotlighted, the movements came naturally, her body remembering the light steps she'd taken years ago during her college dance class.

The class where she'd met Paul. The man who'd become her partner, who'd so entranced her they'd each taken a second semester of dance despite the fact their athletics requirements were fulfilled after taking the first class.

"You have done this before, yes?"

Startled, Emily almost answered Hector before realizing he'd addressed the statement not to her, but to Victor.

"A few classes, that's all."

A glance in the mirror confirmed that Victor moved seamlessly, his light walk emulating Eva's perfectly. Given the ease with which

Victor picked up the subtleties of the movement, Emily suspected there'd been more than a few classes in his past.

Eva demonstrated embellishments to the basic walk—a swish of the foot against the floor, a lift and turn of a knee—then encouraged them to give it a try. After an initial error, Emily embraced the exercise, swooping her feet lightly across the floor, taking the time to feel the music. Much as Emily had resisted when Rita and Maryam begged her to take the dance lesson along with Victor, she knew she'd have craved moving with the music had she been relegated to the sidelines. And, in retrospect, it would make for a better episode with two people learning to tango rather than a solo dancer.

Emily finally began to relax into the steps, feeling the rhythm without having to concentrate as much on the placement of her feet, when Eva stopped the music and informed them they would move on to the embrace. Within seconds, she found herself with her arm high across Victor's back, her hand spread across his shoulders, while her other hand rested lightly in his grasp. As his hand came to her back, sending a wave of warmth through her, she told herself to think of anything else. The street noise outside, the croissant she'd eaten at breakfast…anything but the way it felt to be held in Victor's arms.

Again, Eva instructed them to walk. "The embrace is the focus of the dance. It is not simply the physical connection to your partner, but the means to define your movement on the floor. The man uses the embrace to communicate to his partner, to guide her without words. The woman must be patient, she must feel for the guidance of her partner and adapt to his lead." Eva came up behind Emily and framed her hips, shifting Emily's pelvis closer to Victor's so that Emily might better anticipate his movements. "She must wait through his pauses. She must not hurry, but feel his intent. Yes?"

Emily kept her gaze locked forward, over Victor's shoulder, and hoped against hope she didn't look as heated as she felt. His muscles moved beneath her fingertips as his feet glided across the floor in the slow, sensuous walk Eva had demonstrated.

"Let him guide you," Eva reminded her. "Do not think of your steps. The tango is not about steps, but about the music and the connection to your partner. When you think of your steps, you lose the passion of the dance. Tango is the dance of passion. Even when slow, it is powerful."

Rita's low voice carried across the dance floor. "I'm going to need a stiff drink when we're done. Maybe a cold shower."

"Me, too," came Mike's response. "And yes, we'll edit out our comments."

Victor paused, his energy coiling as the music reached a crescendo. Not expecting it, Emily slammed her knee into his.

"Shoot," she muttered. "I'm sorry."

"Do not apologize," Hector said, rounding them to stand where she could see him. "A man wishes to be lost in the dance. Hearing his partner apologize is a break in this dream of tango, yes? Accidents, they happen from time to time."

Emily nodded her understanding even as Victor whispered, "It's all right. Occasionally I deserve a good kick in the pants."

That was enough to drain the tension from her muscles. The next time Victor paused with the music, Emily was relaxed enough to follow his lead. For the next hour, they danced to set after set—*tandas*, Hector called them—occasionally switching off so Hector could partner with Emily and Eva with Victor. There were definite mistakes, both on Emily's part and Victor's, but the lesson became more engaging the longer they danced. When she broke from Victor for the last time and thanked him according to custom, as Eva instructed, Rita and Mike broke into applause.

Emily dipped a gracious curtsey, glad for the distraction. The separation from Victor after nearly two hours in each other's arms left her with an acute case of loneliness, one that reached to the marrow of her bones.

The realization left her reeling.

For months, Rita had accused her of hiding her need for companionship in her life with her work. She'd heartily denied it and believed every word, which was why she'd been stunned when Victor made a similar accusation after he'd kissed her. *At Home Abroad* kept her invigorated. It gave her purpose. It wasn't easy to serve as both host and co-executive producer, but the hard work wasn't without its rewards. Not only had she made terrific friends—and deepened her long friendship with Rita—the show was her every aspiration come to fruition. Each time an episode aired, she felt an enormous sense of pride.

But now, as Victor expressed his gratitude to Hector and Eva and complimented them on their teaching technique, she realized that Rita may have had a point. While Emily loved her job, she'd become so used to physical isolation it had become her natural state. She'd forgotten how much she enjoyed dancing, how banter with an attractive man her own age challenged her. How it felt to be held close, to breathe in a masculine scent, and—dammit—to be kissed with passion, the way Victor had kissed her last night.

"We ready to move on?" Rita asked, jarring her from her thoughts.

"Yes. Absolutely." On both fronts.

CHAPTER 12

RITA'S BROW rose in concern, making Emily wonder how long her friend had been trying to get her attention.

"I'm sorry. Distracted." By the memory of Victor's mouth melding to hers, of the hard planes she'd felt under his shirt when she'd placed her hands on his chest. Of his body fitting against hers.

How could a man about whom she knew so little, a man with whom she was supposed to be acting professionally, occupy her thoughts so completely?

"We need to decide about the *practica*. It's being held in a park with an outdoor pavilion a few blocks from here. It's all of a two-minute walk. They start in about fifteen minutes and we have permission from the organizers to film."

"That's perfect."

"The downside is that you'll likely be dancing on stone, not a dance floor. Are your feet in any condition to keep going?"

Mike angled a thumb toward the windows. "The light's still good. We have another hour or so to get the best shots. If not, I have a lot of good footage from the lesson alone."

A glance at Victor confirmed he was fine to continue. She turned back to Mike. "Let's give it a go. They're expecting us and I can certainly handle an hour."

Hector cleared his throat. "Before you go, there is one more thing you must learn. You will not need it at the *practica*, but if you ever attend a *milonga*, it is important."

Emily started back to the center of the dance floor, but Eva held up a hand. "It is not a step. It is the look. *El cabeceo.*"

"A…look?" Rita stepped back to study Victor and Emily's clothing.

"No, you misunderstand me." Eva rested her index fingers at her temples. "The look with the eyes. In Argentina, a man does not ask a woman to dance with the voice. He must ask with the eyes, then with a nod of his head. It is more subtle. It allows for a woman to say no without the difficulty for the woman or the man."

"Without embarrassment?" Rita asked.

"Yes. Without embarrassment. Here, Hector and I will show you." Eva crossed the dance floor to the bench where Emily put on her shoes at the beginning of the lesson. Back straight and hands perched atop one knee, she managed to appear relaxed and confident as she sat, rather than stiff. "At a *milonga*, there are often many tables around the room. When you arrive, the host will seat you at a table of their choosing. A woman should always sit with energy, like this. Men wish to dance with a woman who is pleasant and would make a good dance partner."

Eva patted the space beside her and waited until Emily sat, imitating Eva's form while Hector strode to the opposite wall. His gaze swept the room, as if he had dozens of women from whom to choose.

To Victor, Hector said, "The men, they will find a place to stand with a good view, or they might walk about the room in search of partners. Their eyes, they move, yes? You do not stop on one woman until you are sure. You must be…cool."

"Cool. Understood." Victor couldn't hide the amusement in his voice at the old-school traditions Hector and Eva presented.

With a wave, Hector urged Victor to his side. "Now, your turn.

Take your time. Be a mystery. Search for a woman who has spirit, but is not too eager. If you have already seen her dance, that is even better. Then you know she might be a good partner. When you have made your choice and a new *tanda* is about to begin, you meet her eyes."

Victor flicked his gaze past Eva to Emily. Hector caught his shoulder, urging Victor to keep his line of sight fixed. "Now. She is looking at you. You have made the contact and she is not looking away. This is good, but you must be sure. So continue on." He released Victor's shoulder, then tapped the button on the wall that restarted the music. "Let your eyes move, but without stopping on another woman. Then, slowly, come back. See if she looks at you again, if she captures you with her *mirada*."

"This is what you must perfect," Eva said to Emily. "Your *mirada* is subtle. It is a look that lets him know he is safe in asking you to dance. But if you give him your *mirada* and he doesn't respond with *el cabeceo*" —she shrugged— "you are not bothered. It is you who are cool."

"This is hilarious," Rita said to Mike as he followed along with his camera. "We're being schooled in the art of flirtation."

"No, no," Hector corrected, though he kept his focus on Victor. "Not flirtation. Invitation. Now, the woman has met your look again. If you know she is the one and you are confident she will say yes, you must nod, like so. If she does not look away, then that is acceptance."

Hector locked eyes with Eva and gave a slight tip of his head. When Eva's attention did not stray from his face, Hector moved across the floor, acting as if he were making his way through a crowded room. He paused a few feet from his wife. "The man should stop at the woman's table or at the edge of the dance floor closest to her. He should keep his eyes on her as he approaches so she knows that he wishes to dance with her, and so that the women nearby do not mistake his intent."

Hector signaled for Victor to imitate his action. Slowly, Victor allowed his gaze to travel past Mike and Rita, past Eva and Emily, then he drew it back to Emily and lingered. Despite the fact it was nothing more than an exercise in etiquette, Victor's subtle perusal sent adrenaline rushing through her veins.

"Yes, that is it!" Eva clapped her approval. "Now, Emily, you may look away, but if you wish to dance with him, don't look away for very long. Only enough to be certain he intends to dance with you and not a woman sitting behind you. Then, once he gives you *el cabeceo*, you must keep your gaze on him if you wish to dance. If you have made a mistake and do not wish to partner with him, then look away again and do not look back. Do you understand? This is the polite way to say no, without embarrassment."

Eva encouraged Emily to return her gaze to Victor's. Much as she tried to be cool, she found it impossible. The man had a way of seeing through to her soul when he looked at her that way, as if he knew she was envisioning the kiss they shared outside the park. As if he knew it turned her inside out and made her ache to do it again.

Did the whole room see the same smoldering heat in his eyes that she saw? Did they know her face—her entire body—flamed in response?

Fixed on his destination, Victor strode across the floor with the smooth, controlled power of a lion after a trapped gazelle. When he was nearly across the floor, Emily rose, but was corrected with a quick rap on the knees from Eva. The contact wasn't painful, but surprised Emily enough that her rear hit the bench with an unladylike thump that made Rita wince.

"Wait until he is at your table," Eva said. "Do not stand or approach him. You must be certain that you are his target. Remember, you must be cool, never too eager. No big smiles."

When Victor finally stopped in front of Emily, his eyes still riveted on her face, Eva motioned for Emily to stand. "Do not speak. Approach him, then he will lead you to the floor. You are then expected to dance the full set. Usually, this is four tangos. You may speak quietly between dances, but not during the dance. It is considered rude. When the music plays, you speak with your dance and with your energy."

Once again, Emily found herself in Victor's arms. The slight pressure of his large hand against her back calmed the nerves jangled by Eva's censure. He guided her through the basic steps until Hector stopped the music and asked them to run through *el cabeceo* again. This time, Emily waited before she stood.

"Well done." Eva clapped her hands and smiled. "A very good first lesson. You should enjoy the *practica*."

They said their goodbyes, thanking Hector and Eva for opening the tango school to *At Home Abroad* and letting them know when the episode would air. Noting the declining outdoor light, Mike took the lead as they made their way down the stairs and onto the street. His long strides across the cobblestones were quickly matched by Victor's. Music wafted down the narrow road as they approached the neighborhood park where the *practica* was already underway.

"That was amazing," Rita noted once the men were far enough ahead that she was confident she wouldn't be overheard. "You two looked so elegant. And *hot*. My gosh, Emily. Our ratings will go through the roof if we use that footage to promote the show!"

"I'll reserve judgment until I see the edit." Much as Victor appeared both suave and talented during the lesson, she doubted the same held true for her. She'd felt like a bumbling teenager at her first school dance. If she looked confident, it was only because she'd forced it. Even her remarks to the camera hadn't come as naturally as they usually did.

"Trust me. It adds exactly the right amount of sex appeal to the episode." Rita looked over her shoulder to take in the sight of an accordion player perched on a wooden stool so old its green paint had peeled, his arms moving in and out with the rhythm of his song. "That's what I love most about Argentina. It's unapologetic about the role romance plays in its culture. The art, the food, the tango…all of it. And it's so gracefully done."

Emily couldn't stop her wry grin. "I kicked Bob, if you didn't notice."

"I did. I promise, we'll edit that out."

"And I stood too fast. Can't forget that the romance here is of the old-fashioned variety." With impeccable timing, an elderly man with a robustness that defied his wrinkled countenance strode out of a café near the corner, then paused to hold the door for his wife.

"Nothing wrong with that. Old-fashioned romance can have its charms." Rita didn't bother to hide her admiration of the couple as the man took his wife's hand, then tucked it in the crook of his arm while they made their way down the street.

"Most of the time, I'd agree. But in the tango lesson? The man chooses, the man asks, the man approaches. And naturally, a woman cannot be too eager." She pulled a face. "As if by standing up I was showing I was desperate."

"Well, the tango *is* a traditional dance, with very specific gender roles. In that instance, I can understand it." They rounded the corner and caught sight of Victor and Mike, who were nearly to the park. "But as to eagerness in general…I think Eva is wrong. A little eagerness is a good thing. That's what passion is all about, right?"

There was a deliberateness in Rita's words that made Emily cock her head. "Are you talking about the episode? Or is your one-track mind still in its usual groove?"

Rita hitched a shoulder, then made a point of looking ahead at Victor. "Does it matter?"

"It most certainly does matter." Emily needed to nip Rita's match-making in the bud. Otherwise, who knew what Rita might say to Victor, and likely at an inopportune moment. "If you're talking about anything other than our episode, passion is overrated. Don't get me wrong, it's a lot of fun in the moment, but it can drive some stupid decisions."

It wasn't a statement she'd planned to have come out of her mouth, but she meant it. She'd rather have secure friendships, adventures in new places meeting new people, intellectual stimulation, and a solid job than risk giving up all of that for a man anytime soon.

Perhaps she'd needed to say it aloud to keep it in mind.

"Maybe. I know I've made a few stupid decisions as a result." Rita slowed her steps as they neared Mike and Victor, who were leaning against a wrought iron fence bordering the park. "But aren't the greatest rewards enjoyed when we take risks? And that's all risks are…

decisions that go against common sense. It's no different with a man than with a television show. We took a risk pitching to the network. A show like ours hadn't been done before. It requires a big budget and an agreeable host nation. It means a lot of last-minute scheduling and finding guests who might fit our profile, then helping them get comfortable with the camera. But we left it all out on the table when we walked into James Owens' office to sell our show. We didn't play it cool. We let ourselves appear eager. And look at the payoff."

"Rita, it's not the same." And they needed to drop the subject before Mike and Victor wondered about the nature of their conversation.

"Of course it is. We all need that deep, internal drive—that *passion* —to succeed. Allowing others to see our passion gives them the confidence to trust us." When Emily remained quiet, Rita's tone changed. "Bob isn't his name, is it?"

Emily shook her head, then quickly explained the situation. Rita listened, squinting as she looked toward the men. "I'm not surprised that he isn't a Bob. Or that you agreed to his terms."

"It wasn't for the reasons you imagine."

"I know that. In any case, Bob—Victor—wasn't the only one who's danced before. You picked up those steps very quickly. And when you danced, the expression on your face was one of a woman rediscovering an old love. Maybe it's time to pull out that flag and let it fly. Quit keeping it hidden away."

"Good thing your husband is flying in after we wrap. You've let the romantic atmosphere get to you."

Rita grinned as she looked toward the far side of the park, where dozens of dancers moved in time to a sultry rhythm while tourists and locals watched. "For once, so should you."

VITTORIO HAD LONG AGO LOST track of the number of times he'd danced in public, let alone the number of women with whom he'd danced, given that he lived in a palace boasting the largest ballroom in Sarcaccia and that ballroom was well-used. At least once a week, one member of the royal family or another hosted a charity event, a state dinner, or a celebratory gala, nearly all of which involved dancing in front of an army of photographers. But never had Vittorio danced in public quite this way, nor had he ever enjoyed his time with a partner more, despite the rigidity with which Emily held herself. What was it, he wondered, that made her so tense? So afraid to feel the romance of the dance?

"Relax," he murmured near her ear as he guided her in slow counterclockwise circles through the mass of dancing couples. "Mike isn't zooming in. He's going for atmosphere. We're nothing more than another set of faces in the crowd."

"I'm relaxed," she argued, though even as the words left her mouth, her hand twitched against the space between his shoulder blades. "Besides, we're not supposed to talk during the dance. Only in between, remember?"

"It's a *practica*. I'm practicing. Mistakes are expected."

Her foot connected with his ankle. "I'll keep that in mind."

Taking a chance, he glanced at her. One side of her mouth curled into a smile despite the fact she bit down on her lip to keep from laughing. Satisfied her tension level had dropped down a notch, he swirled her toward the center of the crowd, where the pace was slower and the beginners tended to dance. She didn't object, but the way her feet caressed the stones with each turn made him all the more certain this wasn't her first time in a tango embrace.

It was one more mystery in the web of mysteries surrounding Emily Sinclair.

When he'd asked her to join him in his lesson, he'd assumed she protested because she wasn't an experienced dancer, but from the moment they'd walked side by side in Hector and Eva's studio, he discovered that wasn't the case. She glided over the floor with a lightness that only came from experience. And not simply experience dancing, but dancing the tango. When Eva demonstrated embellishments to the basic walk, Emily imitated the moves precisely. Then, when he'd held her in that first embrace, she'd moved fluidly, following his lead with ease.

So it wasn't embarrassment due to a lack of skill that made her hesitate when he'd issued his invitation in the café. Nor did he buy her excuse that she shouldn't be, as she'd put it, "part of the story." As he'd predicted, the minute Rita heard he'd opted for the lesson and the *practica*, she had urged Emily to join him and Maryam quickly located the necessary clothing and shoes. Emily hadn't argued when both Rita and Maryam pointed out the opportunity it presented to have the host dancing on camera.

He could only conclude that Emily had declined for personal reasons. His ego wanted to believe it was the temptation of physical contact, given the intense kiss they'd shared two nights before, and perhaps that was part of it. But as he'd taken her into his arms at the studio and they'd moved through the steps of their first dance, he could've sworn her mind was elsewhere, just as he sensed it was elsewhere now, despite the fact she'd teased him with a kick to the ankle.

The last chords of the tango floated across the park, signaling the transition that would allow dancers to take a break and find new partners. As etiquette dictated, Vittorio escorted Emily to the edge of the dance area. Rather than the rough-hewn tables common at a *milonga*, however, the park afforded only a few benches and a low stone wall upon which dancers could stash their belongings or sit for a quick sip of water.

"I have everything I need," Mike said as Emily gratefully accepted one of the bottles of water Rita had been thoughtful enough to purchase from a nearby cart. "Mind if I call it a night? I'll go over the footage with Ignacio in the morning. If we still need to, we can always duck into a *milonga* tomorrow to grab some filler footage."

"Go ahead." Rita waved him off. "A cousin I haven't seen in years offered to take me out to dinner and an outdoor orchestra performance. Now that I know we have a good handle on the episode, I'll let him know I'm available."

Emily nodded as she set her bottle on the top of the wall. Behind her, the streetlights flickered to life. "We can't thank you enough, Bob. You've gone above and beyond to help us make our finale great."

"We never could have gotten this much material with the couple we originally planned to feature. You've truly been a blessing to us." Rita put a hand on his arm and smiled. "So tell me…have we been any help to *you* at all? Are you any closer to a decision on an apartment?"

"I have a better sense of what's available in different neighborhoods. I'm looking forward to seeing the building in Barrio Norte tomorrow."

"Wonderful. We'll meet there at noon if that still works for you." At his nod, she gave him a quick pat on the knee, then asked Mike if he wanted to share a taxi back to Recoleta. Turning to Emily, she asked, "What about you?"

"Hector said I could use the changing room at the studio after the *practica* if I wanted, so I'll head there first. You go ahead."

"Bob?" Rita asked as she slung her handbag over her shoulder.

"Same as Emily. I'll change, then I'm going to find dinner." It had been fine walking from the studio to the *practica* in the slacks and tango shoes, but he didn't want to wear them in the taxi or to dinner if he could help it.

Once Rita and Mike left, Emily stood, shouldered the bag Rita had been holding for her, then tossed her empty water bottle into a nearby recycling can before turning in the direction of Hector and Eva's studio.

He wasn't sure what possessed him, but he put a hand on her shoulder, urging her to wait.

"What's up?" Caution clouded Emily's gaze, and he didn't blame her.

His feet throbbed and his stomach rumbled in response to the smell of beef grilling somewhere nearby. Despite that, every fiber of his being wanted to stay. He needed to dance—truly dance—with Emily. Just once. No cameras, no instructors. He needed to see her reaction to him and to the music, to understand why she'd been distracted during filming. Why she held herself at a distance, even when her kiss proved she found him attractive. There was more to her actions than a desire to appear professional, he was certain.

"Have a seat." He lifted the bag from her shoulder and set it on the wall, then indicated the spot she'd just occupied. The moment she sat, he turned on his heel and walked away.

"Where are you—"

He didn't wait to hear the rest.

CHAPTER 13

AFTER CIRCLING his way around the dance area, he took up a position on the opposite side, near a group of local men who'd found a bench where they could sit back with their cigarettes and chat while they watched the dancers. Slowly, Vittorio turned and let his gaze scan the crowd, taking in what he hadn't been able to see before, when he'd been focused on dancing with Emily.

Women in summery dresses and skirts sat on benches, along the top of the wall, and in the grass off to the side of the dance area. Some chatted with friends while others discreetly watched the crowd. Men ambled along the periphery, studying the dancers, listening to the music, and subtly checking out the women. The notes wafting through the air indicated the start of a new *tanda*, and throughout the park men caught the eyes of the women with whom they wished to partner.

Vittorio looked straight at Emily. She frowned, then her eyes widened as she realized what he was doing. Raising a brow, he sent her the silent message to play along. Her lips parted as if she were about to protest, then she snapped them shut and let her gaze drift away. Her posture changed to mimic the pose Eva struck at the studio that afternoon. The sight stilled his breath; he knew he'd remember her like this until the day he died. A Degas ballerina couldn't hold a candle to Emily as she perched on the stone wall in the twilight, her skirt swirled around her legs, the straps of her dance shoes highlighting her slim ankles.

Sit with energy.

That was the phrase Eva had used, and it fit. Though Emily's gaze traveled lightly over the crowd, the edges of her mouth lifting a fraction as she spied a pair of teenagers taking the first tentative steps of the dance, she radiated elegance and a vibrancy that made it difficult for Vittorio to drag his attention from her as Hector had instructed. Dear God, she was beautiful.

Her eyes snagged his through the masses of dancers moving to the center of the dance space. Yearning flashed in their depths, then was quickly hidden before she slowly turned her head to watch a talented couple move to the strains of the classic song, their bodies in perfect unison, their feet sliding across the stone as one.

Still, he couldn't turn away.

Look at me.

As if she'd heard his thought, her expressive eyes locked with his. This time, he took a step forward and angled his head in *el cabeceo*. Only the twist of her fingers in the soft fabric of her skirt betrayed any emotion as she casually moved her attention beyond him, then across the park to where the orchestra played.

Look at me.

She shifted, angling her body away from him. The moment hung, her head remained still...but a heartbeat later, her eyes—and only her eyes—turned toward him. This time their gazes held. She didn't smile, didn't move a muscle, yet she captured him as surely as if she'd physically pulled him to her side. He forced himself to count to five before he slowly rounded the dance space and approached her, his attention never leaving her exquisite face. Never in his life had naked desire scorched his veins as it did in the seconds he stood an arm's length in front of her and waited for her to take his hand.

He wanted her. More than that, though, he wanted her to live. To come to the same realization he had during the past few months: her obligations weren't what defined her. It was her joys, her curiosity, and her zest for life. The very things she claimed drew her to film *At Home Abroad* in the first place. It was in the contained vibrancy he witnessed as she sat on the wall at this very moment, waiting to dance, when she wasn't burdened by thoughts of budgets or schedules or ratings.

If dancing with her in an open park at dusk to the sounds of a dozen Argentinian musicians encouraged her to grab life by the horns, to let the energy within her free, then he wanted to dance with her more than he wanted anything else in the world.

Silently, she rose from the wall and accepted his invitation, touching her palm to his before gliding across the smooth gray stone in his embrace. His eyes drifted closed as her head came just below his and he caught a brief whiff of her hair. She didn't miss a step, matching him move for move, pause for pause, their bodies guided by the music. Without thinking, he swished one of his feet in the way he'd been taught during his teenage lessons before easing her into a sultry dip. When he lifted her and they spun into the next steps, she whispered, "You're very good."

He couldn't stop the burst of happiness that filled him at her words. How long had it been since he'd heard a compliment and known it to be sincere?

"I know," she added, "I'm not supposed to talk."

He brought her closer in their embrace with gentle pressure from his hand. "Do whatever feels right. No one is watching."

He couldn't see her expression, but sensed her smile. They danced with abandon for the rest of the *tanda*, enjoying each classic tango as it flowed into the next. All too soon, the tempo changed, signaling that the set had come to its end. Vittorio eased toward the wall, then released Emily and swept into a bow as she curtsied.

"Thank you, Victor. I wouldn't have thought to stay, but that was fun." Her cheeks were flushed from dancing. "Even if you bullied me into it."

"Bullied?"

Amusement lit her hazel eyes. "I couldn't exactly leave politely now, could I? Despite what Eva said about no embarrassment, that would've been horrific."

"Would you have said no if I'd simply asked?"

"Guess you'll never know." She patted his forearm, then grabbed her bag from the wall as the strains of the next *tanda* began. "We should get changed. You have a dinner to go to, right?"

"I don't have anything planned. It's simply time for a meal." Behind them, dozens of couples partnered off while others broke away, searching for taxis or walking in the direction of the nearest bus stop. "But it seems like this is likely the last dance of the evening. Maybe it'd be wiser to catch a cab now. By the time we change, the *practica* will be over and they'll be hard to come by."

"True." She gave her skirt a twirl. "Guess the drivers are used to seeing outfits like this around here."

"As much as they are shoes like mine." He spied a taxi stopped at a light on the far side of the park. "I think I can catch that one. Follow me and I'll escort you back to your place."

He scooted past a knot of young men who'd stopped to watch the dancers, then around an older woman walking two Yorkshire Terriers to exit the park and flag down the taxi at a corner. Once the driver pulled to the curb, he opened the door and held it for Emily, then circled the cab to hop in behind the driver.

He instructed the driver to take them to the Recoleta park where they'd walked the night before last, then turned to Emily. "That was good timing. He may have been the last free cab for a while."

An inquisitive look crept across her face. "You like to be in control, don't you? You're used to it."

He shrugged. "You're pretty comfortable with it, too. You wouldn't be in charge of *At Home Abroad* if you weren't."

Emily's eyebrows raised briefly in acknowledgement, but she said nothing, keeping her focus on the scenery. The last vestiges of sunlight skimmed the tops of the trees and peeked between the buildings. The main roads were thick with taxis and buses, and pedestrians clogged the sidewalks as the taxi made its way into Recoleta. Here and there, friends exchanged kisses before parting ways for the evening. A few *porteños* wandered into restaurants, though the tables wouldn't fill until later in the evening. The city was large, bustling, and a hub for business, but in many ways retained its Old World charm, even outside the traditional districts like San Telmo.

Emily pulled a face when she thought he wasn't looking.

"What?" he asked softly.

She started, realizing she'd been caught. "Oh. Nothing."

He jerked his head back and wrinkled his brow in open skepticism.

A slow blush crept across her cheeks. "You'll think I'm being silly… it's just, well, I love the history of this city. All the architecture, the traditions. On the other hand, the over-the-top male dominance drives me nuts. Did you see that group of men catcalling back there on the corner? How obnoxious is that?"

He'd missed it, though he wasn't surprised. Men in Buenos Aires tended to be bold. "I imagine the women here are used to it."

"Perhaps." She worried her lip before continuing, "Don't get me wrong…there's a graciousness that exists here, too. Men tend to open doors for women, allow them to go first into elevators, all the classic niceties. I just wish—" She waved her hand, then started digging in her handbag. "Whatever. I'm being silly."

The taxi pulled to the curb not far from the spot where they'd entered the park to walk to their respective hotels two nights ago. He went to pay, but Emily beat him to the punch. "I told you, the show has you covered. And you've paid for nearly everything so far."

He acquiesced, making sure he got around the vehicle to open her door for her. He didn't miss the amused look on her face as he swept a bow, then thanked the driver.

They jogged across the street while the signal was in their favor. A few strands loosened from her bun, reminding him what a long day they'd had. Once they slowed to a walk and entered the park, he asked, "It wasn't the catcalls, was it?"

"That cemented it, but no, not really. It was the dance lesson.

When Eva smacked my knees as if I'd committed a crime simply by standing."

As before, the park's overhead lights were on, casting shadows along the sides of the walkway where young couples sat chatting, sharing containers of ice cream, or kissing. On a rectangular court behind one couple, four men who appeared to be in their fifties or sixties finished up a game of bocce.

"Traditions are held dear here," Vittorio pointed out, angling his gaze toward the group of men.

"I know, but as much as I appreciate the graciousness of it, it bothers me that men get to decide everything. Tradition or not, a woman should be an equal partner. If she stands a moment too early, is that really so bad? Shouldn't a woman be able to make the same choices without being judged for them?" Laughter bubbled from deep within her. "I know, I know. I'm fighting what *is*."

"A woman can always say no to a man's invitation."

"Yes, I suppose she can."

"And be as much a professional in the workplace."

"True." They were halfway through the park now, approaching the colossal ombu tree that served as its focal point. Emily stopped walking and faced him. "Wait a minute. Are you talking about my job now? Or is this a discussion about what happened the other night?"

"All of it." It didn't escape his notice that she stood under the brightest lights of the park to ask her question. "I gave you my word and I'll keep it. But I have to say…this afternoon you moved like a woman who's graced more than one dance floor. I suspect this wasn't your first lesson. Maybe not even your first tango lesson."

Her shrug was casual, but he didn't miss the flicker of wariness in her eyes. "Back in college I took ballroom dance."

"Aside from Eva's reprimand, you were having a good time. You miss it, don't you? Dancing like that?"

"I do." She started walking again, and he fell into step beside her. "But that was a long, long time ago. Another lifetime."

A note in her voice made him realize what she didn't say: she no longer had the opportunity, given her schedule. And that it had been by choice. "So why'd you refuse when I asked?"

"I told you, I didn't think it'd be appropriate for me to be part of the story. Rita disagreed, so I did it."

"Bullshit." It came out as clipped as Eva's correction, but in this case, it was warranted. "I think you were afraid."

A choking sound emerged from her mouth before raucous laughter bubbled from her, likely because it was the first time she'd heard him swear. "Um, you're calling bullshit on me? You, Mister I-Want-To-Be-Anonymous-On-Camera? If anyone's afraid of—"

"You misunderstand. I don't think you were afraid of the camera capturing a mistake." He stopped walking as they neared the park's edge and lowered his voice. "I think you were afraid of me. Or you were afraid of the emotions dancing might bring up. Either way, you were concerned about what your coworkers would think of you. That they wouldn't view you as a professional. That's why the catcalling and Eva's rap on the knees bothered you."

It hadn't clicked for him until this moment, but given the way she'd acted all day, it made sense. He frowned. "Do you feel like they don't respect you as much because of your gender? Because from what I've seen over the past few days, that's not the case. Your coworkers think you're fantastic."

"I like to think so. I've worked very hard to earn their respect. They're the best in the business."

"But that doesn't answer my question. Why didn't you want to dance today when it's obvious that you love it? What were you afraid of?"

"I'm afraid of my show being cancelled." The night breeze carried the loose strands of her bun into her face and she swiped them away. "That's it. Period. I can't let them down."

Risking her ire, he took a step closer and looped the wayward hair behind her ears. "You won't. They know you're working day and night to make the show a success. They admire you. They *like* you. I can't imagine them thinking you're any less competent because you're female or because you're dancing on camera. If it'd been a male host and a female guest—"

A ragged breath escaped her, betraying the emotion she struggled to keep hidden. "Victor...stop."

"I told you before, I understand what you're going through. I've spent my entire life working day and night to make other people secure. I've put my own needs and desires aside because I felt like they wouldn't trust me otherwise, and I couldn't help them if they didn't trust me. But I've learned the hard way that I need to put myself first."

He cupped her face in his hands, needing to drive his point home. "I know it's cliché, but life is short. You need to enjoy it. No one will begrudge you a dance if that's what makes you happy, let alone when it's integral to the show you're fighting so hard to keep on the air. It's a hell of a lot better than running off for a five-month vacation."

She could have it all, if only she could see it. Instead, she lived in a cocoon of professionalism, hoping it would protect her. He'd learned the hard way that—no matter how careful one might be—no one could insulate themselves from pain.

"I *do* enjoy my life," she protested. "Hesitating over a dance segment doesn't mean I'm not happy. Just...would you please stop looking at me like that!"

He raised an eyebrow as if to say, *like what?*

"Like you're going to kiss me again."

"I told you I wouldn't, and I keep my word." He let his hands fall away from her cheeks. "Though I must point out that your coworkers wouldn't think less of you if you kissed someone now and then. Frankly, Rita would encourage it."

"In that case, stop looking at me like you can see through me and know what I'm thinking. It's utterly unfair when I don't know you at all." She stepped back, wrapping her arms around her waist. "I still feel like I should. Like I know you from somewhere. But I won't pry, because you know what? I keep my word, too."

The air stilled between them. Their eyes held. Neither moved toward the street, where they'd be compelled to say goodnight and go their separate ways.

"My name is Vittorio." He almost gave her his last name, but caught himself in time. Her lips parted in surprise, but she said nothing. "I didn't want to tell you that morning in the café for the same reason you don't want to dance or enjoy a goodnight kiss. It's a risk. Both professionally...and personally."

She exhaled, then glanced at a bus lumbering down the street that separated the park from her bed and breakfast, as if she needed the distraction to corral her thoughts. "Why are you telling me now?"

"Because I want you to trust me and to realize I have no ulterior motive for what I'm telling you. I'm simply a man who's made mistakes and I'm trying to prevent you from doing the same. That's all." He spun on his heel and covered the last few paces to the street. If she slept on it, maybe had a few days to get through the production and reflect on what he'd said, she'd realize he was right.

He punched the button for the crosswalk and waited for the light to change. Emily stood beside him in silence. He was about to hit the button again when she wrapped her hand around his wrist. Rather than looking at him, her focus was on her bed and breakfast, a contemplative crease bisecting the space between her brows.

"You're right. I made a bad decision once and it's made me sensitive to how I'm perceived." Her voice held a mix of apology and regret. "I've never considered that I'm oversensitive. Or that I may sometimes overreact as a result."

"We all do it. No one's perfect." Though as she stood beside him now, with her mussed hair, wispy tango outfit, and thoughtful expression, he decided she came as close as a person could. Emily Sinclair was, bar none, the most beautiful woman he'd ever met. It wasn't her long, lean legs or the smooth skin of her bare shoulders than enticed him most, it was the vibrancy of the woman within, the gratitude she expressed to those around her, and the intellectual curiosity with which she viewed the world...even if she tried to insulate herself from the risks it posed by throwing every ounce of her being into her career.

"I know. Even if perfect is what's expected. Or what we expect of ourselves, even when no one else cares." Her fingers flexed around his arm. "Just for that, I'm letting you out of it."

The light changed at last, but confusion made him pause and look down at her. "Out of what?"

"I'm letting you out of your promise."

Ignoring the stopped cars and blinking crosswalk light, she stretched on her tiptoes and brushed her lips against his.

CHAPTER 14

"Thank you," she whispered against his mouth.

Victor—no, *Vittorio*—remained immobile, his expression betraying nothing as she briefly touched her lips to his once more. When he didn't respond, she dropped flatfooted to the sidewalk. Behind her, a car honked. She forced a lopsided grin, let go of his arm, and turned to the crosswalk.

She'd utterly confused him. Well, what did she expect? In the five minutes it'd taken them to walk across the park, she'd gone from agitated to defensive to amorous. What he didn't know was how his words affected her in those five minutes. How he'd affected her from the moment they'd met. He'd challenged all her assumptions about who she was and the direction she'd fought to take her life ever since she allowed Paul to upend it.

And, dammit, Vittorio was sexy as hell. Even with his scratchy beard and longish, wavy hair, which generally wasn't a look that attracted her, he possessed an undeniable gravitas that drew her as powerfully as if he'd grabbed her and demanded her attention.

He was the first man who'd ever made her feel lonely for not having him in her life.

"Emily, wait."

"It's all right. I wasn't saying you *have* to kiss me, only that I'm not going to hold you to your word. Come on…we're going to miss the light."

Before she could step off the curb, he palmed her bare shoulder and spun her to face him. His other hand came up to bracket her in place. "Aren't you worried about your colleagues?"

"Deep down, I am. It's habit. But you're right. I need to trust that my work stands on its own merits and stop second-guessing what others might think of me. Besides, we're adults. It was a ridiculous thing to request—"

His thumbs slid from her shoulders to her neck. Before she could comprehend his intentions, his mouth was on hers. Blasts from a car horn echoed behind her, followed by a half-dozen more and even a youthful whistle, then the rev of engines as the cars proceeded through the light.

None of it mattered. All she could process was the man before her. The heady sensation of his strong hands cradling her. His warm mouth opening against hers, inviting her to deepen the kiss. The firm muscle of his back as she wrapped her arms around him. The heat of his body radiating through the soft, cream-colored tango shirt as her fingertips lingered near the base of his spine.

Then his tongue touched hers, retreated, returned…lingered. She rose on her tiptoes, aching for more.

She'd lived in a state of denial for so long, telling herself it was for the good of the show and the preservation of her career, she'd forgotten what it was like to be the object of a man's hunger. Or to experience that same, soul-deep hunger herself.

But it was never a hunger like this. Never.

His hands slid from her shoulders and neck to her bare upper back, but unlike the last time they kissed, he didn't pull away. He took his time exploring her mouth, treating her as if she were a gift to be savored. Gently, he moved his lips from her mouth to her cheek, then exhaled as he pulled her hard against him. In a voice thick with desire, he said, "Not that anyone in the park cares, but I'm not in the habit of doing this in public."

"Nor am I." She wasn't in the habit of doing this at all, as he'd astutely pointed out the last time they'd kissed. "We could go to my room."

Probably not the wisest choice, but everyone was either out or in the office, so the risk of being seen was lower than if they continued outdoors, across the street from the bed and breakfast. All she knew was that she wasn't ready to stop.

"My place would be more private. But only if you're comfortable."

"I'm not comfortable at all." His arms tensed and his lips stilled against her temple, eliciting a smile of delight from her as she continued, "But I'm uncomfortable in a good way. Your place it is."

His mouth found hers again briefly, then he twined his fingers through hers and led her across the street, zigzagging through stalled traffic before guiding her down a narrow side street to a boutique hotel situated in a gracious whitewashed townhouse. The front desk area was empty as he keyed in. Without preamble, he steered her toward the steep, narrow staircase leading to the rooms on the upper floors. When they reached the fourth floor, he paused outside the single door without turning the key.

Her heart pounded against her ribcage, more in anticipation than from the rapid climb. "What's wrong?"

His golden brown eyes found hers in the semidarkness of the landing. "I just want you to know...I have no expectations. I'll walk you back to your place anytime you want."

"A woman's right to say no?"

"Exactly."

"The same goes both ways. I'll leave whenever you give the word."

"Don't expect it anytime soon."

She put her hand over his and turned the key. "Good."

Possessive hands wrapped around her waist, then he nudged the door with his hip and swung her inside in one smooth motion. Her bag fell to the floor, landing with a thud somewhere near her feet. She caught the flash of a dimmed crystal chandelier overhead before he kicked the door shut behind them.

Then she was lost, trapped between the man and the thick wooden door. Hot and demanding, his mouth conquered hers in a no-holds-barred acknowledgment of the sexual tension that had kept them both on edge all day. She opened to him without hesitation, her knees softening even as his arms locked her against him to hold her steady while he fit his lean hips to hers. Heat pooled low in her core as he kissed her with an intensity that defied the coolheaded persona he showed the world.

She wanted to know him. Not only his body, but what drove him, what mattered most to him, why he felt it vital he keep his identity shrouded.

His lips parted from hers, but only long enough for him to press a kiss to her cheek. A masculine sound of satisfaction rumbled from deep in his throat.

"Your name is really Vittorio?" she breathed.

"Yes," he ground out as he dragged his mouth from her cheek down the column of her neck, the friction from his beard making her want to crawl out of her skin from the blissful mix of pleasure and pain.

"And you're really from Italy, aren't you?"

"No. I was telling the truth. And if you recall, I never said my name *wasn't* Vittorio. You interrupted me before I could answer."

"Then—?"

His tongue danced at the base of her throat, the pressure making her back arch in desire. One of his hands came to cup her breast, teasing her nipple through the fabric of her strapless top. "Not only are you too curious for your own good, you're too talkative," he murmured. "Let's leave a little mystery, shall we?"

"Mmm…" Her mind shut off as she freed his shirttail from his pants, then worked her fingers under the hem to explore the planes of tight muscle that wrapped his sides and rippled across his abdomen. He shifted, leaving enough space between their bodies to enable her to unbutton his shirt, then push the fabric aside. Gingerly, she spread her hands across his chest, awestruck at the perfection of his torso. Muscle covered every inch of his upper body, yet he wasn't garishly huge, like a bodybuilder who lived in the gym. Vittorio was lean. Honed. *Hers.* Even if only for tonight.

Closing her eyes, she eased forward and touched her tongue to his chest, savoring the taste of him. She heard him draw a sharp breath through his teeth as her mouth drifted toward his nipple, then stilled, allowing her to tease and lick and explore. She thought he hissed her name, but the metallic purr of a zipper being undone and the wash of cool air against her lower back distracted her. Then her top was off—her bra joining it on the floor with a quick snap—and his palms shifted to the underside of her breasts, supporting their weight even as his thumbs grazed the edges of her nipples.

"Too fast?" The question emerged as an afterthought, the habit of a man to whom propriety was second nature. A quick shake of her head drew a husky "thank God" from him before their mouths met again. Talented fingers worked magic against her breasts, coaxing her nipples to taut peaks. A moment later, his tongue followed and he fell to his knees before her, suckling one breast while he held her waist to keep her from tumbling over in ecstasy. Her hands tangled in his hair, then her breath came in gasps as he forged a path to her navel with his tongue.

"Please." Her head fell back as the word escaped her lips.

The snick of the door being locked echoed through the dim room, then he was standing before her, lifting her, encouraging her to wrap her legs around his waist. Her mouth found his once more as he strode away from the entry, through a darkened sitting area to a bedroom. Without setting her down, he used one hand to pull the shade.

"Last chance, Emily." He uttered it as both a promise and a warning.

She tightened her hold and groaned out her need. His fingers dug into the flesh of her backside as he kicked off his shoes, then lowered her to a luxurious bed, the kind a person could curl into for days. Easing back, he pulled her black tango skirt over her hips, tossed it toward the corner, then pressed his mouth to her ankle as he stood beside the bed and worked the strap of her shoe. Slivers of light cut around the edges of the window shade to partially illuminate his face as he dropped the first shoe to the floor and turned to work on the second, giving her a heart-stopping view of his profile.

She'd thought him stunning when she'd first approached him in the café. This didn't compare. Long lashes swept down toward his cheekbones as he caressed her foot, lashes any woman would kill to have. But it wasn't the lashes that caught her attention; it was the way the shadows cast his skin and facial hair into a single tone, giving her an image of what he might look like without the close-cropped beard. He radiated confidence and a quiet strength that made her body tighten with longing.

Then he was over her, his hands flattened on either side of her head, his amber eyes ravishing her.

"You are so beautiful," he murmured, but she arched from the bed to shush him with a deep kiss. Urgency built within her, so hard and fast she teetered on the brink of control...though they'd hardly started. She worked the front of his slacks, managing to undo the hook and zipper at the very moment Vittorio's hand covered hers in an effort to help. Then he was free, slacks and underwear lost somewhere in the bed or on the floor.

They needed to slow down. She couldn't. Primal instinct took over, sending rivers of fire through her every nerve ending as her fingers curled around him. She marveled at the heat of him, the length and breadth of him. He swallowed hard, watching her with intense, hooded eyes as she stroked his silken skin.

His chest rose and fell as her pace intensified, then he swore and scooped a well-muscled arm under her shoulders to roll her on top of him. He eased her hands from him and kissed her fingertips before placing them on either side of his hips. "If you want to enjoy this, don't touch me for a minute. Just...let me..."

Vittorio parted her with his fingers, then inhaled sharply as he encountered her moist heat and realized what touching him had done to her.

He encouraged her to sit up and lean back, allowing him greater access. Masterful hands found the spot just above her entrance and it was her turn for an agonized expletive. Her head fell back as a fresh surge of desire overtook her. The flower Rita had pinned into Emily's hair for the tango segment bounced down her back as her hair cascaded from the bun she'd so carefully arranged that morning. Her breath refused to fill her lungs, but he didn't relent. His thumb worked her most sensitive spot as he entered her with one finger, then a second. It occurred to her that he was watching her, that she should be embarrassed, but she wasn't. All she wanted was more…and more…then she couldn't take any more.

Her hands fisted in the sheets. "Vittorio—"

"I'm here."

She squeezed her eyes shut against the impending rush. "Yes—"

The pressure building within her erupted, drawing a gasp from her lips as wave after wave of bliss enveloped her. He sat up and lifted her fully into his lap, allowing her to collapse against the curve of his shoulder while his thumb continued its decadent movement until every ounce of tension left her body. When the last tremor subsided, he eased her to the mattress, pillowing her head with his hand.

"You can say no, you know," his teasing whisper came to her ear.

"Not if I can't breathe." She wrapped her leg around him, anchoring his body against hers. "And not if I don't want to."

"Good." He reached behind him and located a condom. Sheathed, he pressed a worshipful kiss to her forehead before entering her in one sweet, unrestrained stroke she knew would drive her erotic fantasies for years to come. The heavenly awareness that he was fully inside her sent her reeling. He felt so good, so right, as if she'd been waiting her entire life for this one exquisite moment.

"Dear God, Emily," he ground out as he slowly withdrew, inch by agonizing inch, then plunged deep once more. She clutched at his corded arms. She could feel him resisting, fighting to slow himself down despite her obvious need. Near her ear, he whispered, "You are amazing."

"Show me." She turned her head, meeting his mouth in a fierce kiss as she wrapped her legs tighter around his hips, encouraging him to let go. He did just that, driving into her hard and fast, ratcheting up the tension in her body until she didn't think she could take another second…only to have him change his angle, touch her in a new spot, and take her even higher.

She cried out his name as she reached her peak, then sensation engulfed her as she plunged over the cliff. A deep moan of pleasure exploded from her, her back lifted from the bed, and she scrabbled for purchase against the headboard with one hand while clinging to Vittorio's broad back with the other.

Through the haze of ecstasy, she heard her name, then an Italian phrase spoken so low and with such passion she couldn't begin to translate, though his meaning was clear. A beat later his body tensed, his chin dropped, and great shudders took him as he found his release. A deep, masculine sound of satisfaction echoed through the small room before he collapsed to her side, his powerful arms holding her fast against his sweat-slicked body.

Eyes closed, she threaded her fingers through his hair, aimlessly massaging his scalp as they recovered. Craving the heat of his skin and the rapid thrum of his heart against her own, she shifted so he lay partially on top of her.

She dragged in long, deep breath, savoring the roughness of Vittorio's scruff-covered cheek where it rested against the tender area just below her collarbone. Gradually, she allowed her fingers to drift down his neck and across his back, to memorize the texture of the supple skin that covered powerful muscles. To trace his shoulder blades and marvel at the contained strength he hid under his casual shirts. To wonder at the complexity of a man who proclaimed to have simple needs, yet who'd apparently endured such challenges he'd needed five months of solitude an ocean away from home to regain his equilibrium.

He shifted, disposing of the condom in a trash can near the bed before caressing her side in the haphazard manner that only came from being thoroughly sated. She couldn't resist kissing the top of his head. Into his hair, she said, "Would it be wrong of me to say that you are an absolutely gorgeous man?"

"Absolutely not." Exhausted laughter rumbled through his back to her fingertips. "This is perhaps the time a man most wants to hear compliments."

"Are you fishing for more?" she teased.

"Only answering your question. But say what you will and I'll do the same." He pushed up to his elbows so his face hovered inches above hers. She expected his expression to be lighthearted, but was surprised to find his brow creased in sincerity. "You are not only stunning to look at, Emily Sinclair, you're endlessly fascinating. Meeting you has been the highlight of my time in Buenos Aires."

She smiled and kissed him again. She intended it to be brief and carefree, but it quickly morphed into more as he cupped the back of her head and nipped her lower lip. She yelped in delight as he pressed her into the sumptuous sheets once more, his mouth possessing hers completely.

Just as she was certain they'd end up making love again, she sensed a change in him. He playfully rolled over, pulling her on top of him and fanning his fingers over her hips. "When you approached me in the café, you promised that filming would be fun," he said. "Never in a million years did I expect this."

"This" —she rose to straddle him, then waved an index finger between them— "isn't being filmed. I also said doing the show would be an adventure to share with your friends and family. That definitely doesn't apply here."

He let go of her, tucking his hands behind his head and gazing up at her in a mix of curiosity and amusement.

"What?"

"I was trying to tell you that I'm really enjoying myself. Are you trying to tell me that filming your show is more fun than this?" He gestured from himself to her, mimicking her.

"Well, I do live for my show. But on the fun scale" —she caught his hand— "it doesn't compare to this."

Never before had she thought of sex in terms of fun. It'd always meant something more. Commitment. Personal risk. Expectations. With Paul there'd been the added fear that if she couldn't satisfy him, he'd leave her and she'd have nothing.

Well, Paul *did* leave her. Despite her sacrifices, despite his claims that he loved her, he needed more. For months afterward she'd agonized over what she could've done differently, if anything. In the end, she'd emerged from the broken relationship stronger, and she'd pursued a new career, one that reinforced her sense of self. She'd sworn never to be that vulnerable again.

Thankfully, *At Home Abroad* kept her so busy and fulfilled that giving herself entirely to a man hadn't been an option. But having fun with a man…well, tonight she'd discovered the joy of it and realized that no-commitment sex, sex without fear, gave her an adrenaline-fueled high. It made her feel confident and free.

Who knew?

Without warning, Vittorio sat up and eased her backward, sending her head to the foot of the bed as he moved over her on all fours. Just as when he'd fixed her with *el cabeceo* during the tango lesson, she experienced the sensation of being a gazelle caught in the sights of a hungry predator, unable to tear her gaze from his.

With a grin, she gripped his thighs, kneading her fingers into his dark hair and rock-hard muscle. "What do you think you're doing?"

"Having more fun."

"Already?"

One of his hands clamped down on hers, sliding it to the inside of his thigh…then further.

"It would seem so," she murmured.

As she shifted her grip, his mouth thinned and his eyes drifted closed. "Or maybe not. That was the only condom I had. I really meant it when I said this was unexpected."

Her hand stilled. "That's—"

"A tragedy," he finished. "But one I can rectify if you're able to hang on for five minutes while I run to the shop we passed a few doors down."

She angled a pointed glance toward her hand. "You're not in a condition to run anywhere. But it's up to you." When his eyes widened, she added, "Pregnancy isn't an issue for me. And I have physicals every six months as a condition of the show's insurance policy, so I can assure you, I'm not carrying anything scary or contagious."

And as he'd shrewdly pointed out when he'd kissed her outside her bed and breakfast, she hadn't been kissed—let alone bedded—in a long time.

Wariness caused a divot to form between his brows. "You're positive pregnancy is a non-factor? Because—"

"We're completely covered on that front," she assured him. He hesitated, then she caught a change in his gaze and a deep understanding passed between them.

"Then by all means, carry on." Though his smile was wicked, the gravity in his tone let her know he was taking a huge leap of faith in trusting her, one he didn't take lightly. At the same time, it conveyed a pledge that she was perfectly safe with him, that he'd never put her health or career at risk.

She shifted her hold and planted a quick kiss on his lips. "Vittorio, your wish is my command."

CHAPTER 15

UNFETTERED SEX. Who knew?

A deep sense of gratification filled Vittorio as he nestled Emily against him and let his racing pulse settle from their second round of lovemaking.

Until this moment, it never occurred to him how contained he'd kept his sex life, but that's exactly what it'd been. Concerns always lingered at the back of his mind when he dated a new woman, concerns that magnified on the rare occasions he allowed their relationship to move to the bedroom. Were they enamored with him, or with the potential of becoming Sarcaccia's future queen? Were they—God forbid—faking their interest in order to keep his attention? If the relationship ended, would they sell their story to the highest bidder?

With Emily, that apprehension didn't exist. She knew nothing of his title, only had hints at his wealth, and had no expectations of a relationship. When the show wrapped, she'd head back to New York and her busy life. He'd go back to Sarcaccia and his. He even believed her when she assured him she'd taken precautions against pregnancy...a statement he never in his life thought he'd accept from any woman.

This was sex for the sake of sex. The sheer enjoyment of another person's body. And it was divine.

He pressed a tired kiss to her temple, reveling in the scent of her shampoo and the light sheen of perspiration at her hairline.

"Stay," he whispered against her soft skin. "We'll get you home in the morning with no one the wiser."

She sighed her assent. He closed his eyes and relaxed into his pillow, satisfied knowing her lush body would warm his the rest of the night.

Less than a minute later, he squeezed his eyes tighter against the swell of emotion rising in his chest. He was kidding himself. He wasn't satisfied at all.

Tonight wasn't divine because it was unfettered sex. It was divine because it was sex with Emily. And as he listened to her quiet breathing and enjoyed the sensation of her silken, honeyed hair splayed across his shoulder, he knew he wanted more than a one-night stand. Emily made him want a relationship.

She shifted, tangling her heavenly legs with his.

His experience with Carmella made him believe he'd forsake marriage until absolutely necessary for the future of his country, and then only because it was his duty to produce offspring. He'd hoped he'd be able to find a woman he could trust, one who'd grow to become his partner and a friend. But he'd never pictured he could experience this, even for a single night. This was all out, soul-twisting lust for a woman he admired deeply. A woman who'd stepped between him and an armed man.

Making love to Emily went beyond a craving for carnal pleasure, even beyond a need for comfort. He knew, deep in his bones, that this was meant to happen. That when he'd come to Buenos Aires, Emily was his destination.

She'd shattered his reason. Challenged him. Made him realize there was still good in the world.

She'd made him care about his future happiness, not merely in his future survival.

But now what? The situation was impossible. As Emily's foot slid up his calf, he tightened his hold around her and dragged his lips over her hair.

A mere six months ago, he'd been openly dating Carmella. Betting lines across the European continent leaned toward them getting engaged within the year, and he'd been mulling the possibility of a future with her. The gossip tabloids had barely moved on from the news of their surprise breakup when she'd died by suicide, sending her fans reeling and the tabloids buzzing anew. In order to protect his family and hers, he'd been obliged to say only the best about the up-and-coming actress, leaving her reputation intact. To step out with a new girlfriend at this point could elicit the worst kind of venom from the press, from Carmella's fans, and even from his own countrymen.

Even if a such a relationship was accepted, how could he possibly explain meeting her? Because the moment their liaison became public, everyone would clamor to know the details, and no good could come of it. He had no illusions about the personal hell public opinion could create for each of them if their relationship ever came to light. It was the kind of hell that destroyed one's spirit. It could throw his abilities as a future monarch into question. It would kill Emily's career.

And that would kill everything inside Emily that made her...*her*. Her openness, her optimism, her zest for life.

She reached to pull the plush coverlet over them both. Just as he settled his arm in a more comfortable position, an insistent hum came from the direction of the front door. He frowned. He'd been at this hotel for several days, but hadn't noticed a buzzer of any kind.

"Of course," Emily muttered, making him realize it must be her phone. "I hate to say it, but I need to check."

"You think it's Rita?"

"If not her, then someone else from the show. They're used to getting quick responses from me and I don't want them to wonder." The edges of her mouth curved as she rose from the bed and looked at him in the dim light. "Of course, it could always be the network saying we're being renewed. Wouldn't want to miss that."

"Any excuse to celebrate?" He gave her naked body an obvious head-to-toe perusal, pausing at her voluptuous breasts.

"Do we need an excuse?"

He laughed as she made her way to the sitting area to retrieve her bag. Perching on the edge of the bed with her phone, she tapped the screen and said, "It's Maryam. Just a text confirming that she's spoken with the real estate agent and we're set for tomorrow's apartment viewing in Barrio Norte."

She deposited the phone on his nightstand and burrowed under the coverlet. His stomach rumbled as she tucked against his side.

Her hand flattened against his stomach. "You didn't get dinner. You must be starving."

"I seem to have worked up an appetite." He cocked an eyebrow at her. "This place has a small room service menu. Would you do me the honor of being my date for dinner tonight?"

She answered with a flirtatious kiss that nearly had him bedding her again. An hour later, they sat in the main room of his small suite, enjoying slices of pizza and a bottle of deep red Argentine Malbec while talking about the apartments he'd toured and the other regions of Argentina she'd visited. In between bites, he asked where she might want to film her next season.

"I haven't given it a lot of thought." She rolled up the sleeves of the blue button-down shirt she'd borrowed from him—one that looked decidedly different hugging her curves than when he'd worn it a week earlier—then stretched her bare legs the length of the sofa. "Rita and I have tossed around a few ideas, but we don't want to invest too much time or effort in any one place until we get the word we're being renewed. Most likely it'll be in Europe. Somewhere warm and visually enticing like Greece or Turkey would be ideal. We did the mountain villages of the Alps in season one, then went to Japan for season two. We want to keep the variety."

He polished off the last bite of his pizza before setting his paper plate on the room's antique coffee table and moving from his chair to take a seat on the sofa near Emily's feet. "Have you always been a glass half-full type of person?"

"I suppose. You?"

He'd never thought of himself one way or the other. "The glass is what it is. Both half-empty and half-full."

"A man who puts practical concerns first." She angled a look at him. "I'm not surprised."

"For the most part it's an attitude that's served me well." He turned sideways on the sofa and stretched his legs beside Emily's. Her hand went to his calf, and though the movement seemed as habitual as if they were a long-married couple, it sent a sizzle of awareness through him that was anything but ordinary.

While she took a long sip of her wine, he said, "I admire you for your optimism. Even when you're under tight deadlines and enormous stress, you're confident you'll land on your feet. You make everyone around you believe things will work out for the best, too."

"I try. Doesn't mean it's easy."

Thinking back to their conversation over croissants, he acknowledged, "I know it's not. But your approach and your resiliency are why I agreed to do your show." Perhaps he was saying too much, but he felt compelled to add, "It's also why I'm so damned attracted to you."

She tsked, but her eyes betrayed her delight at his words. "And here I thought it was because you liked my legs. Don't think I didn't notice you looking when I approached you in the café."

He reached for her calf and gave it a deliberate squeeze. "Your legs certainly don't hurt."

"What's funny is that my biggest failure came because I was too optimistic, too sure I could make everything work in a situation where it couldn't." She shrugged. "A fiasco like that can knock you for a loop."

He understood the truth of that statement more than she knew. "Yet here you are, with a show about to enter its fourth season."

She smiled at that, even as she reached to knock on the top of the wooden coffee table for luck. "I had a choice to make. I had to believe I could survive any failure and even thrive. The alternative was to curl up in a ball and quit. If I'd done that, I wouldn't be doing what I'm doing right now."

He pulled one of her feet into his lap, making note of the bright red polish tipping her toes as he put his thumbs to her arch and pressed. She groaned in pleasure. After a day dancing in heels, he suspected she could use the massage.

"So tell me about this big, bad, terrible failure of yours."

"Oh, you're devious…asking me personal questions while you're doing that to my foot."

"I'm merely paying you back for joining me for the tango lesson." He kneaded her arch, working his way to the ball of her foot. "Judging from the way you danced today, you've done it before, which means you know how much better your feet will feel tomorrow if I do this tonight."

"You're evil." A long sigh escaped her. "If you must know, my big mistake was the dancer."

"The…dancer?"

"Ex-boyfriend. He loved ballroom dancing. We went all the time." She turned her ankle, allowing him to situate her foot more comfortably in his lap. "Obviously, the relationship didn't work out. We met in college and things were great, but once I started working…well, I didn't see what I should've seen all along."

"You're saying you were a bad judge of character? You?" He grinned, hoping to ease what was obviously a painful episode in her past by bringing up the very words she'd used against him when he'd all but accused her of stalking him.

"Yep, me. Which is how I recognized it in you." Though her tone remained good-humored, her eyes reflected a hurt that hadn't completely healed. "He'd given me all the signs, but I was too optimistic to read them. I put everything on the line for the relationship and ended up unceremoniously dumped."

And shattered, though he doubted she'd admit it. "Were your friends and family supportive?"

"In a way. They were all as blindsided as I was. They thought Paul was Mr. Perfect, that I was making all the right choices." An ironic smile lifted one side of her mouth. "Everyone but Rita, wouldn't you know. She never did like him. Told me more than once during the last few months I was with him that she was worried about me. I told her she didn't know Paul like I did."

"What did she say to that?" He couldn't imagine Rita keeping her lip zipped if she disagreed.

"She told me she didn't need to know Paul like I did. She knew me. And she thought I was being naive about the price I was paying to keep him happy."

Vittorio's hands stilled on her feet and he shot her a questioning look.

"I'd left my job for him," she explained. "A job I really loved and that I'd fought hard to get. But my hours and travel schedule were crazy, and eventually he gave me an ultimatum: the job or the relationship. I gave my two-week notice the next day and started looking for a position with fewer hours that'd keep me closer to home." One side of her mouth lifted in a self-deprecating smile. "What Rita was trying to get through my head was that I wouldn't be happy without a career that challenged me and that Paul should've known me well enough to understand that, too. I suspect she also believed that quitting like I did created an unspoken black mark against me in the industry."

Emily's work was such a part of her identity he couldn't imagine her without it. He gave her arch one final deep massage with his thumbs before reaching for her other foot. "Is that what ended the relationship? You missed your job?"

"It should've, but no." A shadow passed over her face, one that spoke to lingering emotional scars. "He ended it. He wanted more than I could give him."

"More than leaving your job for him?" Selfish ass. What man could possibly want more than Emily had to offer? Now he understood why she chafed against traditional male and female roles. When she'd followed that tradition in her own relationship, she'd been burned personally and professionally.

"It's complicated, but yes. I don't blame him, though."

Incredulity roughened his voice. "How could you not?"

"At the end of the day, for a relationship to work, you have to know yourself and know what you want. There were things I couldn't give him. Things I knew, deep down, that he needed to be happy." She polished off her wine and shrugged, her attitude a sharp contrast to the resentment Vittorio felt on her behalf. "It was a tough lesson, but that experience taught me that I needed to go after what *I* wanted, too. And I wanted a career. More than that, I wanted my own show. It wasn't easy, especially since I'd left a great position and it made me appear less than professional, but I put together a pitch for *At Home Abroad* and pursued it. Rita was at a transitional point in her own career and took the chance of going in on it with me. And here I am."

She reached for the open wine bottle he'd left on the coffee table and held it up, offering to top off his glass, but he shook his head.

"Anyway...lesson learned. Happiness found."

Given how easily Emily seemed to have forgiven her ex, Vittorio suspected there was more she wasn't saying—there always was when a woman used the phrase *it's complicated*—but he let it go.

She returned the wine bottle to the table, a pensive look on her face. "It's getting very late. I know you said you wanted me to stay, but if you prefer—"

"I would *not* prefer." His hand tightened around her foot. He'd never had a woman speak to him so candidly, and he valued it more than she could ever know. The thought of sleeping without her by his side tonight didn't appeal in the least.

She extricated her foot before scooting forward and straddling him. She untied his robe and flicked it open before sliding her hands over his chest, then up into his hair, framing his face between her delicate fingers. The excess fabric of the shirt she'd borrowed dipped low, giving him a prime view down the front.

"You make my clothes look very, very good," he murmured, gripping her rear and pulling her higher, leaving only her thin panties and his boxers separating them.

"And you...you seem like a man in desperate need of kissing."

"Astute observation. I'm even optimistic about the chances you'll indulge me."

Her full lips parted as she leaned down to kiss him. A furrow appeared between her brows when she'd only covered half the distance and she drew back. "Before me, you hadn't kissed anyone in quite a while, either, had you?"

CHAPTER 16

"You're torturing me," he accused.

She pressed a decadent kiss to his lips before drawing back. Her lower body remained firmly pressed to his, but her voice softened with a mix of concern and curiosity. "How long has it been?"

He shrugged, mentally counting back. He'd ended things with Carmella just before Sarcaccia's Independence Day festivities, when he'd discovered their entire relationship was based on a lie. It had been a week or two before that, since she'd been traveling to promote a film. "August, I suppose. Not that long."

"Seven months." She eased forward, keeping her hands buried in his hair. "For a man who looks as good as you do, and given your obvious" —she ground her hips against his— "virility, that's a long time."

"Kiss me again and I'll make up for it tonight."

She closed the distance between them and feathered the barest kiss against his cheek before grinning against his whiskers. Without waiting for permission, he scooped her up, pressed his hands to her thighs to encourage her to wrap her legs around his waist, then carried her back to the bedroom.

Laughter cascaded from her as he deposited her on the bed, then sprawled on top of her. "Really? Again?"

"You did comment on my obvious virility."

"Still, a third time seems" —mischief lifted her brows— "optimistic."

"Remember, I am neither optimistic nor pessimistic." He pressed against her. "It is what it is."

This time, they made love deliberately, taking their time divesting each other of what little clothing they wore, then exploring one another with their hands and mouths. He savored the weight of her breasts, the smoothness of her skin, the elegant curve of her waist and perfectly rounded lift of her rear. The tight heat of her as he plunged inside her, then withdrew, keeping their pace tortuously unhurried until she shook with need and begged him to bring her to ecstasy. Later, when they'd recovered, he rolled her to her stomach and kissed his way down her back, settling his mouth at the base of her spine. The sigh that escaped her was the most deeply satisfied sound he'd ever heard.

"Now aren't you glad I learned the hard way to go after what I want?" she said, her voice provocative. "Not only did it result in our meeting, it makes me all the more appreciative of your talents."

"As I," he whispered against her, "am deeply appreciative of yours. You are one of a kind." In and out of bed.

He sensed the change in her immediately and knew his worshipful tone—and the tightening of his hands on her waist as he spoke—gave away too much of his inner thoughts. Feigning ignorance, he traced a path back up her spine with his tongue, sweeping her hair aside so he could place a kiss at the back of her neck before collapsing against his pillow.

She wriggled and rolled over to face him, unwilling to let it go. "You were hurt, too, weren't you?"

"We're all hurt at one time or another. Wouldn't be human otherwise."

"No, not like this. I suspect whatever happened to you is the reason you needed a five-month vacation. And to find an apartment far from home to use as an escape." She flattened her palm against his heart. He couldn't define it, but her gentle touch made him understand she wasn't pressing him for information, but conveying her understanding of a painful event. "I'm glad you contacted your family and that you're going home. I suspect it'll be as good for you as it is a relief for them."

"Is this the point where we swap bad relationship stories?"

She gave a minute shake of her head. "It's the point where you allow yourself to be optimistic about the future and know that, whatever happened, you're over the worst of it."

He smiled and closed his eyes. For all her hard-driving work ethic, Emily was a nurturer first.

"I was deceived by someone I'd come to trust." Love wasn't the right word, though he'd felt a great deal of affection for Carmella. He stroked the lean muscle and fine, downy hair on the back of Emily's arm as he spoke, drawing more comfort from the act than he gave. "I ended the relationship because it wasn't what I thought it was."

Emily was silent for a long moment before asking, "Do you think it was more painful because you lost the girl or because you felt you'd used bad judgment?"

He opened his eyes, surprised by her question. It was an angle he'd never before considered. "Probably both. I mourned the loss of a person and a relationship that never really existed. But I was also angry at myself for not being smart enough to see I was being used." Very angry. "It's taken a long time to get past it. In retrospect, I don't think I could've predicted the full extent of her deception."

Emily's fingertips drifted lower, settling at his waist. "'Deception' is a strong word."

"It fits. She was seeing someone else the entire time. Before she was with me, even. Of course, when I asked her out I had no idea."

The edges of Emily's mouth jerked. "And she accepted your invitation anyway?"

"I was in a position to help both her career and her boyfriend's career. He saw it as a golden opportunity and she agreed. They decided to take their relationship underground so she could pursue me." The muscles of his jaw tightened. "Turned out to be a smart move on their part. They both saw their careers take off."

He knew he was being cryptic about his position, but to her credit, she didn't pry. "I'd say that falls squarely into the category of deception. How long were you together?"

"A couple years, off and on, but we were only serious the last few months."

"Ending it must have been very difficult."

Agonizing was more like it. He'd prided himself on his cautious nature, on always doing what he'd been raised to do—to act in a manner that reflected well on his country and his family—and being confronted with the evidence of her perfidy made him question everything he believed about his ability to make good decisions. His mother had invited him to dinner in her suite. He'd sensed her unease the instant she'd dismissed her staff for the day, insisting that they deserved an evening off and that she and Vittorio would be fine. Her emerald eyes were filled with pain as she confessed that she'd run a background check on Carmella.

He'd reached across the table, putting his hand over his mother's. He didn't like it, he'd said, but he wasn't surprised she'd done it. After all, he was heir to the crown and understood that his mother had only his best interests and those of their country at heart. He'd resumed eating, assuming the subject was closed. He'd been sorely mistaken.

"This was more than a routine check." The gravity in his mother's tone made him set down his fork. This time, she was the one to offer a reassuring touch, covering his fingers with hers. "I know you've been considering a future with her or I wouldn't have been so thorough. She's in the public eye and has an excellent reputation. But I never would've guessed…"

When his normally plainspoken mother struggled for words, Vittorio's stomach had pitched. "Guessed what, Mother?"

She'd told him everything then. A well-known Spanish film producer—one Carmella had introduced Vittorio to on numerous occasions, explaining that the man had backed many of her projects—was also Carmella's lover. Further digging revealed that they'd been together since before Vittorio and Carmella met. When Vittorio had expressed interest in the young actress, the pair mapped out a plan they hoped would boost both their careers.

"How could you possibly know that?" he'd asked.

"She was seen entering the producer's apartment wearing a disguise. Given her odd behavior and obvious familiarity with his neighborhood, I kept watch on her for nearly a month. The man I hired to tail her was able to overhear enough conversations that—when put together with Carmella's and her boyfriend's bank records —painted an irrefutable picture."

"And exactly what is that picture?" he'd asked. He hadn't wanted to delve into how Carmella was "overheard" or how his mother obtained access to the private financial information.

"They knew if Carmella dated you, she'd be followed by the media and photographed. It could raise her profile and help her break out of European cinema and crack Hollywood." His mother rattled off a number of public appearances he'd made with the Spanish actress over the course of their relationship to make her point, then said, "Being seen with you was the tip of the iceberg. Apparently she and her boyfriend began making promises on your behalf, telling studios that they could guarantee your presence at her movie premieres, even claiming that you were willing to help fund certain projects. They knew that with your name attached, they were more likely to get their projects greenlighted. You mean guaranteed publicity for any film."

His mind had reeled at his mother's accusations. "I've been to a few of her premieres, but only when it was convenient, given my schedule. I certainly never offered her any financial backing. How could they possibly cover those claims?"

The queen's mouth had formed a grim line. "Her boyfriend was selling off the gifts you bought her. The painting you sent for her last birthday, for instance."

"She told me her apartment was robbed." The painting was stolen, as were several pieces of jewelry and an antique dressing table he'd purchased for her over the course of their relationship.

"He and Carmella were also leaking information about you to the tabloids…for a price. They've been using that money to finance their projects and to bring in other investors, claiming the money came directly from you."

He'd closed his eyes, hating his mother's words despite knowing in his gut that what she said was true. Carmella had told Vittorio that the producer was an up-and-comer and generating a lot of interest in his projects…and that it was due to his efforts that she was starting to be cast in meaty, career-changing roles. On more than one occasion she'd asked Vittorio if he'd consider investing in the man's projects. Vittorio told Carmella he wasn't comfortable putting his family money into an industry he knew so little about. Once, he'd even asked her why the producer needed his money, if he was getting so much interest from regular investors in the film business. Carmella had turned the question back on Vittorio, saying that she was offering him a rare opportunity and had assumed he'd appreciate it. She'd even said she thought he wanted to pursue interests that distinguished him from the rest of his family.

As his mother spoke, he realized that Carmella had been working him, bit by bit, building her film credits and biding her time until she reached a level of success that would enable her to leave Europe behind. Hearing the truth—from his mother, of all people—had left him feeling emasculated.

Emily shifted at Vittorio's extended silence, the subtle dip in the mattress snapping him to the present.

"You all right?"

He nodded. "Just remembering. We were supposed to go to a charity auction the night after I learned she'd been lying to me. I called her and said I wasn't up to being social and asked if she'd mind having dinner at my place instead. The confrontation was less than pleasant."

"I imagine that's a kind way of phrasing it." Emily's voice was thick. "Did you lose your temper?"

"Surprisingly, no. She was shocked and hurt when I told her I knew, but she didn't deny any of it." All these months later, he remembered the icy calm that settled within him when Carmella swept into his palace apartment that night, all smiles. How the chill remained when she fell apart in front of him.

He lifted a lock of Emily's hair from her shoulder and twisted it around his finger as he spoke. "She insisted that she'd fallen for me during those last few months and that she'd decided to end it with her longtime boyfriend. She claimed she hadn't yet because she was afraid the guy would be angry and want retribution. That he'd do anything to ruin our relationship and both our reputations if he learned that she'd fallen in love with me."

Carmella had even collapsed to her knees before him, oblivious to damaging her cream-colored designer dress, and told him with tears running down her face that he meant everything to her. He'd stared down at her and felt strangely detached, as if someone had simply removed his heart from his chest to keep him from feeling anything while the woman crumpled at his feet. He'd even wondered if it was all a show intended to keep him from reporting her and her producer boyfriend to the police, despite the fact bringing her duplicity to light would harm the Barrali family almost as much as it would hurt her. Her agony seemed out of proportion to the depth of their relationship, and it hardened his heart against her.

He'd callously complimented her on an Oscar-worthy performance, which only made her cry harder.

"The thing is, part of me wanted to believe her. I suspected she had come to love me in a way, but I couldn't look past the dishonesty. Or that she was the type of person who'd gotten into a relationship for career gains—and stayed in it for so long—even if her intent had changed at the end." He let Emily's hair fall from his fingers. "I told her to get out and never to contact me again."

"Given what I know of you, that must've been incredibly difficult." She continued to gently massage his hip as she spoke, her tone one of sympathy rather than pity, for which he was grateful. "I'm sorry, Vittorio."

"Thank you. I'm sorry, too."

A few beats later, she said, "It's human nature to want to be loved. When someone we care for isn't being honest, we can't blame ourselves for not seeing it right away." The edges of her eyes crinkled as a self-effacing smile crept up. "Took me a while to learn that, of course. A lot like you taking a while to learn to prioritize yourself and enjoy life."

He smiled at her attempt to lighten his mood. She only knew part of the story...and couldn't know that there was no way *not* to blame himself for what happened.

"You're not buying it, are you?"

Emily was nothing if not perceptive. "In this case, she actually may have been in love. But I wasn't willing to entertain that possibility until it was too late."

At Emily's quizzical look, he said, "Our nasty breakup wasn't the worst of it. Even knowing she'd lied to me wasn't the worst." Part of him knew he shouldn't continue, but emotionally, he needed to share his grief with another human being, one who had no stake in a tabloid-headlining relationship between a prince and an actress. "She died by suicide a few weeks later. Hung herself with a piece of jewelry I'd bought her." A thick, twisted, golden rope necklace he'd selected because it complemented a gown she'd purchased for an upcoming film festival and modeled for him in the privacy of her apartment. She'd never worn either in public, but several of the articles concerning her death mentioned her unusually formal clothing and the necklace.

The details had gutted him.

Horror and disbelief clouded Emily's wide eyes. Her hand came to his chest, her fingers fanning out to cover his heart. Seeing her emotional reaction—combined with actually saying the words *she died by suicide* aloud for the first time—sent hot tears springing to Vittorio's eyes. He willed them back and ignored the lump forming in his throat. "The news hit me so hard I couldn't think straight. I blamed myself, of course. Never in a million years did I think she felt so strongly she'd believe ending her life was the only resolution. And then it got worse."

He filled his lungs with air, then pushed out the confession in a whoosh. "She was pregnant. She'd arranged to have a sealed letter sent to me a few hours after her death was discovered. It said she felt terrible about lying to me and that she didn't blame me for ending things or cutting off contact. That somewhere along the way, her career became so important to her that she lost her sense of self. Then she wrote that she hoped I understood why she couldn't bring a child into the world under the circumstances and asked me to forgive her."

Tears turned Emily's eyes to glassy pools as she curled her fingers into the hair dusting his chest. He could tell she wanted to say something to take away his pain, but knew she couldn't. "Oh, Vittorio. How devastating."

"It was. It *is*. And I'll never know the truth, will I? I'll never know if that child was mine. And I have to assume there was a child….she certainly had no reason to lie at that point….though if the pregnancy was discovered at her autopsy, no one informed me. Not that her parents would have. What good would it do anyone?" He cursed himself for being unable to contain his frustration. A lone tear flowed sideways from the corner of his eye and into the pillow where he hoped Emily couldn't see it in the shadows.

To her credit, Emily remained silent, her caring expression and gentle touch making it clear she was willing to listen and offer comfort, but at his pace. He hadn't realized until now how desperately he craved it. He covered her hand with his own and exhaled as he closed his eyes. "I tried to tell myself that her boyfriend must've done it. I imagined him as a maniac who'd lost it when he discovered his career plan had been shot to hell. But I knew in my heart that wasn't true." The laugh that escaped him sounded pained, even to his own ears. "Didn't stop me from checking to see where the bastard was when she died. Turns out he was working on a movie set in Berlin with dozens of witnesses. Had been for weeks, since before I'd learned the truth and ended things."

The day after Vittorio received Carmella's letter, Alessandro had caught Vittorio at his computer, searching for information on Carmella's lover. Alessandro placed a hand over the screen and told Vittorio to stop grasping at straws. Carmella's boyfriend may have been a dishonest slime, but he wasn't a murderer, and they both knew it.

Still, what choice did Vittorio have but to grasp at straws? He couldn't fathom why Carmella had taken her own life when she had so much for which to live. Despite their breakup, she still had a career in ascent and a family who loved her deeply. She had to have felt she had no options, and he was the only one who could've made her feel that way. It'd taken several weeks on his own in Argentina to finally forgive her for what she'd done.

But Vittorio wasn't sure he'd ever forgive himself. He could only move forward.

Turning slightly into his pillow, he managed to blot away the tears that had pooled in the outer corner of his eye. It appalled him that Emily might've noticed. "Part of me wonders if I could've prevented her suicide if I'd taken her at her word and given her a second chance, or if I'd tried to look at the situation from her perspective, to see that she'd been trapped between a rock and a hard place with her boyfriend telling her he was willing to blackmail her…."

Emily started to speak, but he shook his head, cutting her off. He swallowed hard, driving back the mass in his throat. "None of it even matters now. I was so focused on my own reputation and on seeing things as black or white, right or wrong, that I isolated her completely. Four times in those weeks between our breakup and her suicide, she tried to call me on my private line. I didn't answer. Deleted her messages without listening to them. Then I blocked her number."

He'd never confessed the phone calls to anyone, even Alessandro. "I was so stubborn, so holier-than-thou, that I ended up with two deaths on my hands."

CHAPTER 17

EMILY ACHED to pull Vittorio to her, to cradle his dark head in the crook of her neck and offer reassurance, but the vehemence in his tone gave her pause. He didn't want anyone to feel sorry for him, and he'd view any attempt at physical comfort as such. She strongly suspected he didn't want to be forgiven, either. He wasn't ready. Too much guilt weighed on him. But he needed to know it wasn't his *fault*. If he couldn't come to believe that, it'd be a festering wound on his soul for as long as he lived. He'd never get to the point where he could forgive himself.

Rather than offer placating words, she opted for a lighthearted approach. "Here I was beating myself up for quitting a job I loved to make a guy happy."

It had the desired effect. His mouth lifted at one edge.

Bolstered, she spoke quietly, keeping her voice matter-of-fact rather than sympathetic. "I can't begin to put myself in your shoes, but no matter what else you believe, your girlfriend's death wasn't your fault. *She* made that choice. And despite the circumstances, the fact is that you didn't know about the baby. Again, it was *her* choice. There's a lot I don't know about you, but I know enough to believe with absolute certainty that you'd never harm another human being. You should know yourself well enough to believe that, too." She tapped his chest. "Even if you are a terrible judge of character."

She half expected him to lash out, to tell her she had no idea what she was talking about, didn't know the people involved or understand how awfully he'd treated his ex. Instead, he surprised her with his steadiness. "Logically, I understand that. But it's another thing to know it in your heart. It takes time." A self-deprecating laugh emerged from him, shaking her fingertips where they lay over his heart. "At least five months."

She was gratified by his response. "She's why you came to Argentina."

"She's why I came. But *you* are why I'm going home. You convinced me it was time."

He said it as a compliment, which touched her. "I'm sure your family is worried, given all you've been through and how long you've been away."

"They don't know about it." One of his eyebrows jerked. "Well, not all of it. They know that we broke up and that she died by suicide shortly thereafter. My mother is the only person who knows of the deception, though she may have confided in my father. She doesn't know about the letter. However, one of my brothers knows of the letter and its contents because he was with me when it arrived. Otherwise, I'd never have told them."

"That's a lot to keep to yourself."

He gave her the barest of shrugs in response. "In the long run it was good my brother was there. He's the one who encouraged me to travel and clear my head. He also knew what to do to ensure I was covered at work. But now it's time to go home."

"Though you'll be back." At the odd look that passed over his face, she clarified, "Given that you're looking at apartments."

"Of course." His brow furrowed as if he'd temporarily forgotten his quest for a getaway spot. "It's a good city for getting one's bearings."

"Funny, I've discovered the same thing."

They lay quietly, only the sounds of their breathing and the low hum of distant traffic breaking the silence. Just as she was drifting off to sleep, Vittorio pushed the hair back from her face, then rolled so she was on her back with his forearms braced on either side of her.

Exhaustion couldn't stop her from snaking her arms around his waist. "Not that I object, but you've got to be kidding."

That drew a wide smile from him, enough to show his straight, white teeth. "No, I'm afraid I don't have it in me at the moment. But" —his voice dropped to a sultry pitch— "if you can handle one last confession?"

"Sounds scandalous. Please, do share."

"I've never had a one-night stand before. Never considered myself the type."

"That's…interesting." She waited a few beats for doubt to creep into his expression at her word choice before she whispered, "I can make that same confession."

One side of his mouth curved upward, turning her inside out. "Interesting."

Once more she wondered what he'd look like without the dark, foreboding facial hair. Given his even olive skin, strong cheekbones, and the bright brown eyes that studied her from behind his thick lashes, she imagined he'd be even more captivating, though perhaps not as mysterious.

His gaze followed his touch as he combed through her hair, spreading it across the pillow before he caressed the outside of her ear and traced her earring with his index finger. "I know this can't last. I'm flying home Monday to face the real world and you're going back to New York to prepare for another successful season of *At Home Abroad*" —he winked as he said it— "but before this ends, I want you to know that kissing you tonight was the best promise I've ever broken. If someone told me I'd have a one-night stand at some point in my life, I'd choose you a thousand times over."

It was the most contradictory yet romantic thing she'd ever heard. Emily reached for his nape, pulling him to her for a kiss. She wanted to remember the feel of his sinful mouth melding to hers, the masterful swirl of his tongue, the electricity of his touch for as long as she lived.

"Tonight has been very good for me. As well as very good…period." The sincerity in his lush accent fired her blood as powerfully as his kisses.

"I suspect we both needed this." He was such a dynamic, resilient man, one who likely had women falling for him left and right. Hell, if she allowed herself, she'd fall for him, too.

"Tomorrow, after your filming wraps, what would you say to a second one-night stand?"

Yes. A thousand times over. A deep sigh escaped her. "Unfortunately, I can't. We always go out for a celebratory dinner on the last day of filming. Rita and I treat the crew and office staff as thanks for the time and effort they've given to the show. The reservations are already made and I suspect it will last until the early morning hours." Taking a chance, she added, "But if you're not busy on Saturday night—"

He cut her off with a kiss. "It's a date."

<hr>

SUMMER WAS WINDING down in Buenos Aires, yet Emily wouldn't have known the date if she had to judge by the temperature. It was barely ten in the morning, yet the cloudless sky and reflected heat from the glass buildings and asphalt roadways combined to raise a sheen of sweat on her skin. Her makeup artist wouldn't be pleased. It was bad enough Emily had been compelled to explain away the redness on her cheeks this morning as a possible case of windburn when the woman dabbed concealer over the abrasions left behind from a night of kissing Vittorio.

Emily smiled to herself. If the croissants she carried tasted half as good as they smelled, perhaps she'd be forgiven for requiring a touch-up.

She ducked into the refurbished apartment building's sleek marble foyer, so grateful for the coolness of the space as she greeted the doorman that she nearly missed Vittorio standing a few feet in front of her waiting for the elevator.

"You're early," she said as he turned to greet her. And gorgeous.

While Emily knew how little sleep he'd had, his appearance didn't reflect it. His hair was neat, his eyes were bright with energy, and his soft blue shirt had been tucked evenly into a pair of summer-weight gray slacks devoid of wrinkles. When she'd kissed him goodbye a block from her bed and breakfast at five a.m. after he insisted on walking her there, he'd been sporting running shorts, a T-shirt, and a serious case of bedhead. He'd watched her all the way to the door, a tired—but satisfied—smile on his face. She wasn't sure which version of Vittorio she found more sexy.

He held the elevator door, ushering her in ahead of him. "Traffic was light. I'm surprised you're not upstairs already."

"I arrived at eight-thirty to meet with the agent, but apparently there was a water leak at her office. We knew you wouldn't be here for some time, so Rita and I told her to go take care of it." She held up the bag of croissants. "I decided to make a run for necessities."

He sniffed the air. "Necessities? Smells like pastries."

"Like I said. I'm craving buttery carbs this morning."

"Wonder why?"

She shrugged, resisting the urge to hit the stop button and kiss him again. Instead, she settled for studying his reflection in the elevator doors. His name fit perfectly. Vittorio embodied exactly what he was, strong, contained, and—she suspected—whip smart. He exuded intelligence without needing to demonstrate it. He struck her as a leader—a victor—and not from the hints he'd given her as to the responsibilities of his job, but from the way he carried himself.

As the elevator ascended, he kept his focus squarely on the panel over the door as it ticked off the floors. "There's a camera in here."

Her gaze went to the black ball mounted in the front corner of the carriage. "You said you wanted a secure building. The feed goes to the security desk near the front door. It's also kept on file for a week in case there's ever a break-in or other issue." Another reason not to kiss him in the elevator.

"Impressive. Though it also means I can't act on what I'm thinking right now."

Her stomach tightened at the flirtation in his tone. "And what's that, Bob?"

One of his eyebrows ratcheted up at her use of the name. "I'll let you guess." The elevator slowed as it reached the top floor and he lowered his voice. "Assuming you don't want me to pick you up at your bed and breakfast tomorrow night, how about I meet you outside the florist shop at the end of your block at eight? We can find a quiet place for dinner."

"That would be lovely." *Lovely* being an understatement. After last night, she couldn't wait to be alone with Vittorio again. To hole up in an out-of-the-way restaurant, learn more about him over a glass of rich red wine, then savor the wonders of a second one-night stand.

She wished there could be a hundred. She doubted she'd ever have her fill of him.

The elevator doors slid open, revealing a brightly lit, rectangular foyer with apartment doors on either side of a spectacular Impressionist painting. She strode to the door on the left, telling herself to focus on business. Much more time in the elevator with Vittorio and her coworkers would notice her flush. They wouldn't buy her explanation of windburn a second time.

"There are two penthouse apartments. Both are available," she explained. "The units are identical, but this one has better morning light and has been staged with furniture, so I expect we'll get most of our footage here. Then we'll go across the hall so you can see what it looks like empty and check out the view from that side of the building."

Once inside, Emily called out her return and announced that she had Bob with her. Vittorio muttered behind her, but she held her laughter in check and led him toward the kitchen, where she could hear Maryam and Rita holding an animated discussion. Given that it was the last day of filming and Maryam's office work was complete, she'd come to the apartment with Rita and they were making the most of the chance to socialize while waiting for the real estate agent's return.

"There's no way that's true!" Maryam sat at the glass-topped kitchen table across from Rita, her back to the entry. "Eleven?"

"I don't know. Kids experiment. Why not?" Rita glanced up from the magazine that was open in front of her. "Bob, give a guy's opinion. Average age at first kiss?"

Of all the topics for Rita and Maryam to debate. Emily set the bag of croissants on the counter and looked over her shoulder at Vittorio. Amusement lit his eyes at Rita's question. "Depends. Are we talking boys or girls? American or worldwide?"

"The article says they polled a thousand American high schoolers," Rita replied. She swept a hand toward Maryam, who'd twisted in her chair to check out Vittorio. "By the way, this is Maryam. Maryam, meet Bob, our real estate guinea pig."

"Ah, you must be the woman responsible for saving my feet yesterday." Vittorio crossed the spacious kitchen to shake Maryam's hand. "Thank you. I can return the shoes with the shirt tomorrow. I sent the shirt to the cleaners this morning, so—"

Emily couldn't help but note the attraction flare in Maryam's eyes as she waved off Vittorio's offer. "They're yours to keep. Rita told me the lesson went wonderfully."

Vittorio made small talk about the tango lesson for a moment, then gestured to the magazine article. "I'd say eleven is young, especially in the United States. But if they're polling teenagers, none will admit their first kiss came later than they believe their friends had theirs. Boys, especially. They'll shave a year or two off the truth."

"Told you," Rita said to Maryam before pushing back from the table. "Just for that, Bob, I'll pour you a coffee and make sure you get the biggest, fluffiest croissant in the bag. Have a seat."

Emily laughed. "I should do a quick walk-through so I'm familiar with the apartment. I assume Ignacio's checking the lighting in the living room so he can avoid magazine debates?"

"The makeup artist is in there, too." Rita swirled her hand at the shine on Emily's face. "You'd better take croissants for both of them. She needs to leave in a minute, but she won't mind pulling out the blotting papers if you pay her off in pastry."

Emily filled a plate and headed to the living room with Maryam and Rita's happy voices in her ears. Much as she hated to leave Vittorio behind with them, she counted herself lucky that the conversation focused on croissants instead of first kisses.

"I SWEAR, the croissants here are the best to be had outside of France. I'm going to miss them when we're back in New York."

Vittorio forced his attention from Emily's retreating back as Maryam leaned back in her chair and sighed over the fresh, buttery scent that filled the air. He was tempted to do the same. Even the croissants served at the palace weren't as airy and melt-in-your mouth as those he'd enjoyed from mom-and-pop bakeries during his time in Buenos Aires.

"On the bright side, it means fewer treadmill miles necessary to keep my incredibly svelte figure." Rita waggled her eyebrows before she passed a croissant-laden plate to Vittorio, then served Maryam and herself. After a few bites of the decadent pastry, Rita flipped to the front of the magazine she'd been reading and emitted a disdainful snort.

"What?" Maryam asked as she washed down her croissant with a hefty swig of coffee.

"Check it out. Val Dempsey's at the top of the masthead. No one told me she left *Today's Royals*. When did that happen?"

"You're kidding. Let me see."

At Rita's mention of *Today's Royals*, Vittorio's croissant hit his stomach like a rock. He kept his head down and his eyes on his coffee mug as Rita pushed the open magazine across the table to Maryam, who scanned a few pages before pointing to a woman's photograph.

"Recently, judging from the Letter From the Editor that's under her picture. A highly Photoshopped one, by the way, unless she's had plastic surgery. Maybe she thought she wouldn't get the top job at *Today's Royals* and jumped ship?"

"Or she ran out of colleagues to torture and needed a fresh batch."

Rita took the magazine back from Maryam and read the Letter from the Editor, grumbling in disgust as she finished. "Guess if we get cancelled, I know where I'm not going to apply."

"Bitch on wheels," Maryam said to Vittorio, by way of explanation.

"Yes, I gathered she isn't your favorite person." It was as diplomatic a comment as he could muster. The fact these two women knew someone who worked at a very popular royalty gossip magazine—one that speculated endlessly about his family—set him on edge.

"Rita and Emily used to work with her," Maryam continued. "I ran into her at professional functions and that was more than enough for me to know to steer clear. Being ambitious is a good thing, but being ambitious to the point that you'll step on anyone you perceive to be a threat is not. And that was Valerie Dempsey all the way."

"I only worked with her for six months," Rita said, making no effort to hide her dismal opinion of the woman. "Emily, on the other hand, was stuck with her for over two years before she left. Maryam and I were hoping Emily would outlast Valerie or at least get promoted above her. Em did such a wonderful job for the magazine."

Years of socializing at high profile events made it easy enough for Vittorio to keep a placid expression in place no matter the nature of the discussion taking place around him. However, he couldn't stop the sickening hole that formed in his stomach, rotting him from the inside as if he were on his fifth cup of coffee rather than his first. "Emily worked for *Today's Royals*?" When she'd told him she once worked for a magazine, he hadn't equated that with a tabloid.

He'd also assumed the job she'd quit—the job she'd told him she loved—was in television. But perhaps not.

"It's where we met," Rita explained. "We really hit it off, even though I wasn't there very long after Emily started. I went from a management position at *Today's Royals* to one with a television production company. I learned a lot in the time I was there. A few months after Emily left the magazine, she came to me with the idea for *At Home Abroad*. I knew the minute she told me about it that we'd be able to make it work. We put together a pitch, and voila" —she swooped a hand through the air— "now we're both in television."

Maryam grinned over her coffee. "When Rita and Emily got the order from the network for a full season of the show, Valerie was the first to predict its failure. Said very publicly at a magazine industry networking event that Emily didn't have the backbone necessary to manage either the staff or the logistics involved for an hour-long show that would be shot outside the country, let alone the talent to appear on air." Maryam made a show of rolling her eyes. "Silly me, that's the very moment I told Valerie I'd decided to go to work for Emily and Rita and that I couldn't be happier."

"You actually said that?" Rita guffawed. "Wish I'd been there to hear it. I have to say, Valerie is a talented magazine editor, which is why she's lasted so long, but when it comes to recognizing talent in her coworkers she's a few tacos short of a combo plate. Anyone with half a brain would've fought to keep Emily at *Today's Royals* instead of letting her quit."

"Or letting you go to the production company."

Rita raised her coffee mug to that.

Vittorio, on the other hand, could only process the word *quit*. The job at *Today's Royals* had to be the same one she'd waxed poetic about the night before. "Did Emily like working there?"

"Loved it," Rita and Maryam said together, then grinned when they realized what they'd each done. Rita continued, "She traveled to Europe all the time. Covered royal weddings in Luxembourg and the Netherlands, and spent over a month in Sweden reporting on the trial of a cousin to the royal family. She always found the best material, the behind-the-scenes stories that weren't being reported in other magazines and moved tons of copies."

"I had no idea." Behind-the-scenes meant private, invasive. The type of personal information that, once released, could irreparably damage both an individual and a monarchy. In other words, information like he'd shared with her last night about Carmella.

And Emily had loved it.

As Vittorio pushed away his half-eaten pastry, Rita's smiled broadened. "I told her not to quit, but all that travel is what gave her the idea for *At Home Abroad*."

"Lucky for us," Maryam said.

Again, Rita raised her mug. Conversation then turned to the outdoor orchestra performance Rita had attended the previous night. Vittorio made all the expected comments, but a mix of sadness and foreboding enveloped him. No wonder Emily kept looking at him as if she recognized him. Sooner or later, she'd make the connection, beard or not. He might not be familiar to most Americans, but given her line of work she'd have heard of him and his family. And if she didn't make the connection, Rita or Maryam eventually might. And what then?

If Emily wanted to save *At Home Abroad*, she had only to do same thing she'd done to sell copies of magazines: pack her show with behind-the-scenes info, the private, salacious material his own family didn't know. Last night, while he'd held her in his arms, he'd served it to her on a silver platter.

It wouldn't just save her show. It'd make her career.

CHAPTER 18

Emily had to give Monica, the real estate agent, a great deal of credit. After racing back to her office, calling in building maintenance and a plumber to repair a burst pipe, then salvaging what she could from her waterlogged desk, Monica made it back to the Barrio Norte apartment a mere half hour after Vittorio arrived. Not only had she kept the show close to schedule, her presentation of the spacious apartment and its amenities was flawless. She hit all the essentials, spoke in a camera-perfect pitch, and took extra care to note the features that matched Vittorio's wish list.

If only Vittorio noticed.

Monica stood beside the master bedroom's expansive windows to demonstrate the room's honeycomb shades, which featured a technology that allowed them to be angled one direction to filter the light while maintaining the view and another direction to completely darken the room, all at the push of a button. Monica's encouraging smile lit the room almost as well as the midday sunshine, but Vittorio only managed a polite nod before testing the shades himself.

"How about we see the master bath?" Emily gestured toward the en suite bathroom, which boasted every feature Vittorio could possibly want. Elegant, soft green glass tiles lined the walls while cream-colored tile cut to mimic the appearance of antiqued white wood covered the floor. A glass-encased shower with multiple sprays lined one wall and twin sinks with ample counter space and sleek mirrors lined the opposite side. A Japanese soaking tub situated under a high, round window dominated the space at the far end of the room. Dimmable recessed lighting and a massive sand-toned urn filled with leafy bamboo added to the room's calm atmosphere.

"What do you think? Will it suit your needs?"

"Other than the fact it's missing a toilet, yes." Vittorio shot Monica a teasing grin, but Emily noticed it didn't quite reach his eyes.

"Over here." Monica moved past the shower to open a sliding door, revealing a private space containing both a toilet and bidet.

"Impressive."

"Nothing's been overlooked. Imagine you're caught in the rain and you arrive home with damp clothes." She gestured to a chrome heated towel rack situated on the wall near the shower. "Hang them here while you warm up in the shower. When you're finished, you'll have a nicely heated towel and dry clothes, too."

Emily made a few closing comments before Rita signaled a cut, allowing everyone to transition back to the living room. "Great job, Emily and Monica. This is going to show wonderfully. Is there anything we missed, Bob?"

"I don't believe so," Vittorio answered. "Monica's been both concise and thorough."

"Perfect. Let's take a five-minute break, then we'll go again." Rita eyed the living room, making sure everything looked good for the second take, then pulled Ignacio aside to discuss the segment while Monica retreated to the foyer to make a quick call to her office.

Vittorio started toward the kitchen, but Emily put a hand on his arm, discreetly guiding him to the far side of the living room, out of earshot of Rita and Ignacio. "Hey, is something wrong?"

He gave a half-hearted shrug. "No. Why?"

"You seem off."

"Well, I did have a late night."

The lack of flirtation in his voice sent worry snaking along her spine. Worse, his delivery was cold, as if she'd offended him in some way. "Vittorio?"

At her whispered use of his real name, his golden eyes flicked toward Rita and Ignacio, then back to Emily. Deep lines creased his brow. "What do you think you're doing?"

"They didn't hear. I want to be sure I have your attention. Tell me what's going on. You seem preoccupied."

"I'd like to make an apartment decision before I fly home and this is a strong contender. There's a lot to consider. That's all."

She understood him well enough now to know there was more to it, but it wouldn't help to pester him if he wasn't in the mood to share. She summoned a smile and let go of his arm. "All right. You want a drink before we start again?"

"I'll grab a bottle of water from the kitchen." His gaze traveled past her once more. "How much longer do you think this will take?"

"Figure another half hour here, then as long as you want across the hall. Another five to ten minutes downstairs to show you the fitness facilities."

He acknowledged her with the barest of nods, then strode past her to the kitchen. As she watched him go, she caught sight of dried dirt on the apartment's wide windowsill, likely from an overzealous watering of the plants. She followed Vittorio to the kitchen long enough to grab a paper towel and dampen it, then returned to the living room, where Ignacio and Rita were finishing their discussion, and bent to wipe the low windowsill. Perhaps she shouldn't read too much into Vittorio's mood. Given the long day—and night—they'd had yesterday, exhaustion had likely set in.

"What's with Bob?"

Emily twisted to look over her shoulder at Rita, who stood with her hands planted on her hips. Ignacio was nowhere to be seen, meaning he'd likely taken a restroom break or decided to grab another croissant. "You noticed, too? I was afraid it was just me."

"It's not obvious, but he seems distracted." Very quietly, she asked, "Should I be worried?"

Emily blotted the last of the dirt and rose. "What do you mean?"

Rita reached out to take the wadded paper towel from Emily. "When we were at our wits' end for the episode and you went across the street to introduce yourself to Mr. Gorgeous, I was all for it. And I was thrilled when you told me later that he'd agreed to do the show. But…I don't know. Today's making me uneasy."

"He's been perfect," Emily argued, surprised at the depth of Rita's concern. "We've seen a good variety of properties, he was perfect for soccer and tango—we certainly ended up with a better story to tell than we would've had with the Winstons—and he's been nothing but gracious. Maybe he's preoccupied today, but all of us have our off days."

"I know, but…I can't put my finger on it. We've never done so little research on a guest. In fact, we've done none. We don't even know his full name. There's no going back now, but what if he turns out to be a criminal hiding from the law? What if—"

Given that Vittorio hadn't done anything out of the ordinary— other than look distracted—Emily suddenly realized what really concerned Rita. "Are you asking for the show? Or for me?"

A guilty grimace crumpled her features. "I should be asking for the show. But in reality? I'm far more worried about you." Her eyes flicked toward the kitchen, then back to Emily. "I know I've been encouraging you to show a little passion, to have fun with him. But then I saw how he looked at you yesterday when you were at the *practica*, like he wanted to consume you. More importantly, I saw how *you* looked at *him* when you thought none of us were paying attention. I've never seen you look at a man like that. Not even Paul."

Consume her? "Rita, no—"

"Then you two stayed after everyone else, and he's acting odd now" —she raised her hand, palm out, to stop Emily from saying anything— "I just want to be sure everything's all right. That something didn't go wrong after I left. Especially if my perpetual match-making caused it."

"Of course not." Emily concentrated on keeping her voice well-modulated so she wouldn't sound like a kid caught with her hand in the cookie jar. "The man's been apartment hunting all week. He got his skull cracked at a rowdy stadium a few days ago, then yesterday he danced for hours. Maybe it's catching up to him. It doesn't mean that anything happened between the two of us or that he's a criminal hiding from the law. I mean...could you imagine? The guy's as far from a hoodlum as anyone I've met."

"Maybe you're right. Maybe I'm reading too much into it, given that it's the last day and my stress level is through the roof. You know how I get when we're so close to wrapping up an episode, let alone a season." She blew out a breath and forked a hand through her dark hair. "I admit, I expected this apartment to rock his world. He seemed fine over croissants and was looking around the kitchen like he was impressed with the layout and decor, but once Monica arrived and we started filming, he...I don't know. He's saying all the right things, so I'm sure we'll be fine."

"I'm sure we will be, too." Part of her knew it'd be best to drop the issue, but another part wondered if they'd hit on a topic that agitated him. "So what were you talking about over breakfast?"

"After that first kiss poll?" Rita shrugged. "The concert I attended last night. Our previous jobs. Oh, and I saw that Valerie left *Today's Royals*, so Maryam and I chatted about her a little—just for sport—then I told him that after you left the magazine, you came to me with your idea for the show and I knew we'd be able to sell it. He asked a few polite questions, and that was about it until Monica arrived."

"Did he ask why I left the magazine?" Though she'd told Vittorio about the circumstances last night, perhaps he had more questions... not that Rita would share that information. She knew what had happened with Paul was personal.

"Nope. Never came up." A wry smile rose to her lips. "Unless our man Bob is related to Valerie somehow, I doubt anything we said is what's bothering him now."

"Then let's chalk it up to apartment-hunting burnout." Or morning after regrets, in which case she'd face the issue later.

Ignacio returned then, indicating that everyone was ready. The second take went much as the first, though Emily did notice Vittorio making more of an effort. However, it was the effort itself that bothered her. With the previous apartments they'd viewed, he'd been a natural, speaking as if he'd been born to the camera, able to comment at precisely the right moment and move to the spots that afforded the best camera angles without having to be pointed there. Today, he acted as if he were going through the motions, like a broadcaster who'd awakened with a migraine and had no choice but to barrel through the morning news with a smile.

She swore to herself as she followed Rita to the kitchen. *That's it.*

Vittorio had given her enough clues, hadn't he? He worked long hours and had a lot of responsibility. He knew how to move in front of a camera, even in a situation as challenging as yesterday's tango lesson. He was reluctant to share his name. He looked hauntingly familiar, yet she couldn't place him. He seemed acquainted with the stresses of her position and his demeanor had changed after Rita and Maryam discussed *Today's Royals*.

He had to have worked in the business. Perhaps still did. And despite the fact Rita had been joking about his knowing Valerie Dempsey, he just might.

As they continued their walk-through, Emily mentally catalogued the reporters she'd met during her time at *Today's Royals*. Though she'd covered royalty solely for print, many of those who'd staked out royal weddings, births, and other events were on-air personalities. Given his name, Vittorio may have had ties to an Italian-language network. For all she knew, they'd shared donuts or coffee outside a hospital once upon a time while waiting for the announcement of a royal birth.

They moved into the master bathroom, with Emily asking the same questions as before and Vittorio again making his where's-the-toilet comment. As he studied the soaking tub and the sinks for the camera, Emily studied him. If Vittorio worked in the business, she should be able to determine where.

"And cut," Rita called. "Monica, that was fabulous."

"Thank you," Monica gushed as Rita led them back to the kitchen, where Monica had stashed her handbag and a folder full of information for Vittorio. "I love showing apartments in Barrio Norte, especially units like these that have been refurbished on the inside while preserving the Belle Epoque architecture on the outside."

"I can understand why." Rita replied. "We really appreciate that you were able to get here, given the emergency in the office. You've made it possible for us to wrap on time."

"And for me to see an apartment I might've overlooked," Vittorio added. "I doubt I'd have found this place on my own before heading home."

"Where's home?" Monica asked as she handed him a folder with information on the apartments. "I keep meaning to ask."

"Southern Europe." He gestured toward the door, making it apparent that, once again, he wasn't going to be more specific. "I'm looking forward to seeing the other apartment. Does it get the afternoon sun?"

"And a spectacular view of the sunset," she assured him. "Makes it very relaxing when you get home from a long day."

"Why don't you go ahead?" Emily said. "We'll have Ignacio do a quick panoramic shot of the unit, but otherwise we're not planning to film over there, so look at your leisure. I'll be over in a few minutes. I need to check on something first."

Rita indicated that she'd accompany them and urged Maryam to come along, while Ignacio said he wanted to take a few final shots inside the furnished apartment now that the light shifted further west. As soon as everyone scattered, Emily grabbed her phone and started flicking through the web pages of foreign news and gossip programs, particularly those that specialized in covering royalty. A few faces on the staff profiles pages looked familiar, though none resembled Vittorio. When Ignacio reentered the kitchen and indicated that he was heading across the hall, she gave him a wave and promised to join everyone shortly.

More and more, she was convinced she'd seen Vittorio before, and somehow it related to her job at *Today's Royals*. Given that they were about to have a second one-night stand, she burned to know everything she could about him.

She paused on a page that caught her eye. Her Italian was mostly limited to words that pertained to food, but the photo beneath the headline was enough to still her breath. With trembling fingers, she expanded the photo so she could see more detail.

It can't be.

Dazed, she dropped into one of the kitchen chairs and stared at the screen. The man in the photo had short hair and was clean-shaven, but the eyes...there was no mistaking Vittorio's eyes. A few clicks gave her a roughly translated version of the article. The man in the photo was identified as Sarcaccia's Prince Alessandro. Not Bob, or Victor, or even Vittorio. And Alessandro had been away—or missing, depending on whether one quoted the royal family or royal watchers—for almost five months. He hadn't attended a public event since the funeral of his twin brother's former girlfriend, Spanish actress Carmella Rivas, in October. The article stated that Alessandro's parents, King Carlo and Queen Fabrizia, said that the prince was merely traveling in an area with limited communication, as he often did, and that they expected him to return to the country soon.

He's a prince. A real, living, breathing European prince. No wonder he'd looked familiar. She couldn't fathom what he was doing in Argentina, let alone on her show. Or with *her*.

She tapped the screen to search for more information even as she wracked her brain for what she knew of the Sarcaccian royals. She hadn't been assigned to cover them while at *Today's Royals*—they'd been part of Valerie's beat—but they were familiar to everyone on the staff. The family name was Barrali—not so different from Barr, the name Vittorio had scribbled on the paperwork—and there were six children. Identical twins were the oldest. She clicked on another article and studied the image of Prince Alessandro that popped up on her screen. Taken as he and his twin exited a limousine at Carmella Rivas's funeral, he looked every inch a royal with his dark suit and tie topped by a long woolen coat. Even with the difference in facial hair and dress, the resemblance to the man across the hall was uncanny.

And while it disturbed her that the man she'd come to know had used his brother's name, she supposed if one wanted to travel and keep their identity hidden, why not use a twin's?

But to do it when they made love, and when he'd told her in a choked voice of the tragedy that caused him to flee—

She closed her eyes as the entirety of the truth slammed through her. Last night he'd said it was his brother who told him to leave home, to travel and get some perspective. And if the story he'd told her about his former girlfriend was really his brother's story, well, he was better at acting than Carmella Rivas.

He is *Vittorio.*

He wasn't the one using his twin's name; his twin was using his, posing as the crown prince back in Sarcaccia, leading the world to believe that Alessandro was simply off on another long-term adventure.

She expanded the photograph of the twins, moving back and forth between the two faces, attempting to distinguish them. She couldn't.

Emily put her hand to her mouth and leaned back in her chair. She'd just stumbled onto what was possibly one of the world's biggest scandals, but the shock of it paled in comparison to the feeling she'd been personally deceived. He wasn't a run-of-the-mill European businessman looking for a vacation home as she'd first suspected, and he certainly wasn't a reporter. He was the crown prince of one of the world's last true monarchies. A billionaire with financial interests around the world.

What in the world had he seen in her, when he could have any woman? Why had he *slept* with her, then asked her on a second date? She could've sworn there was more to it than sex, that he'd actually cared about her. Now she wasn't so sure.

Tension sent pain spiking through her temples and hot tears springing to her eyes. Much as she and Vittorio had spoken as if there could be nothing long term between them, deep inside, she knew she wanted more, whatever *more* might mean. Never had a man intrigued her as Vittorio did. When he'd jumped into her cab and grilled her about the show, then agreed to appear on camera, she'd been floored by his generosity. He'd treated everyone he met as if they were his equal. She'd loved their talks in the park, the way she felt in his arms when they danced, the humorous spark in his eyes whenever she called him Bob. The way he'd raced through the crowd at a chaotic stadium when he'd worried about her safety.

He was everything she could want in a lover and friend. But that fantasy could never exist with Prince Vittorio Barrali.

CHAPTER 19

"Damn," Emily whispered, her throat tightening. She had no right to want a future with him, prince or not. No right to feel deceived. But she did.

Then again, he likely felt deceived, too, if he'd learned that she used to work for a royalty magazine. Double damn. No wonder he'd been aloof during the shoot. She had to talk to him, to tell him she now knew his identity and to make it clear she wouldn't betray him, even if he hadn't been completely up front with her. That she hadn't purposely hidden where she'd worked.

Animated voices came from the foyer. Emily shoved her phone into the side pocket of her handbag, blotted her eyes with the pads of her fingers, then rushed to the door with a smile pasted on her face. "Sorry about that. Are you done already?"

"Not much to see. Same apartment with different cabinetry and different views," Rita said. "Ignacio's taking a quick panoramic shot of the living room, then all we have left is the ground floor fitness center."

"Great." She turned to Vittorio. "Well, what do you think?"

"They're both good choices. If I were to buy in this building, I'd go with the first unit." He gestured toward Monica. "It sounds like I can negotiate the furniture into the price, which would save me the headache of shopping."

"Great." Emily sounded like a broken record, but it was easier to answer on autopilot than risk giving away the fact her head was spinning with questions. She desperately wanted to get Vittorio alone. She was about to suggest that she go back through the first apartment with him—claiming she wanted to be sure they'd left nothing behind while offering Vittorio the opportunity for a final look—when Maryam ushered everyone into the elevator, saying she'd close up the apartments and bring the keys down to Monica in the interest of saving time.

A half hour later, with filming complete, the entire group stood in the lobby. Rita spoke on behalf of the crew as she thanked "Bob" for the time and effort he'd given to the show. She handed him a gift certificate for more tango lessons, which drew a hearty round of applause, then revealed that she'd also gotten a soccer ball signed by members of the Boca Juniors, which she presented to Vittorio along with a box of bandages signed by the *At Home Abroad* staff. "We've never had an injury on the show and thought it should be commemorated," she said.

Vittorio moved through the group, shaking hands and wishing everyone well. Emily couldn't help but notice how he made each person feel as if they'd made his time special, a skill he'd likely learned from his parents as they prepped him for his future role as a monarch. He even asked Rita to be sure to let Mike know what a great time he'd had at the soccer game. Finally, he came to Emily.

"Ah, my tango partner." He took her hand and flashed her the same warm smile he'd offered everyone else, giving no indication of the intimacy that had occurred between them. "I'm honored to have danced with the show's host. Thank you for convincing me that this would be fun."

Her breath hitched as she imagined him lying in bed beside her, teasing her about having fun. Cognizant of her colleagues' eyes on her, Emily smiled warmly and said, "It was fun for all of us as well. I know you have a lot of properties to consider, but I hope you'll give us a call once you've come to a decision. We'd love to update our viewers."

"Of course." He angled his body so his back was to the others. "I'll be in touch soon."

The words were polite, but his eyes conveyed a deeper message. Before she could respond, he waved a final thanks to everyone, then disappeared through the glass doors and merged with the foot traffic on the street.

"On that note, I'll take my leave, as well," Monica said. She thanked everyone for the opportunity to have her agency and listings featured, then headed back to her flooded office to check on the cleanup.

"Another season down," Rita said, clapping her hands together. "Mike and the rest of the support staff will meet us at the restaurant in a few hours to celebrate. Until then, everyone rest up. It's going to be a wonderful night."

And a long one, Emily thought, for her most of all.

***

AT PRECISELY FIVE minutes before eight on Saturday night, Vittorio took a seat on the bench outside the florist shop near Emily's bed and breakfast. Despite the exhaustion that overwhelmed him when he'd returned from filming the previous day, he'd gotten little sleep. The idea that Emily might uncover his identity haunted him. If she did, it was his own damned fault. Not for being on her show—he'd prepared for that to be discovered and had warned Alessandro as well—but for opening his soul to her. He'd known he was making himself vulnerable when he'd told her about Carmella, and he cursed himself for it now. But even if Emily didn't make the connection, even if she never knew his real name and position, it galled him that he'd believed her to have a purity of spirit that made her worthy of sharing his deepest pain. No one who worked for *Today's Royals* and loved their job could.

Though the sun had set, the metal bench remained warm. He leaned forward so moisture wouldn't seep through his shirt. Skipping their date wasn't an option. If Emily knew his identity, he'd only be able to assess the damage by seeing her before he flew home and looking her in the eye. And if she didn't, he didn't want to pique her curiosity by failing to show.

He glanced down the street. Seeing no sign of Emily, he propped his elbows on his knees and massaged his temples. The gut-churning horror he'd felt yesterday after learning the truth had morphed into a persistent headache, one that two hefty doses of ibuprofen failed to deaden. Needing to occupy himself after his night of tossing and turning, he'd packed his few belongings, confirmed his flight for Sunday night, then scanned apartment brochures. That had taken him a whopping hour. He'd jumped on his rented bike in an attempt to enjoy his last day of freedom, but found himself in an Internet café by midafternoon, searching for the articles Emily had published with *Today's Royals*.

As Rita had said, Emily had covered a few weddings and had written extensively about the battery trial of a male cousin to the Swedish royal family. The tone of Emily's work was sensationalistic, as was the tone of every article in the magazine, but rather than focus on the man who'd committed the crime or attribute his behavior to the family, Emily's pieces focused on the trial itself. One article covered testimony given by the Stockholm police, another the intricacies of the Swedish legal system. A guide to the Swedish royals and their traditions ran alongside a profile of the victim, a race car driver who'd apparently had a longstanding feud with the cousin over a woman they'd both dated.

Vittorio had almost admitted to himself that Emily's work wasn't so bad when he came across an article about the exorbitant sum spent by a Dutch princess while on a shopping trip to Istanbul. Emily noted that over a two-week period, antique lamps, dozens of handwoven rugs, towels, and spa products were ordered and shipped at a cost nearing a million U.S. dollars to a home the princess had recently built. While Vittorio had no doubt the story was true, the article was exactly the type he abhorred. It said nothing of whether the money was from the princess's personal funds, which were vast, or from her annual state allowance. He'd bet anything that the purchases were made using her personal funds. More than that, the article made it sound like the princess was a spendthrift who had nothing better to do with her time than shop. No mention was made of her extensive charitable work or the fact that following her trip to Turkey she'd spent nearly three weeks in Haiti, where she'd contributed both her time and personal funds to help build a hospital and two schools for those in need.

If that was how she portrayed the Dutch princess, a woman he knew to be above reproach, what would Emily do with her knowledge of Vittorio's relationship with Carmella? Or the pregnancy?

He'd shut off the computer in disgust, returned his bicycle to the rental shop, then walked back to his hotel to change for his date, a date he now dreaded.

Pressing his thumbs to his brow, he resolved to keep a smile on his face and give away nothing. He'd let Emily guide the conversation, assuming she showed up for the date. For all he knew, she'd gotten all the information she needed and was preparing to release it to the world.

He muttered an oath, telling himself to stop playing guessing games.

"Vittorio?"

His head snapped up. Emily stood before him, worry etching her beautiful face. She'd worn her hair pinned up, likely due to the unseasonably warm weather, and sported a soft green dress with thin straps that highlighted her smooth skin and large hazel eyes.

Before he could answer her, she was on the bench beside him, her hand on his forearm. "I'm sorry I'm late. Are you all right? You look like you're nursing a headache."

"I am." Damn if he didn't follow it with, "But it's better now that you're here."

She fairly beamed. "That is the cheesiest line ever."

"Perhaps. But it's true." He and his twin had truly switched roles now, because he was thinking with his nether regions, just like Alessandro at his worst. The mere touch of her fingertips against his skin made him want to pull her body against his, to kiss away all thoughts of their circumstances, to give her the benefit of the doubt.

She must have read the conflicted emotions in his expression, because her eyes clouded and she eased her hand from his arm. "Did you get a reservation for dinner? Do we need to get moving?"

"I thought we could walk through the neighborhood and see what catches our fancy."

"So no hurry, then." Her smile seemed forced, very much like the smile she'd given him when he'd left the apartment yesterday. "In that case, before we eat, I was hoping we could talk."

The pounding in his head returned full force. "How about if we walk and talk?"

At her nod, he indicated that they should head in the direction opposite her bed and breakfast. They made it nearly two blocks before she spoke. "You were quieter than usual during the apartment tour yesterday morning, even though you seemed fine in the elevator when you arrived. Since we're alone now, do you care to tell me what happened?"

He glanced at the menu posted outside a steakhouse before answering. "Contrary to the gut-spilling I did in bed, I tend to keep my thoughts private."

"So something was bothering you."

"Nothing I wanted to discuss. Besides, I wouldn't have wanted to give any hints to your coworkers about what happened between us, especially given our earlier conversation about how hard you work to appear professional. Whispering in a corner of the apartment with you would've done that."

"You don't want to discuss it now, either?"

"You're persistent, aren't you?" He took her elbow to guide her around a young couple unloading shopping bags from the back of a taxi. "I suppose I should've known that from the way you staked out a luxury apartment on the off chance I'd show up."

"And, as I recall, you demanded to know who was employing me, even though I'd already told you my name and that I was the host of a television show." She stopped walking when they reached an empty stretch of sidewalk in front of a dry cleaner that had closed for the night. When he paused as well, she said, "Vittorio...I'll just come out and say it. I think I know who you are."

"I can assure you, my name isn't Bob." Though he teased, he felt the color draining from his face. She didn't think she knew who he was. She *knew*. He could see it in the way she twisted the fingers of one hand in the skirt of her dress, hear it in the nervous note that crept into her voice as she looked around to ensure no one was listening to them.

"I kept thinking that I knew you from somewhere. That we'd worked together or that I might've met you during the season *At Home Abroad* filmed in the Alps. But we've never met, have we?" She didn't wait for a response. Instead, she reached up to smooth her hand over his cheek. "It was the beard and long hair that threw me off. You're normally clean-shaven, and you've never had your hair long enough for the waves to show. You usually keep it short enough to pass a military inspection."

"You don't want to go down this path, Emily." He grinned, hoping against hope for a reprieve he knew wasn't coming.

Her eyes narrowed as she dropped her hand from his face. "It was Rita, wasn't it, telling you that we used to work together at *Today's Royals*? That's what threw you off yesterday. When you went across the hall, I started looking up competing publications, wondering if you were on staff at one of our competitors and I'd somehow forgotten meeting you. But you've never covered royalty, have you? Or worked as a journalist?"

There was nothing he could say, nothing that would save him, so he remained silent, waiting for her to drop the axe.

"I saw an article about Prince Alessandro. He hasn't been seen in public for almost five months. He's one of six children. He lives in a home with antiquated floors and windows, heavy crown molding, and electrical and plumbing systems older than your grandparents," she said, repeating the very words he'd used when describing his upbringing to her. "And he looks exactly like you...but with shorter hair and far more formal clothing."

"Whatever you're thinking, you're wrong." A family spilled out of the building beside the dry cleaner. Two school-aged children barreled past Vittorio and Emily while the parents wrestled with a stroller and called for the older kids to stop and wait. Vittorio angled his head to indicate Emily should walk with him. He kept a quick pace, not caring that she had to race to keep up. He wasn't sure where he was headed; he only knew they couldn't speak in the middle of a city sidewalk. When they passed a narrow backstreet, she grabbed his arm and pulled him toward it.

"You're going to accost me in a dark alley?" He tried for flirtation, but didn't quite accomplish it. "And here I anticipated a warm bed."

"Stop it. Just stop it." A mix of fear and anger flared in her gaze as she paused just inside the alley, where they were away from curious eyes and ears.

"Emily—" He didn't keep the note of warning from his voice.

"I don't think you're Prince Alessandro. I think you're Prince Vittorio. Your brother hasn't disappeared at all. You have." She stepped closer, but didn't touch him. A breeze caught the hem of her dress and blew tendrils of her hair across her face, but she ignored it, keeping her eyes locked with his. "The story you told me about your girlfriend, it was Carmella Rivas, wasn't it? And the producer in Berlin…I saw that a man she'd done several projects with was there at the time. Vittorio, I'm so sorry. It all made sense once I figured it out."

"What made sense?"

"When I showed up at the Palermo apartment that afternoon. You asked who hired me. If I was following you. You thought I was a reporter or a private investigator, didn't you?"

She wasn't going to let it go. Hot, uncontrolled anger surged within him. His words came out with a snarl as he retorted, "Turns out you were."

"Past tense." She brushed a hand against the front of his shirt, as if she could sense the fury rising within him and thought she could stem it. "I wasn't trying to hide it from you."

He fought for restraint, but it was a losing battle. "Didn't that feel dirty, delving into other people's private lives for profit? Who did it benefit? Oh…I know…it benefitted a corporate ledger. A group of faceless, nameless shareholders. And it kept you employed in a job you *loved*."

He knew he sounded like an ass, but he wanted nothing more than to lash out at her. He felt betrayed, dammit, by the woman who'd made him feel more alive, more at home in his own skin, than any he'd ever met. She'd done it in a matter of days. Now she wanted to run him through a shredder, bringing up what he'd made clear he didn't wish to discuss.

"I reported on their public lives, not their private ones. I wasn't digging through their trash barrels or interviewing their exes about their relationships." Her eyes widened as she realized what she'd said. "I'm sorry. That was a terrible example—"

"But an accurate one. It's what all those magazines and gossip shows do. They make money by showing my family at its worst. Or, in some cases, making up stories."

"I'd never do that." She sucked in her lower lip and swallowed hard, as if she were fighting to hold herself together. "Vittorio, you have to know your secret is safe with me. I don't work there anymore."

"What I know is that you have a show that's in trouble. I know you'd do anything for your staff, because they're like family to you. You feel responsible for them. And wouldn't it be something if a missing prince showed up in your finale, rather than average, boring Bob? If you broke a royal scandal, complete with an actress and a secret pregnancy, cheating and suicide and twins switching places?"

She stumbled backward at the vitriol in his tone. Unshed tears glittered in her eyes as she whispered, "Why'd you do it?"

"Why I'd do *what*?" he demanded. As if he hadn't told her everything while they were lying in bed together. He hadn't learned a damned thing from Carmella.

"Why did you agree to do the show if you were in hiding?" Her eyes searched his face, as if she'd be able to see into his mind. "And why…why *me*? Why tonight?"

He propped himself against the alley's cold brick wall and crossed his arms over his chest. She had no idea how she'd enticed him. How he'd appreciated her generosity of spirit. How beguiling he found her, from the way she laughed to the way she danced to the way she alternately teased him and screamed for him when they made love. How he'd been drawn to the nurturing manner in which she'd listened while he'd spilled his guts. How he'd fallen for her, hook, line, and sinker.

He let out a long, painful breath. "If you have to ask, you don't know me at all."

"Apparently, I don't. And you don't know me if you think I'm the type who'd sell out your family for a few bucks." Her voice was raw as she took a few steps backward, toward the main street. "Go home, Vittorio. See your parents. Do your job and I'll do mine."

"Emily, wait—"

"No. I think it's best if we skip the rest of our evening. I was never the one-night stand type, anyway. No point in a second." A wistful smile graced her face for a brief moment before she said, "Thank you for doing the show. It was an honor to have you. Goodbye, Vittorio. Your Highness."

With that, she turned and strode back toward her hotel. The stiff set of her shoulders and determination in her walk made it clear she didn't want him to come after her.

He counted to ten, then followed, keeping his distance as she threaded her way through the families and handholding couples who strolled the sidewalks in search of the perfect Recoleta restaurants. He didn't stop until she ascended the stairs to her bed and breakfast, then disappeared through the door. He waited near the sidewalk's edge for a long moment, watched as a light flickered to life on the third floor, then turned and strode back to his own hotel room.

Part of him wanted Emily to know who he was, title and all, faults and all. But another part of him wanted to attack her for having worked at the very publication that would capitalize on those faults. For keeping that information from him, when it likely would've swayed his decision to appear on her show…though she couldn't have possibly known that.

It wasn't until he shut the door to his room and saw his packed bag and itinerary waiting for him at the end of the bed—and the flowers he'd put on the nightstand for her in hopes she'd be there again tonight—that he realized he'd fallen in love with Emily Sinclair.

He hadn't handled it well. He certainly hadn't been prepared for her to walk away.

CHAPTER 20

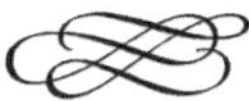

Vittorio awoke with the knowledge another human being was in the room. The familiar smell of the palace's crisp sheets mixed with another scent, one he'd known far longer than that of the latest laundry soap. He cracked an eye to a room cloaked in darkness save for the glow of the lamp he'd left on in the adjoining living room. Gradually, he picked out the female silhouette in the chair near the windows.

"Good morning, sweetheart." His mother's voice was soft, suited to the early hour. "I'm not sure whether to welcome you home and tell you how grateful I am to see you, or to order you to shower and shave."

Vittorio pushed to a seated position so he could better see Queen Fabrizia. Though the room's heavy draperies were drawn, the first rays of dawn crept in around the edges, allowing him to see her hands folded in her lap.

"How did you get in here?"

"I could ask you the same thing," she replied. "Only the rear guards saw you enter, and it was much later than I'd anticipated."

"Flight delay." He rubbed a hand over his head. Now that he was back in the palace, the long hair felt wildly out of place.

"Does your brother know you're here?"

"I wouldn't be sleeping in his apartment if he did. Figured I'd let him stay in mine until I have the chance to shave." He'd need to see Alessandro in the flesh before they could switch back to their normal roles. Not only would Alessandro need to get Vittorio caught up on palace business, Vittorio needed to duplicate his brother's haircut and ensure the tan he'd developed while bike riding through Buenos Aires wasn't deep enough to differentiate them.

"Wise of you." She rose from the chair and strode to the bed, clicking the lamp on the nightstand to its lowest setting, then surprising him by taking a seat on the edge of the mattress and rubbing his calf through the covers. "I missed you terribly, you know. I've never been so worried about one of my children. Not even Massimo, when he was fighting in Africa, though I'd appreciate it if you don't tell him that."

"Mother, I'm fine."

She nodded her acceptance. The queen was dressed for the day in a smart-looking sheath dress of chocolate wool accented by a thin gold necklace and diamond stud earrings. Her hair was down today, rather than in her usual bun. Given the precise ends of her long blonde bob, he suspected she'd had it cut recently. On first glance, she appeared as lean and fit as always, but a closer inspection revealed new hollows in her cheeks and darkened skin beneath her eyes.

"Other than the worry I've caused you, is everything all right with you?"

"Now that you're home, yes, all is well. Stefano and Megan's wedding plans are coming along nicely. And Kelly has moved into the palace with Massimo, though we've managed to keep that quiet."

"And Alessandro?"

"He's done a surprisingly good job in your absence. Your father has handled as many of the government functions as possible, leaving the social engagements to Alessandro." Unspoken was the need for Vittorio to pick up his usual state functions, and as soon as possible.

The queen rose from the bed, smoothed the front of her dress, then smiled down on him. "Sleep for another hour or so. I'll ensure

Alessandro knows you're here, then you two need to formulate a story about where 'Alessandro' has been the last few months. There will be questions."

He bit back a groan. "Press conference?"

"No. We've said all along that you—your brother—merely left on another one of his expeditions. A press conference would grant that more importance than it warrants. We'll simply allow word to trickle out from the staff that Alessandro has returned." She gave him one last smile before she turned off the bedside lamp and strode to the door. "Keep me apprised of what you decide and I'll tell your siblings and your father. We need our stories to be consistent."

"Understood."

Her heels clicked across the apartment's hardwood floor, paused, then came back. He was watching for her as she leaned back into his room.

"Once you're cleaned up, you need to see Dominic," she instructed, referring to the palace's longtime head chef. "He announced his retirement while you were gone. Today's his last day. He's moving to London to be closer to his children. They're both working in the financial sector there."

"You're kidding." Dominic had been a fixture in the palace since before Vittorio's birth and ran the kitchens with the precision of a drill sergeant. "I can't imagine him kicking back in a rocking chair or puttering in a garden."

"He bought an old house just outside of London and has plans to restore it. He's adding a new kitchen and plans to start a part-time catering business. I tracked down his contractor last week and gave the man a call. Your father and I are going to surprise Dominic by paying for the kitchen. We think it's appropriate, don't you?"

"It's brilliant. He'll protest, though."

"He's earned it." She gestured toward the messy bed coverings. "You sleep. See Alessandro and Dominic later."

He waited for the sound of the apartment door closing behind his mother before he eased back against the pillows, grimacing at the ache in his lower back, neck, and shoulders. In an effort to blend in with other travelers, he'd opted for cheap seats near the back of the plane, first from Buenos Aires to Paris, then from Paris to Rome, though that flight was delayed nearly three hours. Once he was certain he hadn't been recognized or followed, he booked a puddle jumper from Rome to Cateri. He hadn't slept a wink his entire time in transit. He could easily attribute it to the uncomfortable seats or the need to listen for flight changes at airports, but it was more than that. Emily dominated his thoughts.

Rolling to his side, he squinted against the encroaching dawn. The room had appeared just like this—a blend of shadows and early morning light—when he'd awakened with Emily in his hotel bed a few days ago. He'd been on his side with her spooned in front of him, the back of her head resting against the front of his shoulder. Low, even breathing signaled she was deeply asleep, the kind of slumber reserved for those who were truly sated. He'd remained still, unwilling to wake her, and inhaled slowly. He'd wanted to remember her light, airy scent—so reminiscent of sunshine after a rain shower—and the way it blended with the more sensual fragrance that lingered in the room after a night of lovemaking. Carefully, so as not to disturb her, he'd spread Emily's hair between his fingers, noticing the myriad shades of blonde and copper strands that combined to create her lustrous honey hue. And he'd been entranced.

When she'd awakened, she'd wiggled tighter against him, reached for the back of his thigh, and sighed. If he'd have died and gone to heaven in that moment, he'd have had no objections.

He allowed his eyes to drift closed, to imagine she was once more in his arms, in his bed. If only he could turn back the clock to that morning, before he knew her full background. When he'd seen only her zest for life, borne out by the joy he witnessed in her face when she listened to the crowd singing at the *fútbol* match or when she danced in his arms. The passion with which they'd made love.

He'd been completely taken by her ability to surround herself with smart, talented, likable people and by her fierce drive to make a success of herself. Her instinct to protect those who worked for her. Her graciousness and generosity.

Driving a hand through his thick, overgrown hair, he swore aloud. He still couldn't conceive a person like Emily working for *Today's Royals*. It would be like his mother working for a tabloid.

The thought sent a guffaw rumbling through his body. Emily *was* a lot like his mother, come to think of it. Emily was deeply emotional, yet she hid her emotions when necessary and projected a sense of tranquility that calmed those around her. She was a natural leader, one who worked efficiently while juggling the multiple projects that would achieve her greater goal. Yet through all her daily stresses, she expressed her appreciation for all those around her, just as his mother made it clear to every palace employee that she cared about their well-being. His mother's idea of purchasing a new kitchen for her retiring head chef was exactly the type of thing Emily would do if she had the resources.

Fabrizia also loved her family fiercely. She would do anything for her children—even cover up one's disappearance, should they need a mental break—and looked at her husband with both admiration and desire in her emerald gaze, even after forty-plus years of a marriage that had seen its ups and downs. She was loyal to a fault. And, above all, she was protective.

Vittorio whipped off the covers and stretched his aching muscles. Now that the cogs of his mind were spinning, sleep was impossible. Wearing only his boxers, he strode through Alessandro's apartment. The layout was identical to that of his and his siblings' palace apartments. Each consisted of a master bedroom, bath, and walk-in closet at the rear of the space. The bedroom suite was accessible through a door at the back of an expansive, fireplaced living room that occupied the majority of the square footage. Windows stretched from floor to ceiling and overlooked the palace gardens, providing a spectacular view and flooding the living room with light when the heavy draperies weren't drawn, as they were now. A library and a smaller bathroom were connected to the living room through a short hallway, while a minuscule kitchen sat on the opposite side of the main room. While the decor was ornate, in keeping with the scale of the grand palace, it wasn't a space meant for the public eye. Personal photos of Alessandro and his friends, taken on various trips around the world, topped the corner desk. Several were snapped at parties, with copious amounts of alcohol and scantily dressed women in evidence, while others showed the men in their climbing gear. A book on Tibet and another on Egyptian archeology rested atop the coffee table alongside an antique Turkish urn that contained God-knew-what. A carved wooden statue with grotesquely out of proportion female anatomy sat on the coffee table's lower shelf.

He and Alessandro might appear identical, but their tastes were far from it.

Vittorio locked the main door to the suite to keep any of the staff from inadvertently walking in on him before he made his way to the kitchen. Though Alessandro had stayed in Vittorio's own apartment for the duration of their switch, the staff kept the kitchen stocked with the bare essentials in the event the wayward prince returned: bread, milk, cheese, cereal, fresh fruit, and several varieties of cold cuts. He opted for the cereal. On a hunch, he sniffed the milk before pouring it over the flakes, then promptly emptied the container in the sink. He could eat it dry. He grabbed the bowl and spun toward the living room only to be faced with a smirking Alessandro.

"Well, don't you look like hell."

"How'd you get in here?" It came out with bite, giving away Vittorio's shock at his brother's noiseless approach.

"My apartment. I have a code." Alessandro leaned against the door frame and aimed his gaze at the bowl. "You're not going to throw that at me for entering my own residence, are you?"

"No onions. You're safe."

"Good. Bad enough seeing you in your underwear and with that growth on your face. That's hideous."

"You don't look like you've showered or shaved, either."

Alessandro ran a hand over his chin, which bore only a day's worth of stubble. "Mother told me to see you first thing."

"I doubt she meant to come now."

"I thought it better to duck in before the day shift arrives. No one saw me enter." Alessandro pushed off the door frame with his shoulder and sauntered to the living room, where he sat on the sofa instead of flopping, as was his tendency. Despite Vittorio's comment about his twin's grooming habits, Alessandro appeared more regal than usual. Perhaps a few months walking in Vittorio's shoes imbued Alessandro with new habits.

Vittorio took a moment to pull on pajama pants, then rejoined his brother in the living room. Once they worked out the logistics of a switch and talked about the crown prince's schedule for the week, Vittorio set down his half-eaten cereal and studied Alessandro. "What will you do now that I'm home?"

"No plans."

Alessandro always had plans. "Surely you've been itching to get out of the palace?"

"Can't do that when I just arrived home, though, can I?"

"I suppose not." Vittorio hadn't considered that the return of "Alessandro" would tie his twin to a number of engagements as the country demanded to see their wayward prince.

A sound that was half huff, half laugh escaped Alessandro. "I've been asking myself, 'What would Vittorio do?' for so long now, I've not thought about what I'd do when you return. After I'm free to leave again, I mean. It's gotten to be habit, acting like you. Extremely boring, but habit."

"What would you have wanted to do six months ago?"

His lower lip twitched, then he grinned. "My choices would've been the blonde, the brunette, or the redhead. All of whom would have perfectly round, perky breasts, of course."

"Of course."

"And they wouldn't expect a damned thing from me but a one-night stand. Maybe two if I'm feeling generous."

The image of Emily sitting astride him flashed through Vittorio's mind, sending an involuntary shudder of pain rippling through him. To cover it, he forced a lighthearted, "Your ego is out of control."

Alessandro knew him too well. "You're still a wreck about Carmella, aren't you?"

"I'm not a *wreck*. And I'm over Carmella, at least as much as a person can get over something like that."

"Then what happened in Argentina? Or should I say who? Did you meet someone? Is that why you stayed away so long?"

He wasn't going to share with Alessandro. With anyone, if he could help it, though that depended on what Emily did now that she knew his identity and had hours upon hours of film to share with the world.

Vittorio leaned forward, placing his forearms on his knees. "I have a better idea. Let's discuss what that irresponsible Prince Alessandro has been doing the past few months. We need a story to share with the press, one that can't be proven wrong."

"One that explains a five-month absence."

Vittorio caught the undercurrent in his brother's tone. "You did a very good job while I was away."

"You were gone a long time. I didn't have a choice."

"You're the one who suggested I go." He held up a hand before Alessandro could make a derisive comment. "But I know you imagined days or weeks, not months. Frankly, so did I, and I should've come home sooner." Though if he had, he wouldn't have met Emily. "Thank you. I won't forget it."

Alessandro merely nodded his acceptance. "I assume you have an idea or two about what we'll say?"

He'd thought of little else, since everything now depended on Emily. He wanted to believe she'd keep his secret, but he'd believed a woman had his best interests at heart before and been burned. In this case, it wasn't a film career at stake. It was the livelihood of an entire staff. And what Emily might choose didn't constitute a crime. He'd put himself in the position of vulnerability.

"Unfortunately, there are still loose ends in Argentina." He ignored Alessandro's inquisitive look and said, "For now, we say that you spent your time traveling extensively, primarily in South America, and you intentionally kept a low profile because it allowed you to see the world in a different way than if you'd traveled as a prince. While you enjoyed yourself, you were also working on a special project for the Crown at the behest of your brother, Vittorio. That project is still underway and details will be released as soon as your brother gives you the word. That will throw the attention back to me."

"And what is this project?"

"Details will be released." When the time was right.

"You've become almost as intentionally vague as I am." Alessandro barked out a laugh as he said it, then reached to his pocket for his cell phone and began punching in numbers. At Vittorio's questioning look, he explained, "The sun is up and staff members are arriving. We won't be able to remain unseen much longer. Time to fix your hair. You can also tell me what happened to the back of your head. That'll need to be disguised."

"You're not calling our barber." He couldn't risk having anyone outside the family—correction, anyone *else* outside the family—catch on to the switch.

"I'm calling Sophia." He made a scissor action with his fingers, then said into the phone. "Your brother's home. Why don't you visit him in his apartment once you're dressed? He'd love to see you. And tuck your scissors into your bag."

Alessandro listened for a moment, then grinned. "Yes. You have your work cut out for you. As do I."

CHAPTER 21

Cold rain pummeled the New York streets, rendering the sky, buildings, and Emily's mood the same depressing shade of gray. She and Rita had spent the morning with the film editor, watching the final cut of the two episodes that would precede the finale. Mike and Ignacio had done a spectacular job capturing the quiet beauty of Córdoba's waterways and Jesuit architecture in the first episode, then the vast scope of Buenos Aires' museums and cathedrals in the second. The real estate guests had been fantastic as well. The couple searching in Córdoba located the perfect home in which to retire, with easy access to grocery stores, restaurants, and hospitals, and in a community where they felt comfortable. The Buenos Aires episode had featured a young woman who'd first come to Buenos Aires with a study abroad program, then decided to return following her college graduation. She'd been searching for a small apartment to match her tight budget, but ended up with a more spacious place by finding a local graduate student with whom to share.

Rita tossed a pile of napkins in the middle of the table where Emily waited with her salad, then took a seat with her ham and cheese sandwich. Long hours in a dark room watching film had mentally exhausted them both. Dodging puddles in order to find a late lunch didn't help matters.

"We'll need to redo the voiceover at the end of the Córdoba episode, but other than that, we're done," Rita said once she'd had a few bites of her sandwich. "We can knock that out this afternoon, then tackle the finale."

"Sounds like a plan."

"We really nailed those two episodes. Viewers are going to love them."

Emily nodded. She couldn't keep her mind off the finale. For the last six weeks, ever since she'd arrived back in New York, she'd been plagued by thoughts of what might happen when it aired. No one knew the twins switched places. News that Prince Alessandro returned to Sarcaccia hit the European papers on the same day Prince Stefano's bride-to-be, Megan, visited an upscale wedding gown shop with their daughter, Anna. The photos of Megan and Anna exiting with smiles on their faces drew attention away from the missing prince's homecoming. It was three more days before Prince Alessandro was seen in public. He told reporters that he'd been traveling and working on a project for his brother, Vittorio, the nature of which he'd reveal when, in his words, "the time is right and all has come to fruition," promising the reporters, "I think you'll like it."

Other than bandying about theories regarding where the prince might've traveled, the story died within a few weeks as the countdown to the royal wedding—the first in a generation in Sarcaccia—fascinated the nation. The only item that bumped nuptial talk from the country's front page was the opening of Carmella Rivas's final movie. Prince Vittorio flew to Paris for its premiere and was captured outside the theater stating that he hoped many people would see it, as he believed it to be her finest work. He took the opportunity to mention the memorial fund he'd established with the late actress's family and the mental health counselors the fund provided free of charge to those contemplating suicide.

She'd watched the clip of his brief interview numerous times. Vittorio had been respectful, saying nothing but the best about

Carmella, her family, and the film, though it had been produced by the very man who'd conned him. Emily couldn't imagine the internal pain it must've caused Vittorio. As unfair as Vittorio was to her when they'd parted, as angry and hurt as she'd been when she'd turned and stalked back to her bed and breakfast, she understood his reaction when she'd accused him of being the prince and asked if his ex-girlfriend was Carmella Rivas. He'd left his wounds exposed and she'd poked at them. He'd lashed out. She'd lashed back.

But then he'd followed her.

She'd felt his presence and resisted the urge to turn around, deciding it was up to him to approach her with an apology. He didn't. But when she stood at the top of the stairs at her bed and breakfast and punched in the entry code, she caught sight of him down the street. Even from a distance, she saw the pain and wistfulness in his gaze and the set of his shoulders.

She'd pretended not to see him. She'd collapsed onto her bed and stared at the ceiling, wondering what possessed him to agree to do the show. Not that she wasn't grateful—who knows what she and Rita would've done at the last minute otherwise—but the risk he'd taken was huge. And then to kiss her, to make love to her, to cradle her foot in the palm of his hand and give her a slow, sensual massage while she wore his shirt and drank his wine…she'd crumpled the bedsheets in her fist and cried—big, messy, breath-strangling tears—for the first time in as long as she could remember.

Over the past few weeks, seeing his face in the news reports with his jaw clean-shaven and his hair cut short enough to eliminate the waves made her ache anew. And with every charity appearance, state visit, and volunteer hour he gave, she realized he'd said yes because he truly cared about those around him. He'd understood what she was trying to do when she'd wanted to use her savings to finance an extended stay in Buenos Aires to wrap the show.

He'd taken the risk for her because he'd felt it was the right thing to do.

"And then we finish with the segment where the elephant crushes the tango dancers. That will really boost our ratings. Elephants always do."

"Uh-huh." Emily took a bite of salad, then paused and looked up at Rita. "Wait. What?"

"I knew you weren't paying attention." Rita's brows drew together. "What's going on, sweetie?"

"You did not just use your mother voice on me."

"I most certainly did."

"Don't. I'm fine. Just distracted from a long day." Emily blotted her mouth with her napkin, then forked another bite of salad. "All right. Let's talk finale."

"Let's. I've been meaning to ask you…have you heard from Bob?"

She snorted at Rita's use of the name Bob. "No, why would I?"

"So we'd know if he ever decided on an apartment, for one." Rita set down her sandwich. "But judging from the guilty look on your face, it's apparent you thought I was asking for another reason. That's what's distracting you, isn't it? Something happened between you and our mystery man."

"Rita—"

"We're going to be staring at him onscreen for the next few days while we do the video and sound editing. You can come clean now, while we're alone, or you can come clean later." There was a hardness in Rita's dark gaze she'd only seen once before, when Emily shared that she was considering leaving *Today's Royals* despite the fact she was about to get a plum assignment interviewing a member of the British royal family.

"I can't talk about it." But suddenly, she wanted to. She'd kept it bottled up for weeks, and there wasn't a soul she could trust more than Rita. "Not here. My place after work if you can make it."

"Done." Rita picked up her sandwich and said, "We'll stop at the liquor store on the way. I suspect I'll want a martini for this."

Six hours later, Emily had second—and third, and fourth—thoughts about inviting Rita to her apartment as she turned the key in her door. Rita deposited the bag of takeout Chinese food on the counter and searched for plates and napkins while Emily busied herself locating a corkscrew for the wine they'd purchased in lieu of making martinis. While they prepped the food, Rita prattled about her daughter's new boyfriend, a Scot her daughter met while studying abroad in London.

"I don't know how serious they are," she finally said. "Distance makes it tough. But who knows? From all she's said, he seems like a great fit for her."

"She's a bright girl. I'm sure she'll make good decisions." Emily finally located the corkscrew in the back of a drawer, then went about opening the wine.

"And so will you." Rita scooped generous portions of food onto two plates, then carried them to the table. "So tell Momma Rita all about your troubles."

"You're the worst." Emily poured the wine, then set the bottle on the counter and shook her head. "And you're the best. That's what makes this so damned difficult."

Once Emily brought the wine glasses to the table and raised hers in a toast to their finale, she told Rita, "Before I say a word, I need to know that what I tell you won't leave this room."

The older woman waved a chopstick in the air before digging into her food. "Like I'm going to blab to the staff about your love life. Haven't done it before, wouldn't do it now."

"This is more than that."

Rita paused with her noodles halfway to her mouth and met Emily's eye. "All right."

"We share a lot, but to share this would put a huge burden on you. It's knowledge you'll want to share."

"A bigger burden than knowing why Paul left you? I've kept that to myself for years. Haven't even told my husband. And you know, it's something your friends would want to know. They care about you and they'd give you support."

"I know that, but it's not a matter I want to discuss." She let out a long breath, then said, "Neither is this, but I need to tell someone."

Rita sucked in her lower lip and set down her chopsticks. "Your cancer isn't back, isn't it?"

That elicited a smile. "No. I'm perfectly healthy."

"Thank God." Rita waved for her to continue. "In that case, anything you have to tell me pales in comparison. I can handle whatever it is and keep it quiet."

All afternoon Emily had debated how to tell Rita…and what to tell her. She'd come up with a million different openings, none of which she liked. But now, with Rita's caring, curious gaze upon her, she simply blurted, "You know Bob's real name isn't Bob."

"We discussed that the afternoon of the tango lesson. A man who looks and speaks like that isn't a Bob. Maybe a Roberto, but not a Bob."

Emily nodded. "Do you think anyone else on the staff questioned his name?"

"I doubt they thought about it one way or the other. Mike and Ignacio certainly didn't. They're oblivious to that kind of thing. Maryam might've, but if so, she didn't say anything. No one else had as much contact with him as the two of us." Rita took a sip of wine, then regarded Emily over the top of her glass. "I'm beginning to suspect that you had plenty of contact."

She nodded. Plenty, but not enough.

"First time since Paul?" At Emily's second nod, she whistled. "Long time, then."

"His name is Vittorio. Vittorio Barrali."

"Vittorio Barrali? I swear, I think I know that name." Subtle pleats appeared on Rita's forehead as she set down her wine and took a bite of her noodles. Then her eyes widened. "Emily! *Prince Vittorio?* From Sarcaccia? But he didn't look like…how could he possibly—"

"Now do you see what I mean by burdening you with knowledge you'd want to share?"

"*Today's Royals.*" The words came from Rita like a curse. "Maryam and I talked about you working there and how much you loved it. He asked us about it. Oh my gosh. I'm so embarrassed. I can't believe… you're saying I've met a prince?" She put her hand to her forehead. "I'm such an idiot. And you walked right up to him in a café and asked him to be on our show!"

"I had no idea who he was, only that he looked familiar to me. And he had no idea I used to work for the magazine. But that afternoon you and Maryam discussed the magazine and he started acting odd, I figured it out." She gave Rita a quick overview of what she'd discovered and that it was Vittorio, not Alessandro, who was gone for so long, though the Barrali family had led the world to believe it was Alessandro.

"It's completely believable," Rita said when Emily finished. "I'm not surprised they've actually gotten away with it. Prince Alessandro is always traveling, going on hiking trips in Nepal or Bhutan for weeks at a time. And the two of them are as identical as twins can get. But why would Prince Vittorio ever take off for so long when" —she set down her chopsticks as her mind connected the dots— "it was because of that ex-girlfriend, wasn't it? Carmella Rivas. Was he still in love with her?"

"You still keep up on all the royal gossip?" Emily had stopped following it after leaving the magazine. Work consumed nearly all her waking moments. On weekends when she could get away, she'd visit with her parents. But even those occasions were few and far between, given her travel schedule. She didn't spend much time watching television or perusing gossip sites.

"On occasion. It was all over the news when Carmella Rivas passed away. Horrible for her family. Have you seen any of her movies?" When Emily indicated she hadn't, Rita continued, "Stunning woman, and a very talented one. When you saw her on screen, she completely became the character. See *Murder One West* sometime. You'll forget you're watching a movie and believe you're watching a true story."

Which was likely why Vittorio hadn't caught on to the scheme Carmella and her producer boyfriend had concocted.

"Was he still in love with her?"

"I don't think so, no. But her death was hard on him. I think it'd be hard on anyone."

"He confided in you?"

More than you know. "A little."

"Oh, sweetie. You're in love with him." Rita sat back in her chair and put her steepled fingers to her lips. "You're in love with a prince."

"Shut up. No." She downed the last of her wine and gave Rita a bashful smile when the older woman promptly refilled her glass. "All right, maybe a little. It doesn't really matter. He's not in love with me."

"You didn't see how he looked at you."

"Nor have I heard my phone ring." She pushed down her disappointment at the thought. It wasn't as if she were expecting him to contact her once he left Argentina, especially given the way they'd left things. "Regardless, I'll get over it. And now that you know, we need to talk about the finale."

"We certainly do. I can't believe we have a finale featuring a crown prince." She let out a low whistle. "An ungodly sexy crown prince, even with that beard and the longer hair. I still can't get over how different he looked. But now that I know who he is, I can see it."

"And viewers would see it, too, if we told them."

Rita lapsed into silence. They had a huge decision to make, and now it weighed on both of them, rather than simply on Emily.

Quietly, Emily said, "You see why I had to tell you? What we do in that editing room will have a profound impact on the show."

"If we were to reveal it, the network would promote the daylights out of the finale and our ratings would go through the roof. Renewal wouldn't be an issue. It'd even get covered on the news." Rita leaned forward and pushed her noodles around her plate. "Wouldn't endear us to the royal family, even if we're respectful in how we present him. And even if we go with the palace's claim that it was Alessandro traveling in South America, rather than Vittorio. On the other hand, if we say nothing, there will be a viewer out there who'll figure it out. They'd think it was Alessandro, but the result would be the same. Big ratings. And a pissed off family, even if the guy agreed to do the show knowing the risks."

Emily slugged the rest of her wine and set her glass on the table, putting her hand over the top so Rita wouldn't refill it. "Exactly my thoughts. Damned if we do, damned if we don't."

"I can't believe he did it." Rita gave her a sad smile. "I think he was really taken with you."

Not taken enough. Not enough to believe she wouldn't betray him. Then again, given the horror he'd experienced with Carmella, why would he?

Because you're not Carmella.

"I'm willing to do whatever you think is best," Rita said at last. "I assume you've been thinking about which way you want to handle it?"

"I've hardly thought of anything else." She shoved her dinner plate out of the way and propped her elbows on the table. "I've come up with a third option, but it won't draw the same ratings and it'll mean a ton of work for the two of us." She blew out a breath and studied her friend. "Do you think you can you convince the network to let us air the finale live?"

"Live?" Rita's expression carried the same incredulity as her voice. "How?"

"We splice in our footage with an end-of-season party. We can use the top floor reception room at the network. Make it festive, decorate it with all things Argentina. I'll act as host, introducing the different segments from a stage at the party and hitting on our theme of passion. But we're going to do some massive editing first. By we, I mean you and me, not the editing guys. I don't want anyone to see this before it airs."

She exhaled, taking it in. "Define massive."

Emily outlined her idea for what she wanted to include...and to cut. When she finished, Rita emptied the wine bottle into her glass. "I like it. I'm pretty sure I can convince the network, but even if they give their blessing, it's a taking huge risk."

"Not really. Taking a risk implies that there's a reward if things go well and this has no upside. If what we originally filmed wasn't going to earn us a renewal, neither will this. But it's the way to go. I know it in my bones."

"I agree. Though if Bob" —Rita emphasized the name— "doesn't see what all of us see in you, he's a terrible judge of character."

The statement made Emily burst out into laughter. "I told him that, though in his defense, he only knew me a week." She gave Rita's hand a quick squeeze and said, "It means the world hearing it from you, though. Thank you."

"I speak the truth, but you're welcome." Rita stacked their plates and shoved them to the middle of the table so they could clean up later, then regarded Emily with concern in her eyes. "Look, when Paul left you, it hurt. I know it did. But even considering the length of time you two were together, I think you were more angry than broken-hearted when it ended. This is different. You made a deeper connection with Prince Vittorio in that week than you did with Paul in years."

Emily felt the same way, but admitting it aloud would make the situation so much worse. "Don't look for the fairy tale, Rita. There was a damned good reason it didn't work with Paul. That reason would go double for Vittorio. He's the crown prince, and that position comes with massive responsibility. I'm not making these edits because I think he'll approve and come riding in on a white horse to whisk me away to his palace. Right now, I'm just hoping to save the show."

Rita leaned over and gave Emily a warm hug. "We'll make this work. No matter the reasons."

CHAPTER 22

THE ROAR of the stadium crowd shook the floor beneath Vittorio's feet. Beside him, Alessandro gave a fist pump as Sarcaccia F.C. put a ball in the net with less than a minute left in regulation. If the team could hold on, they'd have their first victory over A.C. Milan in six years. While the mood in the royal box was jubilant, it wasn't the same as amongst those in the seats below, where fans waved flags and sang, arm in arm, for their team.

While Vittorio was perfectly happy sitting in the royal box wearing a custom-made shirt and Italian silk tie rather than a team jersey and face paint, he knew exactly how the die-hard fans felt, thanks to Emily.

Alessandro turned to Vittorio when an injury time out was called on the field. "You're attending the dinner honoring the Cateri Dog Rescue Society, right?"

"I am. Should be straightforward."

In the two months since Vittorio returned to Sarcaccia, he'd slipped into his role as crown prince as easily as a man slipped into his favorite jacket. Everything fit. The palace's antique dining chairs, the luxurious bed in his apartment, the daily chitchat with the staff, even the sound of his own footfalls against the marble floors in the hallways. It was as if he'd never left. He'd thought that after months away, with no one to answer to save himself, the busy schedule of charity fundraisers, state dinners, and economic meetings would tax his patience. It didn't. He'd been certain he'd ache for the freedom of taking a leisurely bicycle ride through a city park just as the birds twittered the advent of a new day, or the ability to walk up to a window to order a coffee or freshly squeezed juice without anyone snapping his picture. He'd even worried he'd miss the joy of joining a crowd, just as he had when he'd attended the *Superclásico* at La Bombonera, and people-watching from a place of anonymity. Again, to his surprise, he didn't. While he'd enjoyed those pursuits while he'd been in Buenos Aires, he no longer craved the escape they offered from his royal position.

However, he desperately missed Emily. More than once, he'd awakened at night aching to hear her voice. He missed the way she'd touch his arm to get his attention or when she thought he needed comfort. He yearned to see the flush that crept along her cheekbones when they'd visited the men's store after the soccer match and he'd noticed her in the mirror, discreetly watching his movements over the dressing room door, or whenever he teased her for calling him Bob. Most of all, he missed being seen for the man he was on the inside. It was the first time anyone outside his immediate family valued him not for his title or his wealth, but rather for his likes and dislikes, his sense of humor, and his imagination.

It wasn't his pursuits that made him feel most alive in Buenos Aires. It was the company. It was Emily.

He clapped along with the crowd as the A.C. Milan player rose to his feet and shook off the hard hit he'd taken a moment earlier.

It never bothered Vittorio before, being seen through the lens of fame and fortune. His parents had raised him from birth to be a monarch, and Vittorio understood that to the world at large, he represented a country, a government, and a way of life, not an individual with private hopes and dreams. Therefore he strived to show only those aspects of himself that would reflect best on his country, knowing such behavior would keep him and his country safe from the one group of people he'd learned never to trust: the reporters who would drag his family's name through the mud if they thought it would bring in revenue. Anyone else who'd entered his orbit had been vetted. Even those he met at parties were screened long before he met them. They'd fallen over themselves simply to be in his presence or in that of his family. So long as he was gracious, honest, and worked hard to improve his country, he'd believed they weren't a threat.

His experience with Carmella proved otherwise. At any given moment he could fall victim to someone who viewed him only as a target, particularly a beautiful woman. Though it had taken months of work by his mother's private investigators to bring the truth to light, Carmella had deceived him from the start. The evidence was there all along, if only he'd been alert.

Yet two months after they'd each returned home, Emily hadn't betrayed him. He'd checked in twice with Maria Cappalli, the Royal Police Chief Investigator. Maria claimed to have heard no rumblings about the time Vittorio spent in Argentina, though a local news agency was considering looking into Alessandro's time away. Nor had anything suspicious appeared on the usual gossip websites.

He knew the entire story could still come out. His switch with Alessandro, the details of Carmella's fraud, and the letter she'd sent to Vittorio constituted extremely marketable information. But he'd trusted Emily when she'd said she had a potential pregnancy covered. If he could trust her with that—and for some inexplicable reason, he still did—he had to trust her not to divulge his deepest secrets to save her show.

He'd been an ass to her when she'd pulled him into the alleyway and told him she knew his identity. Now he had to fix it, though he wasn't sure how. He only knew he wanted to feel the way she made him feel. She made him want to dance, to laugh, to explore. To view the world with a sense of appreciation and optimism, rather than a sense of duty. She'd made him whole again, if only for the week they'd been together.

"Who's on the guest list?" Alessandro asked, leaning in so only Vittorio could hear him.

Dragging his attention back to business, Vittorio ran through the names he'd seen on the security checklist for the dog rescue dinner. Nodding, Alessandro noted those with whom he'd interacted during Vittorio's time away. "The man who donated the land for the new kennel facilities attended a party Sophia threw just before Christmas. I—you—spoke with him briefly about how much you enjoyed skiing in Switzerland last year. He owns a cottage outside Grindelwald and invited you to use it whenever you wish."

Alessandro discreetly handed his phone to Vittorio so Vittorio could see the man's photo.

"Got it." The brothers knew the easiest way to arouse suspicion at this point was for Vittorio to forget an event Alessandro attended in his place or fail to recognize anyone with whom he'd had more than a passing conversation.

"It's also possible you'll have a wonderful conversation tonight with your future bride."

"Excuse me?" Vittorio forced the surprise from his face and glanced at his brother, though Alessandro kept his eyes firmly on the soccer field, where Sarcaccia F.C. made a terrible pass that was picked off by one of Milan's midfielders to the horrified screams of the crowd.

"Her name is Francesca Lawrence, though she asked you to call her Frannie."

"You think I'm marrying a Frannie?"

Alessandro's lips lifted into a devilish smirk. "Her mother is Sarcaccian, her father is American. They're divorced. The mother lives in Cateri, the father divides his time between London and New York. You danced with her twice at Sophia's party. You would've danced with her a third time, but you know how people talk. As it was, Sophia was giving me the evil eye."

Vittorio tamped down a groan. "Tell me I didn't flirt with this Frannie woman."

"No. Not the way *I* would flirt with her. I still haven't figured out how—or even if—you flirt." Alessandro leaned forward to see the sideline referee, who indicated there would be an extra two minutes of injury time. "But you chatted with her for quite some time. That's how you learned about her parents. I think she was attracted to you."

"Or you."

"Definitely not me. I know how to flirt, but I was pretending to be you." He looked over his shoulder at Vittorio, then eased back in his chair so they were side by side again. "I do think you'd like her, though. She's flat-out beautiful and strikes me as kind-hearted. She's also proper. A true stick-in-the-mud like you."

"That's the best you can do? Stick-in-the-mud? Who even uses that phrase anymore?"

"People like you," he retorted before springing to his feet as the whistle blew to end the match.

Vittorio rose to stand beside his brother and cheer the team's victory. He wondered if Alessandro would be more at home down in the stands with the cheering crowd than in the royal box, where the celebration was more dignified, but quickly dismissed the thought. The past few months wrought changes in Alessandro, too. He'd become quieter, more serious. During a workout with their martial arts instructor this morning, Vittorio noticed that Alessandro didn't even spar in his usual manner. He'd become more calculating. More controlled.

"It's been two months now, you know," Vittorio said. "You could safely take off."

"I might." A muscle in Alessandro's jaw twitched. "Haven't decided what I want to do yet. And you still haven't announced what that project is I worked on for you in South America. I had another reporter ask about it yesterday, when I toured the new wing of the national museum. We'll need an explanation soon."

"I'm working on one." And discarding ideas left and right. "You'll keep me posted on your plans?"

"My only plan at the moment is to go home, put my feet up, and watch *fútbol* on TV with a glass of good whiskey by my side. Maybe take a nap."

At that moment, Vittorio caught sight of a cameraman down on the field. For a split second he thought it was Ignacio, but when the man turned, he realized it wasn't. However, it was a reminder that the *At Home Abroad* finale was scheduled to air in another week. Other than learning that the finale would be aired live from New York and was titled "The Best of Buenos Aires," he'd been unable to find any indication of its content. Nor had there been an announcement regarding the show's renewal.

Far below them, a young reporter with long, wavy hair a few shades darker than Emily's approached the players. The cameraman shifted behind her, his movements mimicking Ignacio's. At that moment, Vittorio knew with every fiber of his being that he wouldn't marry a Frannie.

"Would you do me a favor?" Vittorio caught Alessandro's arm as they made their way out of the box, toward the stairs that would lead them to the car waiting for them in a secure parking spot. "Could you stick around through next Friday night? Something important may come up."

"Like what?"

"An explanation for our project."

Seeing the cameraman not only gave him an idea for a logical-sounding project, it made Vittorio realize how much he needed Emily in his life, despite the fact that at this very moment she could be readying to share his secrets with the world. But before he could put his plan into action, he'd have to make a few phone calls.

The first would be to send his regrets to tonight's dinner and send Alessandro in his place.

So MANY SECRETS. It wasn't natural for one family.

Ironically, despite Fabrizia's hatred of secrets, she was very good at keeping them.

The queen stood at the rear windows of her apartment and looked down at the palace gardens. Though night had fallen, discreetly placed lighting allowed her to see white blossoms dancing on the breeze over thick green foliage. Spring was in full force. In another month Stefano and Megan would be married, which made tonight's private meeting of the entire Barrali clan no surprise to the staff.

"Umberto will keep anyone from disturbing us," King Carlo said as he entered the apartment, referring to the longtime palace guard who watched the staircase leading to the king and queen's residence. "He knows the wedding details are hush-hush for security purposes."

"I assume we're not discussing the wedding?" Prince Stefano took a seat on the sofa beside his soon-to-be bride and draped an arm across her shoulders.

"Actually, we will," Vittorio said. He glanced at Alessandro, who lounged in a chair at one end of the apartment's main seating area, then back to Stefano and Megan. "But first, let me tell you why I wanted the family to meet."

Fabrizia took a deep, cleansing breath, then moved from the windows to stand beside her husband, who'd taken up a spot behind the sofa where Stefano and Megan waited. Across from them, on another sofa, Massimo and Kelly sat with their bodies inches apart, their hands surreptitiously touching. The pair had arrived late—and flushed—and Fabrizia had a single guess as to the cause of their delay.

Good for them.

Fabrizia had been impressed with Kelly from the moment Massimo mentioned her. A professional closet designer, Kelly was skilled at creating order from chaos, which made her a woman after Fabrizia's own heart. That Kelly had found a priceless necklace hidden away in an antique piece of palace furniture and immediately notified Massimo spoke to her honesty, which scored the beautiful young Texan more points in Fabrizia's book. Kelly was exactly what Massimo needed in his life.

God knew Vittorio hadn't had the same experience with Carmella.

Behind Massimo and Kelly, Sophia stood at a buffet and poured herself a glass of Cabernet. Fabrizia was tempted to do the same, but suspected she'd need her wits about her tonight. She'd known from the moment her eldest son returned from Argentina that this night would arrive. What she hadn't expected was that he'd call together the entire family—save Bruno, who was away at school—or that it would be so long in coming.

"I expect you have a public explanation for your time away?" King Carlo always cut to the meat of the matter. "Alessandro's been fielding questions for weeks. Maria Cappalli told me this morning that one of the local news agencies is considering sending reporters to South America to investigate what you were doing there."

"I do, and I believe it will satisfy the reporters' curiosity." Vittorio crossed the room to take the chair beside Alessandro. However, in contrast to Alessandro's more casual posture, Vittorio sat ramrod straight. His gaze took in everyone, ensuring he had their full attention. "Before I share my idea, however, I have a confession to make."

Fabrizia's throat tightened, though she maintained her placid expression. He needn't confess Carmella's lies and theft to the family. It would only serve to make him feel worse. Though if he felt he had to, she couldn't prevent it. Not when he had the family hanging on his every word.

"While I was in Argentina, I agreed to appear on a television show."

Sophia's wine sloshed as she nearly dropped her drink. "You what?"

Massimo grimaced. "Please say it wasn't a dating show or some reality game."

"We thought you were hoping for private time in the wake of Carmella's death," Kelly said, softening Massimo's disapproving comment.

"Let him finish," the king said in a low voice that silenced the room. Though he sounded calm, Fabrizia felt concern rolling off her husband in waves. As everyone turned back to Vittorio, she took Carlo's hand below the back of the sofa, out of everyone's sight. Whatever Vittorio had done, whatever the consequences, they'd weather it together, just as they'd weathered the other storms in their complex life.

"I was approached by the host of an American television show called *At Home Abroad*. This past season was filmed in Argentina. It follows expatriates as they learn about the culture and deal with buying real estate in a foreign country."

Alessandro spoke for the first time since his arrival. "Are you saying that *I* appeared on this show? Or that you did?"

"I did. The host and a producer were sitting in a café across the street from where I was having my morning coffee and reading the real estate ads. The host came over and introduced herself, then said she was filming her show's season finale. The couple she'd been planning to use had been called away on a medical emergency. She pointed out my newspaper and asked if I was looking for real estate. I told her I was, but that I wasn't interested in being on the show."

"You bought a house?" Disbelief filled Sophia's voice. "No wonder you were there so long."

"No, I didn't. And given that I was attempting to stay below the radar, I sent the woman on her way."

"Emily something, isn't it? Gold-blond hair, large eyes, tall?" Kelly asked. "If it's the show I'm thinking of, it's very good."

"Emily Sinclair."

"I saw it a few times before I moved here," Kelly explained. "They filmed a season in Japan. I learned more about the differences between Japanese and American culture than I ever learned in school. Watching foreigners as they went apartment hunting in Kyoto and Kobe was eye-opening."

"If you turned down this Emily woman, then what happened?" Massimo asked.

"Long story short, I learned soon afterward that she was going to drain her own savings to finance the production costs incurred from the delay in finding another guest to feature. The network's executives indicated that they were waiting to see the finale before making a decision about renewing the show, so there was no guarantee she'd even get her money back. I was impressed that she was willing to go to such lengths to try to keep the show on the air and keep the staff employed."

And Vittorio fell for her. Fabrizia knew it clear to her bones, despite the businesslike tone her son maintained. Still, it was an extraordinary lapse in judgment for Vittorio, whom she'd believed to be the least likely of her children to take such a risk.

"The show is scheduled to air this Friday," Vittorio continued. "As far as the show's staff knows, my name is Bob. They know nothing else about me."

"You can't expect not to be recognized," Alessandro said. "No matter that you looked different or that you used a different name. Someone will find you familiar and they'll believe it's me."

"I was extremely careful, but I agree." Vittorio shifted in his seat. "After filming wrapped, Ms. Sinclair figured out my identity. Mine. Not Alessandro's. She apparently used to be a reporter for *Today's Royals.*"

The king muttered a low curse in Italian. At the same time, Fabrizia heard Megan quietly ask Stefano, "Was that who hired the photographer who followed us on the beach in Barcelona?"

Stefano shook his head. "But *Today's Royals* is of the same ilk."

"It's the magazine that claimed I was skipping school and going to all-night boozefests back in college," Sophia said, irritation in her voice.

"You were skipping school," Massimo countered. "And drinking."

"Legally, responsibly, and not all night. And for your information, I had spectacular grades. Does it matter if I missed a class or two if I finished my work on time?"

"Enough." Carlo fixed his dark gaze on Vittorio. His eyebrows knit together as he said, "You believe she's going to reveal your identity on the show this Friday?"

"I have no idea. No word of it has leaked, so I'm optimistic she's decided to keep it to herself."

"The same woman who wanted to save her show so badly she was willing to bankrupt herself?" Sophia spoke as if Vittorio couldn't be more obtuse. "I'd say that's beyond optimistic and into delusional. You're a public figure and you appeared on her show voluntarily. There's no reason she shouldn't broadcast every detail."

"Perhaps. But I have a solution that will defuse the situation, explain where Alessandro went, and will help our country at the same

time. If Alessandro is willing to travel to New York with me" —
Vittorio glanced sideways at Alessandro, who shrugged his assent—
"and if Stefano and Megan will allow me to impose on their
wedding—"

"There will only be a few million people watching," Stefano
replied. "How could you possibly impose?"

"Hold your judgment until I give you the details."

Megan gave her future brother-in-law a warm smile. "Anything
you want to do is fine with me if it helps the family. All I care about is
that Stefano and I are married when we walk out of that cathedral and
that Anna has a good time at the ceremony and reception."

Fabrizia smiled down at Megan. "I'll watch over Anna." The
daughter Megan and Stefano shared was the light of Fabrizia's life.

"I know you will. She adores you."

The simple statement sent a swell of happiness through Fabrizia.
She'd come to truly appreciate Megan over the last few months. It was
hard to believe Megan wasn't already a member of the family, though
Fabrizia knew the long delay in the couple's nuptials was her own
fault. Until the day she died, Fabrizia wouldn't forgive herself for
having interfered in Stefano and Megan's relationship, even if the
harm done was unintentional. She'd been lucky things turned out as
they had. She could only hope matters with this Emily woman would
turn out as well for Vittorio, particularly given all he'd been through
with Carmella.

"In that case, my plan is set." Vittorio let out a long breath and
pushed out of his chair. "If we can work out the logistics, I'm going to
come clean. It's time to let the world know I was in Argentina."

A cacophony of, "What do you mean?" and "Are you serious?" and
"Don't you realize the hell that will break loose?" filled the room as
everyone stared at Vittorio in varying degrees of alarm. Everyone but
Fabrizia, who suspected there was a solid reason her son had decided
to expose his secret to the world rather than confront this Emily
Sinclair before the show aired in an attempt to minimize the damage.

The queen tightened her grip on her husband's hand, then gave her
eldest child a warm smile. "Tell us what needs to be done."

CHAPTER 23

EMILY STEPPED onto the hastily constructed stage that dominated one end of the network's massive reception room. The *At Home Abroad* staff had gone above and beyond, decorating the space with white floral arrangements and balloon bouquets in Argentina's national colors of white and sky blue. Lighting specialists had taken their time highlighting the room's decorative ceilings and gold draperies, making the room appear grander and far more festive than it was in reality. Microphones had been tested, music systems checked, and the champagne glasses had been counted to ensure there was enough for the entire staff to toast the evening and the end of the season. Though the network had been enthusiastic about the idea of a live finale and had advertised it during prime time in the week leading up to the air date, Emily hadn't yet been told there'd be another season.

She flexed her fingers and told herself to relax. Late last night, James Owens, the president of the network, had called her personally, wishing her good luck on the finale. He'd also asked if she could give him ten minutes of airtime near the end of the broadcast, though he wouldn't tell her why. It had taken some last-minute shuffling of the schedule, but she and Rita had managed it.

"They called it a season finale, not a series finale," Rita said, coming to her side. "If they were canceling it for sure, they'd have advertised it that way."

"You're a mind reader, you know that?" Emily turned to admire Rita's elegant yellow cocktail dress, which perfectly suited her skin tone. She wore her dark hair piled on her head tonight and had taken extra care with her makeup. The entire staff had. Emily and Rita had informed them they'd all be on television tonight and to dress to the nines. Rita had even hired cameramen from another one of the network's shows for the night so Mike and Ignacio could join the party rather than film it.

"Only because I'm thinking the same thing you are." Rita scanned the crowd that had assembled in the room now that they were only five minutes to airtime. "Owens is coming for one of two reasons, either to announce a new season or to thank viewers for tuning in and give us a big public send-off. I've told myself he wouldn't announce the end of the series without giving us notice, so I'm hoping for the best."

"I'm doing the same thing." Though deep inside, she knew a public send-off was exactly Owens' style, and that he'd tell Emily later that an on-camera thank you should be seen as a compliment. Emily straightened and swept a hand down her side. "So how do I look? Ready to present?"

"Gorgeous."

Emily had selected a rose pink dress that flared out from the waist in a look reminiscent of the 1950s. There was a subtle sparkle to the fabric that gave it a celebratory air, one she hoped would translate to her mood. She'd worn her hair down, selected a bright pink lipstick, and sported her fanciest heels, a gold pair she'd purchased as a treat to herself after they were renewed following their first season.

She could only hope they'd bring her luck and that the effort she and Rita had put into tonight's episode would be worthwhile. While watching the original film of Vittorio striding through the Buenos Aires apartments with an air of authority, then dancing with the grace of an expert during the tango lesson, she'd nearly changed her mind about the edits. The episode as originally planned was riveting. But she and Rita agreed that they were doing the right thing.

"I hate to ask, but do you know what's going on outside?" Rita angled her thumb toward the large windows that overlooked the front of the building. "There were two police cars out there earlier, and now there are at least a half-dozen news trucks."

"Really?" Emily strode to the end of the stage nearest the windows, then stood on her tiptoes in order to see the street. Sure enough, several news vans were parked outside. At either end of the short block, she could see the red and blue spinning lights of police cars monitoring access to the street. However, she didn't see any reporters or cameras. In fact, the block was devoid of people.

"No idea," she said. "Maybe there's something going on at the museum across the street? A fundraiser with VIPs in attendance?"

"Probably. Glad we had everyone get here early."

Speaking of the time, Emily glanced at the slim gold watch on her wrist, then exhaled. "All right. Let's sell this thing."

She strode to the middle of the stage, gave everyone a one-minute warning, then watched as they got into position. Though she often introduced segments in one take, speaking live got her heart racing. There'd be no second chances. Rita took her usual spot to the side of the cameraman and counted down the time. At her signal, Emily smiled into the camera and welcomed the audience to the final episode of *At Home Abroad's* third season. She quickly recapped a few of the locations viewers had the opportunity to see earlier in the year, then reminded them of the previous episode, which had shown several of Buenos Aires' famous cathedrals and museums, as well as taken viewers on tours of several moderately priced apartments.

"Tonight, as you might've guessed, we're doing something different. Rather than follow an ex-pat through the city, we'd like to give you, our viewers, an idea of what it would be like to live in Buenos Aires if you had an unlimited budget. We'll tour several of the city's most luxurious apartments and give you insights into the neighborhoods where you'll find them. In addition, you'll see what makes locals passionate about their city. We'll take you to a rowdy *fútbol* match and—because my producer twisted my arm—you'll see me learn to tango. And speaking of my producer, I'd like to thank those who are responsible for the great shows you've seen this season."

Crossing the stage, she urged the cameraman to sweep the room. She introduced Rita and several other members of the *At Home Abroad* staff, and said that to kick off their end-of-season finale, they'd visit a gorgeous apartment in Puerto Madero. "It's all about passion tonight on *At Home Abroad*. We hope you enjoy the experience."

The video feed cut from the party to the newly edited film of the Puerto Madero neighborhood and the ultra-modern apartment they'd visited. The staff quieted, looking at each other in confusion as the images filled the screen.

Ignacio spoke first. "You cut Bob?"

"We did," Rita replied. "We needed to do something different to draw in viewers and get the network's attention. This is it."

Mike ran a hand over his head, then puffed out a breath. He uttered what Emily thought was a curse, but she couldn't hear him clearly, as he'd dropped his gaze to the floor.

"That footage was spectacular," Maryam said. "He was a great guest. I'm not questioning your judgment—not at all—but I'm shocked."

"He was," Emily said. "And I know it's a surprise to everyone. But like Rita said, we needed to do something different for the finale. If it's a bust, blame me. This was my call."

"It must have been a hell of a lot of work in the editing room," Mike said.

"Hopefully the viewers will be happy with the result." To the room at large, she said, "Let's get our party faces back on. The feed goes to commercial, then it's back to us. Everyone grab a glass of champagne. We'll have the music turned up" —she signaled the young man working the sound— "and by the end of tonight's episode, we'll all be dancing. Give the tango a go if you're so inclined. And make it passionate! We have one chance to get this right."

Maryam glanced from Rita to Emily. Lines of concern etched the corners of her eyes, but she nodded and turned to face the room with a smile. "You heard her, everyone! Let's get this party started!" She let out a whoop and made a beeline for a long table at the side of the room, where the champagne bottles rested on ice and dozens of flutes stood ready to be filled.

"Good job on the intro," Rita said quietly. "Let's keep it going."

***

"You're not in it."

Vittorio didn't bother looking at Alessandro, who stood beside him watching the live finale of *At Home Abroad*. Shock, gratitude, and a deep sense of relief filled him. At the same time, he wondered what Emily had been thinking to have cut him completely from the episode. The show's viewers had been conditioned to expect an expatriate guest, one they'd follow on a cultural adventure. Hadn't Emily constantly told him that a key to the show was to put the audience in the shoes of the guest? Instead, she'd chosen to focus on the city and its heritage, the thrill of its sporting events and the vibrancy of its music and dancing scenes, the quiet beauty of its parks, and the variety of its high-end residences.

The only footage they'd used of him so far were a couple quick glimpses of his back as he'd danced with Emily. Even then, Vittorio's focus was drawn to the expression on Emily's face as she allowed herself to be caught up in the passion of the dance. He imagined that the show's fans would be mesmerized, as well. It wasn't every day they saw this side of their host's personality.

Vittorio felt his brother's hand on his shoulder, then Alessandro leaned in close to Vittorio's ear. "There's time to back out. Allow the network head to make his announcement, but cut our video. No one has seen it but the two of us and Mother's cameraman. I'll get on the phone to stop the broadcast in Sarcaccia."

Vittorio pushed back the question of why Emily had done it to address his brother. "We're keeping it."

Alessandro released his grip and stepped away, his surprise palpable. "You don't need to do this."

"I do." Vittorio kept from meeting Alessandro's eyes, instead turning at the sound of approaching footsteps. James Owens was in his mid-fifties, a native New Yorker. He wore a smartly pressed navy suit with a lemon yellow tie. His shoes were polished to a high shine and his graying hair had been neatly groomed. When he spoke, his words were friendly, but measured. Though he kept a busy schedule, he'd taken Vittorio's call a few days earlier, then invited Vittorio to New York once Vittorio explained how the Barrali family could raise the network's profile. All in all, Owens was a typical network executive. If a proposal would increase the company's coffers, he was willing to consider it.

He gave each of the brothers a polite nod. Vittorio could tell that Owens wasn't sure which twin was which, so he saved the man embarrassment by stepping forward. "Alessandro and I are glad you could meet with us. Thank you for taking my call. This will be a win-win for both your network and my country."

"It's a pleasure to meet you in person, Your Highness," he said, extending his hand first to Vittorio, then to Alessandro. "I'm honored you came to personally address our audience."

"The feed is set?" Alessandro asked. "Once Prince Vittorio finishes speaking, he only needs to give the cue?"

"That's all," Owens assured them. He peeked through the curtain that had been erected behind the stage and gave Rita a sign. "Looks like we have about thirty seconds. They don't know you're with me. It will be quite a surprise."

"Appropriate that it's a party, then."

Vittorio could hear Emily speaking to the camera, wrapping up the final segment. "Before we go, I've been asked to grant the microphone to a very important person, a man without whom this entire season would be impossible. Please welcome our network president and CEO, Mr. James Owens."

Owens parted the curtain and jogged up the stairs to the stage. Before the curtain fell closed behind him, Vittorio snagged a glimpse of Emily. A broad smile lit her face as Owens approached her. She looked even more stunning in person than she did on the backstage television monitor.

"You're in love with her." Alessandro's voice was barely above a whisper. "That's why you're doing this."

"You have no idea what—"

"I know you as well as I know myself." A low grunt escaped Alessandro. "Guess that explains why she cut you from the show."

Finally, Vittorio angled his head to meet his brother's assessing gaze. "What are you talking about?"

"Sophia was right when she said there was no reason for Emily to keep your identity quiet. Her career is at stake—her whole show is at stake—and you handed her the story of a lifetime. But she did keep your secret, and there can only be one explanation for it. She loves you."

Vittorio had no time to respond. James Owens' voice came through the microphone loud and clear, announcing that the network had decided to renew *At Home Abroad*, which sent thunderous cheers through the room. Over the din, he said, "We have two very special guests here to announce the location for season four."

Knowing it was his cue, Vittorio parted the curtain. At the opposite end of the stage, Emily had her face turned toward Rita, an expression of joy over the renewal morphing to a questioning lift of her brow. Vittorio assumed it was because the two women had always determined where the show would be filmed. He hoped they wouldn't mind having their role usurped, given what Emily had revealed about the destinations they were considering.

"May I present His Highness, Prince Vittorio of Sarcaccia, and his twin brother, Prince Alessandro!"

CHAPTER 24

Emily ripped her gaze from Rita to James Owens. She couldn't have heard him properly. But she had. Without thinking, she pressed a hand to her stomach. Shock over hearing that her decision-making power was being torn away was quickly replaced by shock over the sight in front of her. The twins strode across the stage, one behind the other, to resounding applause from the excited, flabbergasted staff. Though they wore slightly different suits—one a shade darker gray than the other—the men were as identical as two human beings could be. They each had close-cropped jet-black hair, golden eyes framed by long, thick lashes, and a broad-shouldered, lean-hipped build. Before they made it across the stage, Emily knew which was which. Vittorio's intelligent gaze had haunted her dreams for months. Now that she could see them together, she realized that Vittorio's brows were straighter across than his twin's. And there was no denying the recognition in Vittorio's eyes as he shot a quick glance her way before accepting the microphone from James.

"Thank you for such a warm welcome. As you can guess by my presence and that of my brother, Alessandro, next season you'll experience what it's like to be at home abroad on the island nation of Sarcaccia."

The crowd in front of the stage erupted. In the midst of the din, Emily heard Ignacio say the name "Bob," then Mike saying, "Are you kidding me? I went to a soccer match with a prince? Which one?" He said more, something about what Rita knew and when, but it was lost in the noise. Emily didn't turn to look at them. Her gaze remained locked on Vittorio.

How could she not have recognized him? True, he looked vastly different with a clean-shaven face. But it was more than that. It was in his carriage, his facial expressions, his smooth, commanding voice. This was a man who knew he was destined to rule a country and took the obligation seriously. He was also a man used to getting exactly what he wanted. She suspected that what he wanted in this case was to control the story. Not the story she told in her episode, but his own story.

To the camera, Vittorio said, "As you can hear from the reactions in this room, this news comes as a surprise to the entire *At Home Abroad* family. To explain how this came to be, I'd like to show you what is being broadcast at this very moment on Sarcaccian television. It's quite late there, but I felt it was important to explain to my countrymen at the same time I explain it to you, the fans of this wonderful show."

Vittorio gestured to the man running the feed, and the screen switched to a newscast in Sarcaccia. Vittorio was on the screen, sitting in a chair in what appeared to be a hotel room, with Alessandro in a matching chair on his left. Vittorio said a couple words in Italian that appeared to be the end of a speech. He smiled, then said, "and now in English, for those of you in America who are watching the finale of *At Home Abroad*'s Argentina season."

Emily's mouth went dry as dust as Vittorio crossed the stage to stand beside her. "I can't believe you're here," she whispered, grateful she didn't sound as rattled as she felt. "How long have you planned this?"

"Just watch."

On the screen, Vittorio said, "Many reports covered the fact that my brother, Alessandro, was away from late October through mid-

March. During that time, our family was repeatedly questioned about his location. We responded that we were not worried and that it is common for Alessandro to leave for months at a time. Both of those statements are true. When he was reported to be home in mid-March, I stated at a press conference that he had been working on a project at my behest. Now it's time to reveal the details of that project, one I believe will greatly benefit our country's economy."

Alessandro spoke next, a wry smile pulling at the edges of his mouth. "The truth of the matter is that I never left Sarcaccia. Vittorio did. As children, we occasionally switched places for fun. This time, we did it for the betterment of our country."

Once again, Vittorio took over the newscast. "As was covered in the press, I was shocked by the sudden loss of Carmella Rivas, my former girlfriend. I was deeply disturbed that a woman who had so much promise, a woman I thought I knew well, would find herself in such a dark place that she believed she had nowhere to turn. After establishing the Carmella Rivas Memorial Fund to offer free, confidential counseling for those contemplating suicide, I needed time away from the spotlight. First, to grieve, and second, to reassess my role as the heir to Sarcaccia's throne. It became more imperative than ever that I make a difference. Alessandro offered to fill my role at my father's side, literally stepping into my shoes so that I would have the privacy I needed. We stayed in frequent contact, as it was important to him to act as I would, and I believe he did a remarkable job."

As she watched the screen, Emily's heart went out to Vittorio. He'd endured so much more pain than anyone knew, more than anyone would ever know. She twisted her fingers in the side of her dress in an attempt to keep her emotions in check, only to have Vittorio's hand briefly come to the small of her back. In that moment, she knew his thoughts followed the same track as hers. The touch was his way of thanking her for allowing him his privacy.

Onscreen, Vittorio's expression brightened, as did his tone. "Now, I'm finally ready to share what I did during my time away. After a brief stop in Canada, I traveled to Argentina. While in Buenos Aires, I was fortunate enough to meet the producers of an American television show called *At Home Abroad*. The show gives its viewers a look at a foreign country's culture through the eyes of an expatriate hoping to relocate to the country. I spent a great deal of time with the staff as they filmed their season finale. I was impressed by their professionalism as well as with the quality, entertainment value, and educational aspects of the show. More than that, I saw what a boon the show is for the country in which it is filmed. No doubt those who've watched the Argentina season will want to travel there to experience its wonders firsthand."

The camera moved to Alessandro as he spoke. "Our brother, Prince Stefano, has been working the past few years to improve Sarcaccia's transportation system in order to better serve both locals and tourists. Our country also recently opened a new conference center in the capital city of Cateri, a state-of-the-art facility that caters to organizations of all sizes. New hotels have been constructed along the waterfront in recent years, with expanded capacity to account for both tourists and business travelers. Given that modern infrastructure, we knew the time was right to show the world all Sarcaccia has to offer."

"This week, I spoke with James Owens, the head of the network that broadcasts *At Home Abroad*." Vittorio's smile lit the screen, making Emily's heart do a slow flip. It was as if he were smiling directly at her when he sat in front of the camera. "I made my best pitch, asking him to consider having the show film in Sarcaccia. I gave him an overview of our country's rich history, our unique architecture, our picture-perfect beaches, and, of course, the real estate market for those who might want to purchase a vacation home or a more permanent residence. He agreed that our country would be the ideal location for season four of *At Home Abroad*. The first episode will be filmed in a few weeks, following the wedding of Prince Stefano and Megan Hallberg. And" —he winked to the camera— "I happen to know that the show will have access to some behind-the-scenes moments at the wedding that will give viewers a peek into our country's traditions."

Gasps and cheers filled the reception room as Vittorio finished with, "Alessandro and I hope you will be as excited to see *At Home Abroad* in Sarcaccia as I am. Thank you, and good night."

Vittorio moved from Megan's side to stand next to James Owens as the finale cut from the video back to the stage. Owens took the microphone and said, "Our time is short, but I ask that we all raise our glasses to toast Emily Sinclair, Rita Bragna, and the entire crew who brought us to Argentina this season. It was a joy to see Emily tango" —he accepted a champagne glass from a staff member, waited for Emily and the princes to receive theirs, then tipped his glass toward Emily in salute— "and to experience Argentina's vibrant culture. We'll see you again in Sarcaccia!"

He passed the microphone to Emily, allowing her to make a final toast, then the screen cut to black as the network moved on to its next show.

Vittorio murmured near her ear, "I need to talk to Owens before he leaves. Then I suspect Rita, Mike, and Ignacio will want a moment. Don't disappear."

"Believe me, I'll be the last one out of the room." Part of her wanted to pull him behind the curtain and throw herself into his arms, but another part wanted an explanation for all this. Was he doing it because he wanted to save her show? Because he was afraid she'd reveal his switch with Alessandro and wanted to control the flow of information by making a public speech before she could? Or was he truly hoping to improve Sarcaccia's tourist business?

He certainly hadn't apologized for the accusations he'd made in the alley the night of their scrapped date, when he'd all but accused her of being a tabloid reporter with no moral compass.

Emily made her way through the crowd, congratulating the staff on their hard work. Finally, she reached Rita near the refreshment table. They stood side by side in the food line, smiles on their faces, but they knew each other well enough to gauge each other's tension.

"You had no idea about any of this, did you?" Rita's voice was inaudible to anyone but Emily.

"None." She glanced over her shoulder. Vittorio and Alessandro were near the stage talking to James Owens, who was about to take his leave. "It seems our editing didn't affect the renewal one way or the other. Vittorio did."

"I'm glad we made the changes, though. The show was fantastic, even without them showing up here" —Rita's gaze shot toward the twins— "so our ratings should be good. Better yet, the network is bound to rebroadcast it, which should help our viewership for next season."

"True." Emily accepted another glass of champagne, then picked up a chocolate chip cookie. She'd earned them both this week. Once they'd moved a few feet from the table, she asked Rita, "Do you think we would've been renewed without Vittorio's phone call?"

Rita's lips drew taut. "Maybe we shouldn't look a gift horse in the mouth."

"I want to know we earned it."

"We did the moment you walked across the street in Buenos Aires and pursued a new guest. You worked hard on this episode. We all did, and we knocked it out of the park." Rita emptied half her champagne flute in one long drink. "The bigger question is, what now? What happens when we're in Sarcaccia?"

"We have a whole season to plan, and fast. And I'm worried that Owens might not give us as much freedom as he has. He did this without consulting us at all."

"There's that. There's also the fact that you'll be in close proximity to a certain tall, dark, and handsome royal. He wouldn't have lobbied to have the show brought to Sarcaccia if not for you, and I think we both know why."

"Don't be too sure." Emily took a bite of her cookie. It was decadent, but not enough to soothe her nerves. She didn't know what she wanted where Vittorio was concerned. Despite what happened between them in the alley, she loved him desperately—she couldn't deny it anymore, at least not to herself—but after her fiasco with Paul she wasn't going to have her career dictated by a man, not even a man she loved. In Vittorio's case, the issue was moot. Even if he loved her in return—which he'd never indicated—she couldn't have a relationship with him. It would end the same way her relationship with Paul ended, and for much the same reason. She refused to go through that heartbreak again.

"My husband just walked in," Rita said, setting her half-empty glass on a nearby tray. "Must've taken him awhile to get past the traffic outside. Guess we know why the street was blocked. I'll catch you when the crowd clears."

She gave Rita a nod, then waved over the heads of the crowd to Rita's husband as Rita went to greet him.

Emily turned back toward the table only to be faced by a tall, broad-shouldered man in a suit, one whose gaze was fastened on her with a mix of amusement and curiosity. He balanced a glass of champagne and a cracker topped with salmon, capers, and onion in one hand while gesturing toward the refreshment table with the other. "I'd offer to refill your champagne, but you seem to have beaten me to it."

Extending her hand, she said, "Prince Alessandro, it's a pleasure to meet you."

He took her hand and raised it to his lips, his rich eyes never leaving hers. She should've been surprised by the gesture, but she wasn't. Nor was she surprised it didn't set her heart racing as it had when Vittorio did the same thing in the café the morning they met.

"You can tell us apart," he said once he released her hand. "I doubt it's because I'm wearing a different tie. How?"

The question made her grin. "You move differently. And your eyebrows aren't the same."

"Our...eyebrows?" His shot up. "That's a new one to me."

"Yours have more of an arch." She angled her head, studying him. "And you have a scar under your left eye that he doesn't have. Didn't see that until just now, though. But there's something else—"

"I'm far better looking."

That drew laughter from her. Alessandro's entire demeanor differed from Vittorio's. Where Vittorio studied and listened in order to learn, she suspected Alessandro would dive right in. "I'll let you debate that with your brother. What I was going to say is that Vittorio wouldn't eat what's in your hand."

Alessandro frowned. "You know him well."

"We ate out once and he picked the onions out of his meal. Told me he despises them."

"That's an understatement." A mischievous grin lit his face. "We're alike in many ways, but my tastes are far more refined. *That's* how you tell us apart."

"I'll keep that in mind." She sensed he was about to move on to talk to a network executive who lingered nearby, waiting for the opportunity to meet the prince. Unwilling to let Alessandro get away without telling him what was in her heart, she lowered her voice and said, "He appreciates you a great deal. What you did for him...I know it was a great political risk for both of you, not only to switch places, but to admit to it on television with no idea what the fallout may be. I suspect your countrymen will fail to consider that you essentially gave up your life for five months so he could find his purpose again. If no one else thanks you, I will. That was uncommonly generous. Vittorio's lucky to have you as his brother."

"I've tried to convince him of that for years, but to no avail." Alessandro's tone was teasing, but Emily saw appreciation in his eyes and knew her gratitude meant more to the prince than he'd admit. "I suspect that he's lucky to know you, as well. I look forward to seeing more of you when you get to Sarcaccia, Emily."

He moved on, greeting the network executive while leaving Emily stunned by the sincerity in his voice. Had Vittorio told his brother what happened between them in Argentina? She went through the rest of the evening in a daze, accepting thanks and congratulations from staff members as well as their spouses and significant others, many of whom had come to join the celebration and were thrilled to discover themselves in the presence of royalty. Mike teased her about using the name Bob White, while Ignacio seemed genuinely taken aback that he'd spent so much time with a prince and that Vittorio had his head smashed against pavement while on their watch. Emily admitted her horrible name choice to Mike and confessed that she didn't know he was a prince at the time, while assuring Ignacio that all was well as far as Vittorio's injury.

As she shifted from one conversation to another, she was bumped from behind. She twisted to look over her shoulder and was met with a smile from Vittorio that sent her stomach into a spiral. He leaned in close and asked, "How good is your memory?"

"Why?"

His words were low and deliberate. "The Plaza. Royal Terrace Suite, twentieth floor. The key is in the side pocket of your purse backstage. Easier to talk there." One of his dark eyebrows raised fractionally. "You have it?"

She nodded just before he turned away and was swallowed by the sea of people.

CHAPTER 25

VITTORIO STOOD in the living room of his two-story suite looking out at the view of Central Park. He and Alessandro left the network's headquarters nearly two hours ago, as the party was starting to wind down. Emily would stay until the end, but surely it had been over for a while now.

He ran his hands over his hair, then folded them against the back of his head, elbows akimbo, and closed his eyes. She wasn't coming.

As the realization sunk in, he dropped his hands and muttered a choice four-letter word, then loosened his tie, having long ago tossed his jacket over the back of the plush sofa. He'd give Emily another fifteen minutes, then go upstairs and change for bed. In the meantime, he wanted a drink. He crossed the spacious room to the butler's pantry, which consisted of a sink, microwave, refrigerator, and a full selection of liquor. It wasn't lost on him that the suite was larger and better stocked than his palace apartment and a world away from the modest hotel rooms he'd occupied while in Argentina. Though his assistant reserved the smallest of the Plaza's suites for Vittorio and another for Alessandro, they'd both been upgraded to far more luxurious rooms. When one held the title of prince, it was difficult to avoid preferential treatment, and the hotel had been keen on having an actual royal stay in their Royal Terrace Suite.

He laughed aloud as he poured two fingers of whiskey into a crystal tumbler. He'd managed only meager sips of champagne at the reception following the *At Home Abroad* finale. He'd been engaged in conversation after conversation, teasing Rita about her flirtation, telling Ignacio and Mike how much fun he'd had at the soccer match despite the head injury, and assuring Maryam he didn't hold it against her when she'd talked about *Today's Royals*. Seeing their reactions tonight had been entertaining, having met them all without the expectations of his name and heritage intruding on their initial impressions of each other. Even tonight they were far more relaxed in his company than most people he met, and he relished it. They were able to see each other for who they really were. No special treatment, no façades.

Then there was Emily. During his weeks away from her she'd constantly occupied his thoughts. Still, he was unprepared for the intensity of the desire that rushed through him at the sight of her standing onstage in that breathtaking pink dress, her glowing smile bewitching the crowd. Another emotion struck him as he stood near her watching the newsfeed from Sarcaccia. It took him a few moments to identify it, but when he did, it startled him.

Homesickness. Not for his island home, but for Emily.

The soft scent of her hair, the familiar feel of her lower back when he'd gently placed his hand there. Standing beside her on that stage felt like coming home. A crazy thought, since they'd only spent a week together in Argentina. Oh, but what a week it had been. The sex had been phenomenal, certainly, but it was more than that. It was the woman. Her resourcefulness, her wit, her talent. The light of her smile. The way she felt in his arms when they danced the tango. Her playfulness as he practiced *el cabeceo* in the park. And—though he'd failed to value it—her honesty.

He raised the whiskey to his lips. At the moment he took his first swallow, a knock sounded at the door. Frowning, he set the tumbler on the counter and made his way down the hall. A peek at the eyehole revealed a woman awash in pink. He couldn't open the door fast enough.

"You didn't use the key." He stepped back to let her in, but she remained in the hallway clutching her gold purse in front of her.

"I've never been handed a key to a hotel room that wasn't my own. It seemed wrong to simply let myself in."

"How long have you been knocking?" It was an inane question, but her obvious discomfort kept him from saying what he wanted to say, which was along the lines of, *Forgive me, talk to me, don't ever leave.*

"Only once. Rita and I stayed to help the janitorial team, then we stopped in my office to set up a few meetings to plan the new season." Her look of uneasiness grew. "It took me awhile to get here. If it's too late, I can—"

"Never." He reached for her elbow and gently guided her inside, then led her down the hall, past the study and the floating staircase, to a seat on the living room sofa. He watched her face as she took in the suite's high ceilings, restored marble fireplace, and luxurious furniture and rugs.

"It's not like the room I had in Argentina," he admitted.

"That was nice. This is...something else." She withdrew the room key from the side pocket of her purse, where he'd slipped it earlier, and placed it on the alabaster-topped coffee table.

"Extravagant? Over the top?"

"Befitting a true prince."

"About that" —he sat beside her on the sofa and waited until she lifted her face to meet his gaze— "I've been wanting to talk to you for weeks, but wasn't sure how to say what needs to be said."

Her expression remained calm, though he didn't miss that she buried her fingers in the skirt of her dress. "Straightforward is generally best."

"I was an ass our last night together in Buenos Aires, when we talked in the alley. You were right to let me know that you'd figured out who I really am and I was wrong to get angry with you for having figured it out. I accused you of conduct I associate with those who've wronged my family in the past despite the fact you never showed the slightest tendency toward it."

"Writing made-up stories? Stalking royalty so I could expose their private lives?"

"Exactly." He leaned in, hoping he could convince her of his regret. "I was wrong not to trust you when everything you did and said proved that I could. I'm sorry."

"Thank you." Her voice was soft and accepting, but her gaze dipped from his face to the front of his shirt, where his tie hung loosely around his neck. Gently, he cupped her chin and raised it so he could look into her eyes.

"Emily?"

She blinked, as if gathering her thoughts. "You could have called and said that."

"It's not the same." He ran his thumb along her jawline before releasing her. "I knew I was in the wrong by the time I returned to my hotel room that night, but I wasn't sure an apology would fix it or if it would even matter to you. But the longer we've been apart, the longer things went unsaid between us, the more I realized that it mattered to me. I owed you a personal apology, even if you didn't want one. Frankly, I owe you much more than that."

She remained silent, though he could tell her mind was going a mile a minute. Finally, she said, "Is that what all this is? Did you make that call to James Owens and fly here from Sarcaccia because you… you think you owe me?"

"Of course not."

She didn't bother hiding her skepticism. "You know I wanted the show renewed more than anything. But I don't want it this way. Not as an apology or a gesture, no matter how lovely. I wanted it renewed because it earned its place."

"I *am* apologizing, but bringing *At Home Abroad* to Sarcaccia isn't part of that. It's separate." She didn't look convinced, so he edged closer and took her hands in his, needing her to understand the truth of his words. "I attended a soccer match last weekend and it reminded me of the one we saw in Argentina. My brother Stefano has been working on boosting tourism, and it occurred to me that the timing would be perfect to have Sarcaccia featured on a show like yours. You said you were looking for a country with sun and beaches, so" —he shrugged— "I picked up the phone and called James Owens at the beginning of the week. I introduced myself without mentioning that I'd met you and asked if there would be another season of your show. He said yes."

Skepticism laced her tone. "He told you this days ago? But not me?"

"He asked me to, and I quote, keep it under my hat, as he wanted to make the announcement during your live finale. He told me that the show's ratings spiked over the last few episodes, enough for him to justify the renewal. Then he praised you and Rita to the skies, telling me how creative you were with the show. He asked why I was interested, though given the compliments he'd just heaped on the show, I suspect he knew why I was calling."

Vittorio couldn't keep the broad smile from his face as he remembered the conversation. "I told him almost word for word what I said on the news broadcast tonight, that the Barrali family would love to see *At Home Abroad* in Sarcaccia, and that it would be good for us and for the network. I promised limited but exclusive access to Prince Stefano's wedding if Owens could arrange to feature Sarcaccia in the coming season."

"And he jumped on it, even though location has always been a decision Rita and I make together."

"He did. I told you, I'm very good at managing people." Though the person who mattered most to him wasn't smiling. "I hope you're not angry."

"No, I wouldn't say angry. Commandeered, maybe." She slipped her hands from his and stood. He waited while she paced in front of the windows. At long last she turned to him and said, "You genuinely want the show in Sarcaccia? Not that I have a choice anymore—the announcement's been made—but I need to know whether this is truly for tourism or because you have a misdirected sense of guilt—"

"Tourism. Plain and simple." He crossed the room to stand at the windows. Through the parted curtains, he could see the lights on the far side of Central Park. Quietly, he asked, "But is it wrong of me to want you there, too?"

She stopped pacing and opened her mouth to argue, but stopped short, her hazel eyes wide.

"The show is business," he said. "You, on the other hand, are personal. More than anything, I want to know that you can forgive me for my lack of trust in you."

"Of course I forgive you," she touched his arm, then pulled back as if afraid of prolonged contact and turned to stare out the windows. "I don't like that you didn't trust me, but I understand it. You were horribly betrayed before you left for Argentina and your family's been burned by reporters in the past. You had every reason to be leery of me."

"You gave me every reason *not* to be leery of you. You were nothing but generous and kind." As he stood beside her looking out into the night, another thought occurred to him, one he'd had briefly backstage as he watched the finale. "Speaking of generous, why did you edit me out of the finale? Was it because I lost my temper with you in the alley?" Or because, as Alessandro seemed to believe, Emily felt something for him?

She shrugged. "It was the right thing to do. You signed on as an apartment hunter, not to share your entire life. If we'd put you on the air, that's what would've happened. You'd have eventually been recognized." From the corner of his eye, he saw an ironic smile light her face. "Of course, we had no idea you'd out yourself."

"Guess I could have saved you some editing time."

"Maybe. In retrospect, it turned out to be a better episode with the edits, and that's even before you came strolling onto the stage with your brother." A gentle laugh bubbled from her. "He told me that he's the better looking twin, by the way."

"Of course he did." Typical Alessandro. "Owens never saw the original footage, did he?"

She shook her head. "He's not involved in the show itself, only in programming. Rita and I are the only ones who knew your identity before tonight." Emily shot him a remorseful look. "I had to tell her why I wanted the changes. She'd have taken it to her grave."

"I imagine she would've." He'd suspected Emily would have to tell Rita at some point, given that they were equal partners in the show. More and more, he could see why the women had become fast friends. "How does she feel about going to Sarcaccia next season?"

"We talked after you left." Emily's eyes narrowed as she gazed outside. "We agree it's a good location with a lot to offer, but we're both bothered that we didn't have the opportunity to scout it first and that you and Owens arranged it without our input, let alone any warning." Angling her head to study him, she said, "We also agreed that public announcement or not, we won't do it if you or your family want to control the content."

"I'm not surprised." He couldn't help but grin, remembering their debate about gender roles as they'd walked through the park in Recoleta. He would prove to Emily that he wasn't anything like her ex-boyfriend. That man had been a fool. "I have no intention of controlling anything you do for the show, though I'm happy to provide whatever support or resources you need. It just so happens I'm well connected in Sarcaccia."

He reached for her then, unable to stop himself from running his hand along the shoulder of her dress. He'd never thought he'd love pink until he saw it on Emily. "Use me however you wish."

Vittorio had no idea what his touch did to her. Or perhaps he did, and that was why he took his time tracing his way from her shoulder to her back as he complimented her on her dress.

This was so dangerous. Standing in a romantic hotel suite with a man whose tie was loosened enough to reveal the dark, tempting skin of his neck. She craved the taste of him, the feel of his pulse beneath her lips. Swallowing, she forced herself to keep her attention on the twinkling lights outside.

He stepped behind her, framed her shoulders in his large hands, and looked out at the night. His masculine scent teased her senses in invitation. If she went to Sarcaccia, what would it mean for the two of them? Was he looking for a string of one-night stands or something more? She couldn't ask without sounding presumptuous, yet she couldn't let him believe there could be more between them. It was a relationship destined to fail, no matter how much he might care for her.

She closed her eyes, though the city lights still flickered in her vision. The burn of tears welled inside her. She wanted him to love her, desperately, but knew the more she allowed herself to crave it, the more agony she'd endure in the long run.

"You know what this makes me think of?" His warm breath caressed her ear.

Grateful his face was far enough behind hers he couldn't see her fighting against tears, she said, "Tell me."

"A woman standing on a balcony, looking down on a city, singing 'Don't Cry For Me, Argentina.'"

Oh, he knew how to make her laugh. "This is New York. And it's not a balcony."

"But you're every bit as brave when faced with a challenge." His hand slid to hers. "Come with me."

Trepidation filled her as he led her toward the staircase. Given what she'd seen of the suite so far, she guessed that it led to the master bedroom. She could not, would not, allow herself to go there.

"I'm taking you to the real view," he said with a smile, accurately reading her hesitation. "How often do you get to see Central Park from the twenty-first floor of The Plaza?"

She followed him upstairs, through a spacious bedroom boasting every amenity, right down to a fancy upholstered headboard, a sparkling crystal chandelier, fresh flowers, and fluffy pillows topped with mints. Vittorio opened the doors at the far side of the room to reveal a long, narrow terrace. Though it was the middle of the night, the air was light and warm and the city pulsed with life, beckoning her outside.

"Oh wow," she couldn't help but exclaim. The breeze carried the smell of the trees from Central Park. Far above them, stars littered the night sky.

"It's as clear as I've ever seen the stars here," he said, following her gaze.

"It's like a scene from a movie." She moved to the wrought iron railing and took in the view. The contrast between the ribbon of streetlights surrounding the park and the darkness of the treetops filled her with awe. "Thank you. I can't imagine anything more heavenly."

For several minutes, they stood side-by-side, alternately watching the activity below and the show of stars overhead, until the wind kicked up and sent an involuntary shiver through her.

"Cold?"

She shook her head, but his arms came around her anyway. It was all she could do not to lean back into him, to allow his warmth and the magic of the location to envelop her. Softly, he said, "There's a road that runs north from Cateri along the Saraccian coastline. My sister once showed me a hidden beach below the roadway that offers views across the Mediterranean. I suspect the stars are even brighter there. I know it's warmer. I'd love to take you there."

"For the show?" She knew it wasn't what he meant, but needed to hear him state his intentions aloud.

"No. It's not a place I'd ever reveal to the public." With one hand, he smoothed the hair back from her neck and dropped a gentle, lingering kiss there before turning her to face him. The breeze caught a chunk of her hair and blew it across her face, but he captured it and smoothed it back again, then spread his fingers into her hair. "I want you in Sarcaccia. Show or no show. I missed you."

She closed her eyes, needing to think. His mouth was on hers before she could utter a syllable, warm and daring and oh-so-knowing. There was a familiarity to the way he kissed her, but his need seemed to run even deeper than when they'd been in Argentina, as if he'd been holding his breath underwater and finally came up for air. Much as she wanted to resist, she felt the same. A moan surfaced from deep inside her as she opened to him and wound her arms around his lean waist to the tight muscles of his back. He tasted of whiskey and mint, and she found herself craving more, ever more of him, as if she'd never have her fill.

With a rough groan, he deepened the kiss. A wash of heat settled low in her belly at the same time he pressed his body against hers, allowing her to feel his arousal. She knew she should stop, for both their sakes, but he felt too perfect. As he shifted to kiss the delicate spot in front of her ear, she hissed out a satisfied breath at the feel of his smooth cheek brushing hers, so different than when he'd sported the beard in Argentina.

"Admit it. You missed me."

"I missed you." The words were out before she could consider them.

His smiling mouth danced over her jawline, then moved to her throat. She let her head fall back and he took advantage of the access, dragging one hand from her hair to trace the hollow in her neck, then to cup her breast through the fabric of her dress. The sensation made her wobble on her heels, drawing a low laugh from him as he stepped backward, pulling her along with him. "This is not for the outdoors."

The lack of a breeze and the click of the terrace doors snapped her to reality. "This would be a mistake," she managed, even as his mouth found hers again.

He eased back enough to look her in the eyes, but didn't loosen his hold. "Emily, I want to be with you. Not just for a second one-night stand. For the long haul. I know your job requires travel, but you'll be in Sarcaccia for several months. After that, we can work out any obstacles with distance and your shooting schedule. Just be with me."

Tears pricked at her eyes. He was such a good man, everything she could ever want. If only she had the ability to give him what he needed. But she didn't, and she never would. "Vittorio, I'm not the—"

"Shh." His finger came over her lips. His gaze followed, and she ached at the desire she saw there. "I know you're used to being in control and that I make that difficult. It's the nature of being in a relationship with a royal. But I know it can work. Even my parents have made it work. They're opinionated individuals with their own interests. Despite being in the public eye every day, they have a strong marriage."

Marriage. Her heart swelled even as she was certain it would break.

She drew a deep breath, dreading what she had to say. Reluctantly, she reached for his hand and eased it away from where he was tracing her mouth. "Vittorio, that means more to me than you can ever know."

"So be with me."

"I can't. Even if we could make the day to day work between us, I can never give you what you need." Her gut twisted as she finished, "Vittorio, I can't have children."

CHAPTER 26

THE STATEMENT COULDN'T HAVE STUNNED him any more than if she'd given him a sucker punch to the kidneys. Vittorio stepped back. "You don't want children or you can't have them?"

"Can't." A wan smile etched her face as she pulled away from him and dropped into the Victorian-style chair in the corner of his master bedroom. "When I told you I wouldn't get pregnant back in Buenos Aires, it wasn't because I was using birth control. I had cancer when I was twenty-three. Hodgkin's lymphoma."

The shock of her pronouncement must've shown on his face because she held up a hand and said, "Cancer's gone," then knocked on the wooden arm of the chair. "I'm healthy as the proverbial horse. But when I was diagnosed, I had a choice to make. The most successful chemotherapy regimen at the time for my particular type and stage of cancer can cause ovarian failure. There were others I could try, but I worried that if I pursued those avenues first, the cancer might advance to the point that it'd be tough to treat. I decided to go with what was most likely to work and risk it."

"That must have been traumatic for you and your family. I'm sorry you had to endure it."

"It worked." She waved a hand. "I'm here. I have nothing to complain about."

He took a seat on the ottoman that footed her chair and wrapped one of her small hands in his. She'd been so young, starting her career, with her whole life ahead of her. To be faced with such a diagnosis and decision must have been life-altering. "You look at the world with such optimism."

Her shoulders lifted for a moment, then she grinned and said, "I'm fortunate. I really am. In the long run, it made me appreciate my health and my friends. Rita was there when I was diagnosed and offered her support without being smothering or patronizing. She hosted my parents when they came from Oregon to see me and kept them updated when they were home. I'll love her forever for it."

Once again, he was in awe of her inner strength. He ran his thumb over hers. Would he ever learn all there was to know about her?

Her voice turning serious again, she continued, "Even so, the odds of me having a natural pregnancy are zero. I went through menopause at the ripe old age of twenty-four. I did have eggs harvested first, but it's much tougher to have a successful pregnancy from a frozen egg than an embryo. It's not likely to happen."

She squeezed his hand briefly and then stood, as if needing to put distance between them. "I know that's a terrible information dump, but it needed to be said. I found peace with it long ago, but I'd never expect any man I date to settle for that, let alone a man whose position requires an heir. The minute you mentioned the long haul...." She shrugged. "I'm not right for you. No matter what we might feel for each other, a relationship would end in heartbreak for one or both of us. I can't go down that road."

"And here I was worried that the biggest barrier to a relationship would be public opinion, that I'd moved on too quickly after Carmella. That it might hurt your career to be seen dating a prince who'd appeared on your show...though you took care of that issue." There was a smile in his voice, but his expression turned serious. "So tell me...what is it you feel for me?"

"That's not a fair question." Her voice was steady, but her jaw trembled as she said it.

"It's entirely fair." It was all he could do not to launch from the chair and take her in his arms. "Because I know what I feel. I'm in love with you, Emily. Crazy in love."

"You can't be," she protested, an ache in her tone. "Not when I'm—"

"When you're what?" He couldn't resist. He was beside her in two steps, framing her shoulders with his hands. "Intelligent? Beautiful? Creative? Resilient? I could go on forever. I *want* to go on forever. Unless you were planning to end that statement by saying, 'Not when I'm not in love with you,' but I don't think that's true."

The pain in her gaze reminded him of something she'd told him when they were on the sofa in his Buenos Aires hotel room, and she'd been wearing his shirt while he kneaded the arch of her foot. "Emily, I'm not your ex-boyfriend. That's why he ended your relationship, isn't it? Why you said it was complicated, but that you couldn't give him what he needed and you understood?"

"He wanted a family. There's nothing wrong with that."

"No, there's not. But I want you more."

"For now." She exhaled and said, "Look, when I was with Paul, I put a lot of pressure on myself. I felt like I had to be everything to him —I had to make up for the family he'd probably never have if he stayed with me—and I couldn't do it. I can't do that for anyone."

He smoothed her hair back from her face and smiled. "Do you know that when I went back to Sarcaccia, I watched every single episode of *At Home Abroad*? Not just this season. All of them. You were all I could think about. I've never felt this way about a woman. In fact" —he angled his head so he could search her eyes— "I've never told a woman I love her, because I never have. But I love you. You see me for who I am and encourage me to be the best version of myself. You make me laugh. You make me happy whenever you enter a room. And you don't have to do anything or make up for anything in order for that to happen. You only need to be who you are for me to love you."

Emotion flickered in her eyes at his words. He knew then that she loved him, too, and it gave him hope.

"Emily, I know in my heart that this is a love that can overcome anything."

"You can't overcome the law. One thing I learned at *Today's Royals* is that your country signed a very specific treaty with Italy to obtain its independence. When the Barrali line ends, the island returns to Italian control. You're responsible for those people. You can't risk their futures for me."

"You risked the futures of the people who work for you when you edited me out of the episode."

"It's not the same and you know it," she huffed. "Besides, how do you know you won't change your mind? A month or a year from now, you might see things differently."

"I won't. Besides, I have an heir."

She leaned back from his grasp, confusion clouding her face. "You…wait, you do?"

"Not a direct heir, but there *is* another heir to the throne. Several. My time in Argentina proved that Alessandro has what it takes to rule. I'd never admit it to him, but if you and I were to marry and not have children, I'm confident Sarcaccia would survive as an independent nation long after I'm gone. And if not Alessandro, there's Stefano. Then Massimo and Bruno and Sophia, though God knows what Sophia would do to the country."

His heart threatened to explode from his chest as he memorized the shape of Emily's eyes, the flush of her cheeks, the plush contours of her mouth. "All I need to know is whether you could love me. If you feel even half of what I feel for you, I'd be happy for the rest of my life."

"You can't possibly know that. The rest of your life is a long time."

His thumbs skimmed her face. "The world thinks I've come clean about a huge scandal, but you and I both know that what aired tonight isn't the whole story. No one aside from the two of us—and Alessandro—knows Carmella sent me a final letter or what was in it. If I can trust you with that, perhaps you can trust me to know my own heart."

He couldn't mistake the fear in her expression, but there was desire, too.

"I'm not your ex, Emily. I can't promise never to hurt you, but I will never change my mind about how much I want you, and that takes priority over having children."

Her voice was near a whisper as she asked, "Do you not want children?"

"I'd love children. But I don't require them to be happy." And he meant it. "I do, however, require you. I'm going to kiss you now. I want you to kiss me back."

Her lips parted as she searched his face. He could read her well enough to know she still worried about the future. True to his prediction, she asked, "But then what?"

"Then I'm going to unzip your dress very slowly and very carefully so I don't damage it, because it's beautiful and I want to see you in it again. Then I'm going to make love to you. Probably more than once. I'm going to ask you to stay the night. And I'm going to ask you to be my date to a royal wedding in a few weeks. Not for the show, but for you. We'll have the time of our lives. Then I'll ask you for another date and another, for as long as you'll say yes."

"Yes." Her face crumpled and she slid her arms around his neck. "Yes, yes, yes."

A few minutes later, after he'd thoroughly kissed her, he did exactly as promised, spinning her around and gently easing the zipper of her dress toward the small of her back. As he placed his lips to the soft skin along her spine and slid his hands inside the fabric to push it open, she said, "Do you know when I was first attracted to you?"

"Tell me."

"When I saw you at Café Luchana writing in your newspaper."

He laughed as he lowered the dress to her ankles, then helped her step out of it. "You wanted me for my real estate?"

"No. I knew you were different because you were reading a real newspaper instead of holding the latest electronic gizmo, and it looked like you were doing the crossword, which meant you had brains."

"Sorry to disappoint you." He laid her dress over the chair as she spun to face him. "No crossword. Not at that particular moment."

"I'm only disappointed that you're wearing more clothing than I am." She reached for his tie and slowly unlooped it from his shirt collar before tossing it over her dress. "Because in addition to having a fine set of brains, you're very easy on the eyes. And I'm very, very much in love with you."

He wanted to close his eyes and collapse in a mixture of relief and bliss. Instead, he bracketed her waist and drew her gorgeous body flush to his. Lowering his mouth to within an inch of hers, he murmured, "Prove it."

And she did.

CHAPTER 27

Emily leaned her head against Vittorio's shoulder and sighed.

"You're not falling asleep, are you?" he asked.

"Nope. I'm in my happy place." She smiled as the band played a kicky pop number that sent Stefano and Megan's daughter, Anna, and a few of her friends onto the dance floor amid squeals of delight. This, she thought, was the way family should be.

Stefano and Megan's wedding had been straight out of a fairy tale. A Rolls Royce brought Megan to Cateri's famous cathedral, where she walked down the aisle on the arm of her father. Anna had served as flower girl. Afterward, an open-top carriage drawn by four horses took the newlyweds on a circuitous route through the town's medieval center, past cheering crowds, to the palace. The couple made an appearance on the narrow balcony that surrounded the palace clock tower and shared a kiss for the throngs of onlookers and television cameras gathered at the palace gates.

Before the ceremony, Emily had taken the *At Home Abroad* cameras through the decorated cathedral, given her viewers an overview of its history, then briefly interviewed a tuxedoed Prince Stefano, who outlined the elements of a traditional Sarcaccian wedding even as he readied for his own.

The palace reception, however, was strictly for family and friends. Stefano had surprised Anna by flying in some of her former schoolmates from Barcelona. Several of Megan's past coworkers were in attendance, as well. Emily had spent a hilarious half hour listening to Dominic, the recently retired palace chef, debating the proper preparation of various seafood dishes with Santi, the head chef at the Barcelona hotel where Megan used to work. Never had she met two men who talked more with their hands or laughed so uproariously.

"I despair of ever hearing a tango," Vittorio murmured as he planted a kiss on top of Emily's head. They'd danced numerous times, but the laid-back vibe of the reception meant a tango was unlikely, despite the glorious surroundings and talented musicians.

"That's all right." She sat up and grinned at Vittorio as a thought occurred to her. "You know, it's a very good thing you got so mad at me that night in the alley."

One side of his mouth cocked up. "And why is that?"

"Because now this is our first real date."

"I'll alert the press."

"Oh, I suspect they've already got it covered." They'd both seen the cameras aimed in their direction as they'd entered the cathedral together.

"Speaking of news" —Vittorio's voice dropped— "I've heard a bit. I hate to bring it up here, when we're having such a good time, but it's about Carmella's boyfriend."

That caught her attention. "What is it?"

"He was arrested in Spain on charges of tax evasion. The authorities are also looking into allegations from one of his business partners who claims to have been cheated."

Emily absorbed that. "How do you feel about it?"

"It's hard to say." He shifted in his chair, then made a face at Alessandro as Alessandro grabbed their sister Sophia and spun her around the floor to the wild music, despite Sophia's protests. "I'd hoped never to think of him again. But if he was stealing from others, then yes, I'm glad he's been stopped."

Emily reached for Vittorio's hand. "You'll never have to go through anything like that again."

"I know." He brushed her lips gently with his, then said, "And I have other news, if I can trust you to keep a secret."

"I don't know" —she let her voice go intentionally wicked— "can you?"

"Massimo and Kelly are planning to announce their engagement as soon as the mania surrounding this wedding dies down."

"Really?" She'd only spent a brief time around the pair, but they struck her as a couple very much in love and well-suited to one another. "That's wonderful."

"I think so, too."

The song wound down and the kids started to clear the floor. As the band began the next song, Vittorio straightened, then rose from his chair.

"Where are you going?" she asked, but in the next breath, she realized what was happening. The first strains of a tango were being played. And Vittorio was about to play, as well. A few couples had migrated to the floor, including Massimo and Kelly, to enjoy the dance. But Vittorio skirted the floor and perused the women in attendance before looking back to Emily with *el cabeceo*. She gave him a look of mild interest, then turned away. They had fun with stolen glances, then he pegged her with a sultry look of invitation that took her breath away. She remained riveted, her eyes on his, until he came to stand in front of her. Slowly, she stood and took his hand. When he spun her onto the floor, she thought she'd died and gone to heaven. She let Vittorio and the music guide her, matching his pauses, sweeping her foot to caress the floor, then following the pressure of his hand. Nearby, she heard a whistle that only could've come from Alessandro.

"I think we're making a scene," she whispered.

"No talking until we're between *tandas*, remember?"

"We don't know how many songs will be in this set. My guess is that this is the only one."

"Not if they keep going like that."

He spun her so she could see the opposite side of the floor, where King Carlo and Queen Fabrizia danced a tango as sensual as any she'd seen in Buenos Aires. Every eye in the room was riveted on the pair, who were so circumspect in public Emily never would've believed what she was seeing if it wasn't right in front of her.

"Wow," she whispered as Vittorio guided her through the next crescendo in the music.

"Guess they're happy about the wedding," he murmured. "Or something."

"They're very—" she struggled for the right word. It seemed wrong to describe them as sexy to their own son. Sultry and hot were right out, as well.

"I know what you mean. No need to describe it," he said.

"I suspect the acorn didn't fall far from the tree."

His grip tightened on her as quiet laughter shook him. As the first tango morphed into a second, he steered her off the dance floor.

"I know I'm not supposed to protest, but shouldn't we finish the set? I thought that was the tradition."

"I'll make it worth your while." A moment later, he'd scuttled her through the crowd, then ducked through a small door to the side of the ballroom.

"Where are we going?"

"This is a service hallway. The staff use it to move between sections of the palace during big events so they're not seen. And this" —he pushed open a second door to reveal a curtain, then lifted the curtain aside— "is a hidden entrance to the palace library, where we can have a moment alone."

Emily drew in a sharp breath. She thought she'd seen it all today, but this room topped everything. Though the palace's grand ballroom lived up to its name and Cateri's cathedral had been steeped in history, the darkened library had a magical quality. Ancient hardwood floors had been topped with Persian rugs that softened the sound of her footsteps as she made her way to the windows. "I can see the whole garden from here."

"Turn around," he urged. "You like?"

"Oh, Vittorio." Thousands of books lined the floor to ceiling shelves. While several sections contained books that appeared centuries old, most of the shelves were filled to bursting with modern works. Paintings hung in the gaps between the shelves, but rather than musty portraits of Vittorio's ancestors, richly colored Impressionist works brightened the space. Even at night, with a single lamp projecting light from one corner of the room, the canvases took her breath away.

"I had a feeling you'd like it in here." With a hand to her lower back, he guided her past one of the library's two seating areas toward the far end of the room from where they'd entered. "Look closely at the shelves here. Eye level."

She leaned in. "Travel guides."

"And in the center?"

A thick book on Buenos Aires. She pulled it from the shelf, surprised to find it so light in her hand.

"Open it."

She looked at Vittorio to gauge his intentions, but he gave her nothing more than a lift of his brows. Slowly, she opened the book. It was hollow inside, the pages cut out to create a compartment that held a key.

"You never asked me if I bought an apartment in Buenos Aires," he said.

"I completely forgot." She lifted the key from the book, then set the book back on the shelf. "I assume from this that you did?"

Again, he only raised his brows. The devil. "Which one did you get? Puerto Madero?" When his expression didn't change, she shook her head, dismissing it. "No, in the end I bet you went for the traditional place in San Telmo. The one with the chandelier from the old mansion."

"The Sarcaccian chandelier, you mean?"

She laughed, remembering. "I'd forgotten it was from Sarcaccia! I can only imagine what went through your mind when I talked about it on camera."

"I was certainly amused. But no, I didn't buy either of those places.

I bought something else entirely." A wicked glint entered his eyes. "I bought a hotel."

She nearly dropped the key. "You…what?"

"I bought that little hotel where we had our one-night stand. I told you I wasn't the one-night stand type. Well, I bought the place when I discovered that the owners wanted to retire. I kept the staff, installed a new boiler since the old owners couldn't afford to, and now we have a place to stay whenever we're in Buenos Aires. In fact, I talked to Rita this morning and confirmed that you'll be done shooting this season well before Christmas and won't need to start planning season five—"

"I've barely started season four!"

"—until mid-January," he finished. "So the week after Christmas, I reserved that same room for the two of us. We'll have all the privacy we want for that second one-night stand I ruined back in March. If you'd like, perhaps we can fly up to Oregon afterward. I'd love to meet your family. That is" —he wrapped his strong fingers around hers, which still contained the key— "if you'll accept this key as my first-date gift to you."

She suspected it was the first of what would be many wonderful surprises she'd receive from Vittorio. Who received a hotel as a gift? And what prince would speak with such excitement about the possibility of going to Oregon? "This is the strangest and sweetest thing anyone has ever given me."

"So you accept?"

"I most certainly accept." She angled her head to smile at him. "Though you do realize that we're well past a one-night stand already?"

"Shhh." He lowered his mouth so it lingered a breath from hers. "Just kiss me. Then dance with me. Then stay with me."

She would. Forever. "I love you, Vittorio Barrali."

"And I love you more."

She wanted to tell him to prove it, but before she could, he busied himself doing exactly that.

EPILOGUE

Nine Months Later

FABRIZIA WAITED on the garden bench as Prince Massimo and his new wife, Kelly, stood on a gravel walkway behind the palace waiting for the photographer to finish taking his shots. Near her hip, Massimo's purebred Sarcaccian Shepherd, Gaspare, waited patiently for his master, enjoying a stealthy head scratch from the queen. As handsome as Massimo appeared in his dress uniform and Kelly did in her wedding gown, Fabrizia's attention kept drifting to Vittorio and Emily, who stood nearby.

Vittorio had proposed to Emily just after Christmas, whisking her away on a trip to Buenos Aires and presenting her with a stunning pink diamond ring he'd designed with the family's longtime jeweler, Conti & Fancetti. When the couple returned, Fabrizia overheard Vittorio telling Sophia that he knew it wasn't traditional, but he'd selected the stone because he loved seeing Emily in pink. It warmed Fabrizia's heart to know Vittorio had put so much thought into the ring and its design.

Emily, for her part, loved it. In fact, she was playing with it now, using her thumb to subconsciously twist it on her ring finger as she watched Kelly and Massimo with a smile on her face.

"Your mind never stops, does it, my darling?" Carlo rested his arm on the back of the bench and spoke quietly. "What is occupying it now?"

"It was a lovely ceremony." Smaller than she'd have liked, though she understood, given Massimo's desire for privacy since he'd returned from a grueling military assignment in Africa. Massimo called the family together only three days ago to inform them that he'd arranged to fly Kelly's family to Sarcaccia from Texas, then to marry Kelly this morning in the palace's private chapel, a space that held fifty people at most.

"It's what we want," Massimo had explained to his parents. "Very low key, with only family and a few close friends. We can issue a press release after the fact and thank the country for the support they've shown us since we announced our engagement."

Carlo's instinct was to object, Fabrizia knew. The citizens of Sarcaccia wanted and expected a public wedding ceremony for a prince. But to his credit, Carlo had asked once if Massimo and Kelly were certain, had nodded at his son's confirmation, then cleared his schedule.

His gaze pointedly followed Fabrizia's. "Odd that you're studying Vittorio and Emily, then."

Fabrizia smiled. Her husband knew her well. She put her hand on his knee, which she rarely did unless they were behind closed doors. "We have a lot for which to be thankful."

"But?"

His expression remained pleasant, though she understood what he was asking.

"I fear it'll come crashing down."

"It won't."

The photographer asked for Massimo's siblings to join their brother and his new wife for the next photo. As everyone shifted positions, Fabrizia turned to Carlo. "We never found out who was asking questions in Croatia."

"No. But Vittorio's return likely made whoever it was realize they'd made a mistake."

Fabrizia didn't believe that. She'd seen the photos of Teresa's son boarding that yacht in Dubrovnik last year. Rocco Cornaro's resemblance to Vittorio and Alessandro was uncanny. "I understand that he's still separated from his wife. And Teresa is ill. Advanced liver disease. I don't know the details, but I'm afraid it could be terminal."

A muscle in Carlo's jaw jumped. "Not only does your mind work overtime, my dear, so do your investigators."

"She hasn't told you?"

He gave a minute shake of his head.

"Perhaps she's waiting for the right opportunity. I'm sure it's a difficult time for her." The relationship between Carlo and Teresa was a complicated one. Fabrizia couldn't imagine how he'd take the news of her health issues. But that wasn't her emotional battle to wage; it was Carlo's. He'd confide in her if he needed to.

The queen forced herself to relax against the bench and smile in the direction of her children, though she stole another quick look at her husband. "If ever the past were to come to light, it would be now."

"Perhaps." He shifted closer to her on the bench and covered her hand with his, then lifted it to his lips for a brief kiss. "If so, I won't allow it to harm us. I love you. You love me. That bond cannot be broken. And our children are happy. Look at them."

His smile widened as he watched his sons and daughter elbow each other in front of the camera as if they possessed all the maturity of grade schoolers. It made Fabrizia's heart swell to see Carlo so joyful. He deserved it.

He released her hand, but the happy expression didn't leave his face. "When I asked what you were thinking, I was afraid you were worried for Vittorio and Emily."

The newly engaged couple had asked to have dinner with the king and queen a week after returning from Buenos Aires. When the four of them were alone, Vittorio told his parents about Emily's health history and explained that she might have difficulty getting pregnant. While they were anxious to have children and had already met with a fertility specialist, they felt it important to inform the king and queen.

"Knowing you, Mother, you'd find out another way if we didn't tell you." Vittorio hadn't bothered to hide the accusation in his voice, though he'd laughed as he said it. They didn't want the information to be shared with the family, however. Even with Alessandro. "There's no point in placing that burden on him until we know we're out of options. And right now, we're optimistic."

Emily had been quiet for most of the meal, but Fabrizia caught the young woman's smile at Vittorio's declaration of hope. When Vittorio had finished speaking, Emily turned to Carlo, her expression sober once more. "All that being said, Your Highness, before we publicly announce our engagement, we would like your blessing. Between the amount of travel I'll do for my job in the coming seasons and the challenges we would face starting a family, I understand if you feel it would not be in the country's best interest for us to marry. I take Vittorio's obligations as seriously as I know you do."

When Emily uttered those words, Fabrizia saw in Vittorio's face that he hadn't been expecting Emily to make the request. Nor would Vittorio have asked for such a thing himself; he was determined to marry Emily no matter what. That flash of fire in Vittorio's eyes, more than anything, convinced Fabrizia that the two of them belonged together....children or no children. She'd spoken before either Carlo or Vittorio could open their mouths.

"Of course you have our blessing." Gladness filled her as she looked across the table at Emily. "If we can help with wedding planning, finding the best fertility specialists, or anything else you desire, you need only to ask. We're overjoyed that you'll be part of our family."

The formal engagement announcement had been made less than a week later.

The photographer called for the king and queen to join Massimo, Kelly, and Kelly's parents for the next set of photos. As Carlo offered

Fabrizia his elbow, she told him, "I'm not worried about them. They're deliriously happy."

"I think so, too. And in a few short months, we'll be celebrating their wedding. In the meantime, we'll be grandparents again very soon."

"And I plan to spend every moment possible with Anna and my new grandbaby." Megan was due to deliver a son any day now. She and Stefano planned to name him Dario, a name Fabrizia adored.

The king gave his children a broad smile as they peeled off from where they'd been posing with Massimo and Kelly for the photographer, then he leaned in so his words were for Fabrizia's ears only. "Croatia can wait until it needs to be addressed. Until then, let's enjoy the now. It's too good to miss."

Knowing she would scandalize her children, Fabrizia took her place in the photo beside her husband, then raised up on her toes to give him a lingering kiss.

As always, Carlo was right. The now was very good, indeed. She planned to enjoy it thoroughly.

Thank you for reading *Slow Tango With a Prince*. If you enjoyed this book, please consider leaving a review at your favorite bookseller or book club website.

Read on for a preview of the next Royal Scandals book, *The Royal Bastard*.

THE ROYAL BASTARD

Five hours after Rocco Cornaro buried his mother, having tossed the last shovelful of dirt over her grave while wishing her a swift ascent to heaven, Satan knocked at his front door.

More accurately: Satan's driver rang the bell at Rocco's wrought iron security gate.

Rocco stood at a second story window in his Dubrovnik villa, seething at the gall of the woman hidden behind the tinted windows of the rented black Mercedes. The uniformed driver hadn't given his client's name, but Rocco knew. Her appearance was inevitable after she'd phoned two days ago and he'd hung up after informing her that he had no interest in anything she had to say. He'd thought she'd at least give him the day of his mother's funeral in peace, but apparently royals did what they wanted when they wanted, and to hell with anyone else.

Rocco took a seat in his late stepfather's favorite worn leather chair, kicked his feet onto the windowsill, and dragged his palms over his face. Keeping it together while delivering his mother's graveside eulogy was the toughest thing he'd done in his life. Despite the emotion that threatened to overwhelm him, he'd made it through, his voice resolute as he addressed the small gathering of friends and family. He finished a heartbeat before spying his wife watching from the shadows of a tree near the edge of the cemetery. There was no mistaking Justine's stature, still lean and tight as any Olympic athlete, nor the fact she recoiled as he glanced in her direction. He hadn't invited her, and she hadn't intended to be seen.

What was it with women showing up where they weren't wanted today?

Thank God his siblings hadn't noticed Justine standing alongside the trunk of the thick oak. Double thanks that they hadn't accompanied him back to his residence to see the sleek Mercedes now parked outside. It would've spurred even more questions than his wife's appearance.

Rocco leaned forward in his chair to take another look outside. The driver spoke near the Mercedes' cracked rear window, nodded, then returned to the gate and folded his hands in front of him in a show of resolve. On the roadway behind the Mercedes, a red BMW belonging to Rocco's uphill neighbor slowed as it passed on its way to the heart of the city.

"Damn it all to hell."

"Sir?" Kos Horvat stood in the doorway of Rocco's study. Twice Kos had informed the driver that Rocco was not available. Twice the driver had insisted that Rocco would wish an audience with his passenger and that they would wait.

Rocco swirled the amber liquid inside the crystal tumbler he clutched in one hand, then took a long, slow sip, savoring the burn as it made its way down the back of his throat. If anyone could be deterred from darkening Rocco's entrance, Kos was the man to deter them. Not only did he manage Rocco's properties, he had extensive security expertise and a build as powerful and unyielding as Dubrovnik's ancient city walls. But Queen Fabrizia, whose husband ruled the wealthy Mediterranean island nation of Sarcaccia, apparently wasn't one to be put off by a burly, sour-faced Croatian with a voice rough enough to intimidate men twice her size. Nor was she one whose mood would improve with the delay.

"Talking to myself, Kos." Rocco rose from the chair and turned away from the window. "Allow the visitor to enter, but the car and driver stay outside the gates. If this person is so anxious to see me, they can walk."

The corner of Kos's mouth twitched. It was as close to a smile as the big man ever revealed. "Of course."

"Then go home. You've been here around the clock for the last two weeks and worked overtime before that." During those long days, while Rocco's mother had been ensconced in the guest room waiting for the end to come, Kos had been a godsend. "You're due a vacation."

"I've no need of a holiday."

"And I don't need you for the next few weeks. It's April now. The weather should be beautiful. Go while you're able."

Kos regarded him for a moment, then gave a slight nod. "I'll leave once your guest has departed."

"No need to wait. I'll gladly provide a personal escort from the premises when we're finished." Then he could sink into the solitude he desperately craved. He could mourn. He could rattle about the villa with no witnesses, no looks of concern, and none of Kos's silent watchfulness.

"When shall I resume my services?"

"Take two weeks. No…take three. Your wife deserves a vacation as much as you do. She's been incredibly patient while you've been here."

"As you wish." Gratitude flared in the Croat's eyes. "Again, sir, my condolences. Your mother was a great woman."

"She was. Thank you."

As Kos's steps faded, Rocco spun away from the door and set his half-empty tumbler atop the wide mantel that crowned the room's stone fireplace. His mother always described Queen Fabrizia as a worthy opponent. Better he wait to finish his liquor until the woman departed.

With any luck, it'd be his first and last confrontation with her, and it wouldn't take long.

He ran a hand around his waistband, ensuring his shirt was securely tucked in, then straightened his tie. He couldn't imagine what the queen could want that warranted a face-to-face visit. She was one of the most sought-after women in the world. Arriving on his doorstep unnoticed couldn't have been easy.

He sensed Fabrizia's presence before he heard Kos announce, "Sir, your visitor."

"Thank you." Without looking over his shoulder to gauge Kos's shock—for surely he knew the famous face—Rocco said, "I trust your walk up the driveway was a pleasant one? The gardener did a spectacular job with the annuals this year."

She waited until the door closed behind Kos to answer. "You've made a beautiful home for yourself, Rocco." The voice sounded just as it did on television, warm and well-modulated, the Italian accent hearkening to the queen's Sarcaccian home.

"Pity you felt the need to travel so far to see it. I've had an exhausting week and am not in a position to play host. On the other hand, I didn't feel I could leave you at my gate. You never know who might wander by with a camera and I suspect you don't want your visit here noticed."

"You suspect right, though for more reasons than simply exposing our…link."

He turned then, taking in the sight of the elegant queen as she lowered a scarf from her head to her shoulders. He'd grudgingly found her attractive whenever he'd seen her on television and magazine covers, but those images paled compared to the real-life woman. Despite knowing her to be in her mid-sixties, Rocco would've guessed her age closer to fifty. Golden hair cut in a sleek, modern style emphasized her high cheekbones and full mouth. A light spray of wrinkles radiated from the edges of her bright, intelligent green eyes, but her taut physique, fitted black and white silk dress, and matching black studded leather handbag gave her the overall appearance of a younger woman. She held a pair of sunglasses he guessed she'd worn with the scarf to mask her identity.

More than her attractiveness, however, it was her dignity that surprised him. She didn't require a crown to demand attention and deference.

"I don't believe your man recognized me." The queen approached as if she were being introduced to him at one of her palace garden parties, her hand extended and a cordial smile lifting the edges of her lips. "It's a pleasure to finally meet you in person."

He couldn't bring himself to be so rude as to ignore the proffered hand, nor could he pretend graciousness by responding in kind. He kept their touch brief and businesslike. "Fabrizia."

Her eyes lit with a mixture of curiosity and amusement. "So much like your parents."

He merely raised his brows in response. The queen might hold power in Sarcaccia, but not in his home. So long as they stood in his home, in his study, discussion of his parents was off the table.

"Like Teresa, you don't use my title," she added as she slipped the sunglasses into her handbag.

Good for you, Mother. "Titles should be earned. I've never much cared for them."

She moved past him, her fingers trailing across the back of the study's plush gray sofa as her gaze flicked around the room, taking in the tall windows and the clean-lined navy curtains that framed them, then the hefty desk and leather chair he'd inherited from his stepfather, before settling on a framed photo of his mother at one end of the mantel. "For you, on this occasion, I'll grant a pass. You are loyal to your mother and I find that honorable."

"Why are you here?"

She laughed, a true, bubbly laugh that surprised him. "Now that is your father's trait. For better or worse, you prefer to get to the point, rather than learn about others through discussion."

"My father died five years ago. You never met him."

The queen paused near the mantel, then slowly turned to face him. "Jack Cornaro may have married your mother and raised you, Enzo, and Lina, but it's King Carlo's blood you carry in your veins." She lifted Rocco's crystal tumbler and swished the contents beneath her nose. Her eyebrows lifted. "You drink Aberlour."

"I do."

"Interesting. So do my husband and twin sons."

He took a long, quiet breath, waiting for her to get to the point.

After he finished that glass—*if* he finished that glass—he'd find a new brand of Scotch.

"You look like them, you know. It's uncanny, the resemblance between you and my twins." The softness of her voice snapped his gaze to hers. She was studying him in the same calculating manner as she'd assessed his decor.

"Not surprising, as we share a sperm donor." Her damned husband. The man who'd taken advantage of his mother all those years ago, then abandoned Teresa for the aristocratic, wealthy Fabrizia.

Rocco's harsh words didn't deter the queen. "I can understand why you feel that way, but I assure you, King Carlo considers you far more than the result of…that. As do I."

"Don't." His tone made it clear he expected her to state her business and leave.

She set the Scotch on the edge of his desk. "Teresa and I had our differences. Strong differences. However, she was a good mother to you. King Carlo would have been a good father to you, if he'd had the chance—"

"I had a good father."

"Yes, you did. But now you have neither Jack Cornaro nor Teresa. You have soundly rejected King Carlo. Therefore, your care falls to me."

Care? "I'm a grown man, Fabrizia. Older than *your* children, in fact." Including the children Carlo fathered with the queen while still involved with Rocco's mother, the son of a bitch.

"You're a grown man in trouble, whether you know it or not. That's why I'm here."

"Say your piece, then I shall wish you a safe and speedy journey home."

She swept a hand toward the sofa. "May I?"

"You weren't stopped by my gate or my property manager. Why stop now?" He'd never before spoken to a woman in such an abrasive tone, let alone a queen, but dammit, he'd buried his mother today. And he still had the matter of his wife's graveyard appearance to confront.

The queen perched on the edge of the sofa, her back straight. Rocco remained where he was, arms crossed over his chest.

"You remember last year, when every reporter in the world seemed to be searching for my son, Alessandro?" At his grudging nod, she continued, "Your mother called King Carlo and said you were approached at a farmer's market in Dubrovnik by a man who asked if you were Alessandro. Teresa was very concerned. She claimed that the man followed you to the market from your wife's apartment."

"My wife is none of your business."

He regretted the outburst as comprehension flashed in the queen's eyes. She knew she'd pricked his Achilles' heel.

"You handled the situation well by telling the man he was mistaken. However, the incident gave me pause. I put a tail on you to ensure no one inquired further and discovered the truth of your parentage."

"You…*what?*" Fabrizia had been spying on him? Had his mother known? No…she couldn't have. She wouldn't have stood for it.

"It was for your own protection."

"Let's be honest about who needed protection here," he shot back. "It wasn't me." If the world discovered that King Carlo had a stealth paramour and children during the first years of his marriage to Queen Fabrizia, it would severely damage both the king's popular image and the queen's reputation as a savvy, intelligent woman.

"I would do anything to protect my family. Choose to believe it or not, but I include you and your siblings in that group. If your parentage were to become public knowledge, your life would be forever changed."

"So would yours."

"Then we're on the same side, aren't we?" She exhaled and shifted her position on the sofa. "The man who approached you that day in the market was indeed a reporter. He moved on to another story when my son returned to Sarcaccia the following week. However, while investigating the reporter I discovered something far more disturbing. He wasn't the only one watching your movements."

She opened her handbag and withdrew a cell phone, then turned the screen toward Rocco. It displayed an image of a sidewalk café located on a busy street a block from his wife's apartment. "Have you ever seen this man? Do you know him?"

Taking the phone from her, he zoomed in on the face of the man seated at the outdoor table. The man's hawklike nose, lean build, and curly dark hair were familiar. "I don't know his name, but he rents one of the offices above mine."

Rocco first noticed him several months ago when they'd stood in line at a local newspaper kiosk waiting to make purchases. A teenage boy mouthed off to the owner for refusing to sell him cigarettes. The man in the photograph had told the youngster to move along, much to the relief of the elderly kiosk owner. Since then, Rocco caught glimpses of the man from time to time, usually as he ducked in or out of the building's elevator or followed Rocco through building security. He carried a worn, black leather messenger bag and walked in quick steps with his head down, as if he were late for an appointment. If not for the incident at the kiosk, the man would've escaped Rocco's notice entirely.

"Who is he?" Rocco asked.

"Viktor Radich. Twenty-eight years old. Tech expert. His specialty is surveillance equipment." She aimed a glance at the upper corner of Rocco's study, where a security camera was mounted, its form partially obscured by the woodwork. "Mostly custom-designed, high-end systems like yours for a variety of clients around the world."

"You're quite observant."

"It serves me well in my position." A tentative smile lifted the edges of her mouth. "It also doesn't hurt that I live in a residence with superior security. I've made it habit to look for both cameras and exits upon entering a building. A member of my staff once told me he always has a minimum of two escape routes in mind when I'm in a room. I've never needed them, but his words stuck with me."

Rocco suspected the queen was the type to have more than two escape routes in mind, and not because she'd been instructed to do so. Teresa had once described Fabrizia as a wily survivalist camouflaged by designer labels. He didn't doubt it.

"Radich's parents divorced and his mother emigrated to the United States with Viktor when he was a small child. Under the custody arrangement Viktor spent summers with his father in Moscow...at least when the man wasn't being held by the authorities." Her look was hard. "Russian mafia. No charges that stuck long enough to keep him imprisoned indefinitely, but he's still questioned frequently. Radich hasn't been back to Russia since he finished high school. He went on to study electrical engineering and computer science at MIT. Graduated near the top of the class."

"So he's intelligent."

"Very. No criminal record, either, which is necessary if one wishes to work installing security systems. He started his own business right out of college and had several high-profile clients in the United States before moving here, ostensibly to open a second office."

"He didn't install my system, if that's your point."

A twitch of the queen's lips made it plain she already knew that fact. "Tell me, Rocco, how far is your office from your wife's apartment?"

He frowned, unsure where the queen was heading with the abrupt question. "A ten-minute drive without traffic. Twenty with."

"Every other Tuesday, Radich dines at the same restaurant where your wife meets with her girlfriends, about three blocks from her apartment. He arrives a few minutes before they do, like clockwork. He sits at different tables each time, but always in the same section where the women have their standing reservation. He's done it for at least three months now."

Rocco returned the phone to the queen. He forced a calm expression, though a sense of unease prickled the hairs on the back of his neck. "Coincidence. Many people who work near my office live in the same district as my wife. It's a popular neighborhood."

"That's what my people thought...at first. But on alternate Wednesdays, the morning after Radich has eaten near your wife and her friends, he leaves the office building you share to have lunch at this café near your wife's apartment, despite the fact there are any number of places to eat near your office."

"Perhaps he has a standing meeting."

"In fact, he does." Fabrizia turned her phone to show Rocco a different image. "Ever seen this man?"

"No. Never." Taken at the same café, the photo showed a barrel-chested, middle-aged blonde man with a military haircut and dark sunglasses. His face bore bright, raised scars on one cheek, the edges stretched and shiny, as if he'd suffered excruciating burns. The scars extended from beneath the lower edge of his sunglasses and down his jaw to his neck, then disappeared in the collar of his dark leather jacket. A camera sat on the table in front of him as he leaned toward Radich. The pair appeared to be studying the screen of Radich's laptop.

If Rocco had ever encountered this man, he'd have remembered. The guy dwarfed Radich, and Radich, while lean, wasn't short. A scarred man with such a massive build stood out in a crowd.

"His name is Anton Karpovsky."

"Doesn't ring a bell."

"He was honorably discharged from the Russian army after being injured by an IED in Chechnya. He developed a reputation among his men for his patriotic single-mindedness. Very driven, very inflexible. Very unforgiving of the Chechens…or anyone who rebels against Russia, for that matter."

The queen returned the phone to her handbag and met Rocco's gaze. "Karpovsky resented the fact that his injury cost him his military career. His parents hired him to work at their grocery store in Yekaterinburg, which he considered beneath him. Then one night, he shot his wife three times in the head and chest when she arrived home late from work. He claimed he thought she was an intruder, but his wife's sister alleged that Karpovsky was engaged in illegal activities, having become acquainted with members of the Russian mafia while sourcing inventory for his parents' store. His wife had planned to report him to the authorities and file for divorce. The sister-in-law believed Karpovsky killed his wife to keep her from going to the police and testified to that at his trial. He served two years in prison for manslaughter before having his conviction overturned when the sister-in-law recanted."

Rocco spread his hands wide, silently asking what the beefy Russian's presence in Dubrovnik had to do with him.

"The sister-in-law disappeared a few months later while vacationing in Bali. Whether there was foul play or not, I haven't been able to determine, but the woman's claim that Karpovsky is involved in illegal activities is true. Publicly, he once again handles inventory for his parents' grocery store in Yekaterinburg. Privately, he is a gun for hire."

The queen stood, leaving her handbag behind on the sofa as she strode to the window and looked out at her driver. When she turned back to face Rocco, her brow was furrowed. "I believe they intend to kidnap your wife."

ALSO BY NICOLE BURNHAM

ROYAL SCANDALS

Christmas With a Prince (prequel novella)

Scandal With a Prince

Honeymoon With a Prince

Christmas on the Royal Yacht (novella)

Slow Tango With a Prince

The Royal Bastard

Christmas With a Palace Thief (novella)

The Wicked Prince

One Man's Princess

ROYAL SCANDALS: SAN RIMINI

Fit for a Queen

Going to the Castle

The Prince's Tutor

The Knight's Kiss

Falling for Prince Federico

To Kiss a King

BOWEN, NEBRASKA

The Bowen Bride

A ROYAL SCANDALS WEDDING

More Royal Scandals titles will be available soon. For updates, please visit nicoleburnham.com, where you can subscribe to Nicole's Newsletter.

Subscribers receive exclusive content, including the short story *A Royal Scandals Wedding*, an inside look at the wedding of Megan Hallberg and Prince Stefano Barrali from the novel Scandal With a Prince.

ABOUT THE AUTHOR

Nicole Burnham is the RITA award-winning author of over twenty novels, including the popular Royal Scandals series.

For more information or to join Nicole's newsletter for reader exclusives, visit nicoleburnham.com.

facebook.com/NicoleBurnhamBooks
twitter.com/NicoleBurnham
instagram.com/nicole.burnham